THE
TIME TOURISTS

A NOVEL

GladEye
Press

GLADEYE PRESS
Springfield, OR 97478
gladeyepress.com

Published by GladEye Press March 2018

ISBN: 978-0-9911931-6-5

Cover photography by S.K. Nelson

This is a work of fiction. Names, characters, places, and incidents either
are the product of the author's imagination or are used fictitiously, and
any resemblance to actual persons, living or dead, businesses, compa-
nies, events, or locales is entirely coincidental.

Set in Garmond, an old style typeface inspired by the famed French
printer Claude Garamond in the 16th century.

For Dad,
who told me not to worry about failure;
worry about the chances I'd miss if I
didn't even try.

"Photography is a form of time travel."

—*Neil Degrasse Tyson*

"Which of my photographs is my favorite?
The one I'm going to take tomorrow."

—*Imogen Cunningham*

1

More than two thousand years ago, Aristotle said, "Time is the most unknown of all unknown things." Not much has changed since then. Like Aristotle, Imogen Oliver spent a good deal of her time thinking about time, researching time, and traveling through time, yet why and how she was able to do it remained a big, fat mystery.

It was strange to think that just a few short years ago her life so far had been consumed by shoe shopping at the mall, watching progressively bad reality TV, drinking beer and singing karaoke with friends at the bar on Friday nights, and wondering what the hell she was going to do with a liberal arts degree in history.

But history, as it turned out, was actually quite a useful major for her line of work as a time-traveling private investigator. From the discovery that she possessed this unusual gift—the ability to step into the scene of any photograph and become part of that time—Dead Relatives, Inc. was born. If the name seems sort of morbid, there is a perfectly good reason behind it. Imogen knew that if she wanted to attract the kind of business she was after—discreetly locating the whereabouts of lost friends, relatives, misplaced objects—she would need to choose a name that stuck out.

As with any job, but especially bearing in mind the complexity of time travel, there were, of course, rules, quite a few as it turned out, but the three basic ones were: you can't bring anything back from the past with you; you can't run into yourself, and you can't alter established history; for instance, changing the results of an election, or going back and killing Hitler when he was an infant—a common time-travel trope. Luckily, however, following the rules was made a bit easier by a self-correcting universe, meaning that even if you deliberately tried to break a rule, the custodians of the cosmos would not allow it.

Yet, as satisfying as it was to bring the answers, lost items, and long-buried secrets forward, helping her clients embrace closure or find hope for a brighter future for themselves and their kin, as a private investigator, she was also a pragmatist. She understood that humans were unpredictable creatures, not all of them possessed a moral compass. What they did with the information she provided was out of her control and besides, like everyone else, she needed to eat and pay her rent and feed her always hungry cat.

Time travel. It was the focus of prodigious discussion and debate, covered from diverse angles using myriad devices and means in works of literature, on television, and in the movies. There were paradoxes and conundrums and questions that begat more questions, none for which Imogen had sufficient answers. Was it magic? Something else? Perhaps it had something to do with growing up in close proximity to photographic chemicals and materials, or the fact that both of her parents were photographers. She had once heard of a super-secret society that evidently knew all about what she could do, but so far, that was an unverified mystery too. What she did know was that it happened to her the first time when she was four.

Time tick-tick-ticked as Imogen, eyes wide open, stared up at the swirly patterns on Grammy Iris' plaster ceiling. She was supposed to be taking a nap. Naps were for babies. Shoving the quilt off and tossing Horace the stuffed horse aside, she sat up and began to slowly inch toward the edge of her wagon-wheel themed single bed, but not too close, and not before looking down first to make sure that a witch's gnarled claw wasn't sneakily inching up and out from under the bed to snatch hold of her ankle and drag her down to some scary dark underworld beneath it. She was just ready to put her toe down onto the tile floor when Grammy walked into the room. Imogen quickly pulled her foot back up, laid out flat on the bed, and squeezed her eyes shut, feigning sleep.

"Imogen!" Grammy said, trying to stifle a snicker. "Are you taking a nap?"

Imogen opened one eye and replied, "Yes?"

"For some reason, I don't think you're really asleep," Grammy said, coming over to the side of the bed, and reaching down, tickled her granddaughter's neck, sending Imogen into spasms of giggling.

Imogen sat up. "I'm not sleepy, Grammy. Can I get up now?" she whined.

Grammy sighed. "Okay, come on, you," she said, taking Imogen by the hand and leading her out to the living room. Hoping she might get drowsy looking at it for the millionth time, Grammy Iris pulled out the big, dusty family photo album and placed it on Imogen's lap. Inside, dozens of faded, sepia-tinted pictures of Grammy's grumpy family were pasted on hard cardboard backing—people with funny names like Aunt Ada and Uncle Paul and Aunt Phyllis and Uncle Gordy and second cousins Percy and Viola from Missoula.

Because the pictures were attached in each corner with four white tabs that looked like miniature envelopes with their flaps open, she could easily take them out, turn them over, and sound out the names and dates and locations that were handwritten on the back with gold ink in Grammy's fine cursive script. The lines had lots of loopty loos and curly qs that Imogen tried once to copy with a crayon on a piece of paper but could never get to look quite the same.

There were pictures of frowning babies and squirmy toddlers propped up on divans—boys and girls alike dressed up in frilly, white lace gowns and buttoned up leather shoes. There were a few candid street scene photos with blurry carriages, and buggies and horses going by, and even the turn-of-the-century equivalent of today's photo bomb, a youth speeding through the photo's background on an old timey bicycle waving his hand behind a smiling Grammy in the foreground, a young girl of 18; and a later one of her looking as dour as the rest of the relatives did in a studio posed photograph with Grandpa on their wedding day. There were even a couple of really, really old pictures, ones that were so faded out you could scarcely see the faces on the small pieces of metal.

When Imogen closed the album and started to scoot off the couch, a different kind of picture fell out. It wasn't black and white like the others. It was in color and shaped differently, more square. Imogen picked the photo up with her stubby fingers and held it in front of her face to get a good look. She immediately recognized the woman in the picture. It was mommy. She was standing on a beach. Turned slightly away from the camera, her hand shaded her eyes from the bright sunlight as she glanced at something in the distance.

Imogen couldn't say how it happened, but as she stared at the picture, it began to wiggle-waggle and jaggie-jiggle like instant Jell-O, she thought—just slightly around the edges at first, but then all of a sudden, things got sort of all weirdly warbled and crazy feeling. It was dark and she felt afraid, but then there was light again and she could feel her feet sinking down into warm sand and smell the fishy scent of the ocean. Mother looked down at daughter with a look of surprise and bewilderment. Imogen reached up and touched the tips of her mother's fingers.

"Hi mommy," she said.

"What are you doing here Imogen?" Francis asked, and then whooosh, an invisible something pulled her away, and just like that she was back again, sitting in the big chair in the living room, sunlight dancing across the TV where an episode of Grammy's favorite daytime soap *As the World Turns* continued to play on. Imogen suddenly felt tired. A nap sounded very good.

2

Although most people think of time as a constant, physicist Albert Einstein showed that time is an illusion; it is relative—it can vary for different observers depending on your speed through space. Henceforth: kid time.

"Kid" time is very much quite not the same as "adult" time. Kid time is measured by birthdays and first and last days of school; by Santa Claus and Halloween and seasons. If you were ever a kid yourself, you know that kid time goes by s-l-o-w-l-y. Up until about the age of 10, it takes forever for Christmas and birthdays to arrive; it seems like you're eight and a half for time without end; there is no concept of days, weeks, hours, minutes, months, years—it is math problems to be solved with number two pencils on worksheets handed out by the teacher, or like when the big hand was on the three and the little hand was on 30 and it was half past three, but essentially, it plays no relatable role in a kid's life.

Rather, they are much more attuned to their senses—of sight and sound and smell and the way things feel. Instead of a clock, time is measured more by the position of the sun or the moon or the season; by the sweet aroma of lilacs in spring, fresh mowed grass, the mossy forest smell and hamburgers barbequing on the grill in summer, the way the leaves crunch under your feet or how the air smells just before it rains in the fall.

In the summer, if your parents woke you up early in the morning before the sun came up it could mean something good was happening, like that you were going on a long vacation or camping at the lake. When you heard the first faint bars of a familiar jingle, you knew it was late afternoon. Was it? Yes! It could only be the ice cream truck! And from every corner of the neighborhood, the sounds of balls and bats dropping, wet children immerging from pools, second base abandoned, as children made a mad dash home for change. The sno-cone man was coming!

Brimming with a freezer full of sno-cones and missile bars and juice bars, the truck finally made a slow roll around the corner and the tattooed ice-cream man began to recite his sno-cone flavor rap: "Straw-berrry, cherry, grape, ah-lime, orange, ah-root-a-beer, cinnamon, Ringo, Elv-is Presley, the New Dude and Red D'Mickie!" And even though the arrival of the Pied Piper of popsicles was a summer staple, it was as though kid time somehow prevented the children from remembering that this was an everyday occurrence.

In autumn, when the leaves began to crinkle up and turn their bright colors, the rain would start soon after, which meant it was almost Halloween and Trick-or-Treat candy. And when the last leftover piece of turkey was devoured, and the decorations went up downtown and the stores began stocking toys and glitter-filled, twinkly light displays, and the air was so cold it took your breath away, it could only be Christmastime. Then, when you saw the daffodils and crocus poking out from between the frozen patches of melted ice on your way to school, you knew it was only a matter of time before the Easter bunny arrived with more candy, and it wouldn't be long after that until school ended for another year and it was glorious summertime again!

Kid time is when existing in the world seems like a normal state of being; something that is and always will be; no worries about tomorrow or next week or bills or taxes or divorce or growing old alone or lying down for that last, long sleep.

When only good things happen during kid time, it's great, the slow-moving events become treasured childhood memories, but if something bad or horrible occurs—bullying, death of a parent or sibling, abuse, divorce—the trauma and pain can feel like it will never end, that it will last an eternity—until it does, when kid time ends and adult time kicks in and time speeds up, and therapists, who make their living delving into the childhood issues of their adult clientele, step in to try to patch up the wounds. The long, difficult slog through kid time began for Imogen in the autumn of her ninth year.

Niles and Francis Oliver were what you would call natural-world people; they recycled, grew their own vegetable and herb garden; they listened to NPR, shopped at the co-op and sprinkled nutritious granola on Imogen's Cheerios every morning. Niles, tall and lean, affably charming, and most comfortable when wearing an old flannel shirt, a pair of khaki shorts and hiking boots, his hefty camera bag slung over one shoulder; and Francis, tall, dark-haired, reserved, but with a rare contagious laugh, made a handsome couple, and both were adamant about raising their daughter as naturally as possible without any predetermined rules to obey or dogma to follow.

As photographers they were intuitively curious about the world around them and eager to document everything, which meant exposing their daughter to endless excursions, hiking and camping and museums; boundless opportunities for picking up rocks and leaves and bugs and examining them under a micro lens.

Imogen learned to be patient while her folks set up a shot and to appreciate sunrises and sunsets, that special time when the magic hour happened for photographers. She explored odd and out of the way places and learned to love science and to marvel at the surprises in nature. Of course, they had named her Imogen, after Imogen Cunningham, a famous turn-of-the-century female photographer known especially for her botanical photography, nudes, and industrial landscapes.

She was content in the company of her parents, although mother at times appeared aloof, or maybe she was merely distracted, but nonetheless, she often rebuffed Imogen's exuberant efforts at hugs and affection. Luckily, dad made up for it. His cavalcade of silly games amused and delighted Imogen for days. They played catch and she danced to swing music on his shoes. They waded through streams together looking for pollywogs, and at night she leaned into the crook of his arm as he read fantastic stories to her about magic and wizards and fairies and undiscovered lands faraway.

He convinced her that trolls lived in tunnels and that the only way to get past them was to hold your breath from the beginning of the tunnel until the very end of it. Memories of daddy and Imogen counting down 3, 2, 1, entering the tunnel and both sucking in air; mom crying, "Niles, stop it, it's dangerous," but laughing as she said it. The blur of diverging headlights bouncing off the reflectors on the walls and roof; the thump, thump, thump of the tires on the tracks along the road inside the tunnel; the cacophonous echo of multitudinous horns honking. There was something deliciously terrifying about a tunnel, no matter how long or how scary it was. It might be haunted if it was abandoned, or creepy and dumb like the dark scary ride at the Fun Zone in Newport Beach was; or mysterious and confusing like Willie Wonka's hallucinatory boat ride through the tunnel that led to the chocolate factory. Trolls or no trolls, because of their special game, tunnels held a special appeal with Imogen.

Imagination was Imogen's best friend, with books coming in a strong second. Curious about everything, Imogen was a voracious reader. She loved nothing more than an afternoon spent losing herself within the pages of a book, visiting new places, sharing the adventures of remarkable characters, and most of all, learning new words.

One day, bored with her own age-appropriate chapter books, Imogen decided to inspect her parent's vast library collection of books. Choosing a hardbound book called *To Kill a Mockingbird*, Imogen was instantly drawn into the Depression-era story about the little girl named Scout Finch and her brother Jem. And oh goody, there were lots of new words for her to look up! Early one Saturday morning as she was curled up reading in bed before anyone was awake, Imogen stumbled upon a word she'd never heard before. At breakfast, Imogen looked up from her bowl of cereal and asked, "What does rape mean?"

Niles and Francis stopped eating mid-chew, looked over at each other, and then back at their seven-year-old daughter.

"Uh," Niles mumbled, calmly setting his spoon down and looking to his wife for guidance.

"May I ask where you learned that word?" Francis asked Imogen calmly.

"From a book," Imogen said.

"What book?" Niles asked.

Imogen didn't wait to launch into a detailed synopsis. "Well, in *To Kill a Mockingbird*, there's these kids—Scout and her brother Jem and their dad, Atticus, who is a lawyer and he stands up for a black man named Tom Robinson who raped a white lady, but . . ." Imogen was clearly frustrated. "I don't know what that means and I don't want to read anymore of the book until I do because it won't make any sense."

Niles had to cover his mouth with his hand to suppress his amusement at his daughter's dilemma. Neither was exactly prepared to have this discussion with Imogen right now or so soon, but after they explained what the word meant, it opened the doors to further conversation about the deeper social issues, like racism, addressed in Harper Lee's powerful novel, and the beginning of many more such discussions and learning opportunities between the Oliver's and their most-inquisitive child.

On the outside, Imogen was sufficiently cute and pleasant enough, an average child, unusual but in a likeable way. On the inside, she was an introvert, a misunderstood oddball, a little ball of social ineptitude, but not shy, which made her a bit of a confusing enigma. She had a tendency to either inappropriately talk too much, or at other times, too little.

Although she was an only child Imogen wasn't a spoiled un-pleasant kid like some "onlys" she knew. She didn't get everything she wanted, in part because Imogen never thought to ask. And besides, her parents were more inclined to put her in a room full of books than a room full of toys.

Still, as much fun as they enjoyed as a threesome, Niles and Francis worried about their daughter; they wondered if she should have more social interaction with other children. They did their best to encourage her to make friends, but the handful Imogen had collected over the course of growing up so far were more like playmates than true friends, moving in and out of her life like ghost children, never sticking around long enough to make a real connec-tion.

But ever championing their daughter to experience new things, Niles and Francis meant well when they tried to encourage Imogen to play with others, to stop living in her head so much, even if it sometimes meant enduring an unpleasant afternoon or two spent with someone truly dreadful.

Jeanie Bean, one of a parade of superficial "play date" friends her parents naively exposed Imogen to, was a poster child for bad "only" children everywhere. Prone to indiscriminate whiny outbursts, lengthy fits, and foot-stomping tantrums when her hapless parents failed to dutifully gratify the loathsome little princess, Jeanie was a disagreeable mess.

More like a mini-suite than a proper bedroom, Jeanie's room was mostly inhabited by Barbie dolls of all stripes, and all the ubiquitous pink and bejeweled Barbie accessories and paraphernalia that accompanied the Barbie franchise. The centerpiece of the altar of pink was the majestic two-story Barbie dream house along with its many accoutrements, the Barbie convertible and every conceivable Barbie fashion outfit—from catwalk model mod to princess plush. She also possessed Barbie's posse of friends and relations—Ken, Skipper and Scooter Sport, Christie, Midge, P.J., Jewel Secrets Whitney, Todd, and Tracy.

At her house, Imogen owned exactly one Barbie doll, although she wasn't called Barbie; Imogen had renamed her Q and turned her into a punk. Using her trusty lefty scissors, she had, like the evil witch in Rapunzel, snipped off her long, blond Barbie locks, and then taken her assortment of multicolored, fluorescent magic markers and expertly tinted Q's new short, spiky hair in a bevy of bright magentas, majestic purples, and bold limes.

Spending an entire afternoon cooped up in a room alone with Jeanie Bean was bad enough, but to make matters worse, peculiar little Jeanie would not allow Imogen to touch any of her stuff the entire time she was there. She had evidently missed the unit on sharing in school. In her twisted little "lonely only" mind, Jeanie Bean was desperate for attention, but at the same time she couldn't bear to share her possessions with anyone else, insisting that Imogen sit quietly in a chair in the corner and watch her play.

For hours, Imogen observed this pathetic little girl cycle through Barbie's vast wardrobe or pretend to have her take a spin in the hot pink convertible with Ken for a night on the town.

Pressured by her parents, who wanted to know if she was having a good time at her new friend's house Imogen finally disclosed what went on during afternoons spent with Jeanie Bean, to which they abruptly changed course, figuring that allowing their daughter to live in her head was far better than exposing her to someone as clearly damaged as Jeanie. The play dates mercifully came to an end.

Years later, Imogen was not terribly surprised to learn that Jeanie's needy pleas for attention had followed her into adolescence and adulthood. Pregnant at 16, she had dropped out of high school, and after being arrested copious times for drugs, eventually relinquished her child to protective services. Last she'd heard, Ms. Jeanie Bean had finally found her captive audience dancing for dollars at the Cheetah Lounge down near the railroad tracks at the edge of town.

Nonetheless, with or without friends, Imogen was perfectly content to amuse herself in myriad ways—reading, of course—the library was her most favorite place in the whole world. She liked to draw, or sometimes, using Francis' fancy nail polish, which she had secretly pilfered from her mother's vanity, she painted names on the shell houses of snails and lined them up for an all-day race.

She made up counting games as she swung back and forth on the rope swing in the backyard or climbed up high into the uppermost branches of the elm tree to think and peer down at the world below without anyone knowing she was there. She made up intricate stories that ran like a movie in her head, complete with multiple characters and storylines and dialogue, while she rode her blue bicycle round and round the blocks of her neighborhood. But that summer, things were about to change for Imogen Oliver.

The house on the corner had been empty for so long she'd stopped paying attention to it anymore, that is until one morning when Imogen stepped out onto her front porch and noticed that someone had mowed the lawn over there, and a girl, just about her age and size, was standing on her porch looking back at her. Imogen may not have had a lot of social skills, but she certainly wasn't shy, and without hesitation, marched over to introduce herself.

"Hi, I'm Imogen," she said, sticking out her hand. "What's yours?"

"Jade," the girl answered shyly, rocking back and forth on one foot and the other and twisting with one dainty finger one of several tiny braids that encircled her head. From the instant she heard it, Imogen liked that name a lot—Jade, it matched the girl's greenish eyes, which reminded Imogen of the color of a lovely crystal clear deep lagoon she'd seen in one of her parent's travel photography books.

Everything about Jade was compelling; her chestnut skin, her round eyes and long eyeslashes, which Imogen thought made her look like the baby deer Bambi; the spattering of freckles that dotted each cheek. In contrast to Imogen's light skin, honey-colored hair, and blue-gray eyes, they were polar opposites. But the best part about Jade was her hair, which wound all over her head in tiny braids held together with half a dozen little plastic barrettes in every color of the rainbow. It reminded Imogen of the Hydra in the stop-action movie *Hercules*. The second labour Hercules faced was a fierce reptilian female that instead of hair had a head full of live snakes. Jade didn't look at all like the Hydra, of course, but the braids sometimes looked like they were moving on their own when she ran or danced or bounced around.

Jade, as Imogen would soon find out, lived with her mom Monique and her chubby baby sister Sasha. Monique was the color of espresso, soft-spoken, and very, very tall. She reminded Imogen of a beautiful statue. She liked the casual way she insisted that Imogen call her by her first name. It made Imogen feel grown up. She liked that it had a *Q* in it. Any word that had a *Q* in it was a good word in Imogen's book.

Something about Jade and Imogen clicked right away. Everything felt easy and effortless and special as if the universe had planned it. From that first day forward the girls were inseparable—two puzzle parts that fit together absolutely—one dark, the other light, like an Oreo cookie, Imogen the fluffy cream inside to Jade's chocolate crunchy outside; or maybe a chocolate/vanilla ice cream swirl; or yin and yang. Laughing, playing, talking, holding hands, skipping, everything they did together created a divine and lovely synergy.

Yet, as much as they were of one mind, to others they seemed as different as night and day. Imogen, awkward and accident-prone, stumbling over every loose rock, tripping on every stairstep or crack in the sidewalk, where jade glided effortlessly through life like a graceful gazelle. Jade was a whiz at math; Imogen could spit water through the small gap between her two front teeth. Imogen aspired to be calm and lithe like her friend; Jade secretly wished she could be as free-spirited and uninhibited as Imogen; yet together they completed the picture in the photograph.

During the summers before Jade came along, Imogen liked to linger in bed for a while, enjoying the early morning lying between the cool, crisp linen sheets. But that summer, she broke her routine and woke up early, sometimes even before the sun spilled over the horizon in the east, leaping from her bed and pulling on shorts and shirt and donning a pair of flip-flops, eager to start another day with the best friend she'd ever had in the whole world.

Mornings were spent huddled together in the tree fort talking or playing board games and drawing up plans for the day. Sometimes they took the chalk and drew fantastic murals on the sidewalk or played hopscotch. Jade loved to read too, so during the hot part of the day, they sprawled together, tanned legs akimbo across Monique's bed situated directly in front of the water cooler so the cool air could breeze across their skin while they read chapter books.

In the evenings, it was tacos and dancing to Monique's smooth jazz records at Jade's house, or eating hamburgers that Niles expertly grilled up for them on the backyard barbeque, and posing together, or dressing up or making faces together while Imogen's parents snapped black and white photographs to add to their studio portfolio.

Sometimes one or the other spent the night. Most of the time Jade stayed over at Imogen's because Monique didn't want the girls waking Jade's baby sister. It was a small house with only two bedrooms, so Jade had to share a room with Sasha, which meant that when Imogen slept over the girls had to take blankets and pillows out to the living room, which was like camping out. Underneath their blanket fort they stayed up late talking and giggling and making shadow puppets with the flashlight.

Imogen knew that Jade's mother Monique was alone, but one night when they were talking under the blankets, she asked her about her father.

"Do you have a daddy, Jade?" Jade hesitated and Imogen could hear her drawing in her breath in the darkness. All of a sudden Imogen felt really bad for asking. "I'm sorry Jade," she said. "It doesn't matter. You don't have to say."

"My daddy is in jail," Jade said in a quiet voice. "He's in jail," she continued, "for hurting us."

"Oh," was all Imogen could think to say.

Jade stifled a muffled sniffle into her pillow. Not sure what to do, Imogen scooted over next to her and put her arm around her shoulder, and they both fell asleep like that.

When the girls got bored playing or reading or dancing or skipping rope, they spied on Teddy. Imogen and Jade mostly gave him a wide berth, but sometimes, out of boredom, they pulled the stepladder up to the back window to peek in at the awkward teenager who worked part-time in Imogen's parent's studio.

Teddy Diamond was 18 and had just graduated from high school in June. He lived at home with his kooky mother, Mimi Pinky Diamond. Although Imogen didn't know this until much later, Teddy was a nerdy, socially inept mama's boy with no motivation, no direction, and no desire to leave his mother's comfortable home where he was doted on, cleaned up after, and cooked for. When one of Mimi Pinky's many boyfriends weren't around, she doted on him, calling him her little teddy bear, which he hated. Imogen had seen him balling up his fists behind his back a time or two. Teddy seemed angry and Teddy was a bully.

She remembered him being nicer to her when she was littler, but as he'd grown older, something happened to him and he turned mean. In fact, last summer he'd nearly burnt down their house and Imogen along with it after he put firecrackers in her Malibu Barbie's head. Since then, he'd been a bit more contrite, like he was afraid of her, or maybe he avoided her because he figured she was trouble he didn't need. Still, avoiding him was a difficult task considering that he lived in the yellow house two doors down. Imogen's parents had felt sorry for him and hired him to work part-time after school and during the summer in their studio.

He mostly kept to himself, filing photos or sweeping the floors, but in July when the high school girls started coming in to pose for their senior portraits, Teddy became creepily obsessed. Several times, the girls saw him sneak out copies of photo proofs to take home with him.

"What do you think he does with them?" Jade asked Imogen.

"Probably hangs them on his bedroom wall and kisses them," Imogen said, and they both giggled.

Neither was brave enough, however, to spy on him there and confirm that theory. He seemed to be taken with one girl in particular though. She wasn't as cute as the others and she didn't load up on the makeup like some of the girls. She seemed shy and sort of awkward like him, but they had observed him talking to her a couple of times and she seemed to welcome the attention from an older guy, even if that guy was Teddy Diamond.

One afternoon, while they were surveilling him, Niles came into view and approached Teddy. Niles was holding some photos in his hand and his face was deep-set with anger. Teddy hung his head, staring down at the floor the whole time Niles was talking. The girls watched as Niles left the room and Teddy stowed the broom back in the closet. The girl that he seemed to like never returned, and by the end of that summer everyone would be gone, including Teddy.

As late August approached, the girls made excited plans for the approaching school year. They hoped they would be in the same class together. Who would be their teacher? Would Skyler be there? Skyler was the ginger-headed boy with freckles that Imogen had a crush on since last year when he tossed orange peels at her to get her attention when she was hanging upside down on the monkey bars. They talked about the books they wanted to read and about buying matching pairs of Jellys, the shoes they both loved to wear.

Yesterday when they had ridden their bikes all the way to 7-11 to get Slurpees and Now and Later candy they had spotted trucks and workmen setting up a carnival in the Montgomery Ward parking lot. Would it all be set up today? Might they both be tall enough to ride the Hammer this year? It was just too exciting for words.

Imogen popped out of bed as she always did, eager to spend another day with Jade. And had she mentioned that the carnival was here? She zipped up her jean shorts and pulled her She-Ra Princess of Power T-shirt over her head, pushing her toes into a pair of flip-

flops while she walked toward the kitchen. Francis and Niles sat at
the kitchen table sipping herbal tea or something nasty when Imogen breezed by on her way to the fridge.

"Hold up there, Imogen, Niles teased, "What's on the big agenda for today?" He winked at Francis and she smiled back at him. As
much as they enjoyed spending time with her, Imogen was usually
bored out of her mind by the end of summer. They were pleased
that their daughter had finally found a friend.

Imogen opened the refrigerator to grab the carton of juice.
"The carnival's here!" Imogen shouted breathlessly from the other
side of the door.

"Wow, Imogen," Niles said patting his ears, but laughing when
he said it.

"Can we go, Niles?" For some reason a few months back, Imogen had started calling her parents by their first names. It made her
feel grown up and they hadn't seemed to mind.

"The carnival, eh?" Niles looked at his wife. "I don't know,
Imogen," Francis said as she brushed back a stray piece of hair from
her eyes. "I don't really think they put those rides together very well.
It scares me."

Imogen's eager smile immediately collapsed. Her shoulder's
drooped. Clearly, she was crushed.

"We'll see, Imogen," Niles said.

"Pleeeeease," Imogen whined, drawing out the please the way
kids do.

Niles gave her that look that said don't be that child, and said,
"Go see how Jade's mom feels about it first."

Imogen didn't wait to hear more; that was as good as a yes. She
was out the door in a flash and running across the asphalt street,
which was already starting to warm up in the summer heat. She
jumped over the little crack in the sidewalk that they always jumped
over and ran up the steps to Jade's front door. It seemed odd because the screen door had been left wide open. Usually it was closed
and locked. Oh well, she thought, as she knocked three short times
followed by a pause and one more—that was their secret signal. She
waited. Maybe they were still asleep.

Standing on the porch this long she realized she had never
noticed before how shabby the little house was; how the green paint

on the wood shakes was peeling, showing that the house had been white before it was green, and blue before that; that the screen door had holes in it and that the metal was rusting. She had never had to stand waiting on the porch this long before because Jade always ran out, sometimes even before she had a chance to knock even once.

Imogen began to fidget, rocking back and forth on her heels wondering if she should knock again. She did. Three times, wait, one more. The neighborhood seemed oddly quiet; no one out mowing the lawn, no dogs barking. Weird. Frustrated and impatient, Imogen walked over to the front window. The curtains were closed, but there was a tiny gap between the panels. But peeking through it she could only see a sliver of sunlight reflecting through the pane. Maybe they had gotten up early and gone shopping or something, Imogen thought.

Shrugging, she pivoted and started to head back home to wait when something sparkly in the grass caught her eye. Imogen hurried over and bent over to pick it up. It was Jade's necklace with the carved jade Buddha, a gift from Jade's mom. Jade never went anywhere without it. She wore it to bed every night. It seemed odd that she would leave it behind, unless she meant to. Maybe it was a clue for Imogen to follow.

As Imogen examined it, turning it over in her hand, she didn't notice a late model, two-toned Ford pickup truck rolling up to the curb driven by a scruffy little brown man wearing a Blazers cap. Imogen recognized him. She couldn't remember his name, Juan or Jose or Jesus, it started with a J, but anyway he was the guy that sometimes mowed the yard and trimmed the hedges when the house had been empty before. The back of the truck was full of rakes and shovels and other implements for yard work, the mower, and a bin filled with cleaning supplies. Jose, Juan or Jesus got out of the truck and walked past Imogen without saying a word, heading straight for the front door. She watched him as he fumbled with a key, jiggling it in the lock for a second before it clicked and he pushed the door open and disappeared inside.

Imogen did not want to envisage why this man was going into Jade's house without asking, or what was or wasn't inside, but as the minutes passed, curiosity got the best of her. Shoving the necklace into her jean pocket she forced herself to walk back up on the porch to take a peek inside the house. It was mostly dark because the curtains were closed, and surprisingly, there was still quite a lot of furniture inside. It hadn't occurred to her before that the furniture didn't belong to them, but it appeared to be the case because as she stepped inside and took a look around, she could clearly see that only their personal belongings were missing.

All the baby pictures of Jade and Sasha that had been lovingly placed on the mantle were gone, yet there was the couch where they'd spent so many lazy afternoons reading about poets and ponies and princesses, and the end tables that they'd pushed together like bookends to create their blanket forts during sleepovers; the kitchen table where they'd laughed so hard at jokes they blew chocolate milk out their noses, and where they'd drawn pictures together of unicorns and rainbows, where'd they'd eaten tacos and rocky road ice cream with Monique. Reduced now to mere inanimate objects, they became sad and lonely remnants of a room once bursting with life and laughter.

She was adrift in these memories when the man walked into the room and barked in a sort of growly voice and a Spanish accent, "What you want?"

Alarmed, Imogen started to turn to run outside, but then abruptly changed her mind. She needed to know what was going on.

"Where did they go?" she demanded, "the family that lived here yesterday; where did they go?"

"Don't know," the man shrugged. "Left during the night, I guess. Got a call this morning to come over and clean the place up. S'all I know."

"Adios chica," he said tapping the brim of his hat in a salutary gesture. He turned and shuffled out the door and across the yard and started pulling work tools from the back of the truck, leaving Imogen standing alone in the house.

Left during the night? How was that possible? Imogen wondered. Why would they do that? Unless, unless, she thought, they felt threatened? She remembered what Jade had said about her dad being in jail; could he have gotten out? Would he have come after them? Imogen would spend many, many days and nights pondering that particular question as well as many others, never knowing anything for sure, except that Jade, her only friend, was gone for good.

Niles and Francis ramped up the activity meter the remainder of the summer, treating Imogen to day trips to museums and water parks and carnivals, all geared ostensibly to either cheer her up or make her forget, but it might have been enjoyable if she hadn't met Jade. Now it all just felt forced. She enjoyed doing stuff with her parents, but without Jade it wasn't the same—like all the joy in the world had been sucked out of her. Imogen lost more than a friend that summer; she lost her ability to trust. Before Jade came along she had been content to entertain herself, but now that she knew what it felt like to have the love and companionship of a true friend, she was left wanting only more. She had built up such a good wall and now she felt vulnerable, exposed, and afraid like she never had before.

At night when Niles tucked her into bed, he noticed how sullen and altered his once sunny daughter had become and it saddened him deeply. Since she was little she had this habit of playing with the fold of loose skin on his elbow as they chatted about their day before she went to sleep; she had stopped doing that. Before school started, Niles and Francis and Imogen visited a natural history museum and for the first time, the displays of fosseled rock and ancient mummies weighed heavy on Imogen's childlike mind. Imogen knew that Jade hadn't meant to hurt her, to leave her behind, but she couldn't help feeling angry and betrayed, like the rug had been pulled out from under her. August faded into September and schoolwork and piano lessons and dodge ball soon occupied her time.

She hung Jade's Buddha, made of the stone for which she was named, from the side of her bedroom mirror for safekeeping, in case she ever came back looking for it. A few weeks later, Imogen received a letter—actually more like a note—from Jade in the mail. Although it looked like Jade's handwriting, the tone sounded more like an adult had told her what to say. In it, Jade thanked Imogen for the fun summer and apologized for having to leave, but her mom had been offered a job. She also enclosed a photograph of herself standing in front of a house in some other town. She was smiling, but Imogen thought her smile looked artificial. The postmark was local, so she probably wasn't too far away, but when you're nine, across town might as well be the moon.

Over the years, she had often thought of Jade, of her braids and doe eyes and freckles, and wondered what had become of her and Monique and baby Sasha. She thought of doing an internet search for her, but realized she'd never thought to ask Jade what her last name was. Asking her just hadn't seemed that important at the time, which made it virtually impossible to find her lost friend.

3

Typically, when Imogen arrived home from school, either one parent or the other was there to greet her, but on this particular Tuesday afternoon in early October, Imogen arrived home to find Grammy waiting for her at their house instead. Grammy lived in a smaller house on their property that they called mother-in-law quarters.

"Hi Grammy," Imogen said cheerily as she wriggled from her backpack straps and set it down on the couch. "Where's mom and dad?"

"Imogen, I have something to tell you." Grammy's brow was noticeably fraught as she inched toward her.

"What is it?" Imogen asked, concerned.

She took Imogen's hand, guiding her over to sit on the couch where she joined her. Taking both of her small hands in hers, Grammy paused before delivering the sentence that Imogen would never, ever forget.

"Your parents . . . they were killed . . . in a car accident," she said, "They were on their way home from . . ." Grammy's voice trailed off and after that Imogen didn't hear anything more. The floor seemed to sway beneath her and she felt like her body was floating away.

The next thing she recalled was a strong odor of ammonia and Grammy's voice, saying "Imogen, Imogen, wake up!" Imogen's eyes fluttered open. She was in her bedroom now, lying on top of her bed underneath her quilt, but she couldn't remember how she had gotten here. She tried to sit up, but Grammy gently pressed her back against the soft pillow.

"Everything's going to be okay," Grammy said, "you fainted, that's all."

But Imogen knew that everything wasn't okay and that it never would be again. Grammy's unimaginable words came rushing back into her head. "But it's not okay," she sobbed, turning on her side away from Grammy.

The days that followed were a blur. There would be no funeral, they said. Little children don't understand funeral rituals anyway, they said. One day, while sitting on her bed in her room, numb, unable to cry, incapable of processing anything still, staring across the void, Imogen glanced over at her vanity and saw something she hadn't noticed before; Jade's necklace. It was gone.

When she searched the drawer for the letter and discovered that it too was missing, everything became abundantly and painfully clear—the happy part of "Kid Time" was officially over. Without the joy and expectation that accompanies the leisure of childhood, all that was left in Imogen's heart was a black, empty hole of sorrow and endless ache. From now on, there would be no more magic hours, no more carefree, fun-filled days, no holding her breath through tunnels with Daddy, no more carnivals or skipping through time as if there was no tomorrow. Everyone leaves. Everyone dies.

The photography studio was padlocked shut, and Imogen moved from her parent's house into Grammy Iris' smaller house next door. And not long after that, Grammy found Jesus. Newly baptized, she got right to work at saving Imogen's soul, which basically meant filling up most of her time with church-related activities. Even though Sunday school was sort of fun for a kid, and certainly distracting for a recently orphaned one, there were parts of it that even Imogen, with her fantastic imagination, did not comprehend.

A precocious child of progressive parents, she had questions, questions about infinity and about heaven and about hell, and about where her parents were now. Infinity, in particular, kept her awake at night. In relation to God it meant that he had always existed. There was no beginning. He was eternal. Trying to wrap her brain around that made her feel like her head would explode! Who created God? If no one created God, then how was he always there? Night after night she tortured herself with these mental exercises. How could there be no beginning, she wondered as she tried to envision a straight line that went on and on . . . well, to infinity.

Heaven and hell were problematic as well. This place, hell, sounded really bad—endless fire, gnashing teeth, horrible stuff; but heaven, as far as she could tell, didn't seem like much of an improvement. And the more she heard about what heaven would be like, the more convinced she was that she didn't want to go there either.

Reverend Powell's message was straightforward. Be good, try not to sin, ask Jesus to forgive you so that when you die you'll be taken up to heaven to live with him forever and ever. Again, that word "forever"—just another word for "infinity." And if she was going to spend anywhere for infinity she darn sure wanted to know whether she was going to like it or not. The answers that Grammy Iris offered were more than a little vague.

"Well, in heaven," she had explained, "there will be no fighting, no wars, no arguments, no violence; and the streets, the streets will be paved with gold."

"That sounds good, tell me more," Imogen asked eagerly.

"Well, you'll get to see your mommy and daddy; you'll recognize them and they'll recognize you . . ." But, oh," she conceded, "there are no family connections in heaven, everyone will love everyone and be happy and pain-free forever and ever and ever . . ."

That didn't make any sense and only created more questions in Imogen's mind about heaven, like what would a person do all day, every day, forever and ever? And how did Reverend Powell and Grammy even know what it would be like when neither one had ever been there?

Imogen never received a proper answer to that question. Even as a little girl she was thinking about the reasons why humans treasure life so much—that we cultivate relationships, we debate, we fight and make up; we draw and paint and read; we take pictures and make music. If none of those things exist in heaven, where is the joy? Where is the love? Where is the passion? Where were mom and dad? More importantly, why would anyone want to spend their entire one life trying to get to such a place? She was a girl who thought too much—a gift or a curse that would follow her into adulthood.

In middle school, Imogen attended the church's youth group. One Sunday evening, instead of the customary frothy message from the hip young youth pastor and typical puerile junior high horsing around, this night a screen was set up for a film called *A Thief in the Night*, a distressing, end-of-times film designed primarily, as Imogen would soon discover, to frighten the children.

Purportedly, the rapture would happen when god finally decided he'd had enough; these people were just way too wicked, it was time to extricate the good ones and leave the bad ones behind. All the people, dead and alive, on earth that had accepted Jesus would vanish—poof—into the clouds. And the poor souls who are "left behind," which should be a lot of people if you think about all those other religions that don't worship Jesus, will have to deal with a magnitude of horrible events—the rise of the Antichrist, wars, famine, petulance, raining frogs—you name it; if it's bad, it will happen.

In the film, while the mom is mixing up a cake in the mixer, all of a sudden, she's gone and the mixer goes right on mixing and mixing without her. After seeing it, it occurred to Imogen that maybe her parents had been prematurely "raptured." Maybe they had been so darn good god had wanted to bring them up to heaven first for a sort of pre-rapture tour of the place. It was a nice thought, but like every other rationalization for their deaths she'd latched onto, this one didn't seem very likely either.

By the time high school rolled around, Imogen had grown increasingly disillusioned by the biblical stories that didn't make any sense, and the phony church people who talked a lot about being good and kind, but didn't much live by it, and finally, she stopped going to church altogether. Grammy had firmly embraced religion after her parent's death—Imogen had called it Grammy's "true believer" phase. The God that Imogen would later discard took front and center in Grammy's life, yet despite her fervent displays of religiosity, to Imogen Grammy didn't seem all that happy, as if no matter how hard she prayed or how loud she belted out the hymns, redemption managed to elude her.

Still, that didn't stop her from packing Imogen off to the annual summer and winter camps, the primary draw being the social opportunity for intermingling with members of the opposite sex. But trying to make friends with kids who didn't fixate on things like infinity or wonder why do humans matter? Or what is the purpose of life and death? And why would anyone want to go to heaven? was more than a challenge. Imogen predictably became frustrated with their lack of depth and curiosity, and they just thought she was weird. She finally gave up trying.

Depending on your rank in the hierarchy of things, high school can be either brilliant or brutal. You may fall into one of three categories: invisible, picked on, or popular. If you're gay, or a stoner, a geek, or a redhead, wear glasses, or dress remotely weird, play the sousaphone or join the drama club or the debate team, the likelihood that you fall into one of the first two is moderately high, with invisible being the preferred option, because flying undetected under the radar is a much better alternative than getting picked on. Freshman year, Imogen was singled out by a couple of the popular girls as potential cheerleader material, but when they found out that her interests were all over the place, well beyond the controlled realm of clothes, cute shoe shopping, makeup, and boys, she was cursorily terminated from their exclusive inner circle.

Sophomore year she made brief connections with a girl genius named Alice and a closeted boy named Drew. Alas, Alice was much too clever for public high school and, like Jade, soon abandoned Imogen to attend an elite private school up north. Drew, whom she adored, became so worn down from the constant barrage of bullying he dropped out of high school for good his junior year. He had always said he wanted to join the circus, but landed instead with an opera/theater troupe in San Francisco, ultimately finding true love with a tenor.

With their triad disbanded, Imogen floated about for a while, trying on different groups for size to see how they fit, finally coming to the depressing conclusion that none did. A consummate under-achiever, she mostly sleepwalked through classes, flunking out of Algebra and PE, but outshining her peers without even trying in subjects that held her interest like English and drama and history.

Nevertheless, without friends or a group or any real sense of belonging, Imogen was lonely and as time went on her worldview began to darken. It was just easier to retreat to her bedroom where she could put on her noise-erasing headphones and get lost in music, particularly her newfound interest in darkwave tunes from groups like Faith and the Muse, Christ vs. Warhol, or Virgin Prunes.

She loathed shopping, but discovered she liked going to thrift shops because of their funky array of costume jewelry and clothes with a slightly retro vibe. She cut her hair herself and like she'd once done to her Barbie doll, transformed herself into a live version of Q—her hair all spikey and short and dyed. She passed for Goth, but decidedly rejected the Goth label. She couldn't really identify with their angst-ridden mantra of being perpetually moody and pissed off, that everything sucks, everyone hates you, and life is unfair. Imogen considered herself more of an orphan. She had no parents, no siblings, only a grandma—an orphan. And most of the time, all of what she felt inside was nothing as she navigated alone through a hostile, unforgiving, endlessly boring world.

More by accident than design, she stumbled upon a loose-knit group of miscreants who loitered at the park. They were an odd assemblage of morose underachievers who were probably closer to the Goth ideal than she was. They proclaimed their hatred of everybody and everything, even her, but they did have access to beer and good drugs. During this time, Imogen pierced her nose and her eyebrow and she lost her virginity one night to Dylan, a pimple-pocked perpetual stoner who offered to share a joint and six-pack of beer with her. Although she continued to attend the church youth group, mainly to appease Grammy, it became increasingly awkward to listen to the leaders railing against all the things she was doing.

Imogen felt like a poser. She was a poser as she sat there nodding her head in rote agreement, reading scriptures about drinking and drugs, and sexual sin, and wondering if she was going to hell, and more importantly, whether she really cared or not. She eventually extricated herself from the group, and church in general, and ever so effortlessly let go for good of the nice fantasy that there was a special friend living inside her head. It was okay for other people; she would never begrudge them their beliefs, but it wasn't for her, she decided.

She wordlessly drifted further away from the church, and away from her grandmother, away from people, and from herself. Sometimes she envisioned herself as one of the floaters you sometimes see darting around the edges of your peripheral vision; no reason for being there, but just jetting around with no purpose. She missed prom, ditched most of her classes, faded into the woodwork; didn't care.

One night, Dylan scored a baggy of psychotropic mushrooms and the two of them had retreated to Imogen's bedroom to consume and then chase them with a pint of whiskey. Once settled comfortably numb and deep within the squishy nadir of the large orange bean bag chair waiting for the shrooms to kick in, Dylan asked her, "So, like what do you want to do, Gen?"

She shot him a bored look. "What do you mean," Imogen asked.

"Well, like after all this, you know, high school bullshit; what do you want to do? My parents keep hassling me all the time about stuff, saying I need to get serious and shit like that. What about you?"

Imogen rolled her eyes in his direction and expended a weary sigh. For being her boyfriend, he sure didn't know a fucking thing about her. "Honestly, I wish I had parents to hassle me," she answered sullenly. "Maybe I'd want more for myself if I'd had a chance to know what they wanted for me."

Dylan grimaced. "Sorry," he said. "I didn't mean to bum you out or anything."

Imogen shrugged. "It's okay. Everything's copacetic, man."

Not long after, perception began to shift ever so subtly. Her depth of field began to change. Although the dashboard hula dancer was doing her thing on the nightstand like always, things began to look closer than they appeared. Mushrooms were nice that way. They came on slow, giving you time to ease into it.

Imogen watched the light from the portable TV shift and elongate for a while. Bored with the flickering lightshow and with listening to Dylan's voice transform into a tedious drone, she got up to pee, and the last thing she remembered was sitting on the toilet, glancing over to look at the framed photo on the shelf of dad, Jade, and herself, wishing she could step back into that happy, problem-free time and see them both again, and then quietly murmuring, "Where are you daddy?" under her breath.

And then, in an instant, she was somewhere else, or at least it seemed like a real place, even in her mind-altered state. She was outdoors, lying on grass, gazing up at a sky full of billions of stars, and wondering how in the hell she had gotten from inside to outside so quickly. Drugs were strange, but remarkably, she could feel the real sensation of blades of grass gently poking the palms of her hands, and when she sat up and looked around her, there really was nothing there. Seriously NOTHING. No grandma's house, no tree in the front yard, no street, no lights, nothing but lawn and stars.

Although she couldn't see a thing, somewhere in the distance she could hear the faint sounds of a conversation going on; people, adults, and children talking and laughing—and was that barbeque she smelled? She could feel the panic rising and expanding in her chest. What was this shit? Where the hell was she? Right now, this minute, she wanted nothing more than to be back safe in her bathroom and far, far away from whatever this crazy upside-down place was.

All of sudden, everything shifted to the left and the world went *baloomp*. The blinding fluorescent lights above the bathroom mirror assailed her eyes and a sharp, excruciating pain in her head momentarily took her breath away. Imogen realized she was back sitting on the toilet again. Swiftly pulling up her pants, she burst through the door to her bedroom. Everything was the same.

"What the fuck just happened?" she wailed. Dylan, still in the beanbag chair smoking a joint, looked up at her and shrugged. Imogen was frightened. That was it. She was done living like this.

4

Imogen ducked into Professor Furtado's Econ 101 class, sliding unobtrusively into a seat way up near the rear of the big forum style
classroom. First term university freshman, and so far, college had
been basically okay. As a history major, she liked those courses best.
The rest—the math, literature, sciences—the core classes, were a
means to an end for Imogen. Why she was more interested in events
of the past than anything else was a bit of an unknown, although
she had always been fascinated by the people and places and objects
and clothes and signs and roads and architecture she saw in Grammy Iris' raggedy old photo album. She felt weirdly drawn to them
sometimes, wondering if maybe she belonged somewhere else.

At any rate, here she was, sitting in a huge forum surrounded by
150 or so other bored students, each here to fulfill a course require-
ment toward their own various academic pursuits. Imogen pulled the
cumbersome economics textbook from her backpack and placed it
on the desk alongside her notebook, which she had opened up to a
fresh recyclable page ready and waiting to be filled up with copious
notes on capitalism and commodities, income distribution and GDP,
Karl Marx, Adam Smith, and supply and demand. Some people
had brought their laptops along with them. In a few years, everyone

would be taking notes with their tablets. Imogen had a serviceable desktop computer at home that she used for her homework. She couldn't afford a laptop just yet, not on her meager coffee shop barista salary.

Carrying notes and a leather briefcase, the professor bustled into the hall from a side door and the decibel level dropped as students finished fishing supplies out of backpacks and duffle bags, brought their conversations down to whispers, and settled in for the 50-minute lecture; everyone, that is, except for the couple seated directly in the row in front of her. Their heads tucked together like a pair of conjoined twins, they appeared oblivious to everything around them as they continued to whisper and snicker back and forth. The girl's naturally tightly coiled brown hair fell midway across her back and arm, which was casually draped around the guy's shoulder. His hair was dark and curly too, but unkempt and longish in the back exuding a messy, just-rolled-out-of-bed vibe.

Imogen was mildly irritated, but refrained from saying anything until the professor started to lecture and they still hadn't stopped chattering. Imogen did something uncharacteristic. She tentatively poked the girls' shoulder with the eraser end of her mechanical pencil. In unison, Pixie & Dixie both turned around in their seats to glance back at her.

She expected the girl to either be totally okay with someone pointing out that she and her buddy were being jerks, or annoyed at being poked. Imogen braced for the latter, but strangely, the girl didn't say a word, instead, she smiled and then lifted her notebook up for Imogen to view. All along the top of the page was a series of lined tallies and the phrase "at the end of the day . . ." Imogen nodded, immediately understanding. She'd noticed it too, but hadn't thought about actually documenting it the way they evidently were. The professor had this annoying habit of repeating the cliché all during his lectures.

Something happened. Imogen was thrilled to be in on the joke. She felt giddy, in fact, like a schoolgirl. Well, she was a schoolgirl, a bigger version, but she felt like she'd just now discovered something that normal kids take for granted. Strangers, potential friends willingly inviting her into their innermost sphere of friendship was something new, or maybe something forgotten—Jade was the last person to completely open up to her, to let her in, to accept her, flaws and all. Remembering how nice that felt, instead of turning away like she normally would, she smiled back at the pair, taking note of the date that she met these faces.

Throughout the rest of class, the professor probably repeated the phrase "at the end of the day" a dozen or more times, which elicited enough lines to fill the page, and igniting yet another round of stifled snickering for Imogen to share with the interesting new people sitting in the row in front of her. After class ended, they turned around again to face Imogen and the three of them literally exploded with pent up laughter.

"Oh my god," the girl finally managed to say as she brushed away tears that were careening down both cheeks. The feeling between them was immediate and contagious and uncontrollable and Imogen hadn't felt this happy and uninhibited since forever, and never with strangers.

The girl stuck her hand out to shake Imogen's. "I'm Rachel Brewster," she said. Imogen shook hands back.

"Imogen," she offered.

"Im-O-gen," the boy said accentuating the "o" and ostensibly pondering the sound of her name for a minute before offering her his own hand. "I like that name," he said. "I'm Fletcher Brown."

The fact that his rather large hand lingered a little longer in Imogen's small one didn't go unnoticed, and along with it a peculiar chemistry passed between them; peculiar because it felt sensual and familiar, comfortable and easy, calm and odd, all rolled into one. After some preliminary introductory chitchat about classes and schedules and the mutual need for caffeine, the threesome headed out together in the direction of the Starbucks down the block.

5

As the first person in his large family to attend college Fletcher Brown hadn't known what to expect, but as it turned out, it had been amazing so far, way better than he expected. It really was true that college, if anything, was about being exposed to new ideas and learning how to think critically. Still, Fletcher was a country boy through and through, born and bred. He loved country music and boot-scootin' and nothing better than knocking back a few beers on Sunday afternoon on the porch. And sometimes the good ol' boy mentality seeped through, despite his newfound global awareness. Archaic ideas about gender roles and masculinity; about how women should look and behave and recognize their natural place, a perspective that just didn't fly in this progressive college environment. His outspoken and unpopular views often got him into trouble.

Yet, Fletcher was such an amiable guy, polite, and downright respectful that people often forgave his backwoods views. Although the education would be helpful on the ranch, and for maybe later when he wanted to start up a business, he didn't see himself going off to "find himself" in the big city or backpacking through Europe or hiking the Pacific Coast Trail, or any of the myriad things other young people dreamed of doing. No, the post-college life Fletcher envisioned was more in line with returning to Idaho, finding a nice local girl to marry, raising a couple of kids, and growing old together there.

He had already met a lot of nice people, Rachel, in particular. Rachel was fun and full of life and big ideas, and even though they'd sort of tried doing the girlfriend/boyfriend thing, it hadn't felt quite right; theirs was a close friendship, one that unbeknownst to them would last a lifetime. And once they got past the awkward romance part, the two were inseparable. They did everything together. She introduced him to Starbucks and Indie films and rock bands and he taught her to boot-scoot and do tequila shots and regaled her with stories of sunrises and cattle and sunsets and wide-open spaces. His relationship with Rachel had become as cozy as his scuffed up boots. He had settled into it, and he loved how easy and hassle-free everything felt between them, but that changed that first term in economics class, the day Imogen Oliver walked into his life and stole his heart away.

It was a moment for sure. One he'd watched at the movies a million times before. He and Rachel had settled into their usual seats up at the top of the enormous forum classroom. It was only the first week of the term, but already they had both noticed how the professor ended or began practically every sentence with "at the end of the day." It had turned into a silly game where they kept a tally of the number of times he repeated it in class.

Way up there in the nosebleed section, they were oblivious to whether or not they were annoying anyone, especially the girl seated directly behind them. But when she poked Rachel with the end of her mechanical pencil and they turned around, rather than being angry, he was pleasantly surprised. Gobsmacked, was actually more like it. When he saw her it was like time slowed way down. In fact, at that moment he was fairly certain that he heard that classic love at first sight flourish from Tchaikovsky's *Romeo and Juliet* overture play-ing on loudspeakers somewhere just outside of his head. Well, he was sure it wasn't really like that, but in his mind's eye it was exactly the way it happened.

Imogen—she exuded a vibe of sweet girl next door-ness meets wild thing, and something about her face made her seem interesting and approachable, like someone you'd want to meet right off the bat, and talk to and hang out with and get to know better. She was that girl that everyone said reminded them of a character on that one TV show; you know the one, but could never quite remember her name. Her hair was pretty, sort of honeycomb colored, her eyes were grayish-blue. When she smiled she had a small gap between her two front teeth; a spattering of freckles marched across her nose.

She wasn't all made up and Fletcher liked that. It reminded him of the girls back home. Her face was fresh, without makeup and rouge and lipstick and mascara and all that girly nonsense the other college girls thought they needed.

It was all he could do to stop himself from turning back around in his seat to gawk at her. And when they finally met after class, the instant he learned her name—Im-O-Gen, and shook her hand, he felt, no he knew, that something like a lightning bolt had passed between them, and contemplations of Idaho, marriage, and kids flew straight out the window.

6

66 Grammy, I need your old photo album," Imogen called out to her grandma as she dropped her keys and purse on the table and headed straight for the wooden bookcase that overflowed with an array of books on every conceivable topic, old scratchy 78 rpm records, dusty knick-knacks, and the bulky picture album she had scrolled through probably a million times or more.

History 103: Intro to recent American history; Progressivism-Present, a simple assignment on the syllabus instructed: Choose an old photo from the turn of the century and write about it—where was it taken? Who/what was the subject, the year, what was happening in the US/world historically at the time the photo was shot, and if people are in it, research the period clothing, cars, whatever was in the photo. Imogen was excited and eager to begin. She didn't always love-love her history class assignments, but for this one, she knew precisely where to get such a photo—Grammy's old photo album. She remembered as a child spending hours propped up on her couch in the living room flipping through the musty pages, enthralled by the procession of solemn faces of people she would never know.

"You know where it is," Grammy called out from somewhere

on the back porch. Imogen found it and pulled the hefty album from the shelf and carried it over to her special looking-through-the-picture-album spot on Grammy's couch. She slowly opened the book, careful not to tear the fragile fading pages, and there they all were like old friends—Aunt Ada and Uncle Paul and Aunt Phyllis and Uncle Gordy and second cousins Percy and Viola from Missoula. Wedged among the street scene photos of blurry carriages, and buggies and horses going by was the photo she was looking for; the one she had always loved the most.

The subject of the photo was a saucy young Grammy, but before she became anyone's Grammy, when she was a youthful Iris Graham, age 18 dressed up in a fetching lacy white dress with pearl buttons and wearing the biggest, most outlandish hat Imogen had ever seen, with peacock feathers poking out of it in every conceivable direction. The photo never quite seemed to fit with the rest of the pictures in Grammy's album, of Kansas and Missouri and other dusty Midwestern destinations, but Imogen had never thought too much about that, only that it was her favorite. In the photo, her head tilted slightly to the left, Grammy, or Iris seemed to be smiling at someone outside of the frame. Funny, Imogen hadn't noticed it until just now, but careening through the photo was a blurry someone on a bike gesturing with his hand behind Grammy in the foreground. As a child, she had detected the blur, but had never noticed that the blur wasn't a mere camera anomaly; it had form and substance and movement.

"Grammy, come here," Imogen called from the couch.

"What is it Imogen? I'm busy right now," Grammy answered. Imogen carefully removed the picture from within the little photo envelopes, set the album aside, and walked into the kitchen where Grammy was busy taking canning jars and seals off the shelf and putting them into a box.

"Grammy, who took this picture of you? Do you remember?" she asked, holding out the photo for her to see. Grammy stopped what she was doing, pulling her glasses up from the chain for which they dangled from around her neck.

"Hmmm," was all she said as she took the faded sepia-hued cabinet card out of Imogen's hand for a closer look. "Oh, I'm quite certain Andre took that," she said handing it back to Imogen and resuming her search for more jars and seals.

"He was a photographer, right?"

"That's right."

"Well, who's this person behind you on the bike?"

Grammy set a jar down and leaned over to take a second look at the picture. "Odd, I never noticed that before," she said. Her lips began to turn up into a smile as though remembering a happy memory. "Why, that must have been Simon," Grammy said.

"Simon?" Imogen asked puzzled.

Grammy continued. "Simon Elliot was Andre's assistant," she explained. "As I recall, I had been wooed out to the park that day by warm sunshine and the promise of wine and a baguette for a photography session. He told me to put on a pretty frock and to wear my feathered hat. Simon was supposed to help with the camera; cameras were quite large affairs in those days, but he was late, so Andre had set everything up himself and he was all ready to snap the photograph when Simon must have rode through the shot on his bike. That's why he's a blur. There was a charming young girl that showed up that day too, as I recall," Grammy said, speaking out loud more to herself than to Imogen. "I think there is a photograph of her, too, around somewhere . . ." her voice trailed off. Grammy continued to gaze at the photograph with a faraway look as though transported back to that sunny day in the park in 1901.

"Well," she said abruptly as if the spell had been broken, "I don't have time for looking at old pictures; there's canning to be done," she said, handing the picture back and turning away from her granddaughter.

"Grammy, can I borrow this picture?" Imogen asked.

"'s'ok with me," Grammy said without looking up, "what do you need it for?"

"Oh, just for one my history classes," Imogen explained. "I'll bring it back tomorrow, I promise. I need to write about what was happening in the world."

Grammy snickered at that, "Courtship and love was happening in the world when that picture was taken."

Later that evening, Imogen sat down at her desk and propped the borrowed photo from Grammy against the computer monitor to use as a reference as she composed her history essay. She wrote about the clothing styles and the Belle Époque-inspired, wide-brimmed hat festooned with an impressive plumage of exotic bird feathers. She wrote about turn of the 20th century events, World War I, the sinking of the *Titanic* and the *Lusitania* and about the wave of innovation and inventions—electricity, cameras, the phonograph, the telegraph, the telephone, the motorized car, and the typewriter.

As Imogen began to dig deeper into the time period, it occurred to her that something about Grammy's story didn't quite add up; couldn't be right. How could this be? Imogen thought, picking up the photo, and turning it over to read her grandmother's familiar handwritten words on the back:

Iris Graham, 1901, age 18

She'd probably looked at that a hundred times without even thinking about it. She was certainly no math wiz, but if what she was thinking was true, if Grammy was 18 in 1901, that would mean she would have been born in 1883, which would make her like a whopping 132 years old!

"That's impossible," Imogen whispered aloud, shaking her head in stunned confusion. Perhaps Grammy had miswritten the dates. That had to be it. She turned the photo back over and gazed intently into the face of the woman in the picture. It certainly looked like Grammy. The eyes were the same, the shape of the mouth, the nose, but how could she be sure? Grammy had always been sort of secretive and mysterious about her age, but this was crazy. Imogen scanned the picture for more clues. There was that person on the bike that she had not noticed before. What had she said? It was the photographer's assistant? He was late? And today she'd mentioned a second photo from that day with a young woman. Why had she never seen it?

As she pondered all this and continued to scrutinize the photo, something strange occurred—something she had felt only one other time in her life, twice, in retrospect, if you counted the drug-induced trip to that dark, nothing limbo-like place where she had heard voices and smelled barbecue.

Although she couldn't articulate it when she was a child, there was no mistaking what was happening now. The walls and floor seemed to wobble. It made that same gulping baloomp noise and then everything around the edges of her peripheral vision began to grow dark and blurry and surreal. It was like she was looking through a frosted lens. She sensed movement and images and people and she heard voices echoing in the distance like they were coming from the end of a protracted tunnel. Imogen squeezed her eyes shut, afraid to open them until whatever was happening was over. A dizzying sensation of motion made her feel sick to her stomach— like her insides were being stretched out and coiled, the pores of her skin teeming with goose bumps followed by a prickly, tingling feeling of hair standing on end, and for the third time in her life, she had that feeling of being somewhere else, not just some other place, but some other time.

Imogen gingerly opened her eyes. Gone was her desk and computer, the mouse, keyboard, chair, and her vintage 80s Elvis Costello concert wall poster. It was no longer evening. The milieu that moments ago had been her bedroom had evaporated completely, replaced now by a park. Once the shadowy vignette of the photograph fell away, it was crisp and clear; the colors bold and the sun bright.

No one seemed to notice that she had arrived seemingly out of nowhere, and as she glanced to her left and to her right, Imogen knew exactly where she was. She was in Grammy's photo, of course. And oddly, she wasn't a stranger out of place or time. Her clothes matched perfectly to those of the other turn-of-the century women strolling leisurely through the park. Every detail—from the button-top shoes that were noticeably pinching her toes to the frilly off-white summer frock with a big blue sash and the oversize hat she felt resting precariously atop her skull—was appropriate for the era. It was as though she'd stepped into a scene right out of *Hello Dolly*.

There was so much to take in—the sights, the sounds, the fragrances. Was that popcorn she smelled? The park was buzzing with summer activity; kites flying through the air and children and dogs frolicking in the lush green grass, women with parasols strolled along the promenade guided by gentlemen in straw hats. It seemed so vivid; so real. But how could it be? Those doubts temporarily drifted away like a wayward balloon when in the distance she heard the circus-pipe music playing from a carousel and breathed in the very real, very sickly sweet aroma of caramel corn mixed in with an oddly tinny odor of magnesium and sulfur that seemed to radiate from the puff of smoke hovering above and to the right of a very large camera. An older gentleman with a salt and pepper beard and a really angry face emerged from beneath the black cloth on the huge old timey camera that rested precariously atop a tall wooden tripod that took up most of the cobblestone sidewalk. He shook his fist and began berating another man in his thick French accent.

"I told you to be here at twelve sharp!" he bellowed at the younger man, expressively waving his hands in the air for dramatic effect. "Thees camera is much too eavy for me to carry alone!"

The younger man seemed frazzled, but genuinely apologetic. "I am so very sorry Andre; I tried to get here as fast as I could," he explained as he hurriedly rolled his bike over to a massive oak tree and leaned it up against it.

The men continued to converse with one another, but in muffled muted tones that Imogen could not quite make out. It was then that she turned her focus on the woman standing beside her also demurely watching the unfolding dramatic exchange between the two men. Stunned, Imogen couldn't suppress the small gasp that escaped her lips. The woman was Grammy, er Iris. There was no doubt this woman was the much younger version of her grandmother. Imogen suddenly felt very uncomfortable, like an intruder that had, well, stepped into this scene uninvited, but surprisingly, it was Iris that put her at ease. She seemed completely oblivious to the fact that this stranger beside her, Imogen, had simply not been there a mere few seconds ago.

Imogen tried to cobble together a memory of what she had last been doing, before all this. She was working on her history paper. Had she dozed off and she was dreaming? None of it made any sense; she had no clue what the rules were, if in fact there were any rules at all. Imogen decided her best course of action was to just go with it, play along, see what happens next. She wasn't entirely sure she could pull it off on such short notice, but she was a history major and luckily, only moments ago, she'd been studying this particular era for her assignment.

Their conversation finished, the two men joined Grammy/Iris, and flanking her on either side, together they appraised the newcomer. Imogen wasn't sure what to do or say, but as it turned out she didn't have to do anything. Grammy stretched one delicate gloved hand forward for Imogen to grasp.

"Hello, she said warmly, "My name is Iris Graham."

Imogen took her grandmother's small, youthful hand and felt her light squeeze around her own. This is so weird, she thought. Even through the gloves, she felt something like a connection, and she sensed that Grammy may have felt it too, but if she did, she did not let on that anything was out of the ordinary. Their hands parted and whatever she felt immediately disappeared. Grammy placed one hand lightly on Imogen's shoulder, turning her to face toward the two men in the party.

"This is Andre. He is a celebrated Paris photographer," she said. Andre took Imogen's hand and gave it a light peck. Imogen nodded; she wasn't sure what the protocol was, but she'd seen enough old movies she was certain she could probably fake it.

"And this is Simon," she said. "He is Andre's very late assistant," she said with a smile so charming even Imogen was captivated. Imogen smiled back with wonder. Wow. Just wow. Grammy was totally awesome.

"Simon Le Bon Elliot" the much younger man said, inelegantly tipping the rim of his straw hat and bowing slightly.

Imogen couldn't help giggling and Simon's brow furrowed as if confused by her reaction to what seemed to be his best, most elegant introduction. Imogen caught herself, realizing that Duran Duran, the 1980s boy band led by the Simon Le Bon she was familiar with wouldn't take the music world by storm for another 80 years or so.

"Forgive me," she said doing her best petite curtsy. "My manners . . . so very nice to meet you Mr. Elliot," she said with a straight face. "Imogen Oliver" she said, extending her hand and allowing it to be kissed as was customary at the time for proper male and female introductions.

Simon took her hand as well, but instead of the light peck that Andre had given away, Simon looked up and into her eyes, allowing his lips to linger on her hand for what seemed like an impossibly long time. It was awkward for sure, but in an oddly pleasant way that Imogen couldn't define. There was something else curiously odd about him, something she couldn't quite pinpoint—an old soul perhaps?

Yet, he looked to be only a teenager, younger than she was probably. It gave her an unsettled feeling that she had to all but ignore because when he finally returned her hand it was her turn to return niceties. It was one thing, sure, to know how to nod and let your hand be kissed and all that, quite another to get the words right; to not completely blow it by blurting out some lame-ass, tortured 21st century verbiage. She took a deep breath, well as much as a deep breath as she could muster within the constraints of the uncomfortable corset she was wearing under her dress, and smiled a nervous smile.

"Hello I am very pleased to meet all of you." It sort of came out in one long sentence without pause, and for a second she was sure they must suspect that she was an imposter, but when they smiled and nodded at her, she knew she had passed as one of them . . . for now.

"Why don't we photograph the ladies," Andre suggested to Simon in his thick French accent. "The sun eese nice overhead, no?" he said bringing his hand up to shade his eyes. Imogen thought it sort of strange that she was being invited into this intimate circle, a complete stranger, although she couldn't be certain if Grammy suspected who she was. But how could she? Imogen had not even been born yet.

From what she had read recently, photography was considered an art form in Victorian times. It wasn't like how it was in her time with people using their smartphones to document every living breathing moment of their existence, from a selfie shot in front of the bathroom mirror and the latte they were sipping at Starbucks that morning to the drunken group mug shot later that night at the club.

No, in this time, people made a big deal of getting dressed up and posing for a solemn portrait at a professional studio equipped with an assortment of fancy props and accessories like balustrades, columns, and trompe-l'œil moldings, which symbolized the power of the middle classes. In the pictures Imogen had seen heavy drapery swags opening onto fancy painted backcloths situated on oriental rugs or parquet floors and jumbled together alongside a variety of chairs and tables was the preferred photography studio set up of the day.

In her history of photography class Imogen had also stumbled upon a macabre practice known as Momento Mori—photographing the dead—which had also grown out of the studio portrait movement around this time. Imogen had viewed slideshows depicting children and adults propped up on stands to appear more lifelike, or lying back as if sleeping next to their parents and siblings. The long exposure times lent itself to this type of nonmoving subject, creepy as it was.

And although lightweight kits and handheld cameras were becoming readily available in the market for amateur photographers, Andre was a purist. Even though his expensive Rochester Commodore field camera was bulky and heavy he favored the gelatin dry plate negatives, and moving the studio camera outdoors to capture people in a more natural environment, a challenging, but preferred method for professionals.

Andre meticulously set up the photo shoot, posing the two women next to each other, adjusting their chins and having them tilt to the left slightly to capture the right light. He rushed back to the camera and his gray head disappeared beneath the camera's black cloth. The flash lamp exploded and Imogen carelessly turned her head slightly to look at her lovely grandmother. A twirling cone of smoke rose into the air as the edges of Imogen's peripheral view began folding inward and dissipating. The bright sun faded away to complete darkness and Imogen realized that in the span of a few short seconds she had been returned to her room.

She felt a little like Dorothy in the movie *The Wizard of OZ*— "My! People come and go so quickly here!" It had to have been a dream, Imogen thought. She must have fallen asleep while she was writing her paper. Yet, she didn't feel at all rested; in fact, it was the opposite and she had a mild headache, and when she'd gotten up to go to the bathroom to pee, she'd felt wobbly and disoriented for a few minutes.

She took a quick glance to see if the photo was still propped up against the books. It was. Nothing had changed. There was Grammy Iris in her crisp white frock, the blurry figure—Simon could still be seen in the background. She felt sure she had been there. She remembered the sunshine and the unmistakable smell of popcorn; she remembered everything, but how could she be sure? Grammy would surely have answers.

7

Imogen rolled over and tapped the snooze alert on her phone. She would have to get up, eventually. She had an economics class later, but she felt extraordinarily tired, which was weird because she remembered falling asleep early last night, within about an hour following the bizarre time traveling experience. Back through time? Crazy. She wasn't even sure that really happened. How could it have? Maybe she'd dreamt the whole thing. That made more sense. But why was she so fatigued? Could it have something to do with the upsetting of the temporal workings of the universe? She smiled at the sheer absurdity of it as she burrowed further beneath the warm comforter, prolonging the comforts of bed. She knew she should get up now if she wanted to stop in and chat with Grammy before class. Grammy lived next door to her in the tiny house that they'd shared up until recently when she'd decided to move back into her parent's home.

Using the spare key, she unlocked Grammy's front door and let herself in. She set her purse and keys down on the side table like she normally did, but when she looked up, Grammy was standing right there by the door.

"Ohmygod, Grammy, you startled me," she said catching her

breath.

Grammy had a peculiar look on her face. "Are you okay?" Imogen asked as she took a step forward placing an arm around Grammy's shoulder.

Grammy looked directly at Imogen and said, "You went back, didn't you?"

Imogen was stunned. "How did you know?" she gulped.

From behind her back, Grammy produced a photo and handed it to her.

Instinctively, Imogen's palm went up to her mouth. In this new, old photo, one that Imogen had never seen before, Grammy Iris, in the same white frock, gazed demurely into Andre's camera, but beside her was a young girl. She had turned her head when the camera bulb exploded so there was a slight blur, but there was no mistaking who it was.

"So it really happened," Imogen cried, "It was you, and I was there, too!"

"Yes," was all Grammy could whisper.

Imogen led Grammy over to the worn couch where they sat side by side in silence and stared at the picture together for a bit.

"Where did this come from Grammy? How did you get it?" Imogen finally asked.

She shook her head slowly back and forth before responding, "I must have forgotten about it, but when you asked me for the photo yesterday, I had a memory of a girl who had posed with me in another photo that Andre took that day," she said. "And I remembered thinking how odd it was that I immediately felt so drawn to her, and then I looked at you and you looked just like her. So I went through my other picture albums and I found this print—strange, I must have overlooked it."

Imogen had been confident that Grammy would reassure her that she'd dreamed it all; that looking at old photos had simply filtered into her subconscious before she had fallen asleep. The last thing she expected was real, tangible photographic evidence that what she thought she dreamt had actually happened. Imogen's mind reeled with questions, but she wasn't quite sure where to begin—how was it possible that Grammy was there? How had Imogen gotten there? She decided to start with Grammy first.

"How could you have been there Grammy?" Imogen asked. "How is it possible? I thought you grew up during the depression."

Imogen thought of all the familiar faces in the album that she'd viewed so many times over the years, the part she had dubbed the "road" section, which was a series of photos that chronicled the family's harrowing 1932 exodus from Missouri to the Northwest in a busted down Pontiac sedan—from dust bowl to deliverance. Hazy black-and-white photos of a lonesome hi-way against a backdrop of desolate and dry landscapes; of a youthful Grammy posing in front of scores of ticky-tack mom-and-pop businesses, motor courts, and roadside attractions like teepees and giant oranges along the road; restaurants and gas stations and old rusty cars, the *Jackrabbit Trading Post, Snuffy's 24-hr Grill, Mr. D*_z diner, a big EAT sign, and smaller signs scattered along the roadway that had the names of the next town on them: Joplin, Adrian, Santa Fe, Winslow, Needles . . .

And the one road sign that showed up prominently in the compilation: Route 66, the *Mother Road*, the road to opportunity, eight states, deeply rooted in the American psyche as a symbol of freedom and mobility and despair. There were also pictures of Grammy's little sister Lillian at age 13, standing alone on the prairie leaning against the rudimentary trailer her father had built from scratch for their protracted trek, looking sadly down at a sagebrush bush in the desert, staring pensively up at the clouds in the sky, always looking away, never at the camera. Imogen had never met Lillian; she had died shortly after their trip, Grammy Iris said. And later, the Oregon photos of Grammy Iris and Grandpa Roy, who had died before Imogen was born, and her dad Niles when he was a little boy. Had Grammy lived a whole other life somewhere else in some other time?

Grammy paused. She glanced up at the ceiling before slowly choosing her words carefully. "We have a gift," she began.

"A gift." Imogen dubiously repeated. "What kind of gift?" Grammy shushed her.

"Be still now and I'll tell you a story."

Imogen settled back against the couch to listen to what her grandmother had to say.

"Do you remember the photos of Lillian, my sister?" she asked. Imogen nodded that she did. Grammy's forehead wrinkled up and the pained look on her face indicated to Imogen that this story was not going to be an easy one to tell.

"Lillian was ill, schizophrenic they said," she continued. "In those days, they didn't know how to treat people like her; they didn't have the medications they have now." Grammy hesitated and took a deep breath, "Suicide. Lillian killed herself," she revealed sadly.

Imogen reached over and took her hand and held it. "I'm so sorry," Grammy. "I never knew that."

"Nobody outside the family knew," she said. "Folks didn't discuss things of that nature. It was a sin, a shameful family secret."

Imogen frowned at that. "You know I don't believe in any of that sin nonsense."

Grammy nodded, "I know. Me either," she admitted, surprising Imogen a bit with her confession.

"I suppose you're wondering what this has to do with how I ended up in that photo." Imogen lightly squeezed her hand, noticing how rumpled with age it was, and nodded.

"Lillian was my best friend, and when she died, I was devastated," Grammy said. "I stopped eating and I became weak and anemic. I got so sick my worried parents sent me off to live in the country with Aunt Phyllis. They thought the fresh air would do me good. They had an old photo album too, like mine, and just like you, one day I walked inside a photo. The only difference was I stayed there for quite a long while."

She explained that her aunt's father had been a photographer and how she had been drawn to several photos in particular. "He had shot a sequence of street scenes from several different angles, of horses and carriages and ladies on foot wearing big hats and parasols," she said. Something about them piqued her interest.

"One minute I was sitting in my room, and the next thing I knew I was standing on a street corner inside one of the pictures. And I was dressed in the same sort of clothes that they wore, like I belonged there. I was part of the scene," she explained. "And like you, I was scared the first time it happened. I thought I had dreamed all of it, that it wasn't real." Imogen nodded in total agreement.

Iris told Imogen that she had come back from that photo, but kept returning there again and again. She liked 1901.

"Times were simpler, less complicated . . ." she said, "and I met someone."

"Andre?" Imogen asked.

"Yes, Andre," Grammy confirmed.

One thing led to another and Iris was spending more and more time there, carving out a new life. "I was young and carefree," she explained. "In 1901, there were no bread lines or economic depression, no rumblings of war yet, only lightness and gaiety and, of course, Andre."

"But you came back, why?" Imogen probed.

Grammy shifted uncomfortably on the couch and drew a deep intake of air before continuing. "I missed my parents, and I wanted them to have grandchildren," she said. "I realized I was being selfish, so I decided to come back for good. Soon after that I met your grandfather."

It was a lot to take in, but Imogen wanted to know more about this so-called "gift." Who has it? Can just anyone walk into a photo or is it only certain people, and why her? That nebulous memory of landing on a beach somewhere and taking her mother's hand when she was four; in high school, the strange place she'd gone when she was high on mushrooms—had she traveled to another time?

Grammy told her as much as she knew about time travel, which turned out to not be very much at all. If there was a concrete scientific explanation, she wasn't aware of it. She discovered some of the details through her own experience and she knew that traveling through time was exhausting, which Imogen already knew.

After Grammy's time spent in the past, she never returned, and never time-traveled again after that, but she did know that when she came back to her time she was nearly the same age as she was when she left, or at least she hadn't aged very much.

"Time had passed," she said "but not at the same pace. When I came back, it was almost as if I picked up where I'd left off."

She had also heard a rumor once about a group called the *Daguerrest Society* who studied and collected old tintype photos. Some of them, she had heard, had the ability to travel through time, but it was all very secretive and hush-hush.

"Whew." When Grammy was finished talking, Imogen let out a heavy sigh and stood up to stretch her legs. "I have to go, Grammy," she said, "but I'll be back later and we can talk about this some more."

But Grammy stopped her. Grasping Imogen's hand, she pulled her back. "Sit down Imogen," she said, "that's not all of it."

"But Grammy, I have class today," Imogen whined.

"Class can wait," she said.

Rolling her eyes, Imogen made an exasperated clicking sound. She had made plans to hang out with Rachel and Fletcher today after class, but she did what she was told and sat back down on the couch.

Grammy's face seemed serious and stern. "If you ever decide to do this again," Grammy warned her, "an important word of caution: Make sure that the photo you go into is in a safe place while you are in it.

"Why?" Imogen asked.

"Because it is your anchor, and it has to stay intact for you to be able to return through it," Grammy said.

That seemed reasonable, of course, and she could understand why Grammy would want her to know that if and when she ever decided to try time travel again, yet something wasn't right. Considering Grammy didn't seem to know an awful lot about how it all worked it made Imogen wonder, how would Grammy know about the portal/anchor thing if something hadn't happened? She didn't want to interrogate her grandma, but the question needed to be asked.

"How do you know this, Grammy?"

All the color seemed to drain from Grammy's face suddenly, making her appear sad and wrung out and old as if she was carrying a heavy burden that her small, shrinking shoulders could no longer support.

Grammy glanced down at her hands for a second before lifting her head and speaking. "Your parents, they also had the gift."

Imogen's jaw dropped. "What are you saying Grammy?" she asked anxiously.

"I was so afraid to tell you Imogen." Grammy's lower lip quivered and tears began to slide down her cheeks. "I thought you were too young to understand . . . I was afraid you might go looking for them, and get lost too."

Imogen couldn't believe what she was hearing. Her parents were alive? All this time? She impulsively flew off the couch and began to pace back and forth, hand to forehead, on the verge of tears and panic.

"I'm so sorry Imogen," she could hear Grammy saying somewhere in the background of noise and confusion churning around in her own head. "I should have told you . . ."

As she paced, shock turned to anger as the magnitude of this information began to register in her brain; the years of lying in her bed at night weeping, mourning them, praying to that stupid, silent god to please, please, please just bring them back to her.

Livid, she spun around to face Grammy. "Where are they?" she shouted. "Tell me. If they're not dead, then where are they?"

Grammy, who had started to sway back and forth on the couch herself, only whimpered. "I don't know, I don't know," she sobbed. "Someone destroyed the photos. I don't know who or why," she exclaimed.

"How could you lie to me Grammy?" Imogen demanded. "How could you tell me they were dead when all this time you knew they were out there somewhere?"

Grammy covered her face in her hands, too upset now to speak, and Imogen, feeling like she might explode if she stayed there a minute longer, tossed her arms up into the air in frustration. The precipitous need to get as far away from Grammy's weeping and excuses as possible propelled her out the door to find a place where she could be alone to gather her thoughts and process this new and profoundly shocking information.

Grabbing her purse and keys she burst out of Grammy's front door, heading straight for her Mazda, which was parked in the driveway. It wasn't until she had gotten several miles away, windows rolled down, music turned up, that Imogen began to feel like she had regained a semblance of control.

She pulled into the wide expanse of a ubiquitous Wal-Mart parking lot and parked in a space way, way out at the outer reaches where people parked their late model campers and Winnebago's for overnight camping. Cutting the engine, she leaned forward, resting her head against the steering wheel. As if a switch had been flipped, the tears came, buckets of them; years of pent-up pain and emotion dribbling wet like rainforest-sized drops down her cheeks and cascading off her nose onto the dashboard, her shoulders writhing as it all spilt out. What was wrong with her? She wondered.

Learning her parents weren't dead should make her feel happy, but they may as well be dead because no one knew where they friggin' were! They were lost to her no matter what. It wasn't fair. She punched the steering wheel with the palm of her hand.

"Goddamn it," she heard herself lamenting to no one.

In between sobs, she heard a faint tapping, and turning her tear-stained face toward the sound, spied an older, bearded man peering in through the window at her. My god, can't a person just be left alone? Imogen thought as she rolled the window down a crack.

"Are you okay miss?" the man inquired, a look of sincere concern on his face.

Imogen quickly wiped the tears from her eyes with the palms of her hands and answered, "Oh . . . yes," she said, feeling embarrassed. "I'm fine, no problem."

"Are you sure?" he asked again, unconvinced. Never sure what a stranger's intentions might be, especially in a Wal-Mart parking lot, Imogen surreptitiously depressed the door lock and started up the car. Nodding a polite thanks to him, she backed out of the space and drove away. The distraction was probably good, Imogen thought. Otherwise, she might have sat there blubbering for a few hours more. She thought about heading to class, she could still make it, but decided against it when she noticed the pair of swollen, bloodshot eyes staring back at her in the rearview mirror. And besides, she would have to make up a story to tell her friends and she totally wasn't up for that. No, she would just go back home. As angry as she felt at her, a picture of Grammy's stricken face was seared in Imogen's mind. She should go back anyway and check on her, see if she is okay, maybe figure out what should be done next.

Imogen parked in the driveway. All the way home, she had rehearsed what she would say to her. She was sorry, not sorry at all. Grammy was clearly in the wrong here, but she did want her to understand that even though it wasn't okay that she had lied to her, she still loved her and appreciated that she'd taken care of her and raised her after her parents were gone.

She paused on Grammy's porch and took a deep breath before opening up the door. Pushing the door open, Imogen called out,

"Grammy?" No one immediately answered. Imogen entered the small living room and looked around. "Grammy?" she called again, feeling concerned now and moving swiftly toward the kitchen. "Grammy!" she cried when she saw Grammy's small frame sprawled out on the floor behind the couch. She wasn't moving. Imogen felt for a pulse. She was still alive, but her breathing was slow and shallow. "Don't worry, Grammy, I'm calling an ambulance now," Imogen said as she dialed 9-1-1 emergency.

8

Reaching across Grammy's bed, she twisted the plastic tube thingy to close up the window blinds in the ICU. Mid-afternoon sunrays had been doing a slow march up the bed as she napped. The doctors said that the stroke was severe, but fortunately, Imogen had gotten to her just in time. Still, because of her age, Grammy might never fully recover. Although the stroke had rendered her left side numb and useless, she was still able to speak but with some difficulty. And speak she had. Ever since she had stabilized on Tuesday, Grammy had insisted Imogen stay by her bedside, to listen. After holding secrets in for so long, Imogen thought it must have been cathartic for her. What worried her most was what might happen when Grammy ran out of stories to tell.

Growing up, Imogen had no clue about her parents "other life." She knew that they were photographers. Period. Grammy told her that they were worried that they would not be able to afford Imogen's college tuition on their salaries, so they had picked up extra jobs on the side. Evidently, they turned their ability to time travel into one of those side jobs. They went back into the past to dig up information for people as kind of time traveling private investigators. One of the stories about her parents—Izzie and Arnold's box—had a happy ending and it had set Niles and Francis on a path to help people, if they could.

According to Grammy, as it was in the present, in the past, life was happening all around you, and you couldn't unsee things that maybe you would like to as evidenced in one of the couple's early expeditions to the past, in which they had witnessed a crime. The outlaw, Rattlesnake Dick was his name, and his gang robbed the stagecoach Niles and Francis were riding in. Stagecoach robberies were common in the Sierra foothills of Northern California. No one was hurt, but the gang got away. Known to bury their loot, a curious Niles and Francis followed the outlaws and watched them bury it out in the middle of nowhere under a lone oak tree at the top of a small hill.

They came back to their own time thinking that they could forget about it, let it go, but it wouldn't go away. Historical records showed that shortly after that robbery, the gang had been ambushed during a bank heist and all the members shot and killed, which meant the money was likely still buried up on the hillside. Niles and Francis knew they could not return the money to the rightful owners, a mix of nameless strangers on a stagecoach, but they could research the land. A quick property search at city hall turned up a report, along with aerial and property shots showing that the old oak tree—much older and knurlier now—was part of someone's land parcel.

Records showed that the house on the property had been built in 1914 and inhabited by several generations of the Beckman family until being sold in 1949 to an Arnold and Izzie McGee. Birth and death notices revealed the McGee's tragic story. Their first child, a daughter, had been stillborn; a second child, a boy was born in 1951, and another daughter was born in 1954. At age seven, the little girl, Ana, died of a rare bone disease. Their son, Timothy died while serving in Vietnam in 1969. If anyone was more deserving of the lost money, it seemed that the McGee's certainly were.

The Olivers took a drive out to the place. The ramshackle farmhouse, big chunks of peeling paint clinging dejectedly to all sides and a falling-down picket fence enclosing the unkempt yard, stood in the shadow of the hill about 50 yards away. Niles and Francis traipsed through the weedy, unmown lawn to the front door and knocked; knocked again, but no one appeared to be home, so they made their way up the hill to examine the base of the tree where they'd seen the robbers bury the money. They were trespassing. They could be arrested, they knew this, but what the hell.

Making a mad dash back down the hill to their car, they grabbed a shovel from the trunk and returned to the spot. Niles began to dig where they'd seen the outlaws digging so long ago. About a foot deep into the hole, the shovel clinked against something hard. He shoveled around it and drew out an iron lockbox. Surprisingly, it wasn't locked and Francis watched as Niles wiped the dirt off and carefully lifted the lid. Their eyes widened with childlike wonder when they viewed the contents of the box.

Inside it, probably more than a thousand gold coins in mint condition. The dates on the coins ranged from about 1847 up to 1894. Niles glanced over at Francis and said, "Imagine what this could buy," immediately feeling guilty for saying it.

Francis nodded in agreement, but replied. "We can't," as she re-closed the lid of the box. "These don't belong to us Niles." She took the box and placed it back in the hole, covering it over again with dirt. Niles picked up some pebbles and loose gravel and leaf debris to disguise that someone had been digging.

A few days later, Niles and Francis returned to the spot, and making certain that no one was at home, they dug up the box again, but this time they filled the deeper hole in with dirt and buried the box in a much shallower hole. Francis strategically placed a couple of dog treats on top of the box before covering it, and another bone beside the hole, hoping that their dog would find it, start digging, and expose the metal for the couple to find. If this didn't work, they would have to go to plan B, but they hoped they wouldn't have to resort to anything more obvious. Niles and Francis drove the car down the road and parked it in a secluded spot, walked back and hid behind some bushes to watch.

They had studied the couple's routine, which included taking their little dog out for a potty walk before entering the house. Today was no different. After parking the car and getting out, the scruffy little mutt leapt from the back seat and began running toward the house. Izzie called him back as Arnold opened up the gate and Winkie ran out the gate.

"Hold up Winkie," Arnold shouted, but Winkie spun frenetically around a few times the way little dogs do, yipped and then made a beeline straight up the hill to the tree where he stopped in his tracks and sniffed. From the distance, Francis and Niles couldn't make out exactly what the dog was doing, but knew that he had most likely found the treats. He whirled and twirled and spun around the spot a few times, grabbing the bone in his mouth and tossing it up in the air.

"Whatcha got there, Wink?" Arnold called as he neared the tree. Winkie dropped it and Arnold picked it up and threw it. Winkie raced across the grass after the bone. Francis looked at Niles and put her palm to her forehead. Oh no, so much for relying on little dogs. They placed the fetch game for a few minutes more until it appeared that Winkie had successfully done his business and now Arnold and the dog were heading back toward the enclosed yard. But then, all of a sudden, Winkie stopped in his tracks, his nose pressed high into the air as if he'd caught a whiff of something new and exotic, and he turned around and raced back to the tree where he began furiously digging, his little paws making short shrift of the dirt that stood between him and the tantalizing aroma wafting up from somewhere in the depths below.

They figured Winkie must have found the treats and the box because he started barking incessantly. Arnold shrugged and walked wearily back up the hill to the tree to see what the silly dog was up to now. They watched everything unfold, as Arnold seemed to stare intently at the ground for a minute before bending down on one knee—not exactly an easy feat for an elderly gentleman. It looked like he was digging, and when he stood up they could see that he was holding the box in his hands. He opened the lid and although the couple couldn't make out his features, they could imagine the look of surprise that must have registered on the old man's face.

Arnold turned slightly and they heard him calling out to his wife, "Izzie, Izzie," as he lumbered down the hill and across the yard and up on the porch toward the front door, still holding the box, and disappearing inside, leaving little Winkie spinning in circles in the yard.

"That was all they had to see," Grammy said. "Niles said in that moment, he felt like Robin Hood."

It was a sweet story, one Imogen had never heard before, and she was glad that Grammy had shared it with her, but it was not the story she needed to hear, not the one that mattered, the one about what happened the day her parents disappeared. But that would have to wait for another day she supposed, because when she glanced again over at Grammy, her eyes were closed tight. She had fallen asleep. All of the talking must have worn her out.

Imogen leaned over, and pushing aside a few stray strands of silver hair that had fallen across her brow, gently kissed her grandma's wrinkled forehead. She couldn't stay angry with her. Inside, she knew that Grammy had wanted only to protect her. She was just a little girl when it happened after all. She would come back tomorrow and maybe Grammy would tell her what she wanted to know, but she needed to get back to her classes, back to something resembling normal. And more importantly, and maybe for the first time in her life, she needed to be around friends.

9

She was first to arrive at the coffee shop. Ordering her usual hazelnut latte, Imogen grabbed a table by the window to wait for Rachel and Fletcher to show up. It had been a nice surprise when these two had unexpectedly entered her life. But they had made it easy by making the decision for her. Had it been up to Imogen, she would have soldiered on through college alone, as she had always done, through grammar school and middle school and high school, never making any real friends and avoiding the social situations where those associations tended to gel. But with Rachel and Fletcher, not being friends had not been an option, and surprisingly, not an option for Imogen either.

As she looked out the window, watching the rain and listening to the comforting tap tapping of drops against the pane, she wondered if she should tell her friends what she'd learned about her parents. She'd missed several classes so she'd have to tell them about Grammy, that she'd had a stroke. But telling them her secret, about the gift, her parents' disappearance, they would never understand that, and besides, she really didn't know them well enough yet. And why would they believe her? She scarcely understood it herself. On the other hand, she desperately wanted to tell somebody. Lost in thought, Imogen didn't feel the light tap on her shoulder until she looked up and saw that Rachel had sat down at the table opposite her.

"Hi," Rachel said breathlessly as she extricated her arms from her wet rain jacket. "Sorry we're late," she said. "Fletcher's in line." Imogen turned to see Fletcher, who glanced over at her and waved.

"So what's up Imogen? Where you been?" Rachel asked.

Here we go, Imogen thought. "What'd I miss in class?" she deflected.

Rachel took a sip from her latte. "Not much, lectures like always . . . Oh, but a full page of 'At the end of the days,'" she said, giggling.

Imogen laughed at that. It felt good to laugh, to be back with her friends drinking coffee inside a warm, familiar environment on a rainy day, the aromatic smell of coffee beans and Norah Jones crooning in the background, far away from the featureless room where she'd spent the last few days with Grammy, listening to the unremitting boops and beeps of the machine she was hooked up to in the taciturn, sterile hospital with its unnecessarily uncomfortable chairs and odd assortment of unpleasant, unidentifiable odors.

Fletcher joined them at the table. "What are you two giggling about," he asked as he set his coffee down and plopped in the middle chair between the girls to his left and right.

"I was just telling Imogen that we added about another full page of tallies," Rachel said. Fletcher grinned and looked over at Imogen, his eyes lingering probably a little longer than they should. Imogen hadn't noticed it before, but although Fletcher acknowledged Rachel when she spoke, when he had turned away Rachel had continued looking at him. It was fairly obvious that Rachel held some feelings for Fletcher.

"So Imogen," Fletcher said, "where have you been? We missed you in class."

She brushed her hair behind her ears and just spit it out. "I've been at the hospital. My grandma had a stroke."

Rachel gasped. "No! Oh Imogen, I'm so sorry. Is she okay?"

"She's okay," Imogen replied. "I mean, she's old. It could have been much worse, I guess."

"Sorry Imogen," Fletcher said without looking up as he fiddled with the paper sleeve on the outside of his cup.

Rachel reached out and touched Imogen's sleeve. "What can we do?" she asked. "We'll give you our notes from class for sure, but is there anything else you need?"

Not since Jade had Imogen felt so comfortable and cared for. It had been so long, she'd forgotten what it was like to have friends, and more than anything she wanted to tell them everything, what happened to her parents, the gift; she wanted to share everything she'd been holding inside for the last few days, and she was just about to when her phone started to vibrate.

"Hello," Imogen said. Rachel and Fletcher listened to her side of the conversation.

"Yes, yes, this is she." She nodded. "Oh." A stricken look crossed Imogen's face. "Yes, of course. I'll be right there."

"What is it Imogen?" Rachel asked, the concern in her voice evident.

"It's my grandma," Imogen said. "She's dead."

10

66 Is there anything else you need, Imogen?" Helen asked as she
    stacked the last rinsed plate in the dishwasher.
Imogen leaned up against the back of the worn couch and slipped
out of her black heels. "Oh, no Helen, I'm fine," she said.

"Are you sure?" Helen asked, a growing look of concern crossing her wrinkled face. "I can tidy up the living room for you before
I go?"

Although Grammy had all but abandoned religion, she hadn't
let go of her church lady friends, and they had come through in a
pinch. Imogen appreciated all of them, Helen and Vivian and Patsy
Parish and Mrs. Pippen—they all stepped up and essentially took
charge of everything, from making the funeral arrangements to
helping Imogen choose flowers—purple Iris, Grammy's favorite.
They baked cookies and made casseroles—so many in fact, Imogen
would not possibly get through them all. They'd been great, but now
all she wanted was for everyone to go away and leave her alone. The
last few days had been exhausting, to say the least, emotionally and
physically.

Helen untied Grammy's apron—the one with the apples on
it—from her waist and walked over and sidled up next to Imogen

on the couch. "Are you sure you're ready to be alone?" she asked, taking Imogen's hand in hers and stroking it softly. "I know you are tired and want everyone to leave," she explained. "But you know, once everyone is gone, they're gone. You'll be all alone then, and the silence can be deafening."

A tear slid down Imogen's cheek and she rested her head against Helen's soft shoulder. "I miss her," Imogen said.

"I know you do," Helen said, lightly stroking Imogen's hair. "You will always miss her, but she lives in here." She patted her heart with her other hand.

Imogen was grateful that Helen hadn't said something virtuous like that Grammy was in a better place or singing hymns with the angels now in heaven. They sat like that in silence for a few minutes together until Imogen wiped her face and leaned forward. "Thank you Helen," she said. "I am so grateful to you and the other ladies. Seriously, I couldn't have done it on my own."

Helen stood up and patted Imogen on the shoulder. "You take care of yourself, honey," she said as she stood up, grabbing her coat and heading reluctantly for the front door. "Give us a call at the church if you need anything."

"I will," Imogen said and meant it.

She watched Helen back out of the puddle-filled driveway in her big Chrysler 300 and drive away, and almost immediately, Imogen fell apart. Cue big wracking sobs and keening, an emotional earthquake and a tsunami of tears that she'd somehow successfully managed to keep at bay throughout the days leading up to the funeral today. Everyone had been super nice, but none of them seemed to notice that she was dancing along the edge of a breakdown, trying extra hard to keep it all together.

When this first round of tears finally subsided, Imogen wiped her eyes with a tissue and then stripped off the plain black "funeral" dress, tights, bra, and undies and slipped into Grammy's claw foot tub for a much-anticipated hot, soothing bath. She could go home to her own house next door, but silly as it seemed, she felt a need to be close to Grammy tonight, to be in her house.

The warm water felt good at first, but after a few minutes of listening to the dull drip, drip, drip of the tub's leaky faucet, she realized that she'd made a mistake. Helen was right, the silence was deafening. She should have turned on some music before getting into the bath.

Before, she could always hear Grammy doing something busy outside the door, humming, or bustling around the kitchen. The TV was almost always on—she liked watching the soaps during the day and shows like *Jeopardy* and *American Idol* at night. Sometimes, she played her vinyl records on the ancient record player, or listened to the radio—Grammy liked everything, whether it was the old timey songs from the Gay '90s to swing and jazz and classical and contemporary pop. Her diverse musical tastes made perfect sense now that Imogen knew that Grammy had spent several years actually spending time in each one of those eras.

When things became too quiet to bear, Imogen emerged from the tub, dried off, twisted her shoulder-length hair into a messy bun, and put on a pair of loose-fitting sweat pants, an old T-shirt, and a pair of fuzzy socks. She thought about putting on some of Grammy's records, but decided against it—too soon and too much effort, opting instead for some mindless television. Luckily, bad mind-numbing reality shows were a mainstay of TV fare these days, so finding something in that genre wasn't particularly difficult.

Imogen plopped onto the couch with a couple of pillows and a blanket, and with the exception of potty breaks and occasionally wandering into the kitchen to make a bowl of cereal or slapping some cream cheese or avocado spread on a toasted bagel, that's where she mostly stayed for the next few days. When she wasn't watching TV, she slept, albeit fitfully, dreaming about crazy, convoluted things.

In one, she made mud pies with her childhood friend Jade. In another, she was riding in the car through a tunnel with her dad as they laughed and held their breath together; the next she was spiraling out of control through darkness complete. She awoke suddenly from one particularly disturbing dream in which she was choking on toxic smoke and running away from a sky on fire.

Upon waking from each dream, she wished only that Grammy would have been in it, but the closest she came to her was the one where she found herself discussing the merits of baguettes with Grammy's photographer friend Andre and his young assistant Simon.

Light spilling into the bedroom through a leaky gap in the curtain woke Imogen up. The drizzling rainstorm that had begun the day of the funeral had finally subsided, and Imogen was tired of being a homebody. Throwing off the blankets, she padded into the bathroom to pee.

"Oh dear," she said out loud as she glanced at her reflection in the mirror. Her messy bun was a crazy blob of chaos, and days of intermittent crying had turned her eyelids into two puffy, swollen pillows. Grabbing a bag of frozen peas from the freezer to bring down the swelling, Imogen sat on the couch and for the first time in three days, turned on her phone, setting off a string of notification pings. With one eye she scanned through multiple "Are you okay? Call me texts" from Rachel and Fletcher. Helen and a couple of other ladies from the church had left messages too, and she had three days' worth of piled up emails, mostly of the spam variety, as well as condolences from coworkers.

After a shower and a change of clothes, Imogen felt marginally human again, physically at least. Today, she planned to tackle what she had been, up until this point, effectively avoiding—going through Grammy's things. Helen had said that it wasn't necessary to do it right away, or even all at once; she should take as long as she needed. A lot of the stuff could stay put for now, the furniture, the knick-knacks, but Imogen wanted answers and whether they were to be found or not, Grammy's personal affects might hold, if not answers, possibly clues. And if anything, being in Grammy's room, around her personal items held the potential for making her feel better mentally, a chance to not only feel close to Grammy in some weird way, but to also maybe learn more about who Iris was.

It had been years since Imogen had stepped foot inside Grammy's bedroom. She always kept the door shut. The rest of the house was unremarkable, functionally practical, so when Imogen turned the doorknob and entered the room, she wasn't prepared for the magic that awaited her inside this spectacular private sanctuary, a wonderland that Imogen would never have imagined existed in this tiny corner of the house. It reminded her of a gypsy trailer overflowing with bohemian artifacts drawn from a mish-mash of periods, a Victorian-era chair over here, an art deco broach over there, a splash of mid-century modern floral-patterned bark cloth curtains adorning the windows.

The focal point of the room, a queen-size wrought iron bed, was made up with a stunning vintage plush velvet patchwork quilt and nearly completely covered in dozens of decorative pillows of every size and shape and fabric and color, some old, some new, some hand-sewn with intricate patterns and beads. And like her granddaughter, Grammy must have loved soft, furry blankets, too—arranged at the foot of the bed was a neatly folded mound of them.

In the corner, resided a stunning vintage waterfall vanity with a large round mirror accompanied by a dainty, leather-covered vanity chair with tassels ringing its edge. In an opposite corner stood an oversized antique wood armoire. A thick tapestry rug covered the hardwood floors, and on the small nightstand, a black shawl was draped lazily over the lampshade of a small desk lamp, Imogen assumed to mute the light and provide a calm, relaxing ambiance.

Antique shops, Saturday Market, Target, and Ikea were Grammy's favorite shopping venues, and there was a little bit of mix of all three in the room. Accents from pictures in antique frames to incense and Yankee candles, tea lights and bamboo were arranged throughout the space. It was quite a busy room, yet it all seemed to somehow work harmoniously together. It was comfortable, inviting, a room you could disappear into for hours at a time. Imogen could picture Grammy sitting at the vanity brushing out her long, silver hair with the vintage comb and brush set, or leaning against a mountain of pillows piled behind her on the bed as she stayed up late into the night absorbed in one of her favorite science fiction novels or worked on the *New York Times'* daily crossword puzzle, in ink.

In her youth, Grammy had hair the color of wheat that with age had turned a lovely silver. She grew it out long and wore it in a loose braid that cascaded down her back, or sometimes piled into a neat bun on top of her head and festooned with a jewel-encrusted vintage stickpin. Even though she was no longer a young woman, Grammy had a way of doing "young." Even as her body aged, in her mind, she saw herself still as that fledgling girl having her photograph taken in the park on a sunny, carefree day.

Maybe it was the way her eyes sparkled when she laughed or the lightness of her gait, but whatever it was, she had aged gracefully, and once the suitors stopped relentlessly pursuing her she seemed to relish her newfound freedom to come and go as she pleased. She could dance with abandon, make jokes, be silly, and be herself, which to Imogen made Grammy one awesome human. She played piano—everything from Bach to Bowie, and made killer chicken enchiladas.

She was curious about all things; she read voraciously. She sewed, she knitted, she wrote and she painted. She did it all. Grammy was what they called a scanner or multipotentiate. Imogen had read up on it when she herself had struggled to choose a college major. Scanners were people like Imogen and Grammy who were interested in far too many things to settle on just one. What if she picked the wrong thing? It made life difficult at times, but Grammy, and now Imogen too, had learned how to just go with it. Everything, they agreed, was worth at least a try.

So standing here now in Grammy's room, thinking of her, imagining her there, Imogen felt torn, as though going through her things might somehow violate Grammy's trust, yet Imogen felt strongly that it was important for her to push through the hardest part first. Rationally, she knew that Grammy wasn't there to oppose anything, although in here, surrounded by her stuff, her presence was palpable. Imogen wished she believed in the supernatural. How great would it be for Grammy's spirit to appear before her right now and tell her that everything was going to be okay? As a child, she had prayed every night to the invisible sky god to please, please bring her parents back. She should be thrilled knowing now that they might be alive somewhere, but it was Grammy that she ached for. Grammy was the one who had raised her, who had been there for her all this time, and now her heart, which felt as raw as an open wound, was breaking in two.

Tears began welling up in her eyes, threatening to spill over again, but dammit, she had to do this. Wiping them away with her hand, Imogen marched across the room and swung open the armoire doors. A delicate aroma of lavender escaped from inside the closet. Grammy's dresses and sweaters were carefully hung on cloth hangers; her shoes neatly lined up in a row at the bottom. Grammy could be quite meticulous about things when she wanted to.

Imogen pulled out a random purple sweater and rubbed the

soft material against her cheek before reflexively burying her entire face into it. It had always struck her as cliché in the movies when someone had died and the spouse or loved one would bring a piece of their clothing up to their nose to smell. But now she understood. Grammy's essence lingered, especially here, in her special space.

Still holding on to the sweater, Imogen pushed some of the dresses aside, and at the back of the closet she found a large sealed garment bag, which she pulled out and laid across the bed. Imogen gasped when she unzipped it and realized what it was. As she stroked the delicate fabric of the lacy white dress with the rows of small mother-of-pearl buttons, she remembered Grammy wearing it that day in the park. It was one thing to look at this 100+ year old dress and remember seeing it in an old photograph once, quite another to have actually just recently stood beside the woman who was wearing it!

Imogen was puzzled though. That can't be right, she thought. She wasn't totally clear on the rules of time travel, but it seemed like Grammy had mentioned that you couldn't bring things back with you from the past. And when she had stepped through into the photograph herself just a few weeks ago, in terms of clothes and accessories, the universe had amazingly filled in all the details, but when she had returned, she was back to wearing her normal clothes.

Leaving the dress lying on the bed, Imogen moved on to explore the contents of the drawers in the vanity. The first drawer contained an assortment of mementos and keepsakes, birthday cards, postcards, that sort of thing. She had to laugh when she pulled out a picture of what she figured was supposed to be Jesus, maybe Moses, or some biblical character constructed of glued-on beans that Imogen had made one summer in Bible school—half of the beans had come dislodged from the paper and were scattered around the bottom of the drawer—along with a few other crazy kid drawing masterpieces she'd created especially for her Grammy. The drawer below held more of the same, except these were older items—pictures her son Niles, Imogen's dad, had made for her in school along with various notes and cards and letters.

The top drawer on the opposite side held some promise—in it, a faded bundle of letters wrapped in ribbon. Imogen untied the ribbon from the pile of handwritten envelopes. The return address

was from Andre. Again, Imogen was confused. How was it possible for her to have these in her possession? Had a postal person
from the past delivered them to the future? She set them aside to
read later. Then, Bingo! Beneath a stack of old postcards were two
journals. She gingerly opened the first book, which looked old; the
faded material covering it and the binding on the spine were starting
to unravel in places.

In Grammy's expressive cursive handwriting, the beginning sentence read: "I am in love, and his name is Andre." Imogen sighed.
"Oh boy," Imogen said aloud. She gathered up both books, walked
over to the one chair in the room, a surprisingly comfortable wing
back chair upholstered in rose, green, and white chintz with shiny
pale green enameled legs, and curled up into it. This might take a
while, she thought as she reached over and plucked a furry blanket
from the bed, pulling it across her lap and settling in to read.

11

Closing the journal, Imogen stared blankly across the room for a second or two. She felt like she'd been sucker-punched. For the last hours, she had been voyeur to Grammy Iris' most intimate thoughts, peering into a secret garden that paramours keep hidden deep within the cobwebbed corners of their hearts, where only poets and lovers and dreamers dare to tread. And the ending, well, the ending was not a happy one, and the fact that the ink was smeared on the page with probably Grammy's own tears made it all the more wrenching. Of course, Imogen knew the story. She knew how it ended before she started reading. Grammy had made the heart-breaking decision to return to her own time, and all of that pain, she had chronicled in her diary.

Imogen felt terrible, like she'd completely violated Grammy's privacy, but nonetheless, the journal had yielded some invaluable details about the logistics of time travel—answers to questions she hadn't gotten the chance to ask Grammy about before she died. First, her question about how all of the 20th century stuff had made it back here had been answered. It was an ingenious work-around, really. Grammy had simply placed any items in a safe place where they would remain undisturbed until she came back to retrieve them later on in the future.

She also wrote about the phenomena of aging. Apparently the past and the future don't move along at the same pace. Although Grammy had spent nearly 10 years living in the past with Andre, when she returned home to her own time, she was nearly the same age as when she left. It was as though her own time was a movie that had been put on pause, awaiting her return. It could be as little as 15 minutes or as long as a few hours.

After taking a much needed bathroom break and grabbing a quick sandwich, Imogen returned to the bedroom to dive into the second journal. This one was newer and the entries were more recent. As she flipped through the pages she noticed that about half of the book was unused, and the last entry Grammy had made was just two weeks ago. A lot of it was mundane stuff about things she was doing, from working on a quilt to harvesting the garden to preparing for canning season. Imogen skimmed over some if it until on one of the pages her own name jumped out at her. *"Imogen has the gift."* It continued:

"I let her borrow a photograph that Andre had taken of me, and it was strange, but a memory popped into my head from long ago. I remembered a girl that had showed up that day and posed with me in the second photo he took. I dug it out of my drawer to check and sure enough, it was her. It was Imogen. I always wondered if she could do it too and now I know. She has lots and lots of questions and knowing Imogen, she will wear me down until I tell her the truth about her parents. I know I should tell her, but I fear her reaction. Will she hate me?

I never wrote about the day they disappeared because I wanted to believe it wasn't true. It was easier to tell Imogen, and myself, that they were dead. They may as well have been. It was unusual because normally they didn't both travel at the same time. Either one or the other stayed behind to look after Imogen, and when I found what was left of the two photos smoldering in the trashcan I had no idea where to even begin to look for them and I couldn't leave Imogen alone to go searching anyway. A lie was easier, but I've carried the burden for that lie all these years. If I tell her, I could lose her too."

So they weren't together. The idea of this disturbed Imogen. For some reason she had assumed that they would be. And Grammy had written that this wasn't normal, that they never traveled at the same time. Why would they do that? Imogen wondered. And the broader question remained, who destroyed the photographs, and why? If only Imogen had prodded Grammy for more information. She had thought they had more time, but now it was too late. This was all she had to go on, and sadly, it wasn't much.

Imogen returned Grammy's journals to the vanity drawer where she'd found them, but as she was setting them down she felt something lumpy underneath the dainty embroidered handkerchiefs. Pushing the hankies aside at the bottom of the drawer was a metal key ring and two keys attached to a round plastic ID tag labeled: "studio".

Her parent's photography studio, a space her dad had converted from an old barn that had stood on the property, had been locked up for years. Because of digital photography, there was really no need for it or the darkroom, with its washes and basins and shelves of abandoned chemical solutions and racks where her daddy used to store his photographs to dry. But knowing it was there behind the locked door was comforting. It reminded her that his presence once filled up that space in the world. Asking Grammy about it had been on her list of questions, but now that she had a key, who knew what she might find inside.

The gravel pathway leading out to the studio behind Grammy's house was muddy and mushy, and the building itself was so overgrown with blackberry vines they threatened to consume it whole. Knowing this, Imogen had come prepared, remembering to grab a pair of hedge clippers on the way out to battle the nuisance vines that had created a snappish obstacle to getting to the studio door. But cutting away the vines took quite a bit longer than she anticipated. As she battled the brambles it reminded her of the times she'd helped her dad clear them away from the garden. Despite their herculean efforts, the plants seemed to have a battle plan of their own, fighting back with nasty razor-sharp thorns that grabbed hold of your hair and latched on to your clothes, and by the time you were through, left your arms scratched up and bloody.

Finally, the last vine plummeted to the ground, and Imogen was relieved to have escaped with only a few minor cuts and scrapes. Pulling the keyring from her pocket, she first unlocked the padlock, then placed the other key in the door's lock and turned it. She heard it click and tried to open it, but not surprisingly, the door, which had not been opened for many years, was stuck. Imogen pressed her body against the door and pushed until it finally cracked open.

Figuring it would be dark inside, she had also remembered to bring a flashlight along. She was correct. It was indeed very dark . . . and creepy. Rationally, she knew that it was just an ordinary structure, but years of scary books and movies fueled her imagination, conjuring up an infinite number of potentially creepy scenarios that could happen in old, neglected buildings. Imogen leaned in through the opening to take a look before entering. The only light came from a small slit between the sagging curtains at the window, barely enough for her to make out much of anything. Switching on the flashlight she walked through the door. Everything was covered in a thin coating of dust, and a network of cobwebs hung from the rafters like slithering snakes. She was a little concerned about that, because where there are cobwebs there are probably spiders and Imogen was not at all fond of spiders, or any insects for that matter, except for ladybugs and butterflies, although even their wispy feelers made her feel queasy when they ever happened to brush up against her skin.

She was pretty sure the building was still hooked up to the power lines and using the flashlight to light the wall she found a light switch. Whether the bulbs in the lights would work, was another story. When she flipped the switch she had her answer all at once. Boom! The entire room was instantly bathed in a virtual flood of bright incandescent overhead lights. It was a photography studio after all; the light was expected, but also rather disconcerting. Imogen decided that it was almost creepier with the lights on than with the flashlight because now she could see every single icky cobweb.

Still, it put her at ease knowing that she was able to see what was in front of her now and she wouldn't have to fumble around in the dark with a flashlight. From floor to ceiling, the dust covered everything. "Ew," Imogen said aloud as she stepped into the room and noticed that the floor was also covered in disgusting trails of mouse droppings. But other than the visible degeneration of the place, it looked much the same as she remembered, disturbingly so.

Everything was eerily untouched, left exactly as it had been before it had been sealed up like a tomb when she was nine. From the stool where many a high school senior had posed in front of the black cloth backdrop ringed by the camera on the tripod facing it, to the various light-bouncing umbrellas, the standard Rembrandt setup of overhead and side lighting essential for any professional portrait studio, everything was sad and silent and the same.

The mouse droppings made a repulsive crunching sound as Imogen made her way across the room and opened up the door to the darkroom and switched on the light. A torrent of unexamined feelings bubbled up inside her; memories of watching her dad make the pictures appear like magic after first dipping them in the developer tub, then into the stop tub, and finally into the fix tub before picking them up with tongs and placing them on the special rack to dry. The large bottles of chemicals and solutions still sat dusty on the shelves.

Honestly, when she'd come out here this afternoon, she hadn't expected the emotions to hit this hard. It had been years. She had grown up, gotten used to them not being in her life, but the darkroom, clearly a trigger for her.

"Oh my gosh, daddy," she cried out into the empty darkroom, as the tears began to spill from her eyes, and roll down her cheeks and across her nose and down her neck. Overcome by this unexpected wave of emotion, she flipped the light off and immediately left the room, shutting the door tightly behind her. It took a few minutes to compose herself, but she pressed on.

In the office area, Imogen's was instantaneously drawn to the wastebasket. There it was, the one Grammy had described in her journal. And when she walked over and took a look inside, she was surprised to see that after all this time the remnants of their photos were exactly as Grammy had described in her journal. Leaning down for a closer look, she could barely make out a trace of an image, but for the most part, they had been completely destroyed, and when she touched the edge with her finger, they imploded like the Sands Hotel in Vegas, collapsing into a small hill of ashes at the bottom.

Imogen stood up and walked around behind the desk and sat down in the leather office chair. Nothing else seemed out of place. Everything was in order; pencils and pens, an x-acto knife in a glass mason jar, paper clips attached to a magnetic plastic holder, a daily desk calendar unturned and stuck on Tuesday, October 7. Imogen's thoughts wandered back to that day. Knowing now what she didn't know then, made the memories feel especially raw.

At first, when Grammy had broken the news to her that her parents were dead, gone, Imogen didn't believe it. She remembered that she started to cry, but after that things were a blur. In retrospect, she must have suspected that things weren't quite right. For one, there was no funeral. It was true that her parents weren't religious people and they didn't have a lot of friends, but still, there were a couple of people they might have invited, plus some relatives. Had she been older might she have questioned Grammy more? If they'd been in a car crash, wouldn't there be something about it in the newspapers? A celebration of life, at least? But as a devastated child who believed she'd just lost both of her parents, Imogen had no choice but to trust her Grammy, the only person she had left in the world.

Imogen figured Grammy did what she thought was best at the time. She didn't report them missing because how would she explain it to the police? She had simply cancelled their appointments, boarded up the studio, and told their handful of friends and a few relatives that they had decided to move abroad.

An incident not long after they were gone made more sense now. She and Grammy were out shopping at the mall one time when they ran into an acquaintance of Francis. Imogen remembered thinking it was strange that the woman had asked Grammy what country Niles and Francis were residing in now. Grammy had quickly changed the subject and shepherded Imogen away from the lady. At the time, she had supposed that the friend didn't know what had happened to them and Grammy probably hadn't wanted to talk about the accident in front of Imogen.

She remained in the office for a few minutes longer, opened a few drawers without finding anything very interesting. She'd come out to the studio hoping to find answers, but the only answer was confirmation of Grammy's story about the photos being burned and that didn't bring the closure she'd hoped it would. One day she'd have to come back and do something with all the equipment, but today wasn't that day. Shaking off the memories the place had conjured, Imogen started to get up to return to the house when in her peripheral vision, something shiny caught her eye—something looked like it was wedged inside of a small hole in the wall over in the corner. She hadn't noticed a hole before. Could the mice have gnawed all the way through the wall? It was possible, she supposed. They had years to do it.

She walked over and bent down to take a closer look. Yep, there was definitely something wedged in there, but Imogen was hesitant to stick her fingers inside it and poke around; what if she touched a mouse? Pulling out the flashlight, she aimed the light into the hole. It looked like something made of metal. She hated to damage the wall further, but figured it would need to be patched up sometime anyway. Imogen walked over to the broom closet and began to scavenge around for something she could use to expand the hole. At the very back of the closet, she found a hammer. "Aha!" she said to nobody, "this'll have to do." Using the claw end of it, she carefully pulled and punched away at the wall on both sides of the hole, sending shards of sheet rock shavings cascading to the floor.

Once the hole was large enough, she was able to reach in and pull out the object. It was old. It looked like one of those old tins they used to use to store stuff in, from seasonings and coffee to baby powder and tobacco and dog biscuits. Although there were some words on it, they were too faded to make out. Imogen shook it. Something that sounded like paper rattled inside. Carrying the tin over to the desk, Imogen carefully pried the lid open and pulled from inside it a stack of sepia-toned photographs.

She fanned the dozen or so photos out across the surface. They were indeed old and probably taken during the same era as the tin in which they were contained, by the looks of them. It was curious; every one of them appeared to be of the same woman, but in various poses and different locations. They weren't studio portraits, which would have been characteristic for that era. In one, the woman, wearing a simple gingham smock over a long-sleeved blouse, her hair pulled up into a loose bun, was outdoors standing next to a covered bridge. Perhaps taken by an enthusiast with a Brownie camera, Imogen deduced.

In most of them she was alone, but in others she held an infant in her arms. Still others featured the same woman a few years later standing beside a young boy of about six, presumably the infant from the earlier photos. In one, they stood in front of a building. Although the boy was blocking it, she could make out a few words on the sign behind him: Crestv . . . What the heck? Imogen wondered. Who was this woman and how did pictures of her end up in the wall of her parent's studio?

As always, Imogen had even more questions, but who could she ask? Briefly, a fleeting idea flew through her mind. If she had this so-called gift that Grammy said she had, couldn't she do it again, just wish her way into one of these old photos and find out who this person was? Yes, theoretically she could, she supposed, except for one thing, she was afraid to. Without Grammy here for guidance, it felt way too risky.

And as she stood there in the vacant studio, Imogen was all of sudden incredibly overcome by the magnitude of aloneness she felt—the silent empty walls around a place her family had once inhabited, a world absent of everyone she ever loved and cared about. It was clear, this wasn't the time for making decisions. She needed more time to process the information about her parents and to grieve the loss of her grandmother. She could barely do those things and focus on school at the same time. Like Scarlett O'Hara in *Gone With the Wind*, Imogen would deal with it later, she decided, after she'd finished school. Gathering up the photographs, she stuffed them back inside the tin and tucked them under her arm. Taking a quick perusal of the studio before turning out the lights, she closed the door, and left the studio to the spiders and mice.

Back at the house, Imogen wrapped a rubber band around the box to secure the lid, placed it inside an empty shoebox, and affixed a piece of masking tape to the top. Using a magic marker she wrote on the tape: Studio photos. After placing the box on the very back shelf of her bedroom closet she climbed down from the folding stepstool and plopped down on top of her bed. It had been a long, exhausting afternoon. Tears again, were starting to pool behind her eyelids, threatening to spill over. Would it ever end? She wanted her goddamn life back, the way it used to be before Grammy died. Jesus Christ, she was only 19. These emotions were overpowering. She just wanted it to all go away. And after today, she couldn't help wondering if believing her parents were dead might have been better than finding out they were alive, and wondering if both of them might be out there right now, on the other side of somewhere.

12

Imogen fidgeted, biting the corner of her lip. She had questioned her motives more than a few times before drumming up the courage to actually get out of her car and walk up the sidewalk to his apartment. Following days and days of marathon weeping, Imogen had turned her phone back on, surprised to find dozens of messages from her friends. Fletcher and Rachel insisted that Imogen get out of the house and come out to eat with them. As it turned out, it was the best night she'd had since Grammy's stroke.

They ate a lot and drank too much, ending up later at Rachel's apartment. Rachel got sick and said she was going to bed, to lock the front door when they left. Being with friends was just what she needed and Imogen and Fletcher ended up talking into the early hours of the morning. They talked about everything, about science and history and literature and philosophy and about their dreams for the future. Imogen even came close to telling Fletcher about her secret gift, but something held her back. She wanted to share it, but was afraid he might think she was crazy.

As the night wore on, tension was building between them, not necessarily in a bad way; more like an unspoken need that they both exuded. She wasn't quite sure how to define it, nor was she ready to fully acknowledge it. Yet, as stimulating as the conversation was, for an introvert like Imogen, it was also becoming exhausting, and so at around 4:00 a.m. she stood up and announced she was going home. Fletcher impulsively reached out, pulling her in close for a hug, which turned into several small smooches, followed by a much longer, more impassioned kiss that surprised both of them. When they finally drew apart, Fletcher touched Imogen's cheek and softly whispered in her ear, "Come back and see me tomorrow."

And so, here she was tomorrow, standing outside the 17th Street apartment building where Fletcher lived, back for more of what she wasn't quite sure. She liked Fletcher; she liked him a lot. He was smart and funny. He was cute, no . . . he was adorable. Seriously, that curly black reckless hair, those thick black eyebrows and the shadowy eyes that were like two pools you could totally get lost in, everything about him was more than attractive; and that kiss, well, the kiss was out of this world. It was probably the most excellent kiss Imogen had ever received from anyone, ever. It was true, her basis for comparison was limited, she'd had only a few kisses in her life and those that she had received were undisciplined, teenage boy kisses—this was something quite entirely different. Although it wasn't exactly a shoot-you-over-the-moon, fireworks-bursting, wildly romantical, only-in-the-movies type of kiss, it was certainly of the variety that left a girl yearning for more of the same, please!

Imogen vacillated between knocking on the door and not knocking on the door. Should she make up some excuse? She wanted to go and she didn't want to go, and there were reasonable explanations why or why not for both scenarios. First of all, they were friends. Why ruin a good thing with romance? That's the way it always went down on TV, in books, and in the movies. Second, what would Rachel think? They said they were just friends, but Imogen saw the way Rachel looked at him. Was she willing to risk losing them both over a careless moment? Is that all this was?

Sure, she was aroused and curious, and obviously, so was he, but it was more than that, too. It felt like a stirring of something good. And all she'd had lately was bad. Was it wrong of her to want for herself just a little bit of good?

The time for changing her mind came abruptly to an end when Fletcher flung open the front door.

"Hi," he said. His heart was beating like a drum.

"Hi," she said back.

"Come in," Fletcher said, gesturing for her to enter the apartment. "Oh, can you take off your shoes?" he asked embarrassed. "My roommate insists," he apologized.

"It's no problem," Imogen said as she slipped off her boots and set them on the floor in the entry hall beside the coat rack. She took off her coat and Fletcher hung it on the hook. Imogen couldn't help noticing how uncomfortable he seemed. He kept his hands in his jeans pockets and stared at the floor without looking up.

"This is really weird, isn't it," she offered.

Fletcher agreed. "A little," he said.

"Is your roommate here?" Imogen asked.

"Uh, no, he's at work," Fletcher answered.

Envisioning them going back and forth like this indefinitely made Imogen feel crazy. She decided to just go for it; pounce and see if what happened yesterday could or should happen again. She tugged at his shirt, teasing. That was all it took. Fletcher leaned in, and cradling Imogen's face in his hands, they kissed again, but this kiss lasted all afternoon.

There was just something about watching a cowboy take off his shirt, hanging his hat on the bedpost, taking a swig from his bottle of beer, then slowly unbuckling his Wranglers and enthusiastically pulling her onto the bed without even bothering to take his boots off. Fletcher was a skilled lover, and being with him was like watching *Dirty Dancing* like a million times; it never got old. She should totally walk away from this doomed relationship. Inside, Imogen knew that it was never going anywhere, yet, how could she? If his tongue was a drug she was hopelessly addicted.

Admittedly, the last few months with Fletcher had been more than great. Rachel had been okay with them seeing each other, they had a blast together, but Imogen had known going in that she wasn't ready for the kind of relationship she suspected Fletcher wanted. He claimed he was perfectly fine with their casual coupling, but she didn't believe it. His actions didn't match his words. Yet, as long as he was willing to pretend their relationship was going somewhere, so was she. That is, until he brought her a kitten.

She awoke to mewing. Sometime during the night, a sweet furry white ball of cuteness had joined her and was now coiled in a perfect sphere under her armpit, one little pink paw draped over Imogen's arm. She pulled him up on top of her stomach. "Who are you?" she asked the wide-eyed critter, his little head cupped in her hands. Fletcher came into the bedroom carrying a cup of coffee.

"I see you found your kitten?" he said.

"What do you mean, my kitten?" Imogen asked.

"He's yours," Fletcher said. "I got him for you."

Imogen eyed the furry dynamo incredulously. "I don't know if I need a cat," she said.

"You need a cat," Fletcher said. "If you won't move in with me, then you need some company. I don't like that you're by yourself so much. You definitely need a cat."

"I like being by myself," Imogen shot back.

Imogen nuzzled the little kitten's nose and stroked his soft ears. "You look like an expensive, high-quality cat," she said, "so I think I shall call you Luxe." Fletcher joined Imogen on the bed. Resting his head on his arm, he scratched Luxe's head.

"Thank you," Imogen said smiling. "He's cute. I like him a lot."

Fletcher sighed.

"What?" Imogen asked.

"Nothing . . . Well, it's just that we've been going out for a while and . . ."

"Oh, not this again Fletcher," Imogen moaned, rolling her eyes as she pushed the small kitten onto the bed and sat up. Fletcher didn't mean to sound whiny and insecure, but it always seemed to come out that way anyway when he brought up the subject of them moving in together.

"I just miss you that's all," he said. I want to wake up next to you every day, not just once or twice a week."

Imogen sighed again and turned to face him. "Fletcher, I can't. I care about you so much, you know that," she said. The distraught look on Fletcher's face almost convinced her to keep quiet, but she continued.

"I guess I'm just not ready for that kind of relationship," she said.

"Are you breaking up with me?" Fletcher asked.

"I don't know, maybe," Imogen said honestly. "I need to sort through a lot of issues in my life right now and I can't deal with that and college at the same time."

"I'll help you," Fletcher offered. "What can I do to help? I'll give you your space. You can have all the time you need." He touched her shoulder reassuringly and Imogen patted his hand and flashed a weak smile. Why did he have to be so goddamn nice?

Later that day as they were hiking the butte and drawing closer to the treeless, rocky summit, Fletcher broke the silence. "Almost there," he said to Imogen who was bringing up the rear.

"Yep, I see it," she said. When they reached the top, Imogen climbed up on the highest rock and took a big swig from her water bottle. The view from up here was spectacular; several notable mountains to the southeast, the city to the north, and a lake and reservoir and the Coast Range to the west. Hearing Fletcher approaching from behind, she turned around but was surprised to see him bending down in front of her on one knee. When he reached up and took Imogen's hand, she knew what was coming next.

"Will you marry me, Imogen?" Fletcher asked earnestly. She was flabbergasted. "I . . . I don't know what to say," she stammered.

"Say yes," he said.

Standing there, on a rock at the top of the world in probably the most awesome, romantic place on the planet for a marriage proposal, Imogen might have gotten caught up in the moment and blurted out "yes, yes, yes!" but almost as quickly as that impulse entered her head, it evaporated and she knew what her answer had to be.

Imogen lowered herself down to Fletcher's level and held his hand. "Fletcher, I can't marry you. I can't."

"Why can't you?" he asked. "And don't tell me it's because you have issues. Tell me the truth."

Imogen sighed and they both sat down on the warm rock. "Okay Fletcher. Here's the truth. I'm not ready to be married. Hell, I don't know if I'm even ready to be in a relationship," she explained. "I care about you. I do, but I know none of this is fair to you. I don't want to lose you, but expecting you to hang around and wait for me is just mean and selfish. You deserve better than that."

Fletcher nodded in agreement, and to Imogen's surprise he didn't seem all that angry. "Fair enough," he said, closing up the ring box and shoving it back into his pocket. "I can deal with it."

"You're not mad? You don't hate me?" Imogen asked, surprised.

"Of course I don't hate you Imogen. I could never hate you. And to be completely honest, I would have been shocked if you'd said yes."

"Really?" she asked dubiously. "Then why ask?"

Fletcher let go of her hand and stood up. "It was a long shot," he said. "Sometimes you just have to go for it, you know, pounce?"

She did know. "You're okay then? We're good?" she asked.

Fletcher nodded. "We're good," he said.

Fletcher had lied. They weren't good. Her refusal to marry him had wounded him deeply, and rightly so. It was his own damn fault for sticking around with someone who was so clearly afraid to commit. He stopped spending nights at her house, and even though it was awkward for a while, they remained friends. She offered to give back the kitten, but he refused; Luxe was hers. Imogen was grateful that he had been there for her after Grammy died, when she had needed him most.

And even though she was upset and sad and all alone again, she also had this feeling in her gut that perhaps the universe had something else planned for Imogen Oliver.

13

When she first stumbled upon this "gift," and Grammy confessed the truth about her parents, Imogen had, of course, wanted to set out immediately to find them, but her decision to wait and finish college had been the right choice. She wasn't at all ready to take on such a task at 19, although that hadn't stopped her from obsessing over time travel. Her research began in earnest, first with devouring as many books on the topic as she could get her hands on—from H.G. Wells' *The Time Machine* and Jack Finney's *Time and Again* to Madeleine L'Engle's *A Wrinkle in Time*. She spent hours watching movies with different variations on the theme: *Back to the Future*, I, II, and III, *The Butterfly Affect, Looper,* all three *Terminator* films, *Bill and Ted's Excellent Adventure,* and *Doctor Who.*

For pure entertainment value she watched episodes of an old television show from the 1960s called *The Time Tunnel,* which actually turned out to be pretty entertaining—what it lacked in poor plot twists, it made up for in cheap special effects and really bad production values. She also got sucked into the vortex of *Quantum Leap,* a super great television show, she discovered.

But despite how interesting and fun the movies and shows and books were, the fact remained, it was all speculative, so Imogen turned to the library in search of more serious answers. She checked out voluminous tomes on various abstruse quantum physics theories to see what science had to say about string theory and parallel universes and how fast light travels and Schroeder's cat and Occam's theory. Again, enthralling stuff, yet still, nothing she could find anywhere came close to explaining what she could do.

Was it something that only photographers could do? That didn't fit, she wasn't a photographer herself; not anymore. She took pictures for fun with her kids camera, but she hated having her photo taken, probably because her parents had made her the primary focus of their photographic portfolios.

Were her special abilities limited only to photographs? Imogen had actually tested that theory. Could she potentially walk or think her way into drawings or illustrations or even paintings; a Salvador Dali, the Mona Lisa, for instance? She tried. Did not work. No matter how long and hard Imogen concentrated, like a hulking bouncer at a trendy NYC club, the universe's sentry barred entrance. Clearly, the world would still never know what had made Mona smile, Imogen figured.

Devastated when she found out that her parents were still alive, she naively thought she knew how to get them back—simple, go back to the time right before they disappeared and note the locations of the photos they entered, maybe even find out who destroyed them. It was easy to find dozens of old snapshots of herself, of Jade, of their house, the studio, but there weren't many photos of the two of them, and even so, as Imogen thought about it, she realized, in all the photos taken around that time, she had always been somewhere nearby, meaning that the standard paradox of running into one's self would likely come into play. Remembering back to high school and that brief and scary trip she took to the shadowy "nothing" place, Imogen surmised that she must have entered the photograph of her dad, herself, and Jade that had been in the bathroom with her at the time, and the universe had stopped her, placing her in some sort of limbo place within the photo, thus preventing her from running into another version of herself.

And then there was the whole area of digital and cell phone photography, which, as she discovered—she tried that too—worked only if you printed out a hard copy of the digital photo to use as an anchor. It seemed another precautionary measure by the universe to keep you from getting stranded, for instance, the result of a device's failed battery, screensaver, the electricity going out, or even a pop-up ad that could temporarily disrupt things.

There were limitations for how far back you could go; obviously because the first photographs weren't even introduced until 1839. Before she died, Grammy had mentioned the *Daguerrest Society*. Louis Daguerre was the first to transfer photographic images to a thin plate. This group supposedly studied and collected old tintype photos, but she couldn't find a single bit of information about them on the internet, which seemed strange, but at any rate, it seemed sort of out there, woo-woo ghost hunter-ish, and she wasn't sure if these were the kind of people she wanted to associate with anyway.

She was also aware that you couldn't bring things back with you from the past. Grammy had written about that in her journal. But by far, the best and most mind-blowing thing of all was that the universe outfitted you in the appropriate period attire. Yet, after all her research, she came to the conclusion that she had no choice but to accept that she did not have to understand how it worked, only that it did, and if there were others out there who could do it, she may never know.

Eventually, Imogen set her preoccupation with time travel aside to focus on her studies. Finding her parents would have to wait, she decided. By the time her senior year rolled around, Imogen was floundering. While her classmates were making big plans, taking on internships and preparing for careers and life post-college, Imogen was beginning to panic. She wished she knew what she wanted to do, but choosing had always been a challenge for her. In grade school, when the teachers had asked the students what did they want to be when they grew up, all Imogen could ever do was shrug her shoulders; she was the only one in class who had no clue. There were too many options, how could she possibly choose a single one?

And now was no different. Growing up hadn't changed anything. She still didn't know what she wanted to do or be, and it was frustrating. What did one do with a degree in history? she wondered. She supposed she could go on to grad school and become a professor, maybe work in a museum; tour guide perhaps? Graduation came and went. Rachel accepted a job offer on a magazine in L.A. Fletcher returned to his family's ranch in Idaho.

She remembered Grammy mentioning that Imogen's parents had used their ability to time travel to supplement their income. Like private investigators they went back in time to find information about their client's dead relatives. Initially, she had really only wanted to use her gift to search for her parents, but why couldn't she do what they did full time? She could look for them and make money at the same time. There was one small detail to address, however. It was scary. Really scary. If she wanted to do it, she would need more practice.

As it turned out, her current job as barista at the Beany Barn, a local coffee shop near campus, was the ideal job for her needs. Lots of young people took gap time after college to travel abroad and experience life before joining the workforce, why couldn't she? The pay was decent, enough to live frugally on, and the hours were flexible, which provided Imogen with opportunities to research and take some trial runs. So while her peers were taking the year off to backpack through Europe or hike the Pacific Coast Trail, Imogen was doing the same, except her mode of travel was somewhat unconventional.

When she wasn't working at the coffee shop, Imogen scoured local antique shops and flea markets for old photographs, archiving them in her metal file cabinet with detailed notations about dates and events. She made a point to visit each era, familiarizing herself with the clothes and the architecture and the points of entry. She took copious notes about how long recovery took each time. She learned how to keep her head down and maintain a low profile, to avoid places of conflict; to ignore crime and not get involved, no matter what, no matter how much she wanted to help.

At home, she compiled lists of potential aliases, names plucked from history and literature and movies and music and pop culture that she could handily pull out and use to disguise her true self.

Although Imogen would probably never fully understand how it worked, she knew that fundamentally, it was a mind slip. She looked at a photo and imagined herself walking into it until she did. That was it. When she wanted to return, she focused her mind precisely on the physical whereabouts of the photo to transport back. Of course, it was never that easy or simple. There were the physical and emotional changes; the prickly skin, the wild tunnel ride sensation, the deep dark, the bright light, not to mention the aftereffects, the jaggies, the headaches, all of it. She couldn't say that she would ever get used to it, but after experiencing it a few times, the sheer wonder of stepping out of one time and into another replaced any anxieties about the traveling itself.

The more she did it, the more things she learned. For instance, because she always closed her eyes during the transition she had assumed that she was traveling through a tunnel, but one time she decided to open her eyes and what she noticed, in addition to light and traveling at a dizzying speed, was that the sides of the "tunnel" had grooves in the sides with a series of white numbers facing backward, which looked like they were placed along a scale, like a ruler. It dawned on her then. The tunnel was not a tunnel at all. It was a camera lens! She deduced that the process was this: she traveled down through the camera lens to get wherever she was going; the piercing light was the photo being taken, and arrival was after the photo had been taken. It didn't explain how or why she could do this inconceivable thing, but it did explain why she was only able to walk into photographs and nothing else.

Another thing she learned was that upon arrival, always check your surroundings first thing. Without prior knowledge about what the environment at the location of the photo might be, for all you know, a bird could be swooping down ready to poop on your head; a plane or a piano or a kite or a flying squirrel could be ascending from the sky above. From the left, a truck may be bearing down on you, a lion approaching, or an angry homeless person charging at you with a machete; from the right, a tree falling, a bull charging you, or someone pointing a gun at your head.

In other words, if you look at a photograph, all you see is that which has been captured by the camera, a flat, two-dimensional rendering within the length and width of the photo. The absence of a 360-degree frame makes it impossible to know what is outside the frame, up, down, or on either side. This not knowing of what was happening outside the frame of the photo always posed a threat, and that's why it was essential to look around before doing anything else. Fortunately, most people taking pictures are mostly not doing it in a dangerous situation, unless they are say, a reporter in a war zone, or at a protest or something.

Mostly, on those first expeditions back through time, Imogen just walked around, checking out the landscape and marveling at the fact that she could be there, witnessing history firsthand; things that other people could only view in an old movie or in photographs or a book.

She experienced the tactile composition of leathers and fabrics, of old typewriters and books and carriages and furniture; she breathed in the sweet petrichor of rain on cobblestoned streets, the pungent bouquets of innumerable liquors and medicines, newspaper ink hot from the press, wheat fields and horse manure and flowers in spring; she viewed the true nature of the apparels and the curtains and rugs and all the things that from the old black-and-white photos burst forth with a blaze of color, coming to life before her astonished eyes. And she watched the humans and their pets, going about their business, living out their lives in another space and time, oblivious to *future girl* standing right there in their midst.

And along with the sights and sounds, she made it a point to squeeze in as many history-making events as she could. In the 1800s, she walked alongside pioneers traveling the Oregon Trail and visited a one-room schoolhouse on a lonesome Kansas prairie.

She rode the first Ferris wheel at the World's Fair in Chicago in 1893, and in 1899 she attended an early performance of the magnificent magician Harry Houdini where he escaped from handcuffs and a strait jacket to an astonished crowd. At the turn of the 20th century, she took a spin in a Model T and stood on Ellis Island and observed humanity filing through. In 1902, she slid into a seat, third row center, at a majestically ornate theater in France to view Georges Méliès' fantastic debut silent film *Le Voyage dans la Lune* (*A Trip to the Moon*).

She partied with drunken sailors at a Philadelphia pub on D-Day in 1945; she stood beside a group of children and their parents bundled up warmly from head to toe in hats and scarves and boots on a chilly street corner in New York City to watch the 1955 Macy's Thanksgiving Day parade pass by. In the 1960s, she shimmied her way past the bouncer into LA's Whiskey A-Go-Go to see The Doors play, watched the moon landing on TV at a community potluck in

Neptune, Florida in '69, and joined a march against the war in Viet Nam at UC Berkeley. She experienced the punk ethos in the mosh pit at a Ramones concert in 1977 at CBGBs in the East village, and in 1973 triumphantly burned her bra alongside the sisterhood at a feminist rally.

In 1985, she bought a ticket for the new movie *Back to the Future*, and had a go at bringing down a section of the Berlin Wall with a sledgehammer in 1989. In 1996, she ate pancakes at Windows on the World on the 107th floor of World Trade Center's North tower. She saw the Eifel Tower being constructed in 1887. In 1923, she joined a caravan taking supplies to Howard Carter and Lord Carnarvon at the excavation site of the tomb of the pharaoh Tutankhamun's in the Valley of the Kings in Egypt.

She stayed far away from Nazi Germany in the 1930s and avoided the American South between 1860 and 1865 as well as a few other places and times that just weren't safe, especially for a woman. She learned that global time travel could be tricky. It was tough enough to be inconspicuous in a strange place and time, but adding to it a language barrier and cultural hurdles often created unforeseen challenges. Still, as she always knew it would be, witnessing antiquity with her own eyes was awesome.

Imogen's first real test "case" came from one of her coworkers at the coffee shop who, during a conversation about unsolved mysteries, mentioned that her uncle Terrance had disappeared in the early 50s and no one in the family had ever heard a thing from him again; they didn't know if he had died or what happened to him. Imogen went home that night and did a search of old newspapers until she found a story about the case from 1953. The photo in the newspaper showed police officers searching a field next to the road where Terrance's car had been found along with an inset photo of Terrance Schwartz. He was a decent-looking guy, Imogen thought. Dark hair slicked back in typical 50s style, and sideburns, like Elvis! Imogen printed out the article and propped it up on her desk to concentrate on. Nothing.

The copy of a scan was grainy. She wasn't sure if the quality of an image might render it impossible to enter it, but she gazed at it again anyway. This time she focused on the officers; there were four. They were standing next to a black and white police car talking. One was pointing in the direction of the empty field. Things began to wobble. It was happening.

When she got there, she started walking out into the dark field when one of the officers called out a warning, "Hey, you better not go out there by yourself, little lady, you'll get lost, too." But he didn't try to stop her. Imogen walked around out in the field for a bit and then came back. The purpose of this trip was more about investigating whether a copy of a scanned photo could be used, than finding any real clues. It could, although she noted that the coming and going seemed a bit jerkier than usual.

In this case, the internet was the real tool. She searched through local papers from the early 50s for a Terrance Schwartz. After a couple hours of old fashioned sleuthing she was pretty sure she had located him. There had been no foul play. "Terrance" who had changed his name to "Terri" was living a quiet life with her husband. Although Imogen was tempted to tell her coworker about her relative's transformation from uncle to aunt, it seemed clear that after all this time, Terri probably did not wish to be "found."

After a year of exploration and travel, Imogen felt like she was finally ready to embark on her new, secret life—polite and unassuming coffee shop barista by day, time-traveling private investigator by night (and sometimes day).

Hanging the proverbial open for business sign on the imaginary storefront façade, she made it official—Imogen Oliver— Private Investigator, Dead Relatives, Inc. She took out a small ad in the newspaper and waited for the phone to ring.

14

Seven and three-quarter miles west of Butternut Bend, the rain-soaked streets of downtown Stambourg seemed darker and grittier than its suburban location might suggest. With the exception of the greenish neon glow emanating from the interior of the all-night fold-n-fluff, a beam from the motion detector situated in the parking lot of the neighborhood convenience store across the street, and a diffuse speck of light coming from the upstairs apartment over Diamond's Pawn Shop, all the businesses that hugged Main Street were dark and curiously empty.

Like the streets below, the only light source in his dimly lit living room came from the large, 65-inch, flat-screen television mounted on the wall above the fireplace mantle. Sometimes the juxtaposition between dark and filtered light was the only thing that came between Theodore Diamond and his migraines. Most nights found the stocky and mostly unremarkable denizen cozily ensconced in his green faux leather Lazy boy stocking feet propped on two elaborately embroidered pillows resting atop the glass coffee table as he enjoyed a light comedic sitcom or the occasional reality show—the kind he liked best required subtitles to follow along.

But on those evenings when the encephalalgia gods hurled

thunderbolts of ache at his throbbing temples, only the soft, over-stuffed couch would do, providing a womb-like nest for him to burrow himself deep into with knees curled tightly beneath him in a near-fetal position. Though Teddy was not fond of the headaches, he accepted them. Pain was joy and punishment that brought him strange comfort.

The one-bedroom apartment above his downtown shop was modest. He could assuredly afford something considerably better, but why? Why attract unwanted attention and blow a damn good thing? The pawnshop afforded him a comfortable and respectable living, but it was the lucrative trading, his side business that fetched the tidy hauls. Nostalgia was huge now, especially with the spate of collectables-related TV shows enlightening people about how much Aunt Pearl's funky lamp with the fringe shade might be worth, or encouraging them to pick and dive through junk tables at flea markets and thrift shop bins and yard sales and old barns. Nostalgia notwithstanding, Teddy had tapped into something innately hu-man—people will pay handsomely for a chance to relive their youth, whether it's via an old tin lunchbox, a 1959 Barbie, or a coveted Action Comics #1, the 1938 comic book that introduced Superman to the world—relics of glorified childhoods and the good old days when life was simpler, they thought.

Scattered throughout his living room was an assortment of old coins and vintage toys, most of them still wrapped in their original packaging, comic books and baseball cards and oddities and collect-ables galore. Cleaning was not exactly Teddy's forte. Mixed into the mess were a sizeable quantity of candy wrappers and donut boxes and other miscellaneous fast food trash. So what if he'd put on a few extra pounds living the dream.

Tonight, spared for once of the pain of his frequent migraines, Teddy sat rigidly in his chair, pursed lips, both feet planted firmly on the floor, hunched over the bright red 50s-era metal-flaked kitchen table eating a Krispy Kreme donut as he scoured the classified sec-tion spread out before him. He checked it every single night, column for column, moving up and down each one highlighting the fine print. So far, nothing . . . nothing until now when he spotted it.

The ad was simple, no frills. It contained no elaborate graphics or even a bit of flair, only a plain blurb of text that read simply:

Seeking discreet information about a deceased loved one, a friend, a distant relative? Unique, local, licensed private investigator available for hire. Reasonable rates. Call I. Oliver today to schedule a confidential appointment. Dead Relatives, Inc.

Teddy clenched unclenched reclenched his fists, a deep-rooted adolescent habit—one he had learned to regularly conceal in public, but not so much at home. His hands felt at once clammy and icky. He hated that. He knew from experience it was essential that he remain calm, focused. He mustn't let anger beset him, but it concerned him mightily that what he had hoped to never see was seen. The ad confirmed it. Almost certainly, the girl had the gift. Yet, maybe she didn't know anything at all. Perhaps the discovery was merely the catalyst for turning her ability into a profitable little side business, as her parents had, as he did. Or—the thought made him physically shudder—possibly she knew everything and the wretched little bitch was snooping into the past right now. Teddy's fist made contact with the hard, metal table—not too hard, but hard enough to cause him to cry out in an eruption of soothing pain. It was all he could do to quell the panic he felt welling up from deep in his gut over the possibility of this line of thinking.

What would Mimi say? Teddy struggled to conjure a soothing memory of her. Of course, she'd say, "Don't be impulsive, Theodore. Rash decisions can't be undone," he whispered to himself under his breath. Oh yes, Mimi Pinky and her nonstop parade of "daddies" knew all about rash decisions, didn't she? Teddy could feel a drop of sweat beading just above his upper lip. She made them all the time, he thought.

Turning away from the ad for now, he tried to consider what must be done, to find a solution. Although he felt no real feelings one way or the other toward her, he didn't necessarily want to harm Imogen. She had been nice to him, once, he remembered, when she was a little girl. And he did owe her parents a note of gratitude for introducing him to his remarkable livelihood, which he had stumbled upon purely by accident just by being at the right place at the right time.

It had been that summer he'd spent working at their photography studio. He was grabbing a quick drag off the roach he'd hidden in the back storeroom when he heard his boss Niles and his wife

Francis arguing in the office. Teddy crept out, and hiding behind the connecting wall, he watched in disbelief as his boss seemed to fade into a photograph.

After the wife had left, Teddy entered the office. The photo looked like a street scene in anytown USA, but as he gazed into it, he started to feel weird, like the Earth was twisting and gyrating beneath his feet, then complete dark and a sensation of being pulled really fast through a long shaft. The next thing he knew, he was somewhere else. The office was gone. He was standing on a street corner and cars were whizzing by him.

"What the fuck?" he'd thought. And then it hit him, he was in the photo, too, and Jesus Christ his boss was probably somewhere nearby. Not sure what else to do, Teddy started to pray. "Please, please, please, God," he silently chanted as he envisioned himself back in the safe place he'd left. "Take me back." In an instant, he was back. "It worked!" he cried, out of breath and thankful to be returned from wherever it was he had just been, but completely freaked out by the experience. Suddenly an excruciating pain, like a lightning bolt, hit his forehead, and dropping the photograph onto the desk, he ran from the office back to the dark storage room. That was the first time.

Once Teddy had time to come to terms with what had happened, the wheels in his head began to churn and he started to ponder the potential benefits of being able to walk into a picture. First though, he needed to see whether or not he could do it a second time. As an experiment, he pilfered a picture from one of Mimi's old photo albums. He was pretty sure it was a picture of the Vegas strip, where Mimi said she used to live before Teddy was born. He was attracted to the flashy neon lights, and it just seemed like a cool place to go.

Hidden back in the storeroom with the photo propped up in front of him, Teddy crinkled up his brow to concentrate hard on the image. Pretty soon, like before, the room began to wobble and the darkness came up before he went slip-sliding into the light. He was right. The place was cool. His senses were immediately assailed by a thousand dazzling, twinkly lights from dozens of hotels and casinos along the strip—The Mint, the Golden Nugget Saloon, Apache Hotel, The Fortune; a sign announced Liberace playing at the Sands.

At the Pioneer Club, a giant 40-foot neon cowboy waved at him and shouted "Howdy Podner" every 15 minutes or so.

Teddy ducked into a smaller casino and sat down at a slot machine. He'd seen these old one-armed bandits before in movies. Nobody seemed to pay any attention to him as he pulled some change from his jeans pocket and plopped a quarter into the slot. He pulled the handle and watched with dizzying excitement as the bells and melons and cherries and bars and sevens on the reel whirled round and around, stopping first on cherry, bell, lucky seven! A winning couple of quarters plunked into the shelf and Teddy was immediately hooked. Three bars lined up and Teddy was delighted by the sound of many more clinking clanking winning quarters as they hit the metal receptacle.

Deciding that it probably wasn't such a good idea to draw attention to himself, considering that he wasn't 21, he scooped out the coins and filled his pocket with them, walking as inconspicuously as possible out of the casino with a huge bulge on one side. The coins in his pocket jingled as Teddy sprinted over behind the building and began to concentrate on Mimi's picture. The bright lights soon began to fade away and he was back in the storeroom. Excited, the first thing he did was dip his hand into his pocket to fish out the bounty of quarters he'd just won. Nothing. "What the hell?" he said out loud. He looked up to see his boss looming above him with a scowl on his face.

"Where have you been Teddy?" Niles demanded, his voice sounding lower and deeper and far more authoritative than usual. Teddy pressed up against the wall as he pulled himself up.

"Uh, nowhere, sir," he stammered.

"Come with me," Niles said, placing his hand on Teddy's shoulder and leading him out of the storeroom and into his office. Expecting to be in trouble or at the very least, fired, he was surprised when Niles began to explain the mechanics of time travel to him, how it worked, the rules, one of which explained why his Vegas winnings hadn't come back with him. Niles encouraged Teddy to use his newfound ability wisely and Teddy promised he would.

"There's one more thing," Niles said, his tone turning dead serious. From his desk drawer he produced an old black-and-white photograph of a girl wearing old timey clothes. "Do you know this girl?" he asked.

Teddy took the photo from him, and confused, shook his head no. Although the girl in the picture reminded him of someone he knew, this girl Tiffany that he had been seeing, her face was sort of blurry and her hair was pulled up on her head. Niles explained that he'd found the loose photo lying back in a far corner of the store-room.

"You didn't take some girl back through time to show off, did you?" he asked him suspiciously. Teddy was still shaking his head.

"No sir, no, I wouldn't do anything like that."

"Because it's dangerous," Niles warned, "You could strand someone if you're not careful."

Teddy eventually figured out how to make money from time travel, despite not being able to bring things back. It took several years of trial and error to perfect his method of stowing items in the past to retrieve later in the future, but stumbling upon the gift had not only made him a wealthy man, but also insured that he would never have to rely on his flaky mother Mimi Pinky.

Teddy closed his eyes and tried to think. When he opened them again he was looking at the big TV. He must have dozed off. On screen, a youthful Michael J. Fox stood in front of Hill Valley High School. He recognized the movie at once. One of the stations was replaying the 1985 film *Back to the Future*. Teddy got up and reached for the remote that was sitting on the coffee table and turned the sound up.

In the iconic scene, Marty McFly is speaking to Doc, played by Christopher Lloyd, outside the school after Marty has mistakenly driven the time-traveling DeLorean back to the year 1955.

"Whoa. They really cleaned this place up. Looks brand-new," Marty says.

Marty and Doc walk toward the building.

"Now, remember," Doc says. "According to my theory, you interfered with your parents' first meeting. If they don't meet, they won't fall in love, they won't get married and they won't have kids. That's why your older brother's disappearing from that photograph.

Your sister will follow, and unless you repair the damage, you'll be next."

"Sounds pretty heavy," Marty says.

"Weight has nothing to do with it . . ."

With as chubby finger, Teddy hit the DVR's pause button. Marty and Doc froze. Pressing the back arrow button, he rewound to the segment where Doc was speaking. Teddy loved this part. All three *Back to the Future* films were entertaining, although they had played fast and loose with the rules of time travel—most glaringly Marty running into himself. Granted, he'd never really taken the time to learn all of the innumerable rules of the universe himself, and no, astrophysics wasn't Teddy's strong suit either.

Teddy was abundantly aware that he was not a brilliant man, but he prided himself on his street acumen or what the hoi polloi might call common sense. Sure, he'd made mistakes, but you didn't need a fancy college degree to navigate time. If there was one thing he knew for sure, times changed, but people didn't. Oh, their clothes and hairstyles, their cars, the music they listened to and the dances they did, the way they spoke; that was a constant, but deep down, the people, at their core, did not change, no matter what era it happened to be. They fought each other over religion and politics and land and race—the same fear-driven issues as always.

Still, he had spent a good amount of time reading literature on the subject, but the information, or course, had all come mostly from the imaginings of his favorite science-fiction writers. As far as he knew there was no real scientific evidence for time travel, and interestingly, in this modern age of the internet where information on any topic was readily available, a mere Wikipedia click away, the "gift" had astonishingly managed to remain hidden. He wondered how that was even possible. It amazed him that anything was a secret anymore, yet his Google searches had consistently come up empty. Somehow it was protected, immune, magic? But none of that mattered now. The most pressing issue at the moment was what to do about Imogen. Teddy turned the volume down on the TV to white background noise level so that he could think.

The next thing Teddy knew, the final credits were scrolling by. He had evidently dozed off again. He looked at the clock. It was midnight, but he felt wide-awake, alive.

15

No one noticed her until they did, generally after blinking or taking a double take, looking away for a moment, then glancing back and observing that someone had slipped into their range of vision.

Imogen paused to briefly survey her surroundings outside the framework of the photo she had minutes ago passed through, making sure there was no danger lurking somewhere outside of her view. Next, she made a quick scan of the clothing the universe had selected for her.

"Damn," she said, rolling her eyes at the ordinary sleeveless cotton print shirt and dreadful loose fitting Capri trousers in drab beige, capped off with an abysmal pair of plain and seriously sensible brown pumps. Clearly not her first choice for swingin' sixties apparel, it served its purpose, but that didn't mean she had to like it.

Scrutinizing the clothes had evolved into rather a fun ritual; a big reveal of what sort of apparel she'd been assigned this trip. She was not, by any stretch of the imagination, a fashionista, but damn the universe, she thought, why couldn't it, just once, throw together something with a modicum of style? How or why it worked this way, she couldn't say, but you didn't question the universe; the universe was at all times accurate.

The briny smell of the Pacific filled her nostrils, and resonating from somewhere near the southernmost edge of the observation deck, she could make out the distant chinkachinka . . . ching ching sounds of small Indian Karatalas hand cymbals, the bomp-abompa of a mridanga folk drum, and the mellifluous tootle-toot of some-one carefully fingering a keyless Bansuri flute.

San Francisco. June 26, 1966. According to the research she'd conducted before leaving, a year from now a spontaneous explo-sion of cosmic proportions would spur a youthful generation to reject the authoritarian constraints of their parents; a revolution so inclusive it would spawn a host of psychotropic drugs, hippies, communes, tie-dye, freaks and feminists, Hare Krishnas, green environmentalists, wide-eyed buses of anthropological tourists ogling the hippy in the wild, antiwar protests, the peace movement and a profusion of mind-blowing new literature, lifestyles, art, and music, an epic time better known as the summer of love. It was already beginning. Even though the craziness was still a year away, one wouldn't know it from the diverse crowd mingling atop the Cliff House' observation deck today. Even if you couldn't see it, you could feel it. This summer's theatrical pranksters, the Diggers would propel next year's hippies and love children into transcendent chaos—a life-altering carnival of awareness for some; a nightmare for others, and Imogen stood squarely at the epicenter of change, an uneasy palpable vibe that the entire country didn't yet know they were bracing for.

An overwhelming surge of excitement welled unexpectedly within Imogen. As a history major it wasn't as if she hadn't read all about it in her textbooks, but actually being here now, laying witness to an amazing immerging convergence in one place of the most unlikely of tribes—a broad spectrum of people, from hipsters and squares to the spiritual and the stoned, was far more intense and awe-inspiring than she could have ever imagined.

But there was something else too, an uneasiness, some such weird déjà vu that she couldn't quite put her finger on. Today's journey had started out uneventfully. Like always, she had secured the deadbolt lock and checked all the windows to make sure they were closed and locked. She had propped the photo up on the desk in her office, and then sat down to concentrate on the coastal scene depicted in the photo in front of her.

For all accounts and purposes, stepping into a photo in one time and place and landing in an entirely different time period is the embodiment of strange, but oddly, in the year and a half since she'd opened her investigative company, she'd grown accustomed to the curiosities of traveling through time. She'd even come to terms with the physical effects, the unpleasant time-lag hangover after each temporal trip, for instance, which resembled the morning after a long night of seriously stupid drinking, and never mind the discombobulating sensation of Mister Toad's wild ride, which was never much fun, even at Disneyland.

She had done all of her pretrip research and homework, yet something about this place and this day felt markedly curious, familiar yet unfamiliar, although she was fairly certain she had never physically been here before—not in her normal life anyway, and certainly never through a photo portal. Although it would have been just like her parents to have dragged their daughter out to see a giant camera at the Cliff House instead of taking her to Playland, a kids paradise just down the beach from here full of midway rides, cotton candy, a fortune teller named Laughing Sal, and games with chances to win a big, cheap stuffed animal from China. She shrugged it off. It was probably nothing at all, the coastal smells intermingled with the wafting scent of caramel corn and hot dogs triggering some old memory of going to a beach somewhere sometime, or any one of myriad stories Grandma Iris had told her growing up.

Just then, an unexpected wind blew up, swathing hot air around Imogen's legs and knees. She shivered, shaking it off. She had to. With or without the odd vibe, or even as awe inspiring as it was to witness history in the making, she had work to do and a limited window of opportunity in which to accomplish it.

Imogen followed the groups of intermingling people who were also following after the sounds of distant rhythmic music that resonated from the southern end of the cliff-top terrace. It was a gorgeous early summer day under a blue, cloudless sky. The combination of excellent weather conditions and the fact that school had let out a week before, created a giddy atmosphere of carefree students and happy families and day-trippers. Kids in shorts, a person dressed up like a clown—before people realized the inherent creepiness of clowns—stood in a corner with a helium tube blowing up balloons. A little girl in a gingham dress began to cry when her daddy's cigarette accidently made contact with her red balloon, popping it, rubber pieces of it exploding and littering the grass around them. Smoking, a lot of smoking, puffs of toxic fumes wafting around her, intermixed with the unmistakable aroma of marijuana and the sick/sweet smell of patchouli oil designed to mask it. This was the sixties after all.

Imogen marveled at the scene that seemed to be straight out of a *Life* magazine ad; teenagers lounging on blankets on the grass drinking Coca-Cola and 7-Up out of glass bottles, the groovy sounds of the Lovin' Spoonful's *Summer in the City* playing on someone's transistor radio; girls with teased updos or straight, parted-in the middle locks strolled by, indistinguishable only by their fashion choices—some in Mary Quant miniskirts, others in bell bottoms or hip huggers accentuated by an ultra-wide leather belt ordered straight out of the Montgomery Ward catalog. Some of the hipper boys wore paisley shirts and twill jacket/slack combos, while others in ratty jeans and sandals seemed not to care about making a fashion statement at all. In the parking lot, people scrambled to park their VW bugs and two-toned buses, long-ass Chryslers and De Sotos and Ramblers and Mustangs.

On the grass, a group of Hare Krishnas, about 25 persons in all, wearing white paint on their noses and loose-fitting elongated saffron colored robes, sat silently meditating or playing musical instruments. That hotish sea breeze whipped around again on the terrace, transporting an aromatic mixture of musky incense and a smokey campfire-ish odor that smelled like burnt toast. A few of the males were clothed in the traditional white Krishna tunics signifying their place as new devotees to the movement; some had shaved their heads and wore the sikha, a small piece of hair in the back to distinguish themselves from Budhist monks who had a similar appearance. Several of the women wore Indian saris of variant colors, while others dressed in contemporary western attire as if uncertain about whether or not to make such a cultish commitment.

A slow sonorous murmur, like the dull drone emanating from deep inside a hornet's nest, began to gradually rise among the crowd of true believers as they recited the Krishna mantra, their bodies rocking to and fro in tantric tandem. With the drum ceaselessly pounding, the bells trilling at a feverish pitch, and the primordial vibrations of many voices rising and falling, the chanting grew louder and faster, and some of the devotees began to shout out loud with hands stretched upward above their heads, rising higher and higher amidst the general chant.

As though filled up with spiritual fairy dust, some sprang to their feet, forming a spontaneous conga line, grasping one another's hands or wrapping their fingers around the loops or inside the back jeans pocket of the person in front of them. Dancing here and sashaying there they wended and weaved their way through the crowd of startled pageboy-coiffed and argyle sweater vest-wearing tourists—the squares, who wanted nothing more than to enjoy the sun and sea, and perhaps view Seal Rock through the pinhole lens of the world famous Camera Obscura housed over there inside a giant camera kiosk overlooking the coast.

Imogen wandered unassumingly along the outer edge of the leaping skipping hopping romping knot of spirited dancers, on the lookout for one person in particular, a girl named Yajna. And then she spotted her, the girl in the photograph, a frail teenage waif with stringy, parted in the middle, dirty blond hair who was zigzagging now in and out of Imogen's view. A flash went off to her right and Imogen momentarily lost sight of her as she turned her head to look in the direction of the burst. A man wearing a panama hat and a drab grayish suit pulled the undeveloped print from a Polaroid camera and began waving it back and forth in the air to dry.

Momentarily distracted by the flash, Imogen failed to notice that the human chain propelled by the unhinged gravity of 25 some bodies were on a crash course with her own, until it was too late and Yajna unceremoniously slammed into her.

"Ow," Imogen said rubbing her shoulder.

"Sorry," the girl said in a barely audible whisper. Their eyes locked on each other briefly until hands pulled her away and off in another snaking direction. The brief interaction allowed Imogen to get a closer look though and she couldn't help noticing how pale and slightly undernourished the girl seemed. It reminded her of some of the rail-thin models pictured on the magazine covers at the grocery store checkout. Apparently, sexy meant looking like someone clearly in desperate need of a sandwich. At least this girl didn't look like she was posing as a skinny hungry girl on purpose. She actually really looked skinny and hungry.

Draped loosely over one shoulder of her small frame was an oversized, embroidered Mexican peasant blouse bound at the waist with a leather cowboy belt and accessorized by large hoop earrings and multistrands of colorful beads and bangles and bells that encircled her neck and jangled on her slim wrists. She wore a red bandana tied up like a choker around her neck, and hanging limply on her hips was an old pair of faded and ripped blue jeans; on her dirty feet a pair of well-worn huarache sandals. Although it was hard to distinguish from her vantage point, the boyishly clean-shaven face behind the brown mop of unkempt hair on the young man she held hands with looked to be about 18. He too was dressed in contemporary clothing—army/navy store-bought bell-bottomed pants with a khaki shirt layered beneath a buckskin vest, all of which appeared soiled and severely slept in. That must be Stu, Imogen surmised.

Two days earlier, Grace Marshall had walked into Imogen's office. Despite being an older woman, Grace exuded a youthful refinement. Random shimmery ribbons of white and flecks of silver running through her shoulder-length gray hair gave it a very cool sparkly appearance. Although she refrained from actually pulling out a tissue to dab the seat, Grace hesitated before sitting down in the beat-up chair situated across from Imogen's metal office liquidation sale desk. From her designer satchel she pulled a faded and cracked Polaroid photo that she placed in front of Imogen, the focal point, a fresh faced young girl in a peasant blouse being pulled along in a ragtag conga line. Her long hair, frozen in photographic time seemed to be in perpetual motion, flying out in a wild tangle that obscured a portion of her face.

Primly crossing her legs and laying her hands daintily on her lap, palms slightly up, Grace leaned back in the chair, apparently waiting for Imogen to make the first move and drag the story from her. The clock on the wall ticked. The stuffy room made Imogen uncomfortable. Imogen started to speak, but finally Grace Marshall reached over and touched the corner of the faded photo of the girl and dispelled a heavy sigh as if she'd mulled this story over in her mind many times before.

"I was 17 in 1966 when my little sister Kari disappeared," she began. From there, the story unfolded. Growing up in Bakersfield in the 60s with two teenage girls residing in the house had made her parents crazy with fear, she explained, especially her dad, but her mother as well, with whom she described as being in a "constant state of semi-controlled panic." Between the rumors of various roving wild, doped-up biker gangs like the Hell's Angels, the Hangmen, and the Barhoppers terrorizing law-abiding citizens on the streets of California's Central Valley, and the nightly news stories about drugs and protests and hippies and freaks coming out of the the San Francisco Bay area, their dad was convinced the world was going to serious hell.

As Grace spoke, Imogen began piecing together her theories about the Marshall's family dynamic. In addition to her body language, which in and of itself spoke volumes about her prim and proper Emily Post upbringing, it was also fairly observable that Grace totally had that big sister sensibleness that younger sis Kari may have lacked. Likely, she was closest to the mom, emulating her, whether it was learning to sew or cook or exhibiting a ladylike reserve that was expected of young ladies in the early 60s. Imogen guessed she probably had a mad obsessive cleaning streak running through her as well. Kari, she surmised was probably a bit of a wild child, opinionated and rebellious, and more than likely, her heart belonged to daddy—something Imogen knew a little something about.

Kari, Grace continued, had been engaged in an ongoing push-pull battle with dad over everything from the too short skirts she wore to school to her 10 o'clock on school nights curfew. Mostly though, the fights centered on her boyfriend Stuart Franklin, Stu for short.

"Dad hated Stu," Grace said. "I thought he was cute," she demurred, her lip curling out in youthful girlish fashion, "but from the first day Kari brought him home, dad decided he was trouble with a capital T." Grace continued, "He didn't like his hair, 'too long,' he said; the way he dressed, 'damn hippy.' He didn't like that he was older than Kari, and why didn't he get a job or go join the military?"

Imogen had devoted some deep time and study to the 60s era, the civil rights movement, the hippies, and the war in Viet Nam.

Open US involvement in the war, which they were calling a "conflict" began in 1964, but until the draft was instituted in 1969, it had been merely an unpleasant undercurrent and not really on the public's radar yet, although small movement against involvement had begun percolating among peace activists and leftist intellectuals on college campuses. After the draft was established, however, the protests escalated and young men started burning their draft cards in earnest.

"I remember that it was June because it was the last day of school and everyone was in a great mood and excited about the start of summer vacation," Grace went on. "Even Dad was in a pretty good mood, for him anyway," she said. "He was in the backyard barbecuing burgers for us when Kari and Stu showed up, um, well they actually sort of stumbled in," she corrected. "They were giggling and Kari had tried to cover up the smell of marijuana on their clothes with patchouli oil, but it didn't matter. They reeked and their eyes were bloodshot and even our parents were hip enough to know that they were high."

Grace shifted uncomfortably in her seat before continuing. "At that point, Dad just lost it. He screamed, 'You little son of a bitch!' Mom and I were shocked. We'd never heard him cuss before, and the next thing we knew he had pounced on Stu. Kari tried to get between them and I think Dad only meant to push her out of the way, but instead she went flying across the room and she bumped her head pretty hard against the table." Grace looked like she might cry, but she paused only briefly and picked up the story.

"At that point, Dad was stunned. He just sort of dropped Stu and walked away. Mom was weeping, which made me start to cry . . ."

Her voice faded away and a slow-moving tear slipped down Grace's cheek. Imogen began to frantically search inside her desk drawer for a tissue, but Grace waved her hand back and forth in a gesture indicating that wasn't necessary. She was fine. Staring silently up at the poster of Paris tacked up on the wall behind Imogen, Grace took a moment to regain her composure before continuing her story.

"Stu jumped up and flew over to help Kari up, and then the two of them darted out of the yard. Kari was hollering obscenities at

Dad as Stu pushed her into the passenger side of his van, and they drove off. That was 1966," she said, "the last time I saw my sister."

Grace leaned forward and pointed to two people in the photograph dancing in a loose conga line. "This was taken sometime after they left. That's her. That's Kari," she said, "and there's Stu."

Imogen looked up from the photo and into Grace' distraught face, "I don't understand," she said. "If you haven't seen her since she ran away, how did you come by this photograph?"

"That's what is odd," Grace said. "It came in the mail one day. Just the photo, no letter or note or anything, like somebody was sending me a clue; as if after all this time, somebody wanted me to find her, or at least find out what happened to her." Grace turned the photo over and showed Imogen a handwritten word on the back: Yajna.

"Was there a postmark?" Imogen asked.

Almost immediately, a stricken look crossed Grace's face. "Oh my god," she said, realizing her error. "I threw the envelope away without thinking. When I saw the photo I was just so shaken up, I . . . I . . ." Grace's hands flew to her face.

Imogen felt terrible for her. Coming around from behind her desk, Imogen touched Grace's shoulder and said reassuringly, "Don't worry, we'll find her."

While the majority of the devotees danced in a comical foxy-trotty sort of erratic, trance-induced fog, Kari and Stu's behavior seemed unusual; more aware, anxious maybe, and they seemed to be scouring the larger outer area as though searching for an opening to make a quick, undetected getaway into the rising crowd should the opportunity arise. Imogen watched as the man in the Panama hat approached the couple and handed them the Polaroid photo. Kari smiled, nodded at the man and stuffed the photograph in the back pocket of her jeans before jumping back into the conga line with Stu.

Watching patiently from the periphery, Imogen waited for an opportunity to unobtrusively extricate Yajna, or rather Kari, from the procession of writhing bodies without anyone noticing. If she could pull her away from the line she might be able to speak to her, maybe pretend to be a reporter, and at the very least, find out what their plans were. It felt a little like playing double-dutch jump rope as a child, she thought, you know, when both of the ropes are whipping back and forth, up and down and to and fro and you're waiting, waiting, waiting for that one clearly defined moment when you can jump in without the ropes either bonking you on the head from above or jerking your legs out from under you from underneath.

She had missed her chance the last time they came around and Kari and Stu were making another dizzying dance loop when Imogen noticed that the warm June breeze had shifted slightly. And that toasty campfire smell she had gotten a whiff of earlier was now growing exponentially thicker. So thick in fact she could actually taste it, a gummy, acrid ash that coated her tongue and made her want to retch.

Before she could fully register what was happening, out of nowhere a billowing dark cloud of smoke that had a minute ago been a mere dot in the sky, seemed to at once race toward her, obscuring the clouds and sun and causing everyone to stop and take pause. She knew it was fire and it was close; she could hear the crackling of flames, the groan of timbers charring and contracting; windows bursting, but where? How close? She didn't know because she couldn't see anything through the black haze that had descended on the terrace like a toxic teenager in a blind rage.

Fire scared her. Perhaps it had something to do with a childhood memory she carried of a pimply boy teenager one minute blowing up firecrackers in the back yard and the next minute her beloved Malibu Barbie's head exploding, hair on fire, and spiraling through the air; a million tiny sparks leaping and twirling and dancing in the autumn breeze; settling in the dry grass and bursting into an inferno of hot bonfire; of flames licking at the hem of Imogen's favorite dotted Swiss dress, the one her mom had sewn for her; the horrible fear as she tried to frantically get away from it as it burned hotter and began to singe the fine blond hairs on the backs of her knees; the boy running the other direction at the very same time her father burst through the screen door, grabbing the still-damp white sheet hanging on the clothesline and wrapping it tightly around her little body.

Like that long ago day, Imogen wanted to run away now, but she needed to keep it together. She hadn't come all this way to lose Kari and Stu now.

The uncontrolled conflagration was burning so quickly and so hot that breathing was becoming difficult. The panic around her was palpable as people began scrambling to get off the terrace and away from the stench and heat, turning otherwise civilized tourists into aggressively nasty individuals.

"Goddammit get out of the way!" a short, stocky fellow, cigarette still loosely dangling from his globular lip, red Marlboro pack rolled up and showing through the sleeve of his white T-shirt, bellowed at a slow-moving elderly couple as he angrily shoved them aside.

"Watch it, tough guy," a man in a suit roared back at short man when the old woman stumbled up against his chest.

In the ensuing confusion, Imogen completely lost sight of Kari and Stu in the crowd, the pair had surely found the diversion they were seeking. Imogen opened her mouth to form words. Where no sounds came out, choking smoke rushed in, filling up her lungs and causing her to sputter and cough. Even if she could make words come out of her mouth no one would have heard her over the cacophony of wailing sirens emanating from dozens of fire trucks arriving to the scene all at the same time.

In an effort to get away from the thick, billowing smoke, the crowd shifted like migrating shorebirds toward the southern edge of the deck. That's when Imogen spotted it, Kari's bright red bandana lying on the pavement. Could Kari and Stu have run northward into the smoke to try and ditch the crowd, specifically from the band of Krishnas they were with? Scooping up the scarf, Imogen wadded it up into a ball and placed it tight against her mouth and nose and plunged headlong into the murky miasma. A few stragglers heading in the opposite direction knocked into her, but for the most part, the path was clear and crowd free. It was difficult to see within the swirling vortex of smoke, and the bandana wasn't helping all that much.

Imogen considered abandoning the search altogether, but then the wind changed direction suddenly creating an opening in the dark and dense cloud, just enough for her to catch a glimpse of blue sky and the source of the fire. The old Sutro Baths building next to the

Cliff House was ablaze. Built almost entirely of wood, the fire had quickly enveloped and overtook the interior of the bath structure.

Once a glorious pleasure palace, the now abandoned Sutro Baths was a large freshwater and seawater swimming pool complex built in 1896 by former San Francisco mayor Adolph Sutro. By the 1950s, the baths, which were no longer profitable, were turned into an ice-skating rink. By 1966 it had been sitting empty for several years and had been marked for demolition to be replaced by a planned apartment complex. While Imogen was standing around on the deck earlier, she'd in fact, overheard a conversation about how the owners had lost so much money on the property they were ready to go bankrupt; they wouldn't be surprised if they didn't burn the place down for the insurance payout.

The clearing didn't last long, however, and again Imogen found herself fumbling forward in the dark. She wasn't sure, but it seemed like she must have found her way to the westernmost edge of the terrace and she was probably the only foolish person over here. Everyone else was going the other direction to flee the smoke and fire, not walking directly into it.

"Damn it," Imogen cried into the bandana. But miraculously, several other people had apparently done the very same thing, including Kari and Stu who she could now see were standing not five feet away from her. Sensing she must seize the moment, Imogen called out, "Yajna!" The girl either didn't hear her or the name didn't register. Imogen called out again, this time louder, "KARI!"

Kari stopped and turned toward the voice. Imogen knew she had only moments to deliver her message. "Kari," she said, locking eyes with her and dropping all preplanned pretense. "I'm here for your sister Grace. I know this doesn't make any sense, but she'll be looking for you a long time from now." Kari looked perplexed, but did not turn away. A good sign. Imogen placed her hand on Kari's shoulder.

"Where are you and Stu going from here?" she asked quickly. The erratic airstream shifted again, this time transporting the swelling smoke in a completely different direction. Stu was tugging on her hand, trying to get her to go. Kari looked at Stu and nodded, and then back at Imogen.

"Tell her Eugene in Oregon, a commune," she said, and then

she turned away and she and Stu were gone, dissolved into the massive wall of smoke. The smoke cleared again briefly and Imogen opened her stinging eyes to a strange sight, a lone silhouette walking on the beach below, seemingly emerging from the flames. The person walked slowly, nonchalantly alongside the flaming structure as though impervious to the danger. As he drew closer to the cliffside, Imogen made out a few details: a man, short, portly, wearing green khaki pants and a pair of Ray-Ban sunglasses.

Even though the smoke seemed to be blowing the other direction now, the air was foul and her eyes and throat burned. Her instincts were intuitively for flight, not fight. It was time to go. Not unlike the Krishnas, Imogen tilted her head back slightly and closed her stinging eyes to concentrate.

Chanting, fire, a conga line, random asymmetric patterns, an odd little man; the images began to dance away from her. Yet, even with her eyes tightly closed she could still make out the fading shapes of the peripheral edges as they folded in on each other, darkening and blurring and vignetting; and over and above the roar of the sirens and the sound of wood beams cracking and falling against one another, she thought she heard the diminishing sounds of the karatalas and the mridanga folk drum and the bansuri flute fading as time stretched out and pulled away from them.

16

As soon as Imogen felt solid ground beneath her feet she opened her eyes and quickly headed to the second-hand futon she'd picked up for $19.98 at the local thrift shop. The Polaroid photo sat untouched on the desk where she'd left it this morning. Despite the aesthetic banality of the rented downtown office space—one room with tiny windows, standard nondescript bluish workplace carpet, white walls, and a small half bath—it was always a relief to get back to her own time.

This was it, office sweet office, where the magic happened, literally. Although nothing special, it was functional and secure and it suited Imogen's needs. Grammy had more than once stressed the importance of keeping the photograph, or portal in a safe place. It served as the entry and exit point, but because you couldn't take it with you, it needed to remain static; to serve as an anchor to your own time. Of all the rules, protecting the portal was the most critical one.

After Grammy died, Imogen had turned one of the rooms in the mother-in-law quarters into an office for receiving clients, but took the necessary precaution of renting the office space downtown for the purpose of time travel because it was fully equipped with an alarm system and had a heavy solid metal door that could be dead-bolted shut from the inside while she was away traveling. It also featured a hidden wall vault where she could safely store all the photographs and other private materials from her clients. The futon served as a semi-soft landing spot where she could recover upon reentry.

She'd discovered how taxing time travel could be the first time she'd accidentally tripped, skipped, fallen into a picture as a small child. She wasn't sure where, or when she had landed exactly—a beach somewhere, at some time; standing next to her mother who was there with someone, a man she thought, but she was there for only an instant; she was just four, so memories were fuzzy and probably unreliable, but what she did remember, vividly, was how incredibly tired she had felt afterward. It had probably been too much for a little kid.

Imogen stretched out on the futon. She would stay prone like this for another hour or so until the jaggies ended. Although Grammy had died before she could lay out the full spectrum of rules, the jaggies, another thing Imogen had discovered, occurred a short time after reentry. You thought you were good to go, and you got in your car and drove down the road and all of a sudden, you felt dizzy and wobbly and completely certain you should not be behind the wheel of a car.

Closing her eyes, she pulled the blanket she kept draped on the back of the futon around her shoulders and spent the next few minutes quietly meditating. "Brick wall, brick wall, brick wall," she recited. It was an odd, yet indispensable mantra she had lifted from a bad 1960s British science-fiction film she'd watched at movie club with her friends Rachel and Fletcher called *Village of the Damned*, in which the village professor tries unsuccessfully to hypnotize the creepy toe-headed pack of alien children with glowing eyes long enough to detonate a ticking atomic bomb that will blow them all to smithereens. For some reason, it had stuck.

Devised more by necessity than design, the meditation trick served a secondary purpose. After the first couple of times she had discovered that not only was she super fatigued, but what followed shortly after was even worse—a bone splitting, mind-numbing headache. On a scale from one to 10, it was at least an 11, possibly 15.

Thankfully, the headaches didn't happen every time, but when they did she was prepared. Meditating eased the throbbing and made the pain subside quicker. Headaches, jaggies—any way you looked at it, time travel could be hard on you.

Later, buried deep beneath the sheets and blankets in her own bed, and surrounded by familiar, homey things—her books, her artwork, her collection of vintage egg cups, her Mid-Century Modern atomic-themed bark cloth curtains, and the baby grand piano Grammy Iris had given her, her things, her stuff, Imogen took pleasure and a measure of relief in the good feelings she felt after returning from a visit to the past; of making it back once more safely and in one piece. Every trip was always a little terrifying. The drive home last night was a blur, but typically it was always like that.

And as usual, afterward she slept hard. She knew she should get up, but lying in bed felt way too comfortable and Imogen rolled over on her side and attempted another round of sleep. She closed her eyes, but no matter how hard she tried, she couldn't keep them shut. Something troubled her. What was it? And then, she remembered, Imogen sat up in bed, "Fire!"

How in the world, she thought, had she overlooked that important detail; how could she have neglected to put the date together with that specific event? It nagged at her because it was so unlike her to have missed a detail as vital as that. She prided herself in being thorough about these things, borderline obsessive, in fact. As tired as she was she felt compelled to check, right now. Reaching for the laptop on the wooden side table, she opened the lid and placed it atop her stomach, punching the bed pillows into balls to prop up her head as she launched a quick Google feeling lucky search for "Sutro Baths fire." Yep, she sighed, June 26th, 1966. She recalled researching this day in history last week and perusing several bookmarked websites she regularly visited to check out what happened on a particular date and time in the world as well as local, big and little events, but somehow, she must have been distracted.

Imogen plopped back against the pillows. "Damn." Just then, a soft, silky thing brushed up against her leg. "Meow." It was Luxe. He must have stealthily slipped in through his kitty-sized cat-flap door without Imogen noticing him. "Meow," Luxe vocalized again louder as he leaped on top of Imogen and rubbed his ears along against the edges of the laptop.

"Ok, ok," Imogen said closing the computer up and setting it down on the bed beside her. Luxe seized the opportunity for needful attention and began to purr and knead Imogen's stomach with his sharp claws, back and forth and back and forth.

"Oww . . . owwww Luxe . . . stop," Imogen moaned. Luxe turned up his internal motor, purring louder. Imogen drew the faux leopard throw draping from the edge of the bed to create a barrier between her stomach and Luxe' razor sharp claws. "That's better," she said soothingly as she petted the soft fur around his ears and allowed lonely Luxey to fully enjoy some quality kitty time. She'd been busy and inattentive lately, but it was nice that her neighbor lady Mimi Pinky was around to feed and care for him when she needed. Although the time trips actually took up hardly any "real" time, her time to and from and recovery time after a trip at the office downtown did, which was too long for a cat who expected his meal on a regular timetable.

Ever since she could remember, Pinky, aka Mimi Diamond (Imogen called her Mimi Pinky) and her creepy son Teddy had lived two houses over from them, although Teddy had eventually moved out of his mother's house—rather abruptly as Imogen recalled. Pinky was one of those silly nicknames that oddly attached themselves to people for whatever reason.

Mimi Pinky claimed she had once been a Vegas showgirl—the toast of the town, and her showgirl persona had lingered, and not in a particularly good way. At any given time, she might wander out into her front yard full of randomly placed pink flamingos wearing a loose-fitting robe, half open in front and exposing her nether regions, or in winter, in nothing but a tube top and a pair of short shorts, although she never . . . ever, went anywhere without her makeup—a layer of heavy foundation, cheeks brushed in two perfect circles of bright rosy rouge, powder blue eye shadow, jet black eyeliner, and deep scarlet lipstick that outlined her pursed lips.

She was a character, for sure. The other neighbors called her Crazy Mimi. Imogen thought eccentric was a better term for the neighborhood kook. It didn't much matter to Imogen as long as Mimi Pinky could make time away from Sodoku club or ghost hunting or any of her other crazy pursuits to drop by and feed Luxe.

"That's enough Luxe," Imogen said, finally pushing the cat off her lap and crawling out of bed. She had work to do.

Anxious to find more information about the Sutro fire, Imogen scoured the internet newspaper archives for the *San Francisco Chronicle* and found several archived articles. She learned that on June 26th, 1966, yesterday for Imogen, just as a wrecking ball was poised to begin smashing in the walls of the legendary Baths (and two weeks before the bankruptcy that would have ruined the owners) a mysterious fire broke out and burned the whole place to the ground. By the 1950s, when the baths were no longer profitable, it was turned into an ice-skating rink. But even that lost money, and by 1966 the owners were about to go bankrupt.

According to the news article, Dolores Bradley, a waitress at the Cliff Chalet, first reported the flames. With so much wood, the fire quickly enveloped and overtook the interior of the bath structure. Fanned by strong winds from the ocean, the angry fire carried cinders and ashes across San Francisco's Richmond District and blew smoke as far away as Berkeley. The same wind prevented the fire from spreading to the famed Cliff House restaurant just south of the baths. Traffic was snarled with Hare Krishna's and Diggers and people en masse. And here was an interesting tidbit, witnesses also reported seeing an individual walking briskly away from the scene, although this person's identity was never confirmed. Imogen had seen that guy too.

The fire burned for three days, a combination of wood, fuel, and heat made it too difficult to access on the steep cliff-side terrain. As it turned out, the building was heavily insured; the owners collected their massive settlement and quickly left town, leaving many suspicions, but no tangible evidence of fraud and arson.

Despite the disaster this expedition had turned out to be, Imogen had still managed to pick up some useful information—which was that Kari, or Yajna, and Stu were headed to a commune in Oregon, near Eugene. With quite a lot of high-quality pot, along with property for communes, Oregon at that time was becoming a haven for antiwar activists, draft evaders on their way to Canada, and formerly mainstream refugees from the East Coast in search of a utopian way of life. From *Bullfrog Magazine* c 1972, Imogen found this quote:

"The Bay Area has become just a little too heavy. Haight Ashbury is a bad place, motorcycle jockeys, addicts, prostitutes have taken it over. Sausalito was nice, but it was discovered too quickly. The same is true of Mill Valley. And if you haven't noticed there is nothing really north of Mill Valley until you get to Eugene."

The good news was she could probably dig up information about Stuart on the Internet, thus avoiding having to make a follow-up time trip. When she had done an initial search for Stuart Franklin, the commonness of his name had returned thousands of hits. But now that she knew where they were headed, it narrowed things down a bit. Imogen closed her laptop again and leaned back against the couch. She could do all this today . . . or not. She really didn't feel like thinking about clients or fire or anything. It was her day off and what she really wanted to do today was see Fletcher, although now that she thought about it, he was probably the reason she had been distracted enough to miss an important detail like a goddamn massive fire that would be occurring on the very day she was traveling back there! In the future, she would have to be more careful.

Grabbing her phone from the bed table, she sent him a quick text: Fletcher? You around? Hang out today?

Fletcher. They had known each other long enough for things to get comfortable, but their relationship was complicated, although they were trying to be uncomplicated. They slept together— friends-with-benefits style. They had gotten together the first time in college. He was polite and strong and oodles of fun and he made it easy to lean in against him and rest there. She wasn't kidding herself. She had needed his comfort more than anything after Grammy died. With no one left in the world, Fletcher was that comfort.

But after college, he had proposed to her and Imogen said no. They broke up and went their separate ways. Fletcher returned to Idaho and resumed a relationship with his former high school sweetheart. Imogen didn't know all the details, but apparently he'd changed/she'd changed and eventually he had decided to come back. He had since abandoned his cowboy persona, but occasionally still wore his boots. He quickly became re-acclimated to his old environment, wearing shorts, flip-flops—boots with shorts, even in the rainy season, a baseball cap, aviator sunglasses, just like countless other young men in the college town they inhabited. As her friend Rachel had commented, he'd become "civilized."

He also made a point to reconnect with Imogen. Imogen knew how Fletcher felt about her; how he had always felt about her. She suspected things with the old girlfriend hadn't worked out because of her. And she felt awful about that, but when he suggested they resume their "relationship," she had been honest with him upfront.

"I can't give you everything you want," Imogen admitted. Fletcher hung his head. When he did that it made her feel like a monster.

But this time he looked up at her and smiled, took her hand in his, and said, "I know and I don't care. I'll take whatever you can give, even if it's only a little bit."

Imogen hoped that someday she would want to give him more, give him everything. It wasn't him. Something had to be wrong with her because Fletcher was perfect. He was smart and cute and funny. He laughed at her jokes, which were mostly pretty corny; he was impressed that she could squirt liquid through the gap in her front teeth, and he liked to cuddle. And, of course, there was no denying the chemistry they still managed to create together.

Still, his timing was exceedingly bad. He had come back just as she was standing at the precipice, ready to dive into this new life she'd been preparing for herself, and maybe along the way, if she was lucky, finding her parents. He thought she was a barista, and she was, but she wasn't ready to tell him about her other job yet, although she had sat him down and tried to explain.

"I have issues to resolve," she said. "I may be gone a lot."

Fletcher shook his head. God, she was a mystery. "What kind of issues?" he asked.

"The kind that I can't discuss with you yet," Imogen said, shutting that conversation down, but not exactly deterring him either.

A notification pinged on Imogen's phone. It was a text from Fletcher. My place or yours?

17

Fletcher grabbed one of Imogen's shorty terry cloth robes from off the bathroom hook, tied the ties around his waist and walked out to retrieve the morning newspaper off the front porch. He knew he looked silly in it, but it was all that was handy. He dropped the paper on the coffee table and walked leisurely into the kitchen. "Who's that spying on you?" he asked Imogen, who was busy pouring water into the coffeemaker.

"Who? What do you mean?" she said without turning around.

"There's a black car parked down the street and I thought I saw a guy with binoculars inside it looking over here at your house."

"Really?" Imogen asked. "That's weird," she said, although her tone didn't indicate much if any concern. "It's probably just another one of Mimi Pinky's boyfriends," she shrugged.

"Mimi who?" Fletcher asked.

"Oh, the neighbor lady, Mimi Pinky. She feeds Luxe when I'm gone. She has some pretty crazy boyfriends."

"So why would her boyfriends want to spy on you?"

"Geez, I don't know," Imogen said grumpily as she brushed past Fletcher on her way to the bathroom. "Nice outfit!" she called back to him.

Fletcher snickered. Imogen was a grumpy-head before she had her morning cup of coffee. Grabbing up the paper, he plopped down on the sofa, resting his feet on the coffee table. Fletcher loved lazy mornings like this with Imogen—coffee, reading the newspaper, hanging out together. He probably liked them so much because they didn't happen nearly as often as he'd like. It seemed like more and more she was gone, away on "business" trips, she said, but she wouldn't tell him where or what kind of business it was.

There was so much about Imogen that he didn't know. She was a barista at the Beanie Barn that much he knew, but he was fairly sure they weren't the ones sending her out on extended business trips. But he knew all too well that pressuring Imogen always backfired. She only dug in farther. Whether it was asking about her business or trying to figure out where he stood in their convoluted relationship, Imogen refused to reveal or commit to anything. It was both annoying and frustrating. Yet, despite the flaws and gaps in their association, he had to admit, she made him feel the happiest he'd ever been.

He had tried to make a go of it back in Idaho with Molly, his high school girlfriend, but the truth was, he didn't love her. Pretending that farming and marrying the girl next door and living an unexciting life in Idaho didn't seem like much of an option, so he'd left it behind to come back here. Fortunately, he'd landed a great engineering job that he loved, so it wasn't like he was giving up everything to be with Imogen.

But it was true, no denying it; he was hooked. He knew it. Everyone knew it. He'd never met anyone quite like her. Aggravatingly stubborn, fiercely independent, she was a hard mountain to climb, but also the kindest, most loving person he'd ever met. And the sex, whoa, the sex was hot. He smiled just thinking about that and it took him back to the day they'd first met in college. He felt it the moment they shook hands. There was an immediate connection, a feeling that something wild and untapped was percolating just beneath the surface, waiting to be unleashed. Indeed, what Imogen lacked in communication skills, she made up for in bed. He knew she had a lot bottled up inside her, but he had sort of made it his mission to be the one to draw it all out.

He got up from the couch and walked over to the window

to peek out through the gap in the blinds. The black car was still parked there.

"What are you looking at, Mrs. Kravitz?" Imogen asked as she breezed by him on her way to the kitchen to pour a cup of hot soothing nectar of life, otherwise known as coffee.

"Who's Mrs. Kravitz?" Fletcher asked.

"Have you never watched *Bewitched*?" Imogen asked, surprised by her boyfriend's lack of pop culture knowledge. "Gladys Kravitz was the nosy neighbor lady in the 60s-era sitcom that was always peeking out through the curtains at the neighbors."

Fletcher shrugged. "I don't know what you're talking about Imogen, but that car is still parked down the street."

Imogen smiled and took a sip from her mug. She was just reaching for the newspaper when her phone rang. It was an unknown number. "I have to take this," she told Fletcher as she got up and went into the other room, closing the door behind her.

"Hello," Imogen said.

"Hi, is this Imogen Oliver, Dead Relatives, Inc.?" a male voice inquired.

"Yes, it is," she said. "How can I help you?"

"This is Josh Turner and I'm interested in finding information about some stereoscopic plates that belonged to my great uncle, H.R. Doran," he said.

Imogen grabbed a pen and scribbled his name and "stereoscopic plates" on a stickie note. She wasn't sure what stereoscopic plates were, but often the most fun about this job was researching items that she'd never heard of.

When she came out of the bedroom, Fletcher was sitting on the couch with his nose buried in the paper. "It's gone now," he said, looking up.

"What's gone now?" Imogen asked.

"The car that was parked down the street," he said. "I told you."

Imogen plopped down beside him on the sofa's armrest and placed her arm around his neck. "Oh good," she said dismissively, kissing his cheek.

"You don't really care, do you?" Fletcher said, trying not to smile.

"Not really," she admitted, amused.

"Well, keep an eye out," he warned, his voice serious. "You need to pay attention to what's going on in your neighborhood."

"Yes, Mrs. Kravitz," Imogen repeated, getting up and heading back to the kitchen to pour a second cup of coffee.

They spent the rest of the morning chilling until Imogen told him she absolutely had work to do and shuffled him grudgingly out the door.

"Aw man, do I have to go?" Fletcher said in his best whiny voice.

Laughing, Imogen gently pushed him out the door. "Yes, you have to go . . . now go."

After Fletcher took his leave, Imogen refilled her coffee mug and retreated to her office to power up her laptop. Stereoscopic plates would have to wait just a little bit because it was time to revisit, figuratively not literally, San Francisco, 1966.

During her initial research, searching for Yajna and Kari Marshall and Stuart Franklin had not yielded any hits, but now that she knew that they had probably left San Francisco and gone up to a commune somewhere near Eugene, Oregon, she might be able to narrow her search.

A few of the more colorfully named communes that existed around that time in Oregon were Footbridge Farm, Mama Keefer's Boarding House, and the Mud Farm in Eugene; Fort Mudge in Dexter; Hungry Hill in Creswell; Rat Creek in Cottage Grove; and Rainbow Farm in Drain, among others in the vicinity. But now instead of communes they were called "intentional communities" and she had found a directory. Hours later, after visiting multiple links and diving deep into community websites, she finally hit pay dirt. A Stuart Franklin was listed as a governing member at Cerro Gordo, a 1,100-acre eco-village near Cottage Grove. Imogen dialed the number listed on the "contact us" page.

"Hello," a male voice on the other end answered.

"Hello, is this Mr. Stuart Franklin?" Imogen inquired.

"It is," he said.

"Mr. Franklin, the reason I'm calling today is to find out if you were acquainted with Kari Marshall, or Yajna, as she was previously known."

Silence. But Imogen could detect breathing on the other end.

After a moment, the voice finally said, "I'm sorry. That's a name I have not heard in a very long while."

Jackpot. "My name is Imogen Oliver and I am inquiring on behalf of Kari's sister Grace," Imogen continued. "She recently received several old Polaroid photos in the mail anonymously and she hired me to see if I could perhaps find out what happened to her sister."

Again, when no one responded, Imogen said, "Hello? Mr. Franklin, are you there?"

"Kari is dead," he blurted.

Imogen wasn't expecting to hear that, although she knew it had always been a possibility. "Oh, I am very sorry to hear that," she said. "Would you be willing to tell me what happened? It would help bring closure for her family."

He was reluctant to talk about Kari to a stranger, but after Imogen provided him with several details that only members of the immediate family would know, he believed that she was indeed working for Kari's sister Grace. Because Imogen already knew the backstory, she asked if Stuart could take up the narrative from the time they left from San Francisco.

Stuart began his story. "The scene was changing anyway, for the worse, and we'd heard there were people living communally up in Oregon, so we hitched a ride up," he explained. "We ended up first with the Rainbow Family because we were both underage and they were the only ones that would take us in."

Imogen had read that around that time the Rainbows had sponsored teenage runaways and delinquents, which, surprisingly, was approved by the county. The family claimed they kept kids out of foster care and gave them a chance to learn responsibility on the farm.

"It was great, at first," Stuart said. "In exchange for helping around the farm we had food and a place to sleep. It couldn't have worked out better for a couple of runaways from the suburbs." Imogen heard soft laughter on his end.

"And so . . . ?" she prompted.

"So," Stuart continued. "Kari got bored with the farm. She was a free spirit. She wanted adventure. She said she didn't want to get stuck in one place, but I wanted to stay. I thought we had a good gig going, but she was adamant, so we packed our backpacks again and took off.

"She wanted to go to the desert, check out Taos; we'd heard that artists were gathering there, so we hitched a ride to New Mexico. We never made it to Taos, but we found a different community, a sort of similar artesian enclave, more remote, less cluttered," he said. We both really liked it and thought we might like to stay there for a while, but then Kari started to get sick, throwing up every morning."

Stuart's voice took on a somber tone as he continued his story. "She was pregnant," he said. "We'd both been doing a lot of drugs and neither of us, certainly, was even remotely ready for a baby. Abortion wasn't legal yet, but we heard you could get one across the border in Tijuana."

Stuart paused. Imogen could hear him breathing on the other end, but didn't interject, allowing him to tell the story at his own pace.

"He botched it," he said finally. "The doctor messed her all up inside. She was bleeding, burning up with fever. We tried to take care of her, our friend Lily and me, but it was too late. We couldn't even get her to a hospital in time."

"Oh my god," Imogen said, stunned. "I am so very sorry Stuart." It both astounded her and pissed her off that even today, women were still fighting over the right to safe, legal abortion.

"After Kari was gone, I decided to return to Oregon. I didn't like the desert heat much anyway, and I couldn't bear to stay any longer in the place where she'd died. I came back and settled at Cerro Gordo," Stuart said. "Been here ever since."

"And you never contacted her parents?" Imogen asked, incredulous.

"I was just a kid," Stuart said. "I should have, I know that now, but every time I thought about contacting them, I chickened out. I thought they would blame me."

"And the photos? It was you who sent them, right?"

"Yeah, it was me," he confessed after a pause. "I found them when I was cleaning out the attic. They were tucked away inside a pocket in my old backpack, along with a few of her other personal items. She also had an address book with her sister's name in it, so I looked her up online and mailed the photos to her anonymously.

I figured she should have them. They were the last ones ever taken of Kari," he concluded. "I didn't think anyone would try to track me down."

Imogen understood now why Stuart had lied. But the hard part would be telling Grace. "Thank you, Stuart," Imogen said, "but I will have to deliver this information to her sister."

"I'll tell her," Stuart piped up. "I'll go in person. It's the least I can do now for Kari and her family."

"I'll go with you," Imogen said.

After ending her call with Stuart, Imogen sat at her desk for a few minutes staring down at the faded Polaroid of Kari, at that lovely, fresh face, so full of energy and life and hope. How very sad it all was. Such a waste of a young life, Imogen thought. In theory, she knew things wouldn't always be easy in this line of work; that there would be times like this when she would have to deliver bad news, but in practice, it was much harder. Poor Stuart. Poor Grace. Poor everyone involved.

18

Despite a mostly sleepless night of tossing, turning, and bunching up his pillows into tight balls, Teddy had gotten up early this morning anyway and was already parked a few doors down the street from Imogen's house, watching for any and all activity through a pair of high-powered binoculars that some tweaker had brought into his shop last week to pawn for drug money. It had been the usual routine things; feeding the cat, walking past the window, coffee cup in hand. And this morning, a guy, presumably her boyfriend, who had likely spent the night, walking disheveled out to the porch in what looked like a girl's robe to retrieve the newspaper, and then later, not so subtly peeking out the window in Teddy's direction every so often.

The discovery last night of the advertisement in the paper, though troubling, was also a relief. Now that he knew for sure that she had the gift, it meant the thing he had dreaded facing could now be sufficiently dealt with.

He'd been keeping tabs on Imogen off and on for years anyway; she lived just two doors down from his mother. He had watched her while she was in college and it seemed like she had been a normal college kid, coming and going, just doing her thing. He expected she'd move away once her grandmother died, but she didn't. Teddy conceded that even he was a tiny bit sorry at the news of Mrs. Oliver's passing. She was one of the few people in the neighborhood to show him any real kindness. Not that he deserved any, mind you, but for some reason, she seemed able to look past his bad acne and the fact that he was a bully. In fact, that summer he spent working for Imogen's parents she sometimes brought snacks out to him in the studio—fruits she'd picked, cookies she'd baked, and she'd ask him how his day was going. She was a decent old lady.

Teddy didn't intentionally aspire to be a bully, but part of the problem was he looked like one. His physical attributes made the decision for him. It is how the girl named Peggy with the upturned nose becomes forever known as piggy, or the boy with the limp becomes Gimp. It is a sad little boy that receives only one Valentine and it is from the teacher. It is the cruelty of children. And what starts in childhood often follows into adulthood, even if it is better left behind. It becomes our destiny whether we like it or not. So with his dark and persistent greasy hair, a face crowded with freckles and a perpetually pursed lip that slightly resembled a fish, Teddy just looked angry. And as the childish taunts about his simmering face escalated Teddy began to slowly assume the character and to cultivate his bullish reputation.

Yet anger at being pigeonholed into a role that he himself had not chosen was only partially responsible for Teddy's behavior. Perhaps it was the taunts that drove the rage to the surface, but Teddy's twistedness ran deep, and the defining moment, the moment that Teddy discovered his power, may well have been that day standing in the milk line with his friend Ray Tanner, who was doing his usual goofy antics to impress the girls, poking them with his pencil, teasing and nudging them, pulling their ponytails. Negative attention, positive attention, any attention was good in Ray's playbook.

For some reason, girls made Teddy feel annoyed. He wasn't sure why, but even in fourth grade, he had a sense that deep down girls held more power than boys. Maybe they didn't know it yet, or maybe they knew, but they were keeping it hidden for some pertinacious reason. And he knew that somehow that power they held had to be extinguished. So while Ray and these girls were distracted, without warning, for no specific reason, Teddy turned around in line to face

Marilyn Newman and violently jammed his knee hard between her legs.

Teddy wasn't sure why he did it, but Marilyn, standing there with that irritating, dull look on her ugly pug-nosed face, infuriated him. He could tell that he'd hurt her, but even though she flinched, she pretended like nothing had happened. This made Teddy even madder, but he knew he could not risk doing it again. Even though tears were pooling up around her eyes, Marilyn looked back at Teddy with steely eyes, before turning and scampering off toward the girls' bathroom, probably to cry Teddy thought. Good.

And he knew she wouldn't tell on him because she'd be way too embarrassed to report him to the teacher, who may or may not have done anything about it anyway because all "good" girls and teachers subscribed to the inequitable notion that "boys will be boys."

For Teddy, it was the start of an emergent need. It empowered him and he knew that like a lab rat addicted to cocaine, he would seek it out over and over and over again because he liked the way it made him feel; how he was in control. After Marilyn, it was easy, especially with the girls. But there were other easy targets too, like pasty-faced Walter Bird with the cowlick and coke-bottle glasses. Teddy and some of the others called him Walter Turd. For a week the class had carefully designed paper lunch sacks festooned with cutout hearts and paper doilies that were hung with clothespins along a clothesline. After the cards had been distributed on Valentine's Day, Teddy had snuck into the classroom and taken all of Walter's cards, except one. Watching Walter "Turd's" pathetic, dejected face when he opened up his bag to find only a single card from their teacher was priceless.

When it came to Imogen; however, it hadn't been so easy. Sure, he pestered her any chance he got, and one summer he almost set her and her backyard on fire with a bunch of illegal firecrackers, but Imogen was different; she was wilier than most girls, tougher. He had an alien thought once about her, respect. For some reason, he wanted Imogen to like him and he wasn't sure why.

And he liked her family. They were nice, and nice to Teddy, which was befuddling. Nobody was nice to Teddy, not even his mother most of the time. He had seen these types of families on the television sitcoms, but was convinced they couldn't possibly exist in real life. Yet, whenever he spied on the Olivers, which happened a lot, they seemed to truly like each other. The parents, both photographers, followed Imogen around taking pictures of her. They took her places and spent time with her; they laughed together all the time. It seemed so far removed from Teddy's own unsatisfying home life with his dysfunctional mother, Mimi Pinky and her endless procession of boyfriends.

He even harbored a secret wish that he could be their boy, the good son that Mr. Oliver would take to the park for a catch; the one that Mrs. Oliver would make her special lasagna for. Mrs. Oliver, Francis, wow, Imogen's mom was something else. Not only was she elegant and beautiful, but that last summer before everything went to hell, Teddy was sure that she had a thing for him. It was subtle, of course, but that way she looked at him sometimes made him wonder if maybe she wanted more from him than she let on, like Mimi did. But then, why was she having an affair? Nothing about that summer made any sense at all.

When it seemed like the boyfriend was getting a little too suspicious, Teddy drove away, parking the car around the corner on the next block and then walked over to his mother's house from there. Mimi, deeply entrenched in her book club and ghost hunting group and belly dance class and an array of other unconventional activities that Teddy didn't much care to hear about, didn't seem to know anything other than that she had been charged with feeding Imogen's cat when she was away, which apparently, might be fairly frequent. And Imogen had given her a key.

"Look," Mimi said, holding up the shiny silver key hooked on to a red plastic coil keychain. "Here it is, Teddy Bear."

Teddy's response was swift and brusque. "Don't call me that, mother." A fleeting look of feigned hurt crossed Mimi's moon-shaped face.

"Oh Teddy," she said, reaching out and stroking his pocked cheek. "You know, you'll always be my little Teddy Bear."

Teddy withdrew in revulsion. "Stop it Mimi," he said trying hard

to temper an angry mantra: don't make me hurt you, he thought. He
rose from the table and poked his head out the front door. The boyfriend had left hours ago, but now Imogen was backing her car out
of the driveway. This was his chance. He knew it was risky, but he
couldn't contain himself. He needed to find out what she was up to.

Modifying his angry demeanor of a few moments ago, Teddy
took a deep breath, relaxed his shoulders, and turned around and
walked back over to the table where Mimi was still pouting. Leaning
in, he planted a quick kiss on her rouged cheek and said sweetly, "I'll
be back in a bit, ma" while sneakily palming the silver key and tucking it inside his jacket pocket.

Standing nervously on Imogen's porch, Teddy did a hurried
survey of the neighborhood to make sure that no one was watching
before quickly slipping the key into the lock, turning it, and entering
the house. Surprisingly, like his apartment, Imogen's house too was
a chaotic mess. For some reason, he assumed that girls were just
inherently better housekeepers, but obviously that wasn't the case.
Teddy walked from room to room until he found the room Imogen used as her office. Unlike the rest of the house, this room was
shipshape. He walked around to the desk opening up drawers, all of
which contained just your usual office type things. One contained
hanging file folders, presumably cases she had worked on already.
Teddy flipped through them without recognizing any of the names
or places.

About to give up, he noticed a notepad next to the phone. On
it was scribbled the words "stereoscopic plates" and a name and
phone number that he did not recognize, and one that he did: "H.R.
Doran."

"Well Shit," Teddy said out loud. That settled it. He knew what
he had to do. Wherever Imogen was going, Teddy needed to follow
and find out what she was up to. He was beginning to feel anxious
about being inside her house and was readying his exit when he
spotted it. The key. He'd seen that key before; used it, even. It was
the key to the photo studio. Teddy knew he should go now. He
didn't know how long Imogen would be gone. No, he shouldn't.
He started to turn away and walk back out of the office, but as if
an invisible hand was tugging him back, he marched back over and
snatched the key from the peg it was dangling from.

"Damnit" he whispered under his breath. He had considered breaking into the studio off and on for years, but something had always deterred him. Now though, with the key hanging there in front of him like that, beckoning to him, it was hard to resist.

Carefully locking the front door of Imogen's house, he dashed around the back in the direction of the studio. Using the key, he entered the studio and groping around on the wall in the dark he finally found the light switch. Amazingly, after all this time, the studio lights came up, illuminating the space and revealing years of undisturbed dust and cobwebs. Despite the neglect, it was the same as he remembered it when he worked here, although back then, the floors were a lot cleaner. He had taken pride in keeping everything sparkling for his employers, well except for that one line of dirt that you can never quite get with the dustpan and broom, that you end up sweeping off into a corner.

It was strange being in here after so long. Over there was the stool where the procession of high school girls had once smiled and posed for their senior portraits against a white or gray or black backdrop. He remembered fondly swiping a few photos of the prettiest girls and taking them home with him where he taped them up on his ceiling so he could pretend they were watching him as he masturbated underneath them on his bed.

Teddy headed straight for the storeroom in the back, his domain, and turned on the overhead lights. Although sweeping floors, lugging heavy photography equipment around to photoshoots, and filing miscellaneous prints and negatives hadn't been as glamorous as Teddy had envisioned, he knew he was lucky to have a job, any job. It could have been worse. With the mild recession that was going on most teenagers that summer were resorting to mowing lawns to fund their beer parties and cigarettes. Plus, it couldn't be beat in the convenience department; the studio was located just two doors down from his house.

While he stood there regarding the dusty still-stocked shelves, a boatload of memories came rushing back, but mostly, memories about Tiffany Rose. Tiffany Rose was one of many inane girls who had come into the studio that summer to have their senior portraits taken. Although he was supposed to be sweeping or stocking supplies, Teddy liked to hide back behind the curtain and watch them posing for the pictures. Tiffany Rose wasn't as attractive as the other girls. Her face was sort of mousy and she was always pushing her of out-of-date glasses up her thin nose. Most of the time, Teddy was careful at concealing himself, but the day Tiffany Rose came in for her photo shoot, he accidently dropped the broom. It made a loud kabang when it hit the floor. Niles, his boss pulled the curtain away exposing Teddy.

"What is going on Teddy?" Niles demanded.

"Uh, nothing, sir," Teddy stammered "Just cleaning up back here."

Niles pulled Teddy aside and said in a whispered tone, "We don't clean in the studio area when clients are being photographed Teddy," he lectured.

Teddy nodded agreement, "Yes, sir, I'm sorry sir" he responded. Niles bent down and picked the broom up off the floor and handed it back over to Teddy. Teddy took the broom and started to retreat to the storeroom, but not before glancing back at Tiffany Rose and noticing that she was smiling at him. Girls rarely smiled at Teddy. He liked that.

Teddy strode back to a far corner of the room that was camouflaged behind shelves to the very spot where he and Tiffany had shared their first kiss; where she had let him feel her up, and she'd once given him a hand job.

Suddenly overcome with excitement the memories ignited, Teddy hastily unzipped his pants and withdrew his penis, and started to frantically rub himself out right there. It only took a minute or so before he came, ejaculating into his hand, which he indiscriminately wiped on his shirt. Spent, his forehead shiny with sweat, he slid down to the floor to wait for his heavy breathing to subside. Closing his eyes, he smiled at the private images in his head that were nearly as intense as the real thing.

After a few minutes, another thought popped into his head. "I wonder if it's still there," he said aloud. Pulling his chubby body up from the floor, he stepped over to the shelves and positioned himself directly in front of the third shelf up from the floor. Reaching into a hole hidden in the very back, he rummaged around until he felt something. "Aha!" he said laughing as he pulled the tightly rolled doobie out. Because Mimi often searched through his room, he'd hid the joint here so that she couldn't find it. His plan was to come back and retrieve it later, but that was the summer when everything went to shit and he lost the opportunity to come back and get it.

Teddy sat down on the floor again and pulled out a lighter that he carried with him. He didn't smoke, but you never knew when you might need to light something on fire. He lit up and took a big drag, holding it in as long as he could before exhaling. The sweet smell of reefer permeated the space around Teddy's head. He instinctually tilted his head back and closed his eyes. Although it was a little brittle and dry, being stashed in the wall all this time, it hadn't lost all its potency. It was still pretty good.

When he opened his eyes again, a single spot directly across from where he was seated came into view—part of the wall was missing, the edges around it frayed as though mice had gnawed through it. And there was something there, something shiny. Teddy scooted on his butt across the floor and began to tug on the edges, making the hole large enough that he could reach his hand inside and pull the item out. It was an old tin box of some kind, and when Teddy lifted the lid to see what was inside, he choked back air, a wave of panic pressing down on his chest like a boulder.

Still clutching the box in his hands, Teddy scooted back over to the shelves and shrank against them. "Fuck," was the only word he could form. This was way worse than he imagined. He stood up, zipped his fly, and jammed the tin into his jacket pocket before scurrying out of the storeroom, and back out through the studio. He was just about to close and lock the door when he remembered the light. "Oh shit," he said as he swung the door back open and pressed the switch down. He didn't want Imogen to know anyone had been inside.

Despite the rising tide of anxiety he felt, Teddy still had to return the studio key. Looking both directions to make sure no one was around, he made a mad dash across the yard, maneuvering around the garden area, and then up the steps of the porch to Imogen's front door. After fumbling with the key, he managed to get it open, rush into the kitchen, hang the studio key back on its peg, run back out, locking the door behind him. He was panting now. "Stay calm, Teddy," he told himself in an effort to self-sooth. "Calm, stay calm." More than anything he wanted to run as fast as he could back to Mimi's house, but instead, forced himself to slow his gait down to a leisurely, semi-natural pace.

"Hey Mimi," Teddy called out as he strolled back into his mother's house.

Mimi Pinky, who was standing on a stepladder hanging a strand of twinkly purple lights above the window, answered in giddy response, "Oh, you're back Teddy Bear!"

Teddy slipped Imogen's house key back behind the saltshaker on the kitchen table, and on his way out, without a hint of emotion, replied, "Please do not call me that, mother."

19

"Damnit," Imogen muttered as she fumbled in the dark trying to locate the front door key. Had she known when she left this afternoon that she wouldn't get back home until well after midnight she would have remembered to turn on the porch light. The plan was to meet up with Stuart and drive together to Grace's house, about an hour away, deliver the news about her sister Kari, two hours tops, and out of there. It didn't work out that way.

She knew he would not look like the youthful Stuart in the Polaroid picture, but when she answered the door she hadn't expected the burly man standing on her front porch. She shouldn't have been surprised really, he'd been living at a commune for the past 40 some years. Bushy beard, tied-dye shirt, jeans, a pair of worn Birkenstocks, round wire-rimmed glasses—everything about Stuart Franklin screamed old hippy!

"Hello," he said pleasantly, extending his right hand for Imogen to shake, "I'm Stuart Franklin."

She shook his hand. "Imogen," she answered, smiling and gesturing for him to come inside. "Thank you for coming," she said.

"No, Thank you," Stuart said. "I appreciate you going with me. I should have dealt with this years ago."

On the ride to Grace Marshall's house, Imogen and Stuart listened to classic rock 'n roll on an oldies radio station and talked about Kari and San Francisco and all the happenings in the late '60s. For Imogen, it was cool to talk with someone who had lived and experienced that era firsthand. By the time they reached Grace's house, Imogen felt as though she'd made a friend. But when Grace came to the door, she was tense and wary of Stuart. The last time they had seen one another, of course, was that night at her parent's house in 1966 when Stu had fought with her dad and then he and Kari had run off into the night. They shared an awkward moment when Stu inquired about her parents and Grace coldly replied, "They're dead."

But Imogen was proud of Stuart. He dived right in to it and didn't sugarcoat anything. He told Grace their story as honestly as anyone could. He didn't make excuses or try to shift blame. The responsibility for Kari, he told her, was all on him and he had failed her, miserably. By the time he finished, it was clear that Grace had warmed up to him. She cried. He cried. Imogen cried. And then Grace got up, walked over, and gave Stuart a hug and thanked him for being there for her sister.

Grace invited them to stay for dinner and afterward, pulled out the photo album and they sat together on the couch drinking pale ale and reminiscing as they looked at family pictures of Kari and her family. By the end of the evening Imogen felt more than confident that Grace had found the closure that she was seeking, and Stuart had finally made peace with the gnawing guilt he'd carried around with him all these years over Kari's death. Before leaving, they had even exchanged email addresses and phone numbers and promises of getting together again soon. Happy endings like this were one of the most rewarding parts in her line of work.

It was late, and after the very long, emotionally draining day with Grace and Stuart, Imogen was tired, but at the same time, sort of excited and eager to move on to her next case and find out more about those stereoscopic plates, although she did not particularly look forward to traveling back anytime before the 1920s, mainly because of the constrictive wardrobe, including multiple layers of corsets and cumbersome long skirts and buttons and tight, laced up shoes.

This would be a local investigation, albeit 100 years removed from the present; the client grew up here and said that his great uncle was a well-known citizen here as well. Unable to sleep, Imogen decided to do a quick search for stereopticon:

"A stereopticon is a slide projector or 'magic lantern', which has two lenses, usually one above the other. These devices date back to the mid-19th century and were a popular form of entertainment and education before the advent of moving pictures. Americans William and Frederick Langenheim introduced stereopticon slide technology—slide shows of projected photographs on glass—in 1850. For a fee of ten cents, people could view realistic photographs with nature, history, and science themes. At first, the shows used random images, but over time, lanternists began to place the slides in logical order, creating a narrative. This 'visual storytelling' directly preceded the development of the first moving pictures."

Next, Imogen went to the archived newspaper site and began searching for news of one visual storytelling event in particular, one that her client's great uncle, H.L. Doran had delivered. Bingo. Imogen glanced at the clock—2:30 a.m. She turned off her computer and cuddled up next to the laundry pile that Luxe was still curled up on. Tomorrow she'd gather up all the information, tell Mimi Pinky to feed Luxe, fold and put away the laundry, and finish preparing for her next trip, to 1912.

20

Imogen shielded her eyes from the mid-day sun, allowing them to adjust to it before taking in her surroundings. It was strangely familiar, yet not. The streets and the buildings of the town she was used to navigating in her time had been rewound. Some of the buildings that still stood in her time were recognizable, but clearly there were many less of them. The sidewalk she was standing on was not made of concrete, but of bricks.

From across the street, Imogen discreetly observed an unfolding spectacle and was quite unable to avert her eyes. A quite nattily dressed man—a dandy, she supposed—was holding sway within a tight inner circle of seven or eight tittering and appreciative young girls. He reminded Imogen of a modern-day rock star as he confidently leaned in close, but not too close; gently lifting every chin, fondly stroked awaiting cheeks, and whispered sweet, soft somethings into the captivated ears of each swooning lass. She imagined this must be what it was like before reality TV. But even more than that, the scene evoked sweet memories from her own youthful summers past; of one in particular in her 13th year when every giggly girl "tween" she knew had been hopelessly madly in love with Irene

Jacopo's older brother.

Nicky Jacopo was 18 and the epitome of cool with the really super great hair and a car, well a Toyota, but a car, nonetheless. In the eyes of a boy crazy pubescent girl, he was dreamy and irresistible. And like this one, he breezed in and out of their imaginings, casually flipping back his sweet locks and flashing that sparkly gorgeous grin that set every nymphet atwitter. Dangerous, yet deliciously out of reach, they all crushed hard.

Even from where she stood, Imogen could see why the girls were taken with this fellow. Like Nicky, the guy exuded charm— the whiteness of his perfectly straight teeth when he smiled, the sexy ponytail falling long beneath his brown felt wool derby, and the round, shaded spectacles, which fueled the illusion of roguish deportment. Like most men of this era, he had a mustache, but in a seemingly bit of added flair, he also boasted a small tuft of hair centered in the cleft between his lip and chin. Clearly a hipster for his time, he was fashionably dressed in a checkered, single-breasted waistcoat and matching vest (with a prominent pocket watch and fob), a wing-collared shirt and bow tie, pull-up trousers, and a dapper pair of kidskin leather, two-toned spat boots. Imogen recognized these fashion accoutrements on account of countless hours researching everything from the era—from clothes to housewares to slang.

Although he was not terribly tall, this Nicky-esque clone stood straight and confident, and his gesticulations seemed deeply controlled, as if he were an actor in a play—the slow, deliberate saunter of his manner and the smooth way by which he kept the girls at arm's length, then drew them back in with a wink and an amused smile, all the while manipulating their delicate girlish emotions in such a way that each believed she was the special one. It was odd, but there was something identifiable about him, like Imogen had met him somewhere once before, but how could that be?

She looked away for only an instant, but when she glanced back again the latter-day groupies had suddenly disbursed. Dismissed, as if by some invisible stagehand, they wordlessly floated away from the charismatic man that moments before had held their enthralled attention. Imogen realized she was staring at him, and curiously, it felt like he was looking back at her. Was he? She wasn't sure. He seemed far enough away, yet she found herself noticeably experiencing the discomfort one might feel during one of those interminably long, super emotionally charged scenes you see in just about every romantic movie ever made—even though movies here were still in their infancy—where the filmmaker slows everything way, way down to capture that first glorious moment of unspoken boy-meets-girl chemistry.

She didn't know if he was looking at her or past her, but she was quite certain she didn't want to find out. Breaking the connection, she looked away, pretending to disinterestedly poke around for nothing in particular in her beaded swag purse. Thankfully, a cabriolet carriage pulled by a big, dapple-gray horse passed between them, mercifully interrupting the awkward moment. Seizing the opportunity for flight, Imogen spun around hoping to make a hasty retreat only to find her face squarely planted in the chest of the very man she was hoping to circumvent.

Oh my god, how did he get over here so fast? she wondered. She didn't dare move. Yet another long and awkward pause ensued until finally the gentleman broke the silence. Like he had done earlier with his group of silly little aficionadas, he leaned in close to her. She could feel his warm breath on her cheek and then he said, "Imogen, it is you! Have you returned after all these years merely to tempt me?"

Imogen stiffened. What the hell? Tempt him? As if! Who did he think he was? And how did he know her name? That was not supposed to happen. Collecting herself, Imogen looked up into that remarkably gorgeous face and replied coolly, "Kindly step away from me, sir, or I will use these extremely pointy boots on your person."

In an instant, the man's smug smile melted away, his face becoming a cocktail of anger and confusion. If she was reading his reaction correctly, it was apparent that he was not expecting such a less than genteel response from a proper lady. But a proper lady she was not.

Immediately, like two pendulums coaxing each other into motion, Imogen managed to extricate herself from the dumbfounded stranger, who was also hastily backing up and moving away in the opposing direction. Despite the challenges associated with walking in pointy laced up boots, and long, flowing skirts and hats and endless ribbons and buckles and bows and sashes and such, not to mention a corset that was seriously constricting her ability to properly breathe, she turned on her heel without stumbling . . . much, and managed to melt into the crowd without looking back and without knowing if he had turned to see where she had gone.

In her rattled state following their brief encounter, Imogen nearly forgot why she had come, but she stealthily circled back making sure that he was no longer around and found what she was looking for. In her experience, nearly every town had a public square where people could leave messages or fliers about upcoming events—sort of similar to telephone poles you'd see downtown with hundreds of stapled over, ripped off, shredded, reattached posters stuck to them. This town and this time was no exception and it didn't take long to find exactly what she was looking for, a brochure that read: "Man in the Making," a stereopticon slide presentation featuring H.L. Doran, tonight 7:30 p.m., downtown Civic Club. No admittance fee. Donations accepted.

"Perfect," Imogen murmured under her breath as she quickly snatched the paper from the board, folding it neatly in half and putting it into her clutch bag. She should have plenty of time to get back to the hotel to relax and freshen up before tonight's lecture.

After several attempts of vigorous jiggling, the pewter skeleton key finally caught in the precise spot to click the pin tumbler into place and unlock the door to her room at the Benson Hotel. Imogen wasn't used to this stupid time and the stupid stuff and all the stupid clothes and oh just 20th century everything. Plus, she was mad and still fuming at the nerve of that guy! She pushed the door open.

"Here to tempt him?" What did that even mean?" she vocalized aloud into the empty room. Who was he? He was cute though. But how did he know her name? That was scary weird. Generally, you don't travel 100 years into the past and run into someone you knew. And she was certain she'd never been here before. It was puzzling for sure, but truly, right now, all she wanted to do was get out of these layers of constricting clothes before she suffocated.

What she wouldn't give for a beer right now, or even a nice glass of wine; even better, a joint, something, anything to help her relax. Time travel was funny. She didn't get the headaches or the time fatigue when she traveled backward in time. It only seemed to have that effect on the return trip. Maybe the universe set it up that way so that you could get right to the task at hand, kind of the way the period clothing mysteriously appeared, she figured.

Because the curtains were drawn, room 213 seemed dark and unwelcoming at first. Setting the key with the curved bow down on the dresser, Imogen made her way across the room to the window and drew back the heavy pair of matching velvet and lace draperies embellished with an elaborate wooden valance. With a sigh nearly as weighty as the drapes she plopped down on the too soft, too frilly comforter atop the iron bed to take in her temporary surroundings.

The room, which was luxuriously furnished in a plush Euro-luxe styling, was actually a bit too florid for her taste, but she actually loved staying in these old hotels. She adored the architecture, the ornate wainscoting and crown molding, the high ceilings, even the overwhelming and moderately overdone rose cabbage-covered wallpaper. Next to the door stood a neoclassical oak dresser, where she'd set the key on when she came in. Resting on top of the dresser was a fancy porcelain chamber bowl with, of course, the same rose motif and centered squarely atop a frilly tatted doily. A velvet settee with claw feet in a rich claret languidly poised on a thick Persian pile rug was situated next to the large bay window. In a way, it reminded her of Grammy's cozy old-fashioned bedroom.

Overall, it presented quite a contrast to the generic, uninspired hotel rooms of her own time: Massive, across-the board beds with more fluffed pillows than any one person required; two end tables with touch lights, a desk, a television; angular patterns of bland, although this turn of the century version also boasted the latest modern innovations of the day—automatic door switches and cir-culating ice water, private baths, and electric lights. And yet, despite this being all quite stunning and exquisite, and far superior to any room at the Hilton, as she glanced around the room she couldn't help also noting how strange it was to be looking at that which she so admired and appreciated in her time for its elegant vintage beauty was something brand new in this time. It felt oddly icky in a way that she could not fully explain.

Nonetheless, the Benson Hotel was nothing short of magnificent. The 12-story building exuded old-world sophistication and elegance. Among the grandest of the day, elements of the Baroque Revival style were evident in the structure's red brick and glazed terra cotta exterior, arched lobby windows, and a French mansard roof with dormers.

Inside, the French baroque styled lobby was a stunning example of turn of the century architectural opulence that featured rare circassian walnut-paneled frames imported from Russia, marble flooring, Austrian crystal chandeliers, and a huge marble fireplace. The ornate plasterwork ceiling showcased designs of acanthus, rosettes, egg-and-dart, and other classical motifs. The grand staircase, also marble, had a cast-iron railing that begged for dramatic entrances. It reminded Imogen of the interior of the ill-fated ship the RMS *Titanic*, which sank in the North Atlantic on its maiden voyage to New York this very year in April. She had watched the blockbuster movie of the same name a number of times for period piece "research" purposes, but the shameless truth was each time she watched it she was drawn into the drama and romance that went along with it.

When she was in the lobby earlier to sign the guest book she had noticed a sign indicating that guests of the hotel received a complimentary morning cup of hot clam nectar. Coffee sounded better, but even as bad as it sounded Imogen thought she'd at least give the hot clam nectar a try, because she was here and why the hell not?

For obvious reasons, Imogen never used her own name. Choosing an alias had become sort of a fun game that she liked to play when she prepared for a trip. Sometimes she used characters from literary works, being extra careful not to choose a character from a book that had been published within the timeframe for which she was entering—she didn't want anyone to recognize the name and call her out on her deception.

So for a trip like this to 1912, she might choose strong female characters from more contemporary works, post 1912, like Katniss Everdeen from *The Hunger Games* or Hermione Granger from the *Harry Potter* books. Sometimes it was a character from TV or film— Veronica Mars or Mrs. Featherbottom. Other times if she was feeling silly, she'd put random names together to come up with Mimsie Katz, Helga G. Pataki, Rosetta Stone, Betty Crocker.

This time, she signed in as Daphne Blake. It sounded appropriate to the era, and nobody other than herself would make the cultural connection that Daphne Blake was the fictional fashion-loving member of the super-sleuth Mystery Inc. team in the animated *Scooby-Doo* cartoon series.

Finished with scrutinizing the room, Imogen hopped off the bed and ambled across the room, plopping down and splaying her legs unladylike on the settee next to the window to begin the tedious task of unlacing her high-top boots. Her feet were screaming. She wasn't used to just high heels in general, so her poor toes, unaccustomed to being unnaturally pinched together inside the ridiculously pointy-toed shoes, ached terribly.

Around the same time that Imogen was upstairs fumbling with the key to her room, Theodore Diamond entered the downstairs lobby of the same hotel. When he observed Imogen tearing off the flier in town he knew that attending the same lecture would be an ideal opportunity for him to keep tabs on both she and Doran. He'd followed her here, and like Imogen, he too marveled at the hotel's well-appointed décor. He seldom had occasion to travel back this far in time. For his business purposes, he typically only went back to about the 1930s—when items he could sell were being commercially packaged. In his pawnshop, he may deal with the dregs most of the time, but he could appreciate some finery every now and then. It was kind of like pulling the wings off butterflies when he was a kid; he could appreciate the beauty even as the doomed insects fluttered to the ground in a death spiral.

Teddy had to think for a second before writing his name down in the hefty hotel logbook. Hotels in 1912 didn't require identification like a driver's license to check in like in his time, so there wasn't really any good reason not to use his real name, but he really liked the idea of using an assumed name, of transforming himself into somebody else. What good was it to travel in time if you had to go as yourself? No, it was much more exciting and dangerously covert to choose an alias, to be like a super spy on a dangerous, highly classified, undercover mission, popping in and out of time, flying undetected under the radar. Plus, it was an opportunity to leave Teddy Diamond behind for a little while.

He especially liked using the names of his comic book heroes, but he was also wary of using the really obvious ones like Clark Kent (Superman), Bruce Wayne (Batman), Billy Batson (Captain Marval), or Peter Parker (Spiderman) out of his always paranoid sense of being watched; of being recognized and called out by someone from his own time who might be familiar with the names.

Sometimes, if he was feeling roguish, he used a villain's name: Lex Luther or Oswald Cobblepot, otherwise known as The Penguin. If he was in a more lighthearted mood, he might go with something like Keith Stone, Ronald McDonald, Buster Brown, Joe Camel, or Mr. Whipple. But his all-time favorite had to be Wesley Crusher, his favorite character on the *Star Trek Next Generation* franchise. The actor, Wil Wheaten had also played Gordie Lachance in the film *Stand by Me*, another of Teddy's favs. He sometimes cleverly combined the two character names to form Gordie Crusher or Wesley Lachance, both equally delightful. Just knowing the hidden meanings—crushing and taking chances—was enough to keep Teddy happily amused.

This time was different, however, because now that he knew that Imogen would be here, it was imperative that he keep a low profile and not arouse suspicion, in looks or in the name he chose, and he would need a disguise. Using the other names was fun, but he needed something old-fashioned sounding, respectful without being overdone. For this trip, Teddy chose Leeroy Jenkins.

As a *World of Warcraft* computer game nerd, it was a clear shout out to one of the most well-known fuckups in computer gameplay history. The story goes that a group of players were discussing a detailed battle strategy for the next encounter while one of their party members, Leeroy, is away from his computer. Their risky plan is needed specifically to help Leeroy, yet is ruined when Leeroy returns and, ignorant of the strategy, immediately charges headlong into battle shouting his own name in a stylized battle cry. His companions rush to help, but Leeroy's actions ruin the meticulous plan, and all of the group member's avatars are killed. Like Gordie and Weslie, Leeroy Jenkins would be his entertaining secret.

The desk clerk let out an exasperated, barely concealed, sigh as he waited for Teddy to begin writing his name, noting that it seemed odd that the short man in the ill-fitting suit appeared to be suspiciously contemplating it, as though he were deciding right there on the spot what it was to be. Teddy couldn't care less that the desk clerk—Marvin was the name embroidered on his jacket—was growing impatient. That was the fun of time travel, you could toy with people, use them for personal gain, whatever you liked, because you didn't have to stick around; you could leave at any time and you never had to see them again. With little control over things in his own time, why not have a bit of fun when he was out of it?

After leisurely taking the pen and dipping it into the inkwell, Teddy entered his name on the line, and quickly scanned the names above his in the hotel guest log, his eyes instantly falling upon one name that stood out in particular: Daphne Blake. Teddy smirked with recognition. That had to be Imogen, of course. Only someone from the future—someone heavily immersed in pop culture, like Teddy was—would recognize "Danger Prone Daphne" aka Daphne Blake in the long-running cartoon *Scooby-Doo*. Teddy suspected that more than the character's signature red hair, lavender heels, or fashion sense—Imogen possessed none of those qualities—she relished a bit of danger.

Teddy remembered her as a child being fearless for a girl, ever ready to try something new or dodgy, whether it was climbing up to the very highest limb in the elm tree or skinning up her knees sliding into home plate at the park. She also took curious interest in Teddy, probably because she was an only child with no friends in the neighborhood to play with. He caught her all the time tagging after him, secretly spying on him from behind corners and bushes and trees.

He rather liked having her as audience to his cruelty—setting insects on fire and watching their spiny legs and antennae curl up and turn black, deliberately pulling the wings off butterflies, or pouring salt on innocent slugs and those snails she painted names on and left to race, turning them inside out on the sidewalk. It gave him an imagined sense of dominance and purpose knowing that he might be making her upset or grossing her out; fortified that she would still came back to watch.

Even that time when the fire had gotten out of control, burning up her back yard and nearly setting her on fire too, she hadn't been mad or nearly as terrified as she should have been. She was strong and resilient, the kind of girl he would have someday wanted to marry, but then Tiffany had come along and spoiled everything, and Imogen would grow up without him.

Teddy was still lost in thought when he heard Marvin say, "Here is your room key, Mr. Jenkins."

Teddy snapped back to attention and took the key from the desk clerk's hand.

"Do you have any baggage you'd like the porter to assist you with?" Marvin asked.

"Uh . . . no," Teddy stumbled. He had brought only one bag along.

"Very well, sir. third floor, room 305. Take the lift or the stairs up, your room will be down the hall and to your right," Marvin pointed in the direction Teddy should go. Teddy nodded without smiling and walked away.

After he'd gone, Marvin gripped the logbook, turning it around to face him. "Leeroy Jenkins my ass," he muttered under his breath.

21

After stripping down to all but her undergarments, Imogen had lain down on the soft, feather comforter and drifted off. Intending to sleep only about a half hour—a power nap—when she awoke, late afternoon rays of hot sunshine were dancing across her eyes preventing her from opening them immediately. Groggy from oversleeping and a bit confused about where and when she was, it took a minute to remember that it was 1912 and she needed to be somewhere. Without a watch, she had no idea what time it was, but the fact that there was daylight meant that she had some time yet to get ready for the lecture.

She was headed across the room to draw the drapes when she tripped over the bulky vintage bag that had this morning been a London Fog Chelsea satchel purchased from Macy's earlier in the week. As always, the universe miraculously managed to transmogrify whatever bag it was into the correct style for the particular era she was currently inhabiting, and then converted the necessary goodies—clothing, accessories, toiletries, and gadgets into their period-appropriate equivalents.

As Imogen discovered during her forays into time, the bag was an integral part of preparation for trips requiring an extended stay in a hotel. Apparently, it was highly suspicious for a woman alone to check in with no baggage. Because there was no roadmap to follow, Imogen encountered this particular problem on a trip she'd taken back to the 1880s a few years earlier. It had been one of her early assignments and the first where she had to go that far back in time.

While investigating some letters for a client she recognized that her task might take longer than she had first calculated, and may even require an overnight stay. When Imogen had tried to check into the local inn, a different much smaller pre-Benson one, the innkeeper had immediately demanded to know where was her traveler's bag, because he absolutely could not, would not, rent a room to an unescorted young lady without a travel bag. It simply was not done. So distraught was he, Imogen apologized profusely, and came up with a nice little white lie on the spot, explaining to him that gosh, dear me, she must have left her bag at the train station as she rushed out with a promise to return with it later.

So now she had to figure out where to get it. Imogen spent a good hour wandering around the town searching for a store. There were plenty of establishments around—a blacksmith, a smoke shop, a bakery and butcher shop, but no store catering to ladies "things". Without GPS or even a map, she was at a loss. She took note to make old city map checking a part of her future research agenda. Her toes were super pinched from the uncomfortable boots she was wearing. It was hot, her ankles were aching and she longed to rest, but she could not return to the inn without a goddamn travel bag!

Soldiering on, she eventually found a mercantile shop on the outskirts of town. Imogen went in and as she perused the shelves she noticed that the shop seemed to carry a little bit of everything— from apples and apothecary, crockery and sarsaparilla to buttons and thread and zippers, although everything was covered in a thin layer of fine dust, which by the way, blew in unremittingly from the unpaved dirt street on account of both big wooden doors on either side being wide open.

Other than two ladies, who were whispering back and forth to each other, seemingly enthralled by the bolt of fabric one of them was holding, Imogen was the only other customer. Every few seconds they looked up and glanced her way probably because with every step she took the wood floors made an annoying creeeek,

creeeek sound. Searching every aisle, she finally came to a dusty shelf with several carpetbags that looked like they might do the trick. But, uh-oh, she wasn't sure if she had any money. She reached into the pocket of her skirt and relieved, pulled out a couple of dollars and some change. The money looked old timey and unfamiliar, and she wasn't sure how far $2 would even go. Would she have enough to purchase the bag? She would find out soon enough she thought as she lifted the hefty bag from the shelf, scattering dust, and headed toward the front of the store to a long wooden counter that accommodated the most enormous brass cash register she'd ever seen.

The shopkeeper, she assumed, stood half-hidden behind the gigantic thing. A smallish man, barely an inch taller than Imogen from what she could tell, sported a large handlebar mustache, slicked back hair, round spectacles, and he was wearing a dingy, barely discernably white, apron. When Imogen placed the satchel on the counter, the man peered at her curiously from around the side of the register. "Going on a trip?" he inquired with a hint of mistrust in his voice and one eyebrow raised. She was feeling more than a little nervous now. After all, this was her first money exchange in another time. What if she said the wrong thing? Gave him the wrong amount of money? Aw heck, she could do this. Pretend it's acting class, she told herself.

Imogen tilted her head sideways and with a forced, but pleasant smile said, "Why yes," her voice lilting up an octave. "Indeed, I'm planning an overnight journey on the train to visit my sister; thought I could use a new bag for the trip," she said sweetly.

The shopkeeper's eyebrow lowered a notch as he warmed up to that winning smile. "Oh, of course, miss," he said. "How delightful. Just let me ring that right up for you. That'll be one dollar."

Imogen was floored. One dollar? Really? She handed him her dollar (later research on 1880s currency revealed that her "one dollar" was equal to roughly $20 today).

"Thank you kindly, miss." The shopkeeper said grinning genially. "You have a safe trip."

She thanked him, picked up her purchase from the counter, but just as she turned and started to head for the door, she bumped squarely into a young woman who was blocking the aisle with a rickety old wicker carriage. She smiled at the young woman, who for some reason seemed out of place although she wasn't sure why. Glancing down at the infant, she was immediately taken by its unusual beauty, a contrast to his mother who was rather ordinary looking, despite a really stunning, thick mane of hair. Imogen wasn't particularly into babies at all, but the chubby cheeks and alert blue eyes of this one gazing angelically up at her from the carriage compelled her to blurt out the first thing that popped into her head.

"My goodness, I've never seen such a beautiful baby," she said looking into the woman's face. Most mothers beam when someone compliments their child, but the woman's expression never changed. Imogen kept going, "Well maybe except for the Gerber baby," she continued without thinking. Oops, she thought, catching herself, but the woman didn't seem to notice her gaff or, thank goodness, ask her who the hell this Gerber baby was. Rather, she put her head down, mumbled something that sounded like a thank you under her breath, and started to move away from her.

Imogen tried to move aside in the cramped aisle to let them pass, but before she could properly get out of the way, out of nowhere it seemed, a very large woman swooped in like an eagle capturing its prey, sidestepping Imogen to get in front of the lady with the baby. Tall, stout, sturdy, but not exactly fat, the woman cast a wide shadow. What was the word? Rubenesque, that was it, Imogen thought. But that wasn't all. Adding to her looming largeness was the ridiculously enormous hat topping her cranium that appeared to be festooned with an atrocious assortment of feathers and godknewwhatall—there was so much stuff on that hat Imogen wondered if a family of squirrels resided in there too.

After bending her large frame down to peer into the baby buggy, the woman turned her attention to the young mother. "Well now," she said, her tone loud and condescending with a distinctive European accent that dripped with a suggestion of presumed aristocracy, "what do we have here? This must be the little bastard!"

The younger woman drew back, clearly distressed by the confrontation and unsure about how to respond or deal with the situation. In addition to her obvious youth it appeared that she was alone and likely unschooled in the social mores, but wont to be respectful of her elders. Imogen couldn't be certain, but behind the girl's hand that she raised up and placed in front of her mouth, Imogen was pretty sure she heard her mutter something that sounded an awful lot like, "fucking bitch."

The next thing she knew, the girl had turned around and managed to spirit baby and cumbersome carriage through the door and out into the street. Imogen tried to navigate around the large lady with the colossal hat, but by the time she got to the door, girl and baby were nowhere in sight.

So that was the bag story. Like the money in her pocket, the modern bag came through time with her, albeit transformed into a bag specific to that era, one of the many quirky little ins and outs of time travel. Going in reverse, she discovered, however, was another story. While items that she brought from her own time could easily cross over and come back with her, albeit often transformed, something new from the past could not go forward, ever.

As tempting as shopping in another time can be, she had learned an important lesson on a trip she had taken once back to 1922, when on impulse she purchased a "flapper" dress, a fabulous flashy sleeveless, glass-beaded chiffon wonder! While she was there, she had worn it out everywhere and love, loved it! Unfortunately, she was also wearing it when she'd decided to return to the future. The result: Nakedness! As soon as she felt the carpet beneath her feet back in her office and the wisp of air hitting her bare skin, she knew she had absolutely nothing on. The dress hadn't made it through! The only thing that saved her from having to drive home naked was the T-shirt and sweatpants she kept at the office to put on while recovering on the futon after trips.

This bag, the one she'd just tripped over, was much larger than the 1880s version, and it reminded her of Mary Poppins' carpetbag. Every time Imogen opened it she half expected to pull from its magical depths a lamp, a mirror, a coat rack, and a tape measure. That never happened, but what the universe generously provided was still pretty magical, for inside of it was each and every item required to complete two ensembles—dressy and casual. From the bag, she began to draw out layers of cumbersome undergarments, lace up corsets—

comparable to modern-day Spanx—designed to squeeze away the belly and give the body an S-shaped line, and uncomfortable bloomers and stockings, as well as the necessary gadgets and gizmos and accessories to go along with all that; dainty gloves, jewelry, boot and button hooks and hat pins and hair accessories.

Did she mention before that time travel didn't come with instructions? So if she was planning to spend more than a day or needed to change her clothes for any reason—like for attending the lecture tonight—getting ready took some time. There was also the problem with her hair. The first time she had come she had to put on a hat and go out prowling the streets to observe how the ladies were coiffed so she could come back and mimic their hairstyle.

Thank goodness though for all those history courses she'd taken on period dress and styles. And the drama classes in high school had paid off as well. Grammy had encouraged her to at least give drama and speech classes a try. She never excelled much at speech, but admittedly, drama had been fun. It was there that she had met a lot of the so-called weirdo creative kids, people that actually turned out to be the most remarkable group she would ever meet, and although she didn't really have the courage or the desire to get on stage herself, her backstage training in lighting and costuming and blocking had sparked an interest in art and history in college, not to mention saved her ass a few dozen times when she wasn't sure how some gizmo from the past was supposed to work!

Imogen got down on the floor and opened the bag, first pulling out of it a most-lovely, sparkly gown. Much more stylish and feminine than everyday apparel, this was an evening dress, something one wore out into the evening to see and be seen. Tiny hand-sewn pearl beads adorned the contours of pale citron shaded fabric of the garment. It reminded her a bit of the flapper dress, but less gaudy. Imogen ran her fingers along the delicate beads embedded in the pleats of the dresses' bodice. A delicate silk ribbon festooned the waist and tied in the back.

She carefully laid it out on the bed and continued to draw more goodies from the bag—petticoats, undergarments, stockings, a pair of white simply de rigueur kid leather gloves, a dainty pair of silk evening pumps decorated with a rosette embellishment, jewelry, and finally, an impressively huge, broad-brimmed hat trimmed with masses of feathers and ribbons and artificial flowers.

"Wow." Imogen said out loud. "Now that is some kind of hat." It was large like the hat the snooty lady had worn at the mercantile that time but less garish.

If there was one good thing about time travel it was that she never had to try on several different outfits like she did at home. After researching the clothing she'd need, she tossed into the bag random clothes, undergarments, hair things, jewelry, gloves, hats, some shoes, and voilá, the universe supplied her with the appropriate period-correct attire.

As Imogen was beginning the laborious task of donning layer upon layer of undergarments, one floor up, Teddy stood before the ornate gilded mirror in his own room adjusting the wire-rimmed glasses and fake mustache he had carefully glued to his upper lip. He adjusted the fancy ascot tie and pivoted a touch to the left and then a tad to the right, admiring his reflection. He was pleased with this disguise. It screamed man of distinction! Teddy rather liked that.

He grasped the brim of his derby, tilting his head sideways in jaunty fashion and said, "Hello stranger," in the deepest, most manly voice he could muster.

It wasn't likely Imogen would recognize him; they hadn't seen each other in years, and besides, he looked just like any other dandy traipsing around town. But he also needed to keep a low profile so that Mr. Doran didn't recognize him either. It was risky letting Imogen get so close to one of his associates from the past, but it was the only way he could get her in a place that he could trail her and see what she was up to.

Tapping the brim of his derby Teddy clicked the heels together of his Patent Leather Buttoned Kid Tops and took a final glance in the mirror before heading out for tonight's lecture and reception.

22

The illustrated lecture was to be held at the Civic Community building on Friday evening at 6:00 p.m. sharp. Fortunately for Imogen, she knew exactly where to find it. Growing up, her parents and grandmother had taken her numerous times to plays and events at the stately brick building on Pearl Street downtown. And the hall was even within walking distance of the hotel. Excellent!

Imogen made her way down to the hotel lobby, through the revolving glass doors, and out onto the sidewalk where only a suggestion of a cool breeze greeted her on this unusually warm late May evening. She was glad she hadn't brought along a wrap; she was wearing enough layers as it was. It had showered a bit this afternoon with intermittent sunbreaks—typically predictable spring weather in the Pacific Northwest and she took a deep purgative breath, inhaling that familiar pungently sweet foresty smell that always filled the air following a good soaking rain.

It was a glorious night for a stroll, and as Imogen glanced around at her surroundings she observed that other people seemed to be enjoying the evening as much as she was. It wasn't quite dusk; not dark enough for the kerosene gaslights to be turned on. Imogen recognized it immediately, the magic hour—that time right after dawn and just before dusk when the sun casts a dreamy, warm glow. The daughter of two photographers, she had accompanied her parent's on more than one occasion as they chased the magic light. It was the best time to capture the essence of a picturesque landscape or the naturally surreal light bouncing off of or from behind a subject's face. Daddy would take her by the hand and shoot photos of her as she romped and ran, skipping and dancing against a naturally backlit sky.

And beyond the light itself, there was something ethereal about it—it was hard to explain, but while you were bathed in the magic hour's soft light you felt as if you had been transported elsewhere, outside of yourself for a while. During that one-hour window, you saw everything from a new and enchanted perspective; experienced something otherworldly.

Imogen could sense it not only within herself, but among the other people walking downtown along with her who were also basking in this extraordinary, muted light. Puddles from the earlier downpour reflected the waning sun's light, turning them into small pink pools. Tiny reflective droplets clung to the delicate roses that flowered outside the stores, and to the petals of hundreds of tiny red blooms on the camellia bushes, reminding her of the overgrown bushes that shrouded her grandmother's porch. The beauty of the hour made perambulating to the theater this night an unexpected treat, and before she knew it she was nearly there.

Turning the corner onto Pearl Street, a small group of people already mingled outside the hall, a big brick building, which curiously, looked much newer than she had remembered. In fact, if it weren't for the people she might have passed it by without recognizing it at all, because, of course, it was not yet covered in the thick coat of ivy that in her time was its identifying feature!

A sidewalk sign out front announced Mr. Doran's lecture and that although admittance was free of charge, a silver offering would be taken. Imogen panicked a little. Did she even have a silver coin? She wasn't sure. Had she bothered to put money into the small beaded purse? She couldn't remember. She pulled it out from the folds in her gown and began to rummage through it—a comb, a makeup accessory with a mirror. She was getting aggravated. Honestly, were these items really necessary? Aha, she fished out a small coin purse and opened it and Imogen's heart sank. All that was in it were a few pennies, no silver whatsoever. What would she do now? While she was fumbling with her purse on the sidewalk more people had arrived, the usher had opened up the hall's doors, and the attendees were beginning to file in. If she had to go back to the hotel, she would be late for sure.

As she stood there debating what to do, she felt a light tap on her shoulder and a man's voice behind her saying, "Excuse me miss."

She turned around to a bespeckled, rather rotund gentleman in an ill-fitting suit with a mustache that seemed oddly askew.

"Forgive me," he said pleasantly, "but I noticed that you seemed distraught. Can I help you with anything?" Imogen had not realized that she had seemed so obviously unnerved, but apparently she had.

"Um," she stammered, "Uh, no I seemed to have forgotten something that's all, but thank you," she said. The man glanced over at the sidewalk sign.

"Admission is free," he said, but if it's the silver you've misplaced, I'd be glad to donate for you," he offered with a reassuring smile.

Imogen felt relieved. "Oh my yes, I feel so silly, forgetting it like that," she said. "My goodness, I should have read the flier before I left."

"Allow me then," the man said politely as he ushered her toward the entrance where he dropped two silver coins—one for him and one for her—into the donation bucket. Imogen felt marginally uncomfortable accepting money from a stranger, but grateful all the same.

After they were inside, the man turned to her. "Enjoy the lecture, miss," he said, tipping his hat and smiling as he moved away, leaving her alone in the vestibule. She couldn't help being relieved that he hadn't expected her to return his generosity in exchange for agreeing to sit next to him during the presentation. Imogen wasn't shy, but admittedly, she was a bit of an introvert. Where some people thrived on crowds and parties and social situations, being around people for long periods of time was a drain. She hated small talk. After such events she felt compelled to get away by herself to recharge.

Nevertheless, she was much impressed with how polite men

appeared to be in this time period, well, other than that arrogant one she'd run into earlier. It seemed like here they at least tried to be courteous and gentlemanly. Although things were changing in her own time, a lot of the guys she ran into were incredibly boorish and cavalier. If they took you out for dinner or bought you a drink at the bar they still invariably expected something in return.

Imogen passed by a hat rack located next to a sign that read: Ladies Kindly Remove Your Hats, and dutifully removed hers, placing it on an empty spike alongside several other equally fabulous millinery creations.

As she followed the meandering crowd inside the hall, she scanned the room for a place to sit, hoping to get as close to the front as possible to get a closer look at those stereoscopic plates, and if possible, even approach Mr. Doran afterward to find out his plans. And to be honest, she was also really excited to see this presentation on evolution. As a confirmed nonbeliever, it seemed that if it were possible for people to become enlightened at the beginning of the 20st century, there might be hope for the 21st century where belief seemed to be at a global tipping point. Incredibly, evolution vs. creationism was still being hotly debated, yet while people were turning away from organized religion in droves, the zealots were clinging ever more fiercely to their dogma, and the Middle East was exploding with religious fanaticism.

A large canvas screen had been set up on the proscenium arch in front of a massive curtain of crushed velvet. As Imogen made her way down the aisle she noticed the waggish gentleman that had given her the silver coin standing at the back of the hall talking to another patron. He seemed to be pointing her out, but when he realized she was looking back he nonchalantly smiled, did a little dip, and tipped his hat. Imogen offered a half-hearted wave in return, but quickly turned away, focusing on making her way to a seat she had spotted third row center. She didn't want to sit in the front row and appear too eager, but at the same time she did want Doran to see that she was interested and thoroughly engaged in his lecture.

Imogen glanced over to her right and something caught her eye. To her dismay, seated in the fifth row back was that foppish fellow from earlier, the one who somehow knew her name. "Oh shit," Imogen softly muttered behind her gloved hand. Leaning back with one foot casually propped on the seat in front of him, he lowered his head when he saw her approaching and tipped his derby at her. That smile, oh so smug, Imogen thought. What was he doing here? He didn't seem at all like the type that would be interested in science. It was baffling, but she wouldn't let his presence ruin her task.

She turned away brusquely showing him that she held little interest in his being there, but before he was out of her sight line, she saw that he was chuckling. She found a seat and sat down and tried to pretend that he wasn't behind her.

The houselights came down as people hurried to their seats, and a few moments later the hall was swathed in complete darkness, save for the white patch of light on the picture screen that was emanating from the stereopticon, essentially a slide projector with two lenses designed to make the images it cast appear to dance. The audience started to applaud as a tall man in a dark suit took the stage. Doran stepped up to the podium and began to speak.

"Good evening, ladies and gentlemen," Doran said in a deep, resonating pitch. His voice had a sonorous, quality that reminded Imogen of the minister at her old Baptist church; a tone of authority mixed liberally with the smoothness of a snake's skin, she thought. It was the kind of voice that could gently lull you into a false sense of security, convincing you that the message was proper and true, even if it was an outright lie.

Imogen had researched these lectures and many of them featured music as an accompaniment, but H.L. Doran needed no such props. His commanding stature, impressive gesticulations, and charismatic voice were enough to keep the audience deeply enthralled. The slides on the glass plates enhanced his speech rather than the other way around. And not even the knowledge that that insufferable guy was two rows behind, his eyes boring into her backside, could pull Imogen away from the man speaking on stage.

"The Making of Man" traced the origins of the species from the billions of cells in a primordial soup that split off and mutated into other organisms to amphibious creatures that over the course of millennia grew legs and walked out of the water and onto dry land by means of four basic mechanisms that allow biological evolution to take place: mutation, migration, genetic drive, and natural selection. It was fascinating, and the realization that these concepts were something entirely new to this audience, was not lost on Imogen. For her, it was a matter of accepted science taught in school, but for these people it must seem like either a fantastically extraordinary new scientific theory or, something highly suspect.

Fifteen minutes into the presentation, a loud POP POPPOP disrupted the lecture as three of the light globes on stage burst consecutively. According to the newspaper account Imogen had anticipated that at some point the light globes would fail, but it was a shame that it had to happen during the most interesting point in Doran's presentation. She sat back and relaxed assuming that some-one would turn the lights back on soon, but something felt wrong. Beyond the audible shuffling and murmuring sounds among the startled audience, when no one came forward to explain what was going on, Imogen sensed a growing unease that something not so good was afoot.

Out of the darkness, the shrill screeching sound of the heavy front door being opened; a beam of light from outdoors swept across the floor, and then the silhouettes of several people, the thud of heavy boots stomping across the floor, then crash! Glass break-ing, the potent smell of gasoline, and then an unexpected burst of fire and sparks began to dance like angry sprites across the stage di-rectly in front of her. Imogen's first thought was, Oh no, not again! What was it with her and fire? This wasn't part of the narrative; a fire hadn't been reported in the newspaper. This wasn't what was supposed to happen!

The flames moved quickly, spreading across the stage in fiery sheets ignited by the petroleum, and then shot up swiftly catch-ing the thick, heavy draperies afire. The polite murmurs of a few moments ago rapidly turned into frightened shrieks as the panicked crowd scrambled from their seats. Several agile men came running toward the front of the stage to try to squelch the fury. Just then, Imogen turned and caught sight of her antagonist heading in the opposite direction, leaping up and over the seats in an effort to beat everyone to the exit, it appeared. Coward, of course he'd save his own hide, Imogen thought.

As the flames advanced, Imogen struggled with her long skirt. These ridiculous clothes were simply not equipped for emergency situations. Finally, she found her way to the center aisle. The hall was fast filling up with a toxic ball of smoke and amid the ensuing chaos she could see people dashing toward the exit. A sea of coughing patrons pulled handkerchiefs from their pockets, program playbills, or anything they could find to place over their mouths.

Through the haze Imogen could see that despite the terrified crowd pressing on them, another group of people pushed them back as others struggled to get the heavy doors open. As she stumbled forward like everyone else toward the promise of safety and fresh air the toe of her pointed shoe became entangled in the hem of her ankle-length gown and she tripped, hitting the wood floor hard. The fine material made an ugly ripping sound as it tore apart, sending the tiny beads bouncing and skittering to the floor all around her. Imogen tried to get up, but a sharp pain registered in her left ankle.

"Fuck!" she heard herself cry out. The crackling noises behind her were getting closer and she could feel the heat. The need for air propelled her forward as she painstakingly scooted herself across the floor. The next thing she knew, a hand had grabbed onto her shoulder. She looked up and it was him. He held out his hand. "Come Imogen," he said, "let's get out of here. Taking her arms, he lifted her up from the floor and gently placed his arm around her waist for support. With his assistance, she was able to hobble/hop through the doors and out onto the sidewalk to gulp in the fresh cleansing air.

Spilling outside on the lawn and sidewalk, the stunned audience stood or leaned on one another, coughing and sputtering and wondering what just happened. Imogen spotted the man who had given her the coin. As he wiped away the sweat from his face with his handkerchief his lopsided mustache curled up and fell off onto the sidewalk. Without the mustache, he looked strangely familiar. Where had she seen him before? she wondered. When he saw her looking in his direction, he quickly turned away, making a hasty retreat down the street. Mr. Doran was nowhere in sight. Now she would never get the chance to speak to him. Was this trip going to be a bust? She realized she was still being propped up.

"I'm alright," she managed to say as she extricated herself from him and pressed down the wrinkles that had formed in the front of her dress.

"Are you certain?" he asked.

"Yes," she answered confidently and then promptly lost her balance and slid down to the sidewalk, her dress again becoming a crumpled mess.

"You don't seem "all right" he said.

"I thought I was," Imogen replied, "but I think I'll just stay right here for a minute."

The deafening sound of the fire brigade's brass bell clanged as the truck roared up, skidding in front of the building. A dozen firemen leapt from each side and sprinted inside to battle the fire. Some of the crowd was dispersing.

Her rescuer bent down and looked squarely into Imogen's eyes. "Stay here."

Imogen tried to say something, but he placed his index finger to her mouth and disappeared down the street leaving Imogen shaking her head in bewilderment. Did he really just shush me? A few minutes later, an ultramodern motorcar came around the corner. At this transitive time when both motorcars and horse-drawn carriages still shared the road with penny-farthings and bicycles, owning a car was considered a luxury. Imogen was impressed. He stepped out of the car and walked over to her.

As he started to lift her, Imogen began to protest, "This is not necessary, I am fine, really. My hotel is just around the corner. I can get there without assistance."

"No, you absolutely cannot get there on your own," he said. "Let's get you in the motorcar now." Helping her to her feet, he helped her over to the car, opened the door, and after scooting a small, box-shaped camera aside to accommodate her, guided her gently into the passenger seat. The motorcar was so loud neither attempted conversation as they journeyed the short distance to the hotel.

They entered the hotel together. The only person in the lobby was the bellhop, who was slumped and snoring behind the broad desk. The bell on the lift registered a loud ping when it arrived at the lobby floor. He slid open the iron gates and as they entered the lift she noticed that the now awake bellhop was craning his neck in an unnatural way to see who was going up.

They rode the lift up to the second floor and he braced her as they navigated the long hall together to her room. The room was as she had left it earlier—a mess of stuff laying on the floor and the bed. Imogen was embarrassed. "I apologize for the disorder," she said.

He only smiled as he helped her onto the settee by the window. Bending down next to her, he carefully removed her shoe and Imogen couldn't help noticing the smooth texture of his hands. They were man-sized, but elegant and uncalloused, and not unlike the kind of hands a girl might like to have touch her, she thought furtively, immediately trying to dismiss that image from her mind.

"I'll be back momentarily," he said as he arose from his crouched position. He returned a few minutes later with a hot water bottle filled with ice, which he placed on her swollen ankle. Although the ice brought a measurement of relief, the pain overcame her.

"Owww, ow ow," she groaned, "that hurts."

He gave her an incredulous look. "You're behaving like a child," he said sternly. "Have you not sprained an ankle before?"

"Yes, of course," she replied embarrassed.

"Be still then."

Imogen complied, but it still hurt, a lot.

After a few minutes, the ice started doing its job, numbing up her ankle nicely and easing the pain. Imogen relaxed a bit. "Who were those men back there?" she asked him.

"They call themselves Crusaders for Christ," he answered. "They are a fundamentalist Christian group with a radical anti-modern platform, which includes, of course, evolution."

Imogen wondered if she had missed something in the paper. Perhaps she could get more information from him. "So they are anti-evolution; but was it necessary for them to practically burn the place down; endanger lives?"

"They accomplished what they set out to do; they disrupted the meeting," he said.

"That is true," Imogen agreed. "But will they be punished?" she asked.

"I'm afraid not."

"And why is that?" she asked.

"The mayor and the city council support the group," he said.

"So what you're saying is it will go unreported?" Imogen asked in disbelief.

"Yes."

Of course, that would explain why it hadn't been reported in the newspapers she had read. They would have covered it up, dismissing it as an accident, attributed perhaps to an electrical fire associated with Doran's lighting equipment.

"I'm curious though," Imogen continued. "Why were you at the meeting? Are you interested in evolution?"

He nervously crossed, then uncrossed his legs. "I have interests on many topics," he answered, "however, I was interested most in learning more about Mr. H.L. Doran."

Imogen leaned forward, resting her elbows on her knees. "Really? And why is that?"

He hesitated before adding seriously, "I believe he was once known as Reverend Doran, and I suspect he may have been instrumental in having someone I loved dearly committed to the sanitarium."

Imogen drew back, uncertain how to respond to his candid statement, and she noticed too that his demeanor had visibly shifted. He seemed uncomfortable, creating an awkward silence between them. Interrupting the blanket of tension in the room, he rose stiffly from the end of the settee announcing, "Well, I presume you are able to tend to yourself now, miss?"

"Oh, yes, of course," Imogen replied. "I have ice," she said, nodding her head and pointing at her ankle, feeling utterly stupid even as she was saying it.

"Very good then," he said as he positioned his derby atop his head and moved toward the door. Midway, he paused as if he had something more he wanted to say. From where she sat Imogen could see his shoulders move up and then down in an apparant sigh. Whatever it was, the moment vanished and he must have decided not to say it because he simply turned to her and said, "I'll be seeing you then."

"Wait!" Imogen called out. He turned back round to face her. "Today when we first met, how did you know my name?" In all the chaos, she'd forgotten to ask.

Where his body language a minute ago was that of someone

clearly distraught, the tension seemed to dissipate from his frame, his face to brighten. When one dark eyebrow shot up and his lip curled into a half smile, she knew everything between them was better.

"Why, don't you remember?" he asked, "We were introduced."

Introduced? Imogen was confused. She'd never ever been here before, well never been here in this time before.

"Years ago, when I was working with Andre and Miss Iris," Simon said.

"You were a photographer?" Imogen asked, recalling the boy on the bicycle.

"Still am, but more as a hobby," he said smiling, "but yes, back then I was Andre's lowly assistant." He removed his hat again and bowed. "Simon Le Bon Elliot at your service."

It had been her first real trip, of course she remembered. "Oh yes, I do remember now," she said, "you had that funny name," she blurted without thinking.

Simon smiled. "As I recall, you had a rather strange reaction to my name on that day as well."

"I'm sorry, uh . . . Simon, Mr. Le Bon, I didn't mean to offend you, then or now," she returned, "it's just that I knew someone else by that name and it surprised me, that's all."

It didn't seem to bother him at all because he walked back to where she sat and gently touching his smooth fingertips to her arm, he said, "It doesn't matter Imogen. I never forgot the day. It was the day you walked into my heart."

And with that, he strolled to the door and opened it, turned back slightly, did a little dip, and was gone.

After the latch securely clicked shut, Simon paused before leaving, pressing his back against the door to room 213. He couldn't believe it. She'd come back. She was back! He had been certain that he would never see her again, but here she was, as fine looking as she'd been the first time he'd laid eyes on her on that sunny day long ago. True, he had seen her the day before; spoken to her even, but he was surrounded by people—girls actually, his affectionate students.

He was overjoyed to see her again, bursting, but felt that he must behave in a certain manner despite that his heart was beating out of his chest! Afterward, he was certain that he had ruined his chances with her, especially after their rather snappish exchange.

And she had run away and he couldn't extricate himself from Georgia and the other girls fast enough to see where she had disappeared to. He was devastated. But then, what were the odds that she'd show up at the lecture? Certainly, luck was smiling on him, or serendipity, or both. Either way, he could scarcely contain himself when he glimpsed her entering the hall this evening. At first, he had thought she was with the portly gentleman who was speaking with her, but then he left her side and she appeared to be alone.

But now, after showing her his better side, he would return tomorrow under the guise of checking up on the condition of her ankle, declare his deep adoration, and claim her as his own! No more games. He would not let Imogen get away from him again.

Once Simon had gone Imogen caught herself doing a very uncharacteristic girly thing—like a love-struck teenager, she sighed deeply. "Wow, that was intense," she said out loud. "And awesome!" How could she have known that she'd made such a big impression on him? She'd only been there really for an instant—barely enough time to make idle chit-chat and have her picture taken with Grammy. Except for the name, she barely recollected him. He was the boy on the bicycle, the one Andre had chided for being late. It was funny that he had remembered her at all. The fact that any of them might have hadn't occurred to her at the time. Probably because it was her first real experience with time travel. Certainly, she was far more consumed with what was happening to her than what was happening to anyone else around her.

Although the thought of returning to her home tonight was tantalizing—propping her injured foot up on pillows, maybe having a glass of wine, and then crawling into her own, soft bed with Luxe—she was way too exhausted. Plus, she had paid for the room. Instead, a bath might be nice. Her clothes smelled like a campfire, and she longed to get out of every single body-squeezing one of them! A shower would be divine, but the claw foot tub would suffice. It would be like taking a bath in the old tub at Grammy's house.

Hopping over to the bath she turned on both the porcelain hot and cold spigots until they were at the correct temperature. While the tub filled, she worked at undoing and unhooking the bazillion buttons and bows attached to the dress, and then removed the layers of uncomfortable undergarments while strategically balancing on one foot. It was too bad about the dress, she thought, and the hat—in the chaos, she'd left that spectacular bonnet behind. When the bathtub was full, she turned off the spigots and eased herself down into the warm water, careful not to bump her ankle against the side of the hard tub. Once in, she relaxed at once, succumbing to the hot water's divinely soothing properties.

Perhaps being confined to the tub would allow her to clear her mind and recall more details about she and Simon's first meeting. It was her first year of college. She'd borrowed Grammy's picture for an assignment and unintentionally stepped into it. She had been so confused and distracted at running into her own grandmother, she'd completely forgotten about meeting Simon. He was cute back then, but now, yowza.

She recalled how she'd snickered when he introduced himself as Simon Le Bon Elliot. She had thought it was odd, but kind of funny that he shared the same name as the lead singer of an 80s pop band, but had dismissed it as coincidence. But now that she was thinking about it again, she wondered, might he be a time traveler as well? It was curious, for sure. She would positively have to do some sleuthing when she returned home from this trip. So there was that, but it bothered her too that she had felt drawn to him immediately, even though he'd known her name, which had confused her, but had also made her both fearful and angry.

If only Grammy was still alive to tell her more about him! She slunk down into the warm water and lamented the passing of her grandma. He had worked with Andre and knew her grandma, so he must be okay, but there were too many questions and no answers, and Imogen was dreadfully frustrated by her own feelings. Well, whatever she felt for him was impossible and silly anyway because, she decided, as she emerged from her bath—they lived a century apart.

After drying off and combing out her hair, Imogen felt considerably better. Her ankle still hurt a bit, but she hobbled over to the bed without putting pressure on it, and without bothering to dress, crawled between the sheets nude, burrowing herself under the heavy comforter, and falling almost immediately into a dense, dream-populated sleep.

23

Her body shuddered as the last remnants of a waning dream dissipated, a dream that seemed so real she wasn't quite certain that she wasn't still in it. Although the details were sketchy, images of animated flame sprites did pirouettes in her head, like those crazy ones she remembered seeing in an old Mickey Mouse cartoon she remembered watching in her childhood called "Fire Brigade", where hot little livewire flames leaped and danced a jig along the keys of the piano, and then chased Mickey round and round the room, the burning hot embers nipping at his heels as he tried to run away. But in her dream, the flames were chasing her and catching up.

Dreams. As far back as she could remember, she had occasionally experienced lucid dreaming. It wasn't a bad thing really. Actually, it was kind of cool, like being the director of your own private movie, only in your head. The dreams were often vivid and intense, but she had the ability to wake up and return to them at will, except for a time after losing her parents when she stopped dreaming altogether. She wanted to. She had this crazy idea that maybe in her dreams they would come to her and tell her what had happened to them, where they were now; that she would be able to talk to them and ask them questions, but they never showed up, and as the years passed, her dreams eventually returned, still rich and interesting, but without any visits or answers from them.

And yet, despite the convoluted dreams and waking up early, surprisingly she had slept quite well, and that was rare. Even with the cool meditation tricks she had mastered for time travel, she couldn't seem to apply those same techniques when it came to emptying her mind at night to go to sleep. Most of the time when she went to bed, it usually took an hour or more to the turn off the rampant thoughts running at light speed through her brain—succumbing to sleep only when exhaustion got the best of her and she could fight it no longer.

Perhaps all the excitement of yesterday—the events at the lecture, and then the memory in the tub last night of meeting Simon for the first time had helped her sleep, but she had no time for lingering in bed analyzing dreams or thinking about Simon right now, even though she sort of wanted to.

Tossing aside the thick comforter, she sat up on the edge, letting her bare feet touch the plush Persian rug that framed the massive iron bed. Putting pressure on her foot would be a test whether or not she could walk today. Using her arms to slowly ease herself up she put pressure on first her right foot, and then the injured left. This morning, it felt more sore and stiff than painful. Moving away from the bed she took a first tentative step and then another.

"Ouch," she said. That hurt more, but the more she walked on it, with each step, the better it felt. Good, it didn't feel as though it was sprained. The ice and the hot bath had worked wonders. And she had things to do today, important things. Number one on the list—breakfast, maybe even giving that hot clam nectar a try, why not? And then, locating H.L. Doran.

Imogen pushed the knob up on the lift and heard the familiar, high-pitched *ping* sound as the creaky pulleys eased the elevator up to the second floor. Thank goodness this morning the attendant was on duty and she didn't have to pull the thick iron gate aside by herself. That sucker was heavy!

"Good morning Miss," the attendant said bending forward in a little bow.

Taking note of the man's name badge Imogen answered politely, "Good morning to you too, Otis," she said as she entered. As

Otis reached for the knob to draw the gate, the stocky man from last night, the one that had given her the silver for the presentation, rushed in. Pressing his back against the back wall of the elevator, he drew in a heavy breath, but managed a smile and bowed slightly in her direction. Interestingly, his mustache was now back in place on his lip. The sound of his heavy breathing made for an awkward ride down. When they got there, Otis opened the door and Imogen stepped out into the bustling hotel lobby. She glanced back to see if the man with the fake mustache was behind her, but he was gone.

As she was looking in the direction, Imogen noticed the clerk at the front desk staring intently at her. Was there something wrong with the way she was dressed? She was fairly certain her appearance seemed normal. Today she was wearing a fresh new frock and a pair of sensible pumps, not as comfortable for walking as her sneakers, of course, but an improvement over the tight lace-up boots from before that pinched her toes so bad.

Imogen passed through the revolving glass doors and stepped out into a glorious spring day, bright with sunshine and pungent of flower. In contrast to last evening's peaceful and leisurely stroll, the city had awakened and become a living thing. The brick streets were bursting with activity—motorcars clipped alongside horse-drawn carriages and bicycles maneuvered perilously in between vehicles and pedestrians. Adding to the chaotic scene, dogs and people dodged the oncoming electric rail car where dozens of daring citizens clung to its copper-plated poles as it zigzagged along its overhead wire route.

It was like playing dodge ball, but Imogen fearlessly lifted her frock and stepped into the frenzy. She wasn't exactly sure where to begin to look for Mr. Doran, but this wasn't such a large town yet; there was bound to be someone that knew him, or at the very least, knew how to locate him. She passed a millinery shop and marveled at the spectacular display of hats in the window—she had felt so cool and sophisticated in the one she was wearing last night, too bad it had probably been destroyed. There were outdoor fruit and vegetable markets and a flower shop, a blacksmith shop, a barber, a butcher, a bank. All the shops seemed charming and quaint.

As she walked, she couldn't help noticing several young women loitering on the sidewalk. Maybe she was imagining it, but it seemed like they were watching her. And actually, she recognized a couple of them from Simon's entourage. No doubt they had witnessed yesterday's tense little tête-à-tête between the two of them. Imogen tried to ignore them, continuing on her way and leaving them to their petty whispers. And then she spotted it. It was the same building now as in her time: the post office. The postmaster may be able to help. Imogen waited for a lull in traffic, then lifted her long skirt and made an unladylike dash across the busy street.

The post office building looked exactly the same inside, except newer. Exquisite marble floors, high ceilings, and a row of ornate, cast-iron boxes with numbers lined an entire wall. She approached the window and spoke to a gentleman, who she presumed was the postmaster, a man of average build, handlebar mustache, indistinguishable from most of the other men she'd seen here since her arrival.

"Hello sir, my name is Imo . . . Daphne Blake," she said, correcting herself. "I'm wondering if you could help me locate someone. I attended a lecture last evening given by a Mr. H.L. Doran. I was hoping to speak to him afterward, but there was a bit of a commotion and we were unable to speak."

Imogen knew she was rambling, but without hesitation, the postmaster smiled and said, "Of course, everyone knows Mr. Doran." He took a piece of paper and wrote down the address for her. "He rents a room over the mercantile, two blocks down on the left."

Well, that was easy, Imogen thought, pleased that things seemed to be going so splendidly for a change. That wasn't always the case, remembering back to a few dumb miscalculations she'd made during past trips. So this was a nice change.

Feeling good, she left the post office and headed in the direction of the mercantile shop. As she strolled along, friendly shopkeepers standing in doorsills tipped their hats and said hello. What a refreshing contrast to the impersonal email messages and texts of her time. The physical act of greeting someone, of making actual eye contact seemed sort of foreign and archaic to her, yet at the same time, quite delightful. She made a mental note to self to make an effort to interact more with people on a personal level when she got back home. As she continued on, basking in the warmth and good vibes, Imogen did not notice the group of girls start following her.

After several blocks, fewer shops lined the street, replaced now by rows of uniform farm-style houses, each with a wraparound porch, various blooms in flower boxes, and carefully tended rosebushes. Springtime in the Northwest was the best, as far as Imogen was concerned. First the small, purple crocus popped up in February, followed by happy daffodils, then a stunning array of colorful tulips, and finally the showy rhododendrons busting out their finest hues of whites and pinks and yellows and oranges and, of course, the most vibrant of reds. The birds came back to town as well—hummingbirds and sparrows and Canadian geese that soared across the sky forming their spectacular V formations, loud honking signaling their triumphant return.

Even 100 years removed from her own life, Imogen realized she could always find something familiar and feel comforted by the knowledge that some things didn't change, even when everything else around you did. Caught up in the soothing sights and sounds and smells of spring, Imogen realized she'd passed the mercantile two blocks ago. "Well shit," she said under her breath. She was always doing things like this—easily distracted, shiny things, all the time living inside her head, it seemed. She turned around and started to retrace her steps back in the direction she'd come, but as she passed by an alleyway, she again noticed that same group of girls that she had observed in town. With their long braids, sailor-inspired uniforms, and pointy, lace-up, black high-top boots, she was certain it was them.

She would simply ignore them again, Imogen decided as she stepped up her pace past the alley, hoping to avoid drawing their attention. But one of the girls spotted her and began to walk toward her . . . really fast, until like a flash she was right there, within inches of Imogen's face. Without hesitation, the girl reached out and grabbed Imogen by the arm, twisting it back behind her back.

"Ouch," Imogen cried out as she wriggled away from her grasp with some effort. "What are you doing?" she demanded. The girl's face was a mish-mash of misplaced anger. Any preconceived notions she had previously held about turn of the century girls sharing niceties over tea completely dissipated. The remaining girls joined their leader, forming a tight circle around Imogen, blocking her escape.

"What is this about?" Imogen demanded in a voice as calm as she could muster under the tense circumstances. Without saying a word, the girl that had grabbed her brought the heel of her boot down, stamping hard on Imogen's toes. The comfortable pumps were now the worst possible choice as the sharp pain registered. Forgetting all early 20th century decorum, before she could stop it, the words rolled out. "You fuck-ing bitch!" she howled.

That was it. She'd had enough. She may be outnumbered, but Imogen was no slouch. She'd been around mean girls like this before, and knew if you let on that you were scared or gave in or tried to run away, it only made them madder and meaner and more inclined to inflict even more pain and hurt. Despite her smarting toes, Imogen moved in close to the toe-stomping girl, making direct eye contact. It was a stare-off that Imogen knew she could win, and did. After about 15 seconds, the girl averted her eyes, and Imogen took the opportunity to shove her away and then bulldoze her way out of the tight circle.

She turned back and glared at the group. "I don't know what your problem is," Imogen said defiantly, "but I'm not afraid of any of you."

The girls were clearly in a flummoxed state after hearing Imogen drop the F-bomb. Possibly, it wasn't a word they were accustomed to hearing, if ever they had, especially coming from another female. Imogen didn't care. She turned and started to limp away. The leader of the mean girls didn't follow her, but issued a parting shot instead.

"You stay away from our teacher," she said. "Keep away from Mr. Elliott."

"Shut up, Georgia!" cried one of the other girls.

Imogen stopped. "Or what?" she called back to her.

With less bravado, the girl replied, "or . . . or you'll be sorry!"

Imogen shrugged her shoulders and kept walking. Simon, a teacher, she thought. Hmm, well that explained his entourage. Handsome young teacher, blushing adolescent girls imagining an improbable love connection; Imogen got it. Freshman year of college, she'd crushed hard for her assistant history professor, a dreamy guy in a sports coat with great hair and impossibly long eyelashes that made all the girls swoon.

Great, Imogen thought as she limped away. Now, in addition to the sore ankle, which had begun to throb, the toes of her stomped-on foot were screaming in agony. And, during the scuffle with the Simon groupie, her hair clip had become dislodged and now her hair was falling all over the place in a sloppy mess. And a seam in her sleeve had ripped apart when the girl had roughly bent her arm back. However in the world could she drop into see Doran looking like this? This trip had been a disaster from the start.

At this point, all she wanted to do was go home, not hotel room home, but home home, but she trudged on. If she gave up now, she'd just have to turn around and come back. No, she needed to see it through for her client. And hallelujah, there it was on the left, finally, the mercantile, which seemed nebulously familiar as well, but she could not remember why.

Imogen mined her satchel and pulled out a fancy ink pen that she could use to wind around her hair for a makeshift barrette to temporarily hold her hair in place. She smoothed down the wrinkles in her dress as much as she could, and entered the store. The store was filled with an assortment of odds and ends—from foodstuffs to medicine to buttons and needles and thread—an early version of a modern department store. Aside from a couple of women with children in tow, who seemed to be engaged in a trifling conversation about the sorry state of the produce, the store was empty. Imogen spotted the clerk, who was busy stocking the wooden shelves with boxes of Cracker Jacks, the first junk food featuring mascots Sailor Jack and his dog Bingo and a prize inside! Instantly, it brought back fond memories of baseball games spent with her dad—sitting up high in the stands eating hot dogs and Cracker Jacks and drinking a Pepsi, belting out *Take Me Out to the Ball Game* together at the seventh inning stretch.

"May I help you?" the clerk brusquely asked. She must have been lost in thought because he seemed rather impatient with her.

"Oh, pardon me," she replied. She pointed to the brightly colored boxes. "I was just remembering Cracker Jacks from the baseball games my dad used to take me to."

The clerk cocked one eyebrow and looked at her suspiciously. "Uh, how did you have them at a ball game? We just got these in; they're brand new."

Quickly realizing her mistake Imogen tried to backtrack. "Well, I mean . . . of course. . . I was mistaken. That wasn't it . . . my memory is all haywire." She spied a box of licorice on the shelf. "I must have been thinking about black licorice," she said catching herself. The clerk seemed unconvinced. Of course he did, this bedraggled lady walks into his store, saying outlandish things about Cracker Jacks, making stupid mistakes, but he must have felt sorry for her because he smiled then and asked, "Can I help you with something, Miss?"

Imogen managed to regain her composure a little bit. "Yes, I'm inquiring about Mr. H.L. Doran," she said. "I was informed that he rented an apartment above your store."

"Who wants to see him?" The clerk seemed suspicious again.

Tired, frustrated, attacked, suspect—Imogen had had just about enough for one day. "Look," she said, pressing in close to the clerk's bug-eyed face. "I need to speak to Mr. Doran . . . now!" She pulled back then and sweetly said, "If you please, tell him that Miss Daphne Blake is here to see him, or please direct me to his whereabouts."

Distrust turned to trepidation about what the angry lady might do, and the clerk responded, "uh . . . yes ma'am, I'll get him for you, right away." With that, he turned and bolted up a staircase toward the back of the store that Imogen had not noticed before.

The two women in produce looked away, pretending they hadn't witnessed the exchange while Imogen nonchalantly browsed the spices and jams. Five minutes later, the clerk emerged from upstairs, coming down the steps with Mr. Doran following behind him.

Doran approached her and Imogen allowed him to take her hand as she gave a little curtsy. "Hello Mr. Doran, I'm Daphne Blake."

"Herbert, please call me Herbert," he said. "How may I be of service, Miss Blake?" he asked in that deep, wonderfully resonating voice of his.

She eyed the shop clerk, who had yet to take his leave. "Mr. Doran, sir, I was hoping to speak to you in private." Imogen said.

"Of course," Doran said. "Come this way. Let's visit the garden round back. It's quite lovely this time of year."

He guided her out through a door at the back of the store. Lovely was an understatement. They stepped into probably the most exquisite English garden Imogen had ever seen—a garden lifted straight from the pages of *Sunset* magazine. She couldn't help marveling at the array of flowers and the care to which had been taken to create such a devastatingly awesome milieu, a place bursting with colorful hydrangeas, fox glove, aquilegia, delicate violets, lupine, peonies and primrose, lavender and Echinacea, and bordered by a small lush lawn.

She followed Doran down a pebble pathway that led to a spectacular gazebo situated beneath the leafy canvas of a large elm tree at the center of the garden. A rippling pond was stocked with neon orange and white Japanese koi and delicate lily pads floated on its top; a small wooden footbridge had been placed over an oval of dry stones. The setting was so bucolic, so magical; it made her feel as though she had been transported to Jane Austen's Mansfield Park.

"Please, do sit down," he said as he gently guided Imogen to the bench inside the coolness of the ivy-encased gazebo. Imogen gratefully sat. "I sense you have not had a pleasant day," he said eyeing her torn sleeve and disheveled hair. "Are you injured," he inquired, genuinely concerned. Embarrassed, Imogen hesitated, looking away and fidgeting with the lace on her dirt-smudged skirt.

"No," she answered finally. "I'm fine, really."

"I am quite pleased to hear that," he said. "What then can I do for you?"

"I attended your lecture last evening," she said. With that, Doran straightened up and leaned in closer. A not terribly unpleasant combination of rosemary root and lavender scent emanated from his person.

"Oh. And did you enjoy it?" he inquired of her.

"Very much," she said truthfully. "It was interesting and informative. I especially enjoyed the narrative on plant species . . ." She could hear herself blathering on and on as though she was writing a term paper when what she wanted to do was skip the preliminary fluff and get straight to the point. Doran sensed this and stopped her.

"Why are you here Miss Blake?" he asked. "I appreciate that you enjoyed my lecture, but I sense that you have something else on your mind, am I correct?"

"You are perceptive, Mr. Do . . . Herbert. I was honestly enthralled with your presentation," she said. "But I am also curious about the people that disrupted the meeting."

Doran shifted in his seat. "Are you a reporter?"

Imogen shook her head emphatically, "No sir, I am not. I simply share your interest in evolution and am concerned about the safety and well-being of those citizens, like yourself, who may, shall we say, publically declare their beliefs in science over superstition."

The robust man who had confidently taken the stage last night to speak seemed to shrink into the depths of the large whicker chair in which he was seated. "You know, I was once a minister," he said sighing, an unsteady whisper of melancholy creeping into his voice. "A good one. An honest one. Not like many of those other fire-and-brimstone tent revivalist types who were out to squeeze every last dime from people, although I did preach in a tent. But I didn't care about money," he said, his voice rising in anger. "I sincerely wanted to help people."

"And what happened?" Imogen asked, hoping he wouldn't think she was prying.

He cleared his throat before continuing. "When I started thinking, I stopped believing," he said. "I discovered that through science; evolution, in particular, caused me to lose my faith, and ultimately, everything."

Imogen did not change her expression while she listened, but something about his story was missing. While evolution was indeed quite controversial, Imogen found it difficult to imagine that his family would turn their back on him over it. She sensed Doran wasn't telling her everything.

He paused for a moment before continuing, "It was difficult enough losing my reputation and livelihood—I expected that to happen," he said. "The hardest part was trying to explain it to my congregation. Of course, they didn't understand, and worse, I had to give up my work with the mentally ill."

Doran explained how he had been instrumental in securing spots for patients to be treated in the new modern state hospital. No longer a trusted clergyman, he had been forced to give that up as well. He leaned forward putting his head in his hands. Suddenly the air felt warm and stifling and quiet as a dreadfully long and uncomfortable silence hovered like a hummingbird suspended in the air between them.

Imogen wished she could say something to ease the man's suffering, but what could she possibly say that would make any difference?

After a moment, Doran composed himself. "I am quite sorry Miss Blake. I ought not to have burdened you with my trials."

"It's quite all right, Mr. Doran," she said. Imogen wondered if the mental health hospital might be the same one Simon had cited, but it didn't seem like a good time to ask. Instead, she took the opportunity to steer the conversation in another direction. "So, your leaving the ministry, was that what prompted you to begin your lectures about evolution then?"

"It was partially, yes," he said. "But considering the violence of last evening I am afraid I cannot continue. It is becoming far too dangerous. People aren't quite ready to embrace science," he said. "Evolution involves so much more, yet they are unable to get beyond the single element that humans descended from apes."

Imogen wondered if he had noticed the clear change in her face when he mentioned that. It was all she could do to bite her tongue and not blurt out the unbelievably austere fact that people were still denying evolution and science and climate change 100 years from now.

"Who are these people that are disrupting your lectures?" Imogen asked.

They are a small group of religious extremists, loosely related to the Ku Klux Klan, but growing in numbers, and becoming bolder. They fear new ideas or ways of thinking.

"If you stop lecturing, what will you do?" Imogen inquired.

Rubbing his fingers through the stubble on his chin, Doran pondered her question for a moment. "Hmmm, well, I can't go back to being a minister," he supposed. "And the further I delve into science and the natural world, the more convinced I am agnostic." But then, before her eyes, his deportment changed again and he seemed to be unexpectedly revivified. "I suppose I would like to learn to fly an aero plane!" he exclaimed.

In spite of herself, Imogen snorted. With the dark cloud of awkwardness vanquished, the world seemed infinitely brighter, and the garden a magical place once more. "An airplane? Really? Are you sure?" she asked.

"Yes," he said. "Indeed, yes!" With a renewed spirit, Herbert Doran spoke at length of having spent countless years following the mishaps and escapades and achievements of the Wright brothers who first took flight in 1903. Apparently, it had sparked something in him in his youth, although he ended up following a different path. But now, now why couldn't he do it? Why not? Imogen listened to him more or less having a back and forth dialogue with himself— should he or shouldn't he? In the end, it seemed he decided he should.

Imogen was pleased to have been potentially instrumental in helping Mr. Doran uncover his new passion for aeronautics, but it was time to get down to business; the whole reason for being here— the stereoscopic plates, projector, and slides. What would he do with them if he was no longer giving lectures? From the records and what the nephew had told Imogen, Doran had never married, had no children to leave them to, and that the setup was eventually sold.

"I reckon I won't have any use for them now," Doran said.

"Would you consider selling them to me?" Imogen asked.

"To you, what use would you possibly have for them Miss Blake?"

Imogen was a little offended that he was clearly assuming that a woman would have no use for the technology, but Imogen played coy. "I have a friend that might be interested in obtaining them . . . for his own purposes."

Doran leaned back, his body language suggesting that he was considering her proposition, but not fully convinced why he should. Without giving him the opportunity to respond Imogen reached into her purse and pulled from it a wad of money. "I can pay cash!" she said. Doran's eyes widenened at the sight of the roll of bills she held in her clenched fist.

"I'll take it!" he said, this time without a hint of hesitation.

With Doran paid and arrangements made to deliver the projector and slides to the hotel storage later that afternoon, Doran thanked Imogen and escorted her back through the beautiful garden. She was sad to leave it. They strode back through the mercantile where the clerk, who was doing some make-busy sweeping, gave her a wary eye. Out on the sidewalk, Doran thanked her again, but before she left, he touched her shoulder, and said, "You are not from here, are you Miss Blake?"

Disconcerted by his candid question, Imogen searched her brain for a quick and suitable reply. "Umm, I am not originally from this city, no," she sputtered.

"I mean, you seem like a modern woman." He said it in such a way that Imogen was certain he must know. But how could he?

"I'm certain I don't know what you mean," she said feigning ignorance.

"Forgive me. You remind me of a young woman, Tiffany, with whom I was once acquainted," he said, fluttering his hand in front of his face, embarrassed for bringing it up. "I will let you be on your way now. Goodbye Miss Blake," he said turning away and heading back through the entrance to the mercantile.

Imogen started to walk away too, but then stopped and called out to him, "Mr. Doran, one more thing. What was the name again of the mental health facility you mentioned?"

"I don't believe I did, but it was called Crestview Sanitarium."

Imogen thanked him, then turned and limped slowly back to the hotel.

24

Arriving back at the hotel after her meeting with Herbert Doran with her sore ankle and freshly stomped-on toes, Imogen dreaded the thought of having to enter the lobby in her disheveled state, but mercifully, the lobby was empty and she was able to slip in undetected. The gruff hotel clerk had apparently stepped away from his post at the counter and Otis, the elevator operator, was away too. The only downside was having to pull the heavy wrought-iron gate aside by herself, and then align the floor even with the elevator box, a feat that predictably took several unsuccessful tries of either stopping too high or too low. Finally, when it was less than a foot above her floor, she decided to simply slide down. She couldn't close the gate, but what did they expect from someone so woefully unskilled in elevator operation? After tidying up, nursing her bruised toes, and changing into a new, clean frock she avoided the elevator altogether, instead opting to limp down the stairs to the lobby.

Because she could not bring the plates and stereopticon back with her, Imogen employed Grammy's method for stowing and retrieving them later. Banks, of course, had vaults, as did some hotels. Part of the research she did ahead of time was locating these places in the past and ensuring that the building and the business were still there in the present, although the receptacles could only store one item at a time, and if she was given a key, it would have to also be stored elsewhere for later retrieval on account of the not being able to take items from the past forward rule. Sometimes, of course, that entailed having to travel to whatever city she had visited to pick the item(s) up, but it was a business expense that she could write off, plus her clients paid her very well.

Of course, presenting a clerk or a teller with an antique key to a lockbox or vault that had been sitting untouched in storage for decades made for some interesting interactions. But Imogen had perfected her story over the years: She'd been bequeathed the contents from crazy Aunt Phyllis, her mother's spinster sister, or wealthy Uncle Henry on her father's side had left it to her, or she'd found it while going through Grandma Pettigrew's attic or Grandpa Henry's basement/shop/desk/hidden vault. Choosing a name and a member of the family was fun. Often, she would scan the local newspaper's obituaries for names to use. If anyone became suspicious, they could easily look up the deceased. And because it was an aunt or a grandparent the obits typically did not list names of relatives other than the immediate family. Grandchildren weren't mentioned by name either, usually only by how many of them the grandparent had.

After Imogen secured a vault at the hotel to house the stereopticon and the plates, she placed the small bronze key the bank clerk had given her into a tin box she had purchased earlier from the mercantile. Checking to make sure no one was around to see her, she found the spot near the Methodist church that she'd prechosen a few feet from a sapling that was destined become a hulking big leaf maple in her time. Using the hand-held garden spade, also purchased earlier from the mercantile, she dug a small but deep hole, placed the box inside it, pushed the dirt over on top, and tamped it down smoothly with her foot.

Of course, it wasn't always guaranteed that the thing you buried or hid in a building would necessarily be there to retrieve later, but with the ability to know the future combined with solid research that the hiding place was still there and unchanged in the future, it was a nearly failsafe plan.

With her tasks completed, Imogen returned to the hotel to

prepare for her departure. She started to head back upstairs to her room, but instead, lingered a while longer in the lobby. With nothing more keeping her here, Imogen could leave at any time, but as much as she hated to admit it, she had secretly hoped that she might see Simon again. He had made no indication that he was interested in that, but even so, she asked the desk clerk if there was any messages just in case. He shook his head no, there were none for her.

Why hadn't she thought to ask how to contact him? Something tugged at her gut. She could leave a note for him, but it was a silly idea really. He lived in the past. She lived in the future. How entirely ill-fated was that? Still, what harm could come from leaving a message, she thought? Chances were he'd never receive it anyway, but she could thank him for his kindness, and at the very least, let him know that twice now they had both existed in the same time and place.

Endeavoring to evoke the proper etiquette for 20th century correspondence, Imogen composed a brief missive on the hotel's stationery:

Dear Mr. Elliot, It is with deep regret that I must take leave without first the opportunity to thank you in person for seeing me back to the hotel last evening and tending to my injured ankle. I wish you well. Fondly, Miss Imogen Oliver

She reread the note wondering what the point in leaving it was. Seriously, the only way she would ever see him again is if she came back, but why would she? She had no clear reason to. Debating whether to leave it at all, she thought about crumbling up the note and tossing it in the trash receptacle, but oh what the hell? She thought. She folded it in half and handed it to the desk clerk before she changed her mind again and went up to her room.

Imogen perched at the edge of the soft bed. Taking a final look around the room to admire the plush curtains and the luxurious settee a last time, she took a deep breath and closed her eyes, focusing on a photograph sitting in an office 100 years from now, and waited for time to peel away.

At the same time Imogen was sitting on her bed in her room up-stairs preparing for departure, Teddy glided out of the lift and into the hotel lobby, rubbing his hands together and whispering under his breath, "good, good." He was pleased how things had trans-pired. Sending that anonymous note to Georgia Bitgood had been a genius move. Igniting the jealous passion of the girl who had a crush on that fellow Imogen had interacted with yesterday had been the perfect distraction. And even though Imogen had managed to track Doran down, he was fairly certain they had only discussed the stereopticon, what she had come here looking for, because he had seen the delivery boy drop it off at the hotel.

Teddy exited the lift and rounded the corner and immediately recognized the man who was standing at the desk speaking to the clerk. It was that same fellow that had helped Imogen back to the hotel last night. Curiously, he reminded him of someone, but Teddy couldn't quite put his finger on who. On the internet, he'd seen old pictures of people from another century that closely resembled celebrities. Maybe it was just some weird genomic fluke. As Teddy drew near, pretending to admire the artwork hanging on the wall, he listened in on the exchange between the man and the clerk.

Simon: "It can't be. I was here just last evening with her. Are you sure no one named Imogen Oliver checked in or out?"

Clerk: "No sir, I am very sorry, but I don't show anyone in my guest log by that name."

Simon: "Are you sure? She was staying in room 213."

Teddy watched the guy's growing confusion, knowing, of course, that like him, Imogen didn't use her real name when travel-ing, which would explain why it wasn't listed in the guest log, but if that was true, how did this man know her real name? Teddy won-dered. Clearly unhappy that she wasn't there, Simon turned away, but the desk clerk called out to him.

"Oh one moment, sir," he said waving a piece of paper in one hand. "Is your name Simon Le Bon Elliot?"

Teddy held back a snicker. Simon Le Bon? Really? From Duran

Duran, the band? And then it occurred to him, could he be another time traveler using an alias as well?

"Yes!" Simon said, abruptly turning back around, his face lighting up like a star.

"Shortly before you arrived, a young woman did leave a dispatch for you, Mr. Elliot," he said as he slid the note across the counter's smooth wood surface toward Simon. After hastily reading it, Simon stuffed it into an inside coat pocket.

"The woman that gave this to you, can you tell me what her name was?" Simon implored.

The clerk wavered, wondering if he should give out privileged information, but then shrugged and ran his finger down through the list, stopping at a name: "Daphne Blake," he said, "room 213."

Simon didn't wait. Spinning around, he raced across the carpeted lobby to wait for the lift, but impatiently decided to take the stairs instead. Taking the steps two by two Simon sailed up to the second floor, nearly knocking over a potted plant as he burst into the long carpeted hallway where he sprinted past rooms 202, 203, 204 . . . he met an elderly couple and made a beeline around them until finally, there he stood, outside the door to room 213 where Imogen was, or Daphne Blake, or where one of them should be.

He wasn't sure where these feelings were coming from. They had only met twice before. The first time he had been enamored; certainly she had made an impression, but after a few years, he'd forgotten about her; moved on, met a plenitude of young ladies, Georgia Bitgood, for one. But this time when he saw her again, it had come roaring back, rushing over him like a sneaker wave—that something that he'd felt years before; an excitement, a stirring, a yearning to know her, whoever she was.

He had never met anyone like Imogen. In their brief time together last evening, he sensed that she was different, curious and smart. Unlike the besotted girls that purred and begged to curl like kittens at his feet, she seemed independent; did not need, nay, even desire a man's care and assistance. It was refreshing. He liked that, and inside, a feeling, a hunch, something, urged him not to let her get away again. Resolute, Simon drew in his breath, lifted a raised knuckle, and lightly rapped on the door.

Simon knocked, hesitated, knocked again. No answer. Silence.

Nothing. Frozen for a moment, his jaw clenched, a look of puzzled apprehension crossed his brow. The clerk had steadfastly confirmed that she had returned to her room. No one had seen her come down to the lobby to check out. But Simon was worried, stricken. Perhaps she had fallen. Her ankle was weak. She could be inside, injured. He pounded on the door, calling out now, not caring if he was causing a ruckus or making a spectacle of himself.

"Imogen? Daphne? Are you in there?" he implored. "Please answer me if you are all right!" He waited, but again, nothing. His first inclination was to rush downstairs and notify someone, but he stopped short when he saw it lying on the floor by the door—a key. Simon picked up the brass key, debating whether or not to put it in the lock and open up the door. What if she was in there but did not wish to see him? What if she wasn't there at all, had pushed the key under the door, and slipped away unnoticed? There was a third option: what if she was hurt, unconscious, and unable to respond? That option cemented his decision and he placed the key in the lock, turned it, and tentatively entered the room.

An oppressive silence greeted him. The space was uninhabited, but as he walked about the room he felt an eerie shiver run up his spine, because the room, not only void of any human, also seemed untouched. The bed was made as tidily as if the maid had recently been there. He opened up the cedar armoire and peered in—no clothes, nothing. No linens, not a thing left behind, nothing out of place, nothing to indicate that a person had been here at all; that Imogen or Daphne had ever existed.

Stunned that she was gone, but not ready to give up, he walked over to the claw-foot bathtub and looked down. There at the bottom, barely visible, lay a pearl earring. Simon reached in and picked it up, examining it in his palm. Could it be hers? He couldn't recall if Imogen had been wearing earrings or not. He poked around a bit more and discovered a somewhat damp linen draped over a chair by the window. She had been here, he thought, but where did she go?

With reports from other guests of a mad man pounding wildly on a door up on the second floor, the desk clerk, followed closely from behind by Otis the elevator operator and Teddy, the three men burst into room 213 to find a confused Simon holding a towel and pivoting slowly round and round as he tried to make sense of it.

"What is the commotion Mr. Elliot?" the out-of-breath desk clerk demanded before noticing the condition of the room himself. Simon shrugged and made with his open-palmed hand a sweeping motion around the room, indicating that no one was here.

"How did you get in?" Otis asked.

"The key," Simon said holding it up for him to see.

"I don't understand," Simon said. "Where did she go . . . Marvin," Simon asked, finally noticing the nametag affixed to the man's lapel. "Was she ever here or did I imagine it?" Simon asked everyone and no one.

Marvin and Otis shook their heads. Only Teddy knew what had happened to Imogen, but pretended to be as dumbstruck as the others. A small group of curious guests began to amass outside in the hallway trying to peer into the room to see what the commotion was about. Marvin raised his hands above his head and barred the door with his body.

"Everything is fine, folks," he said, pushing the group back and away from the door. "Nothing amiss. No need for concern. Just a small misunderstanding."

Otis followed Marvin out the door, helping him distract everyone. "Anyone going down? Free rides!" he said jovially. The group of people chuckled and followed Otis down the hall.

Back inside the room, Simon and Teddy shared an awkward moment until Simon turned to him finally and said, "I've seen you before." Teddy began to fidget, biting his lower lip and clenching his fists behind his back uncomfortably. "Yes. Of course, you were at the lecture, weren't you?" Simon said rubbing the small tuft of facial hair below his lower lip. "I saw you give Imogen a coin."

Teddy nodded, "Uh, well yes," he stammered, "she had forgotten to bring the silver donation."

"What did you say your last name was?" Teddy asked.

"I didn't say," Simon answered, pulling his longish ponytail out from behind his collar and twisting and twirling the end of it around his index finger, "but it is Elliot—Simon Le Bon Elliot."

And Teddy knew why Simon looked familiar. Things were spiraling dangerously out of control. He knew it had been risky allowing Imogen to come back here in search of Doran, but he thought he had that under control, until now. Now that she'd met Simon, this could change everything, if she were to return, that is. Teddy would make damn sure that didn't happen.

25

Once the process of time conveyance had been set into motion Imogen visualized, even with her eyes closed, the matching velvet and lace draperies and the red cabbage rose wallpaper twisting and folding into themselves; the iron bed with the pretty covelet she was resting on dissipating beneath her. For a moment, she thought she heard knocking far off in the distance, but the sound bowed and became nothing but a faint and distant echo, dissolving along with everything else.

When she felt the floor under her feet she knew she was back. Slowly opening her eyes to the familiar surroundings of the rented office Imogen totteringly maneuvered to the futon to begin the meditation trick . . . brick wall, brick wall, repeat. Because she had stayed two whole days in many years past, her head felt like it was filled with dirt—sort of like that groggy, next morning feeling you get after taking a heavy-duty pain narcotic the night before. She'd recover from the trip here in her office for a few hours, but estimated that she'd need at least day of rest to recuperate at home before digging up the key and going to the hotel's vault to retrieve the stereopticon equipment and plates.

One day turned into two. Imogen hadn't taken into account

that she'd also returned with a twisted ankle and battered toes. Sore
and aching all over; lying on the couch with a soft blanket and the
remote, vacillating between sleeping and watching old movies and
Netflix, was all she felt like doing.

Luxe, jubilant at his mistress' return, camped on top of her the
entire time, contentedly purring and cuddling with only minimal
interludes for dining and kitty litter breaks. Barely noticing when she
readjusted or turned over on her side, he rode the changing tide like
a surfboarding cool cat. Yet, her days weren't totally without inter-
ruption. As anyone who works from home can attest, people seem
to assume that just because you are there, it must also mean you are
at all times available. Case in point, Mimi Pinky. Imogen appreciated
that Mimi looked after Luxe while she was away, but she was fast
becoming irritated by her innumerable excuses to repeatedly knock
on Imogen's door.

Could she borrow Imogen's lawnmower—that good-for-noth-
ing son of hers had not been by to mow her lawn. Would Imogen
mind if she put her recycled newspapers in her bin?— each intru-
sion followed by a lengthy bit of unnecessary chatitude. Mimi Pinky
Diamond's curiosity about Imogen was ostensibly a thirst that could
not be quenched—endless questions involving Imogen's love life,
where her travels took her, what she did, why was she so tired when
she got home? and so on and so on. Imogen had already on numerous occasions given her enough information to mollify any normal
person's curiosity, but it was as though each time, Mimi forgot anew.
After the fourth visit Imogen finally told her she needed to rest,
couldn't talk, promised to drop by and visit with her on Tuesday.
This seemed to placate Mimi Pinky for the time being, and so far,
she had left Imogen alone.

Imogen grew weary of lounging about. It was time to get off
the couch and take a much-needed shower. Her hair felt matted and
greasy and just icky in general. It felt like she hadn't bathed in 100
years; oh right, she hadn't. The shower was rejuvenating; the warm
water soothed her aching muscles. It felt almost as good as the
well-appointed soak she'd had in the big claw-foot tub in her room
at the hotel after Simon had gone.

Simon. Besides catching up on TV while trying to thwart the
hourly incursions of Mimi Pinky, her dual-day respite had given her

plenty of time to mull over what had just happened in the distant, yet recent past. Simon Le Bon Elliot happened. That name, it still cracked her up. She could see naming a child Simon; that sounded like a name fairly specific to the era, but why Simon Le Bon? Curious whether it was the real name of the lead singer of the 80s band Duran Duran, Imogen did a fast lookup on Wikipedia. Sure enough, the British pop musician Simon John Charles Le Bon was born in 1958. But how or why would 19th century parents come up with such a name, unless it was a family name, or perhaps, she wondered, an alias?

The truly coincidental part was that she had run into him, not once, but twice, seven years apart, although it had been 11 years for him. It was true, she had visited the same location both times, which slightly raised the odds of two people potentially bumping into one another, but still, it was weird. She had forgotten all about meeting Simon that first time until he had reminded her. Clearly, he had not made much of an impression on her. But then, she had been a little preoccupied at the moment with this whole wow-I've-just-time-traveled-through-a-photo thing. She had to concede though that this time, he'd made an impression on her.

Even during their first awkward encounter in town, there was no denying she was attracted to him. Surrounded by his gaggle of groupies he was an ultra-charismatic presence, and clearly he knew it, relished in it even. Imogen hated everything about his type—self-satisfied, egotistical, and narcissistic, flashy, conceited; could she think of any more adjectives? Probably. And because even though she found him nominally appealing, she also knew that the odds of running into him again were slim to none, considering she'd threatened him with bodily harm via pointy boot, which had totally knocked him off his game and surprised even her.

Certainly, she hadn't anticipated him showing up at the lecture. And his same cocky behavior had been on display. But later on, when the fire started, it was as though he became a different person. He dropped all the pretenses and came to her aid. And at the hotel as he tenderly bandaged her injured ankle she had sensed within him a gnawing discontent. She was no psychologist, but her intuition and ability to read people was pretty darn good and it seemed there was more than one side to Mr. Simon Le Bon Elliot.

In between naps on the couch, events and trifling snippets of conversations weaved in and out of her consciousness—her encounter with Simon, the man with the fake mustache tipping his hat and handing her the silver coin, the gang of mean girls, and the tall one twisting her arm behind her back and stomping on her toes, the smoke and chaos when the fire started, driving back to the hotel with Simon in his motorcar, her conversation in the aromatic garden with H.L. Doran, seeing the man with the fake mustache a second and third time, come to think of it several times during her stay—who was that guy anyway? Simon gently bandaging her ankle . . . it occurred to her that instead of fading away into a filing cabinet located somewhere in her brain labeled "experiences" like they usually did, something about these particular memories stuck around.

That lingering something she surmised was Simon, and the "feelings" were becoming a nascent yearning in her gut—a desire to go back to him. There was also something else that piqued her interest, something that had seemed like an inconsequential morsel of information somehow connecting Simon to Doran. Both had mentioned a sanitarium. Doran had said he had taken mentally ill people to a Crestview Sanitarium to get the help they needed. Simon hadn't mentioned it by name, but he did say that someone close to him had been sent to one, possibly against their will. The name sounded sort of familiar. She would have to look it up. Maybe she'd read about it in a book about local history, or perhaps during her research, had seen it in a photograph. Hmmm, Imogen thought. She loved mysteries; she was a PI after all.

Fully awake now, Imogen turned her phone back on. Fletcher had texted her at least a dozen times over the last two days.

"Imogen are you home?"

"Hellooooo, are you out there?"

"Shit Imogen, do you even have your phone?"

"I give up, text me when you can."

Although he knew she was an investigator, of sorts, and had to be away often, he didn't know about her method of travel and he especially couldn't understand why she never took her phone with her. Of course, she couldn't take her phone, and she couldn't tell him why.

Several more text messages from Fletcher popped up. Good

lord, Imogen swiped over to her contacts and pressed his number. Fletcher answered on the first ring.

"Imogen!"

"Fletcher," she said trying not to sound too eager or too drowsy or too flippant.

"Where have you been? Why haven't you at least texted me back?" he asked, exasperation creeping into his usually calm veneer.

He had every right to be mad. She wasn't exactly behaving like a model friend. She should have contacted him. All she could do now was try to apologize.

"I'm really sorry Fletch," she said. "I was out of town and when I got back I was so totally exhausted I went straight to bed and slept like 13 hours or something."

"Oh wow, where did you go?" he asked.

She hated it when he asked her that question because it forced her to have to lie. Fortunately, she had cultivated a number of fixed responses—places and airports that were particularly difficult to fly in and out of, bad weather, etc.

"Chicago," she responded, maybe a little too briskly.

"Oh," Fletcher said. "Did you have to fly into O'Hare?"

"Yep," Imogen replied. "As usual, I missed my connection and hit delays all the way down the line."

"That sucks," Fletcher said, the crossness in his voice dissipating. "So, can I come over?" he asked.

Imogen felt a guilty pang in her gut. It wasn't like she had actually done anything with Simon. Yet, it wasn't Fletcher who had been at the epicenter of her thoughts over the past few days either. Still, she indisputably missed Fletcher and she could use some company. Luxe was great, but he was a cat. She knew she required some human contact as long as they weren't total energy vampires. Fletcher wasn't. He liked to hang out and get high and that sounded perfect. What was she thinking anyway? Let it go Imogen, she thought. Simon didn't even exist in the now. Fletcher did. He was a living, breathing human being, and one who wanted nothing more than to come over right now and have sex with her.

"Of course you can come over. Come now!" she answered brightly.

She really should go take care of the stereopticon, but it was a lovely spring day, warm, but not too hot, and Fletcher had suggested a hike up the butte. If there was one thing that Imogen and Fletcher both shared it was a great love and appreciation for nature. Maybe it stemmed from the nature excursions her impulse-driven, hippy parents had dragged her out on as a kid, or perhaps it was that unmistakable foresty bouquet of moss and mold and mushrooms that she wished someone would bottle so she could carry it around with her in her pocket.

There was nothing quite like a hike through an old-growth forest to rejuvenate and ground her. With sandwiches, bottled water, and sunscreen loaded into their backpacks, they arrived at the trailhead around 9:30 a.m. for the 2.5-mile hike to the 2,060-foot summit, which began with a trek through a grassy meandering field where in summer you could stop and pick berries.

This time of year, wild iris turned the field an eye-popping shade of purple. It reminded Imogen of the delicate flowers growing in the English garden where she and Mr. Doran had recently sat and chatted. As tempting as it was to run out and pick a few, Imogen knew better; ubiquitously hiding among the wildflowers was poison oak. The trail ran along a line of oaks covered in lichens before another switchback revealed a hillside of sword ferns, so thick that in places they encroached on the trail and brushed against their legs as they walked.

From there, the trees quickly became denser, leading the hikers deeper into the verdant forest. Imogen watched the shifting sunlight as it played hide and seek between the soaring canopies of towering Douglas fir, and breathed in the musty smell that she loved so much. Once they hit the deep woods, she and Fletcher hiked in silence. It was the way they did, each mute, each lost in their own thoughts.

As she walked along, her sneakers kicking up small billows of trail dust, Imogen's couldn't stop thinking about Simon. She tried not to because every damn time she thought about him, his smile, the funny way he twirled his hair with his fingertips, this annoying fluttering sensation materialized from deep down in the pit of her stomach. She knew exactly what that was. In fact, she'd read about it. Thoughts about him was triggering a spot in her brain, the medial insula to be precise, which is associated with the perception of pain and gut feelings, or better known as "butterflies." Whatever you wanted to call it, it made her feel strange, and bad, because she didn't get a hint of that sensation when she thought about Fletcher. But there was something else, too, something about that time, that place, and a vexing tug that she couldn't dismiss, or maybe it was just her medial insula working overtime.

The trail switched back one more time before reaching the summit and an awkward silence fell between them as they trudged past the rock where Simon had once proposed. Neither acknowledged it as they passed by it on their way to the hilltop meadow. Even so, Imogen was determined not to let it ruin her day. She loved this hike and it felt so good to get out of the house. No way around it, journeying through time was just weird. It was like traveling someplace new where the food and the culture and the architecture and maybe the language is different too. It even smells different. And so it takes some time to become acclimated to all these new things around you. But when she returned home, everything was familiar again, comfortable, exactly where it should be.

When they reached the meadow, Imogen and Fletcher unhooked their backpacks and set them on the ground and Imogen took out a couple of bottled waters.

"Here," she said, handing one over to Fletcher and sitting down next to him. A light breeze gently blew through her hair and the sun radiated just the right amount of warmth. A perfect day. They sat quietly like that for a bit, each enjoying that special rush after reaching the top until Fletcher finally spoke.

"I need to know one thing," he said.

Imogen tilted her head sideways and rolled her eyes at him, certain he was joking around. "Oh yeah? What one thing is that?"

"Where do you go," he asked, "when you go away?"

Imogen winced a little, but Fletcher continued, "I worry about you, Imogen. I know you don't have any family. I want you to have someone that you can rely on, someone you can call if you need help." He paused before saying it. "You may not want to marry me, but you still need a friend, someone who knows where you are."

Imogen tried her best to hold back the tears, but no use, here they came and it felt like the dam had burst. She hadn't cried much since Grammy died, so she figured she was probably due. Fletcher knew exactly what to do. He pulled her in close to him for a hug.

Nuzzled against his shoulder, she sobbed, "Why do you have to be so goddamn nice?"

Fletcher was right. Ever since she was nine, she had made a pact with herself to be strong, be independent, but she'd forgotten that people also need somebody in this world that they can count on. She couldn't always go it alone. But this wouldn't be an easy story to tell. She had not shared it with anyone, ever. More importantly, would Fletcher even believe her?

After they'd finished eating their sandwiches, Fletcher leaned back, resting on his arms and said, "Well? Are you ready to tell me everything? All your secrets?"

Imogen returned a weak smile and nodded yes, and for the next hour or so proceded to spill her guts. She told Fletcher about believing her parents were dead, but finding out the truth about them, that they were alive, later from her grandma before she had died. She explained how she had accidently wandered into a photo three times: once as a child, again during high school, and then in college, and as much as she knew about the way time travel worked. She finished off with telling him about starting up her business, Dead Relatives, Inc., and then she sat back and silently observed his face, waiting for his reaction.

Slowly turning his head from side to side, Fletcher closed his eyes and then reopened them, his face a question mark of bewilderment. Whoa, time travel! That was not at all what he was expecting, not to mention a lot to take in at one time. He wasn't quite sure he believed her; it sounded so farfetched, but if true, it would explain a lot about her disappearances and why she never answered his text messages. He had known that she was an orphan, but the idea that her parents were out there somewhere lost in time sounded like something out of an episode of *The Twilight Zone*. Other than that, wow.

He scanned her face, looking for a sign that she might be putting him on, but there was none. She was dead serious.

"So Imogen," he said, "can I go with you the next time you go?"

She wasn't expecting that to be his first question, but okay. "Honestly," she said, "I don't think so."

"Why not?"

"Well, because I've never tried to take anyone else and I don't know what might happen."

"Then we should totally try it, Imogen," Fletcher said, excitement creeping into his voice. "Can we?"

Imogen felt like a mean parent telling her child no. She shook her head. "I don't know enough about how it works. I'm afraid something bad could happen to you."

"Like what?" he asked, sitting up now.

Imogen shrugged. "I don't know, but I just know I don't want to risk it," she said, starting to feel irritated by his probing questions.

Realizing he was making her uncomfortable, he backed off. "I'm sorry Imogen, but you do realize how crazy this all sounds, right?"

She nodded.

"And I'm a little bit pissed that you've been lying to me all this time about airports and flight delays and bad weather and shit, and why you're so tired when you get back. I'm just trying to make sense of it."

"I know," she said, hanging her head and staring down into her lap. "I'm sorry for lying to you." She lifted her head again and said, "Time travel sometimes takes a lot out of me and I need a couple of days to recuperate, that's all."

Tears were beginning to pool around the edges of her eyes and slide down her cheeks again, which made Fletcher feel horrible for pressing her so hard for answers. He stood up, grabbing her hands in his, and pulling her up. "Come on, let's go home now," he said.

When they reached Imogen's house, Fletcher walked her up to the porch. It had been a long day and both of them were beat. For Imogen, it was a relief to finally tell someone. All these years of bottling everything up inside had felt like she was carrying around a bag of cement, and although the unburdening of it had been draining, afterward she felt lighter.

She knew Fletcher would have more questions, but at least he would better understand her, and it felt good thinking that now someone else in the world would know when she was traveling, and take notice if for some reason she didn't come back.

"Do you mind if I just go on home? Fletcher asked Imogen as she unlocked the front door.

"Oh, not at all," Imogen said, shaking her head wearily. "Gosh, I'm pooped, too. I think I'll just curl up on the couch with Luxe and a warm blankie and watch a movie."

Fletcher leaned in and gave her a peck on the cheek, his mouth lingering next to her ear longer than usual. "Sleep well, Imogen," he whispered.

Imogen watched him as he walked to his car. Before getting in, he turned around and waved goodbye and she waved back.

26

In general, Teddy was ever the cool customer. Over the years he had carefully cultivated his persona of honorable businessman Theodore S. Diamond, a man unfailingly in control of his emotions, finally shedding the awkward insecure propensities of his youth once and for all. Yet, ever since his return from 1912, and following the two days of recovery time he'd spent nursing an excruciating migraine, he'd been uneasy, fidgety, sweaty, and unable to sleep. Why did she have to go back there? Everything was going along fine. Now Imogen could potentially screw up his perfectly constructed life. Tonight, he'd managed to work himself up into such a state that he had impulsively hopped into his car and drove over to the old neighborhood and parked down the street to watch her house.

Everything appeared normal. Her car was in the driveway. The lights were on inside; he could see the flickering light from the TV. Mimi Pinky hadn't been assigned cat duty. On a rational level, he knew she was in there, probably sitting on the couch watching a movie, but as Teddy sat alone in his car, in the dark, his mind began to conjure up a much different scenario. He imagined Imogen lounging back on the sofa against a backdrop of soft, velvet pillows, one milky smooth arm extended seductively above her head, the other hand performing a slow, titillating one-woman show for only him. The graphic imagery excited him; made him feel horny and nasty and aroused, the way Tiffany Rose used to make him feel. He also had enough self-awareness to realize how exceedingly creepy it was sitting outside her house in his car fantasizing about her, but he could not help himself. Slowly unzipping his pants, he slipped his hand inside.

When he had finished, Teddy wiped up with a dirty, discarded tissue he found on the passenger side floor, and then zipped up his fly. While escaping into a pornographic fantasy had relieved a modicum of the tension and anxiety he'd be feeling lately, he knew it was fleeting and temporary. Up until recently, he had not touched himself like that in years, and it angered him that the puerile memories of a teenage romance mixed up with a foolish infatuation with his mother's 20-something neighbor could send him spiraling back into the daily compulsion he had struggled so hard to kick.

Ever since he broke into the Oliver studio and found that box with the photos, he'd been sick with worry. Were there more still floating around? What if they found out? His mind reeled at the idea of being caught, not only of Imogen finding out, but also his mother, especially his mother—all of them knowing what he'd done to her.

The summer of 1997 Teddy turned 18. Fresh out of high school, he was bored and horny and a failure in the girl department—girls didn't like him because he was a bully and he was a bully because girls didn't like him. His mother doted on her nerdy, socially awkward son; her little "teddy bear," unless she had a boyfriend, in which case, she ignored Teddy completely. Mama or Mimi Pinky, which is how he addressed his mother most of the time, was a former stripper, a textbook narcissist, and had no business being a mother to anyone.

Mimi's story was that when she found out she was pregnant, she had initially planned to go get an abortion—she didn't know who the father was anyway. But because she was heavily into drug use at the time, she somehow managed to "forget" that she was with child, and by the time she remembered—only when her belly began to noticeably swell—it was far too late to abort. Mimi never missed an opportunity to remind Teddy just how painfully awful birthing him was.

As laissez faire as she was about the pregnancy, she was equally unprepared for the birth. The night Mimi went into labor, she was so drunk she passed out on the cheap Vegas motel room bed, only to wake up hours later in the final, fully dilated, excruciatingly painful throes of labor. The loud shrieks brought the elderly couple in the adjacent room outside in their pajamas to bang on the door, but to no avail—all Mimi could do was lie there and whimper. The frightened man rushed to the motel office and summoned the night desk clerk, who used his universal key to get into Mimi's room where they found her naked from the waist down and bathed in a pool of sweat, tears, and blood. They noticed the movement of a tiny baby on the bloody bed sheets between her legs and called 9-1-1. The ambulance arrived and rushed mother and child to the hospital.

Mimi refused to look at the bloody godawful "thing." But as she was preparing to sign the papers releasing him for adoption, a nurse's aide waltzed merrily into the room, announcing, "Here's your baby boy" and pushing the baby swaddled in a blue blanket into Mimi Pinky's wholly ill-equipped arms. She didn't want to look, but curiosity got the best of her and Mimi looked down at the thing's face, into its needful eyes, at the small nose and puffy lips; scrutinizing the dark tuft of hair on his cone-shaped head, and feeling perhaps for the first time something resembling emotion, an unfamiliar reaction that for once didn't revolve exclusively around her. In that moment, Mimi decided to keep her boy.

Teddy had heard this story at least a thousand times before; how Mimi Pinky had loved him soooo, so much, that she had made the ultimate sacrifice for him—giving up her big dreams of becoming a high-paying Vegas showgirl. According to her, she was teetering right there on the cusp of getting discovered. Any minute, an agent was going to swoop in and pluck her from the strip- club pole and make her a big star, but then she'd gotten pregnant and that ruined her plans forever. Her flawless body would never be the same again, her dreams of dancing under the lights, dashed forever. And she did it all for him, all for her little man; her Teddy Bear.

Whatever emotion Mimi might have felt in the hospital quickly dissipated, however, once she got the squirmy, squawking, endless poop-generating, needy creature home.

And so life began with Mimi Pinky and the constant stream of "daddy's" that wended their way in and out of their lives. None stayed long enough to form any sort of bond with little Teddy Bear; most were shadow figures, others were drunks or violent toward Mimi or to Teddy or both of them, but when they were gone, things were far worse. It was then up to Teddy to step up and be Mimi's "little man" and attend to all of her needs—emotional and physical.

"Come here 'little man,'" she'd say, raising up the blankets and patting the sheet with one of her long, red glittery painted nails. "Come have 'snugggies' with mama."

At first, Teddy liked snuggling with mommy. She was warm and soft and he felt safe with her under the warm covers. Whenever a boyfriend was there he was not allowed to join her in the big bed. He wasn't even allowed to enter her bedroom.

Teddy was around seven when Mimi, who was in between boyfriends, invited him to come rejoin her in bed for snuggies, but to his surprise, this time when she raised up the blanket, she wasn't wearing any pajamas or underwear. He could see all of her and he was afraid.

"It's okay, little man," she assured him. Teddy hesitated. "Come on now Teddy Bear," she said, raising her voice. Teddy did what he was told and got into the bed and Mama wrapped her naked body tightly around his. He could feel her breasts poking into his back.

Uncomfortable as this was at first, eventually, it became the new normal and he got used to her sleeping nude, but then one night, instead of rolling over and going to sleep after snuggles, she reached down into his pants. He knew that it was wrong for her to be doing that, but it also felt really good. As time passed, Mimi told him he could sleep in bed with her and she would "play" as long as he did something for her.

At first, she nuzzled him up against her large breasts, but over time, progressed to other, more sexual activities. This went on until another boyfriend would inevitably come along and take Teddy's place, sending him spiraling into a perpetual state of angst and confusion, endlessly wondering whether his mother loved him, or not.

Teddy also learned early how to fend for himself. Unable to count on his negligent mother to do even the simplest things like cook dinner, or prepare him a school lunch—there was barely any food in the house anyway because she didn't do grocery shopping—or do his laundry—the kids made fun of him because his clothes were stained and dirty—Teddy did the best he could. Out of her neglect, the cruel taunts that plagued him helped cement his future reputation as a bully himself. He had a habit of stealing other kids' lunches and clothes and money. He was especially mean to girls. His mother told him repeatedly that girls were bad, and considering that his mother was the only role model he had, Teddy believed her.

When he was 16, he got his driver's license and quickly discovered that going out for a drive, going anywhere that was away from Mimi, filled him with an overwhelming sense of freedom and control and independence he'd never known before. The only problem was that the car belonged to Mimi and she locked the keys in a safe. Teddy quickly assessed that the way to curry favor with Mimi so that she'd let him borrow her car was through what it had always been with her—quid quo pro, a favor for a favor. He would bed her.

This was no happy sitcom juxtaposed by a laugh track where the teenage boy whines and begs to use the car, promising to get it home before midnight without a scratch. Being with Mimi was no longer pleasant nor comforting, but Teddy felt he had no choice. It was a small price to pay for some necessary time alone, even though it was spent soothing himself, something that would evolve into an unhealthy habit of chronic masturbation, which kept him from ever sharing true intimacy with a real person.

Inside, Teddy was fully aware that sleeping with his mother was deeply twisted and sick. One time he had even went as far as to call up a crisis hotline where he anonymously divulged his sordid story to a sympathetic volunteer named Brittany. It should have been a cathartic outpouring. Instead, excited by his own retelling and by the shocked gasps coming from Brittany on the other end, Teddy climaxed before promptly hanging up on her.

◉

But things were about to change. Newly graduated from high school, Teddy, who had no real aspirations and no college dreams, had been more or less content with taking the occasional car drive and hanging out in his bedroom with his rock, coin, and comic book collections for the first few weeks since school had let out, but Mimi had other plans for him. She'd started dating a man, aptly named Dick, who wanted Teddy out of the house, pronto. She managed to finagle a job for him working part-time as an assistant in their neighbor's photography studio two doors down. Teddy was not overjoyed with the prospect of working, but Mimi said if he wanted to borrow the car he would have to buy his own gas.

Working for Niles Oliver wasn't terrible. Although he occasionally got to help out in the darkroom as well as lug heavy photography equipment for his boss on photo shoots, the job mostly consisted of menial chores like sweeping the floors, filing, and general cleanup.

To his delight, Teddy discovered a major upside to the job—girls, lots of them! Summer at the photo studio meant senior portraits and senior portraits meant teenage girls in sexy dresses and high heels and makeup, hair flawlessly coiffed, traipsing in and out, all summer long. He knew he didn't stand a chance with any of them; whenever they did take notice of him, it was usually with disdain. But Teddy devised a way to covertly get back at them.

One of his tasks was to package up the proofs and send them out to clients so they could choose which poses they wished to purchase for their portrait package. When the proofs came back in, Teddy pilfered the rejected ones to take home and hang up on the ceiling above his bed. Little did those stuck-up prima-donna bitches know that Teddy was jacking off directly below each one of their smiling, plastic faces every single night.

He'd also discovered a secret cubby back in the storeroom where he could stash a few of the photos for breaks. Tucked in behind one of the shelves, the small space provided him with the privacy he needed. It was also a great spot for hiding joints.

Teddy also knew that Imogen and her dumb sidekick Jade, the little black girl, spied on him all the time. They thought they were sneaky, but he saw them climbing up the stepladder to take turns peeking in through the window. He thought of snitching them out to his boss, Imogen's dad, but sometimes he got a kick out of unzipping his pants and exposing himself, just a little bit. As perverted as that seemed, he sort of liked knowing that they were audience to his depravity.

So went the summer, days spent in the studio sweeping and tidying up, nights smoking weed and jacking off. Consumed and distracted by Dick, Mimi left him alone, and Teddy had plenty of gas money now to fuel his nighttime joy rides. It was late August, and the parade of adolescence girls coming in and out for senior pics was winding down.

One morning as Teddy was sweeping up, he heard the bell on the door ding and she walked in, Tiffany Rose Elliot. He knew the minute he saw her she wasn't like the others, primarily because when she looked at him, her mouth didn't instantaneously turn into a scowl. In fact, he wasn't sure, but it seemed like she sort of half-assed smiled at him before putting her head down as if she was embarrassed before stepping back behind her mother. He wasn't used to dealing with clients, but Teddy was the only one in the studio right now.

"Uh, how can we help you?" he asked, leaning the broom up against the wall and wiping his hands on his apron.

"Hello," the woman said, extending her hand for Teddy to shake it. "This is my daughter Tiffany Rose. We would like to have Tiffany's senior portraits taken."

Teddy nervously shook the woman's hand. He'd scheduled appointments before when the boss wasn't in, but all of a sudden it felt unusually hot in the studio; he felt anxious. Beads of sweat were forming at the back of his neck and forehead.

"Um, yeah," he stammered, reaching under the desk and pulling out the appointment book, opening it, and scanning the page with his index finger. "It looks like any day next week is open. Would you like morning or afternoon?" he asked, surprising himself with his professional acumen.

Mother turned to consult with daughter in a whispered voice that Teddy couldn't make out. She turned back around and said, "Thursday afternoon will be fine."

Teddy wrote in her name and asked, "How about 2:00 p.m.?" She nodded, thanked Teddy, and she and Tiffany Rose turned and headed for the door, but not before her daughter turned her head slightly to glance back at Teddy, flipping her curly brown hair back and giving him a sly smile.

The door closed behind them and they were gone. Teddy was beside himself with uncharacteristic elation. This Tiffany Rose, she wasn't as cute as the other girls that had been parading through the studio all summer long, but she wasn't ugly either. He couldn't stop thinking about her. Thursday wouldn't come soon enough.

On Thursday afternoon, Teddy, concealed behind the curtain between the studio and the stockroom, observed Niles instructing Tiffany Rose in how to pose for her portrait. Although she had a thin nose that made her look sort of mousy and wore a pair of oversized glasses, he had to admit, she looked hot in the black dress she'd picked out to wear today for her portrait. From what he could tell, she had a nice rack, but her best feature was her massive hair, which reminded Teddy of a lion's mane. It was a dark brown, longish and curly, and it cascaded past her shoulders like a rushing waterfall.

Knowing this might be his only opportunity, after the photo shoot was over, Teddy awkwardly approached Tiffany and complimented her on her dress. Not used to getting attention from a boy, especially an older one, Tiffany blushed, and when he asked her to go out, she eagerly accepted.

Thus began Teddy's first relationship with a real girl. Teddy made good use of access to the car, taking Tiffany Rose out for long drives in the country and the surrounding hills. It was fun, at first, but Teddy was growing steadily impatient with her. For one thing, she had this annoying habit of always fiddling with her hair, brushing her hand through it or twisting the ends of it with her finger, flipping it back or pushing loose strands behind her ears. It drove Teddy crazy. At times, he had to constrain himself from hitting her and telling her to just stop, but even he realized that if he did something like that, she would stop letting him reach under her blouse and under her bra to touch her soft tits.

One night, while they were parked up on the butte, things began to get hot and heavy between them. Sensing she was losing control of the situation, Tiffany interrupted their foreplay and pushed Teddy away, but Teddy was fed up with playing her games.

"I want you," he said breathlessly into her ear. "Just let me," he whined, pulling at her panties and pressing hard against her.

"No" Tiffany said, trying again to push him off her. "Stop it, Teddy, I mean it," she cried. But Teddy wasn't listening and he didn't stop. Tiffany Rose tried to impede him, but Teddy was stronger than she was. Ignoring her pleas, he grabbed at her panties, ripping them as he pulled them off and forced her legs apart. Pinning her arms above her head he plowed into her with violent intent, ignoring Tiffany's repeated whimpers of, "No, no, no, Teddy," again and again.

She squeezed her eyes closed, praying for it to be over because resisting only seemed to ignite the searing, rupturing pain as Teddy jammed himself into her repeatedly, deep hard angry thrusts meant to hurt and scar and traumatize; each an epitaph of Teddy's hatred of his mother, of himself. He knew he was out of control, but he could not stop. His face was an angry blur above hers as beads of sweat dribbled off his nose, mingling with the tears on Tiffany's horrified face.

Finally, an eternity, Teddy's body shuddered as he came inside her, collapsing on top of her with all of his weight before rolling off the seat and pulling up his trousers. The windows of the car were fogged up with steam, but a stream of light from the streetlamp revealed Tiffany lying limp, a mass of sweat mixed with sticky blood on the seat. This was not how Tiffany Rose had envisioned her first time.

Before pushing open the door and crawling out, Teddy let out a disgusted "Ew" when he noticed the mess on the seat. He walked around to the back of the car, opened up the trunk, and then returned with a dirty towel that he tossed her way. "Clean yourself up," he said as he slammed the door shut and lit up a cigarette.

Teddy's car rolled up to the curb outside Tiffany Rose's house. Without turning to look at him, she exited his car and ran inside.

27

Summer faded into fall and Teddy continued to work at the photography studio, sweeping the floors and filing the proofs. In the evenings, he was mostly content playing his video games and watching TV. Mimi broke it off with Dick, but quickly found a new love interest to replace him, which, now that he was older, was always a relief as far as Teddy was concerned. He was starting to really like working at the studio. He enjoyed working with the chemicals in the dark room and he liked accompanying Niles on photo shoots. In the back of his mind, he had even toyed with the idea of asking Niles to mentor him. For the first time, perhaps ever, in Teddy's miserable life, he felt like he had a purpose, real goals, and hope that he might have the future that he had never anticipated.

One afternoon in late October as Teddy was stocking chemicals in the back room he heard the bell ring on the front door. Niles was in the darkroom processing prints. Teddy came out to find Tiffany Rose standing at the counter and she looked angry.

"What do you want Tiffany?" Teddy asked.

"I need to talk to you Teddy," she said.

Teddy leaned his elbows on the counter, close to where she was standing. "What about?"

Tiffany recoiled, clearly uneasy about being alone with him. "Where's your boss?" Tiffany asked.

"Darkroom," Teddy said, pointing at the red neon "Dark Room In Use" sign above the door. It was sort of amusing to think that he could intimidate her, but at the same time, it didn't feel right either. Maybe he had changed. That was the old Teddy. He didn't want to be mean to Tiffany anymore. Maybe he was even a little sorry for the way he'd treated her. Like Marilyn, the little girl he'd kicked in middle school, and all the other girls he'd abused over the years, including Tiffany, he knew they wouldn't tell, they never did. Who would believe them?

Teddy leaned away from her and sighed, saying, "You don't have to be afraid of me Tiffany. I'm not going to hurt you. Why are you here?"

Tiffany seemed to relax a bit, but continued to keep a safe distance from him.

"I'm pregnant," she blurted.

"What?" Teddy cried, a look of shock registering on his face. Forgetting all that stuff he'd thought moments ago about having changed, and propelled by impulse, he bounced around the other side of the counter and grabbed hold of her upper arm. Tiffany recoiled, instinctively raising her hands up in front of her defensively.

"What do you mean, you're pregnant?" Teddy demanded. "You can't be. It's not mine!"

Tiffany began to sob. "I haven't been with anybody else, Teddy," she cried.

"You're lying," he lashed out at her, squeezing her arm tighter. "We only did it one time!" Teddy was sure that getting pregnant the first time you did it only happened on TV or in movies.

"Owww," Tiffany wailed, "let go, you're hurting me!"

Just then, the red light over the darkroom door went out and Niles pushed the door open. Teddy promptly dropped Tiffany's arm.

"What's going on here Teddy?" Niles asked.

"Nnn-othing," Teddy stammered, moving sideways and away from Tiffany. But Tiffany's telltale tears seemed to provide a different story. Recognizing Tiffany from the photo shoot earlier in the summer, Niles walked over to her and touched her arm, which was beginning to turn red from Teddy's clutch.

"Is there anything wrong Tiffany?" he asked, eyeing Teddy suspiciously. Although she was clearly upset, Tiffany didn't want to involve Teddy's boss.

"I'm okay," Mr. Oliver," Tiffany said, wiping her face with her sleeve. "We, Teddy and me, we just had a little fight, that's all," she said.

"Is that right Teddy?" Niles said turning to face Teddy.

"Yes, sir," Teddy stammered.

Niles wasn't entirely convinced. "Why don't you take a break Teddy," he urged. "You and Tiffany can use my office." The office had a window, which would allow Niles to keep an eye on them. Reluctantly, Teddy led Tiffany into Nile's office and closed the door. Calmer now, Teddy told Tiffany to sit down.

"Okay, so you can get an abortion," he offered.

Tiffany shook her head no. "Why not?" Teddy asked. "I'll pay for it. I work. I have money!"

Tiffany hesitated, and in a barely audible voice replied, "It's too late."

"What?" Teddy demanded. "Did you just say it's too late? What do you mean it's too late?"

"It's too late," Tiffany said slightly louder. "I waited too long. I didn't know. I didn't think it was possible after just one time, so I didn't take the test." She sighed and looked down at her hands. "I waited too long."

Teddy was livid. Balling up his fists behind his back he tried hard to quell his mounting anger. He wanted to hit something. He wanted to hit her, but damn it, Niles was just outside the door. Instead, he took a deep, purgative breath before speaking.

"Okay Tiffany, so what do you want from me?" he asked as calmly as he could muster.

Tiffany shifted in her seat and said, "My dad told me if I ever got pregnant, he'd kick me out." She tilted her head sideways and began to nervously twist a strand of her hair around her finger in that annoying way that Teddy hated. "I won't have any place to go," she said, "so I though we could get married."

"Oh god," Teddy wailed, putting his hands up to his face in anguish. "Get married? You can't be serious," he said. He paced back and forth for a minute before whirling around to face her. "What if

I don't want to?" he asked.

Tiffany, who had stopped crying now and managed to pull herself together, sat up straight in her chair and looked up at Teddy defiantly. "I will tell everyone that you raped me," she said, slowly rising up from the chair and staring squarely into his face.

"And because you are 18, Teddy, and an adult, and I'm only 16 they will come and arrest you and lock you up for statutory rape."

The prospect of being arrested, of going to jail, or worse, his mother finding out, was creating a maelstrom of escalating panic inside him. She had him backed into a corner.

Out of the corner of his eye, Teddy saw movement outside the window. It was Niles and he was tapping on the door. "Everything okay in there?" he asked as he slowly pushed the office door open.

"Everything is good. We'll be right out Mr. Oliver," Teddy assured him. Niles closed the door and Teddy turned to Tiffany. "I need to get back to work," Teddy said. "Let's talk about this later."

"When?" Tiffany demanded. "I need your answer soon or I'll have to tell."

Wheels began to turn in Teddy's head as he remembered back to a conversation he'd had with Niles when he'd first stumbled upon his secret for time travel.

"Tomorrow," he said, the corners of his mouth turning up to form a fake smile, "meet me at two o'clock at the park by the high school."

Leaning up against a tree as he waited in the park for Tiffany Rose to show up, Teddy could feel the sharp corners of the photograph poking his fingers inside his coat pocket. Even though the day was overcast and chilly, several kids had braved the weather; a couple were taking turns pushing each other on the swing; a trio of older boys tossed a football back and forth out in the field adjacent to the park. He spotted Tiffany walking along the sidewalk bundled up in a puffy coat with a dirty fur collar. She approached him, but kept her distance, looking around to make sure there were other people around.

"Well?" she said to Teddy.

Teddy smiled and shrugged. "Well, I guess we're getting hitched."

"Really?" she said, her face brightening.

"Yeah, sure," Teddy said, "why not?"

Teddy nodded and smiled, his thoughts drifting away as Tiffany launched into a litany of things they would need to do to prepare for their wedding. They'd need rings, of course; she'd want to buy a dress and maybe have a corsage and a boutonniere for him. Did he have a suit and tie? If not, they could probably pick one up at the thrift shop.

"But first," she said, "We'll have to tell our parents."

Teddy kept right on smiling, even though the thought of facing his mother with the news made him shudder inside. It wasn't going to happen. Not if he could help it.

"How 'bout a hug?" Teddy asked, extending his arms out wide.

"Oh, okay," Tiffany said. She didn't notice the sepia-colored photo he'd removed from his pocket as she cautiously stepped forward allowing Teddy to wrap his arms around her. They stood that way for a couple of seconds until it started to feel awkward and Tiffany tried to extricate herself from him. Teddy wouldn't let go. He squeezed tighter.

"Teddy," she said, becoming alarmed, "let go." She turned her head sideways and saw that he had his eyes closed tight as if he was in a trance or meditating or something. She squirmed as hard as she could to get out of his clutches, but she couldn't move; he had her body pinned securely beneath his arms and she was starting to get scared.

"Teddy, what are you doing?" she shrieked, but her screams faded into a distant echo. Darkness and spinning and rushing lights enveloped them until they were thrown abruptly into bright, blinding sunshine.

He loosened his grip on her and she collapsed against him unsteadily. Teddy pushed her away and she glanced around. The park and the school and the streets were gone. Where they had once been was replaced with empty fields as far as you could see.

Tiffany gasped, "Where are we? Teddy? What just happened?"

Teddy took another step backward, away from her.

"You didn't really think I was going to marry you, did you Tiffany?" he asked calmly.

Terrified and confused by his sinister tone, Tiffany looked around wildly.

"Goodbye Tiffany Rose," Teddy said. She watched in horror as Teddy vanished into thin air, leaving her lost and alone.

28

In the days following her hike with Fletcher, Imogen had located the tree at the church and dug up the key, which was still safely concealed in the tin, and then retrieved the stereopticon and plates from the hotel vault. She successfully delivered it to Doran's great nephew, who was delighted to have the keepsake back in the family.

Afterward, she realized that she didn't have a single thing on her schedule, which was okay because she sort of needed a break. Fletcher had promised to give her some space, for which she was grateful. He really was a great guy. She loved him. The problem was, she wasn't in love with him, and she knew that was the dumbest excuse ever. It wasn't like she was some middle school girl dreaming about romance. She realized that relationships were made up of much more than that.

Her parents were a good example. Even as a child, Imogen had noticed that her mother was aloof, not only toward her, but to her dad as well. Although they seemed well suited for one another in many respects, they rarely demonstrated affection for each other. For all accounts and purposes, they seemed happy. She knew she could have that with Fletcher, yet, a part of her demanded more; something wild and wanton and powerful and passionate. At this time in her life, she longed to feel something beyond grief and pain and frustration. She didn't want to give up on her search for her parents, but at the same time, would it be selfish to want something for herself, what everyone desires, to be happy? Though a good deal of her time was spent in the past, she needed to make time to live her life here too, in the present.

She remembered once, her mom, in a rare candid moment, telling her daughter that she should always pay attention to the little voices in her head. While some parents followed the archaic notion that children should be seen and not heard, that was not the case for little Imogen. Baby talk was not allowed when Imogen was growing up. She was treated like a small adult, included in grown-up conversations, and afforded a voice to be heard.

But even so, her mom was quite guarded, so it was unusual for her to give her daughter advice of any kind, and Imogen wasn't even sure why Francis was offering up this particular piece of information.

She was sitting quietly at the kitchen table drawing a picture that afternoon, humming a song when Francis stopped sautéing the portabella mushrooms and onions concoction, turned around to face Imogen, and out of the blue, said, "You know, Imogen, if you ever have a strong feeling in your gut about something, you should always listen to it. It means the universe is trying to tell you something important."

Imogen looked up from her drawing, "Huh?"

"Your gut, you know inside you." Francis pointed to her stomach and walked over and sat down in the chair next to Imogen. She seemed distraught and Imogen didn't understand why.

"I hear people talking in my imagination," Imogen proffered, "but not in my gut." Francis placed her hand on Imogen's arm, but Imogen reflexively jerked it away; she wasn't used to her mother's touch.

Francis frowned. "I'm sorry Imogen," she said. "I know you don't understand what I mean. I'm not sure I do either."

A cross between sadness and exasperation cast a dark shadow across her mother's normally stoic face. She looked at Imogen and sighed. "Well, all I'm saying is if you ever have a strong feeling about something or someone, you know, and it doesn't go away, just keeps nagging at you, you should probably pay attention."

She got up then and walked back over to the stove and returned to stirring the contents of the pan. Although she wasn't sure what or who her mother was referring to back then, Imogen was certainly beginning to understand nagging inner voices now.

In fact, she was experiencing a nagging feeling in her gut this second. It was because of Simon and it was crazy, but damn it, she really wanted to see him again. No matter how hard she tried to dismiss it, the voice/feeling, whatever it was, kept getting louder. Had he received the note she'd left for him? Was he thinking about her too? Was he looking for her? Something inside told her that he was. It was nothing more than a hunch really, but the way he had looked at her and the care that he had taken the night she'd injured her ankle, made her think maybe he felt something too.

The only way to know for sure was to go back, but what was the point? How could there be a future for them? Grammy had warned her about the consequences of making emotional connections with people who were dead long before you were ever born. Oh, why did it have to be this difficult? Imogen thought. Grammy had gone back and stayed for a while before returning. She supposed she could always come back too. No matter how things turned out, at least she would know. That was it then, done, settled.

Imogen was relieved that Fletcher had agreed to keep Luxe over at his apartment with him this time. She wasn't certain when she might return, and she really didn't want to deal with Mimi Pinky's interrogations. He actually loved that cat as much, if not more, than Imogen did. Along with being surprisingly understanding, he prom- ised also to keep an eye on her house, pick up the mail, and water her plants.

A few days later, Imogen was seated in the chair at her office downtown, fully prepared to throw all caution to the wind and step back into time via a postcard of the Benson Hotel she had picked up for 50 cents at an antique shop. The caption below the photo read: Benson Hotel, 1913. It was the closest she could find to the time when Simon was there. Even though it was a year later, she hoped she could find him. Squeezing her eyes shut, Imogen braced for the journey, this passage of destiny, to Simon.

29

The valet turned his head slowly in Imogen's direction, oblivious that mere moments ago, the girl had not been there. Imogen took a quick peek at her perfect period-specific clothes, as she always did upon arrival, marveling at the handiwork of the universe's selections.

From the profusion of colorful leaves adorning the tree-lined avenue, she deduced it must be fall. So to counter the crisp autumn chill in the air, she had on a snug jacket over a tailored day outfit consisting of a smart blouse and gored skirt combination. She glimpsed skyward taking in the hotel's towering red brick and glazed terra cotta exterior and forest green awnings, the unique four-bowl bronze bubbler out front, and glass revolving doors, and felt a tingle run up and down her body. It was exciting to be back at the Benson again.

The valet finally took notice of her. "Madame," he said, tipping his droll satin pillbox hat. "May I help you with your bag?"

Imogen nodded and entered the hotel lobby. With its marble flooring and fireplace and crystal chandeliers and exquisite grand staircase, it was as magnificently striking as she had remembered. She strolled over to the wood counter to check in. She had thought about using the name Daphne Blake again, but decided against it. Even though a whole year had passed in their time, she didn't want anyone to remember her and potentially come across the alias in the guest register. And, because this trip was not business-related, she decided to use her own name.

"How may I help you, Miss," the desk clerk asked. He did a not very subtle once-over of her, an appraising glance that began with her face and moved down to her feet, up and down, which made her uncomfortable. She would never get used to the sexist way some men behaved toward women in this time.

The name on his name badge read MARVIN. She sort of remembered him from before, but it didn't seem like he remembered her. "I'd like a room, please, Marvin," Imogen said dismissively, trying to shrug off his ogling.

"Of course," Marvin replied. It was all Imogen could do to keep from rolling her eyes, but she knew she had to play along.

"Oh, and I'd like to request room 213, if it's available," Imogen said sweetly.

A fleeting look of wariness flashed across the clerk's face, like he had a flash of remembrance of something, but he shrugged as he turned away. He grabbed the familiar brass key from the peg on the wooden board and placed it on the counter. "You're in luck," he said, "that room is unoccupied. Kindly sign our guestbook, please."

Imogen wrote her name down in the fancy cursive handwriting she'd practiced at home, ending the "r" in Oliver with an impressive flourish. Sadly, cursive writing was fast becoming a lost art, replaced with keyboards and scrolling and swiping left, it was no longer even being taught in schools.

Marvin turned the book around and glanced at her signature before handing her the key. "Here you go Miss Oliver. Enjoy your stay."

"Thank you," she said in a pleasant, yet reserved tone. As she walked away she could sense that the clerk was watching her. Grrrr, how she hated the stupid gender games of this period.

Imogen strolled over to the cast-iron lift and pressed the button. The bell chirped, and she watched the heavy lift descending to the lobby from an upper floor. Through the gate, Imogen recognized the elevator operator Otis and nearly acknowledged him before realizing that he might not remember her.

He didn't seem to. "What floor, Miss?" Otis asked.

"Second," she answered.

On the second floor, Imogen exited the lift and walked down the long hallway, pleased as she passed by the pair of potted ferns. She placed the brass key in the lock and entered room 213. The room was unchanged. Armoire, settee, porcelain jug, check; iron bed, claw-foot tub, check. In an unexpected way, it felt like home, even though she'd been here only once before. Imogen sat down on the soft bed pondering what to do next. She knew Simon was a school principal, so before the trip she had conducted an online search of schools in the area. There were only a handful, which would make narrowing it down a bit easier. Although telephones, as yet, were not available in individual rooms, Imogen had noticed down in the lobby a wall of built-in wooden booths, each containing a small seat and one of those "nickel-in-the-slot" pay telephones, immortalized by bookies and gangsters in old black-and-white Hollywood movies.

After freshening up, Imogen made her way downstairs to the phone stations equipped with a written list of half a dozen local schools that she would need to call and inquire after Mr. Simon Le Bon Elliot. It took her a few minutes to figure out what to do. A box located on the side had slots for 25, 10, and 5 cents and below it, it read:

DIRECTIONS Call Central Office as Usual. Do Not Deposit Money Until Told By Operator.

Finally, on the fifth call, the assistant that answered asked who was calling for Mr. Elliot.

"Please tell him Imogen Oliver," she said.

"One moment please," the woman said. Imogen heard the dull thud of the receiver being dropped on a wooden desk. A few minutes passed before she finally heard someone on the other end pick it up.

A male voice answered, "Hello." It was Simon. Hearing his voice again suddenly made Imogen feel uncharacteristically giddy and anxious inside.

"Um . . . yes, Simon, I mean Mr. Elliot," she spluttered nervously. "I'm not certain that you remember me, but we met . . ."

Simon interrupted her, "Imogen, it is you, isn't it? he asked.

"Yes!" she answered, delighted that he had recognized her voice.

"Where are you? Are you in town?" The palpable excitement in Simon's voice validated Imogen's decision to come back.

"Yes, I'm at the Benson," Imogen answered.

"Stay there!" Simon shot back. Before she could respond, she heard the clicking sound of the receiver and the line went dead.

Imogen placed the receiver back in its cradle and did a leisurely stroll over to a grouping of wicker chairs arranged in a seating area in the center of the lobby near the huge floor-to-ceiling fireplace. Before taking a chair, she stopped at a side table bearing a sampling of magazines, including a *Vanity Fair* and a *Vogue*, which featured on its cover an illustration of a woman in a striped skirt, brown coat, and plumed hat. She was reclining in a stylish lounge chair, a steaming cup of tea resting on a slender stand in front of her. Choosing the *Vogue* Imogen sank into one of the opulent chairs and began thumbing through the magazine.

It was funny because at home, she had several framed *Vogue* magazine prints from this era hanging on her walls that she'd scored at a flea market. It felt strange now to be holding a practically hot-off-the press version in her hands. The tactile feel of the thick paper stock, the best of its time, combined with the high-fashion publication's quality design, photography, and modern typography was a treat. It was fun flipping through the pages and looking at the opulent Edwardian and La Belle Èpoque fashions, although she knew from her historical fashion research that it wouldn't be long before these trends would become obsolete. With the start of World War I in Europe in August of 1914, designers would start introducing military influenced garments, and hemlines would rise above the ankle.

Imogen tried to focus on the magazine, but she didn't have to look up to know that the desk clerk was still eyeing her from across the room. Like before, she could feel his eyes burrowing into her. What would he think when Simon arrived? What if Simon kissed her? She contemplated that with a secret smile. Why, it could be downright scandalous!

None of that happened. Instead, Simon came bustling in through the hotel doors and the second he spotted Imogen he rushed over. But, instead of greeting her with the expected warm embraces and librettos of love, he took her arm and swiftly piloted her through the lobby doors and outside to the sidewalk. Before she could react or say anything, Simon said, "Why are you here, Imogen? Why now?" Imogen was confused.

"I'm sorry Simon," she said, clearly mystified by his reaction. "Is this a bad time?"

Simon seemed beside himself, nervous, befuddled, rocking back and forth on the heels of his oxfords. As he swayed, he repeated her words back to her, "Is this is a bad time? Well . . . yes Imogen, it's not the best." He looked at Imogen and stopped fidgeting long enough to interject, "You are still so lovely," he acknowledged, touching her arm briefly, before resuming another round of pronounced fretting.

"Simon," Imogen said, "Stop. Look at me. What is wrong? Please tell me."

"What is wrong?" he cried. "What is wrong Imogen is that it has been more than a year since last I heard from you! I thought I'd never see you again."

To Imogen that seemed like it should be a happy thing. "I'm sorry it took so long Simon, but I'm here now!" she said brightly.

Simon frowned and took her arm. "Come. Let's go find a place where we can talk." About a block down, they found an ice-cream parlor. Imogen took a seat at a table while Simon ordered them each a sundae.

After rejoining her, he took one of her hands in his and regarded her from across the table. "Imogen," he said, sighing and glancing down at the table for a moment before raising his head. "When I received the note from you, I was distraught. You'd left no address. I had no clue how to find you." Simon cleared his throat. "Things have changed since I saw you last," he continued.

"Changed?" Imogen asked. "How so?"

Simon hesitated before blurting out the news. "I have become engaged to be married," he confessed.

At that moment, the server, a young boy of about 12, arrived with their desserts. "Enjoy your sundaes," he said pleasantly, placing a pair of beautifully etched glass bowls filled with vanilla ice cream topped with chocolate syrup and nuts in front of them. Simon took a shiny coin from his pocket and handed it to the boy for a tip.

"Thank you," Simon said.

Now it was Imogen's turn to fidget as she twirled the spoon around and around in the bowl. "I . . . I . . . don't know what to say," she stammered. Imogen was beginning to fathom the ramifications of time travel. Although it had been only a few short weeks for her since she'd last seen Simon, more than a year had passed for him. She was wrong to assume that she could just breeze right back into his life.

As a school principal and handsome heartthrob to his female students, Simon was used to easing wounded hearts, but this was something quite different. This wouldn't be nearly as easy, and he wasn't entirely sure what to do. I've ruined everything, Imogen thought. But the reality was beginning to sink in—maybe it just wasn't meant to be. Her instinct was for flight, as it always tended to be, and she began pushing her chair away from the table preparing to leave, when Simon reached over and grabbed ahold of her hand.

"Wait Imogen please, don't go. Let me at least explain."

Feeling utterly deflated, Imogen leaned back against her chair. Out of politeness she would listen to what he had to say, but she already knew that whatever they might have had was over before it had even begun. She would return to her life with Luxe and Fletcher, forget all about Simon and any ridiculous romantic scenarios she might have imagined for the two of them.

Simon explained how when he'd received her message, he'd gone to her room to find her, but she was gone; how he'd spent months inquiring after her. He'd even traveled to several neighboring towns and called up the local operators to inquire after her. After about six months, he had given up his search, resigned that he would likely never see her again. He had started courting a former student, Georgia Bitgood, who was now a teacher at his school.

Where had Imogen heard that name before? And then she remembered. Of course, Georgia; she was one of the girls who had followed her to Doran's home and accosted her in the alleyway. Could it be the same Georgia? she wondered. She had explicitly warned Imogen to stay away from Simon.

Curiosity getting the best of her, when Simon paused, Imogen took the opportunity to interject, "This Georgia Bitgood, is she tall, about 5' 8", darkish hair pulled back in a long, tight braid?"

Simon's face conveyed a look of mild confusion. "Why yes," he said. "Have you met Georgia?"

"You might say that we have," Imogen said, her voice terse. "She and her minions attacked me in an alleyway!"

Simon was shocked. "Oh no, that could not have been the same Georgia. She would never do such a thing," he insisted.

"Oh wouldn't she?" Imogen asked, feeling the anger rising in her chest, her eyes squinting. She told Simon about the incident, how the group of schoolgirls had followed her and ambushed her in an alley; how the one named Georgia had twisted her arm around her back and then stomped on her toes.

"And she warned me to stay away from you," Imogen said.

Simon knew that Georgia possessed a bit of a jealous streak, but he had no idea that she was capable of such violence. Simon was clearly shaken. "I will speak to her," he said.

"You do that," Imogen said, rising to leave and tossing her napkin on the table. She wasn't sure why, but she was even angrier now. She was angry that Simon had given up on her, even though she knew he had every right to. They had no claims on one another. So perhaps disappointed was a better word for the way she was feeling. She was disappointed that Simon would take up with someone as vile and unstable as Georgia Bitgood appeared to be.

"Imogen, wait," Simon said, standing up too and reaching out to grasp her arm.

Brushing it aside, eyes narrowed, she looked at him and said, "Look Simon, you don't owe me any explanations. I really don't even know you all that well."

She continued walking toward the door, but turned around briefly to leave a parting shot. "Congratulations on your marriage, I hope you and Georgia will be very happy," she said as she marched out of the parlor, leaving Simon alone and speechless with two un-eaten chocolate sundaes.

Out on the sidewalk, Imogen stomped away, slowly at first, but as soon as she came to the first alleyway between buildings, she scampered down it. Pressing her back up against the brick wall, she wept. Why did everything have to be so fucked up, she thought, as an endless stream of tears flowed down her cheeks. What had she expected to happen though, really? She should have tried to find a photo from an earlier time, before he had given up on finding her; before he'd hooked up with Georgia Bitgood. She had been careless. That was her mistake. Theoretically, she could go back to an earlier date before they got engaged, but it gnawed at her that he'd given up so easily and had chosen to marry someone who had hurt her, even though he didn't know about that.

Damn it, why was she crying anyway? She should have known it would turn out this way. Simon was nothing but a silly romantic fantasy. She had a pretty good life back home, in her own time. She had a sort of boyfriend and a cat who both adored her. So much for her mother's trifling advice about listening to your gut. She'd let her emotions run amok and where had that gotten her? Standing here in an alleyway 100 years from home, that's what.

She started to wipe her face and retreat back to the hotel when she felt the soft touch of someone's hand on her shoulder. Startled, she twirled around to see who it was. It was Simon. Clearly distressed, his eyes full of sorrow, he reached out and lightly stroked Imogen's cheek, brushing a tear away and then leaving his hand to linger there as he softly caressed her skin. There was no doubting it, his touch was electric. She felt a sudden excited rush of adrenalin, just like that first time when they had met on the street.

She turned toward him and he leaned in slowly kissing her lips so softly and tenderly it seriously felt like the fluttering of hummingbird wings. Imogen closed her eyes then and surrendered to his kiss, going with it, getting lost in it, letting him embrace her about the waist, draw her in close and meld with her in a way that she had never experienced.

It seemed silly, clichéd, but even though she and Fletcher's first kiss had been quite stirring, it in no way measured up to the heated tingling sensations or the buffet of bottled up emotions inhabiting her entire body right this minute. She felt buoyed by two overpowering emotions, one part of her wanted to be reasonable, in control; another part was as malleable as clay, unrestrained and wild, and allowing the moment simply to unfold sans critique.

Oddly, for someone acquainted with the minutiae of time travel, she was unable to gauge how long the kiss actually lasted, but to Imogen it felt like infinity, in a delightful way; neither participant at all eager to interrupt the enchanted spell that bound them together in this single instant. Finally, the deep osculation transitioned into a series of short soft kisses that broke the tempo, and Imogen re-opened her eyes to see Simon looking at her. She expected that the usual awkward pulling away from one another would follow, but that's not what happened. Instead, Simon continued to hold her tightly until the intensity of his gaze became almost too much for her to bear. At last, he broke the spell and turned away from her as though he was ashamed of what they had just done and felt.

"Forgive me, Imogen for being so audacious," he said. "I lost my head."

Imogen gently touched his chin, guiding him to look back at her. "Simon," she whispered, "don't be sorry. I'm not."

The sides of his mouth began to curl up and form a half smile. Imogen returned the sentiment. Simon seemed to relax for a second before looking away again, this time as though he was distracted. He abruptly pulled a gold fob from his vest pocket, looked at it, and grimaced. "Oh dear, I'm afraid I have to get back to my employ Imogen," he said.

"Oh, yes, your job," Imogen spluttered. "Of course, you should go."

"I must see you tonight," he said, grabbing her hand. "Please assure me that you will not leave again."

"I won't leave," she said, nodding.

"Promise?" he asked. There was always a sense of urgency with Imogen. Not only the tension, but the fear that she could vanish at any moment; that he'd lose her forever.

"I promise," she said. "You can reach me at the hotel, room 213."

"Until later then," he said, letting loose of her hand and bending over slightly for a quick bow before dashing off around the corner and leaving her alone again in the alleyway.

As Imogen strolled back to the hotel, she could barely disguise her amusement at the thought that had popped into her head. It sure seemed like she spent a lot of time in alleyways when she was back here; either getting beat up or making out. She was still distracted by that thought when Otis, the lift operator, unlatched the lift's cage allowing her to step inside.

"Excuse me, Miss," he inquired. "If I may be so bold, you rather look like the cat that ate the canary."

"Indeed," Imogen said, "indeed, I did."

30

Although he was beside himself with apprehension over Imogen's unexpected return, Simon could not conceal his growing excitement. Imogen had come back! To be honest, he knew that it was wrong to be feeling so giddy about this. After all, he was betrothed to Georgia. He should dismiss Imogen, immediately. Tell her to go back to wherever she had come from. A true gentleman would not hesitate; someone who was faithful to their fiancée would not be overjoyed that their paramour had suddenly reentered the picture. He was nothing but a dirty, rotten scoundrel.

Yet, as much as he berated himself he could not suppress the surreptitious smile that materialized whenever he had the slightest of thoughts of Imogen.

He returned to his office at school and so far, had the good fortune of not running into Georgia. With school only back in session for a few short weeks now, she was most likely preoccupied with organizing her class, he hoped. That is, until around 3:30 p.m. when Simon glanced up to see Georgia looming in his office doorway.

"Oh," he said, startled, but pretending as though he hadn't been. "Hello Georgia. Come in."

Georgia entered the office and plopped down in a chair across from Simon, who was seated at his big oak principal's desk. "What can I do for you . . . um, darling?" Simon asked, trying hard to retain a semblance of a normal, not at all guilty tone.

Georgia glowered at him before speaking. "Where were you this morning, Simon?" she asked suspiciously.

He had not noticed it before, but her voice had a discordant quality about it, not unlike the sound of fingernails running across a chalkboard. And he was taken aback by her challenging inquiry.

Simon clasped the fingers of his hands together in front of him and replied, "Out, my dear, I had a task that needed attending."

"Oh really?" Georgia said, raising one eyebrow and observing him skeptically. "Because Cordelia told me that after receiving a phone call from a woman, you rushed out without explanation."

"Hmm," Simon said, as he slowly rose from behind his desk, momentarily turning his back to Georgia, hoping to buy a little time to come up with a suitable explanation. He had thought it might be easy to break it off, but he sensed that would not be the case. When he turned to face her, she was standing now, arms crossed against her chest in a defiant expression of ire.

"Where were you?" she demanded again. This time more fervently.

Feeling pressed into a corner didn't sit well with Simon. He had always been around strong women, but he wasn't a pushover and he wasn't about to start now. He strolled around to the front of his desk, crossed his arms too, and squared off with Georgia.

"I had some errands to attend to, that is all," he lied. "Now, I have work to do," he said firmly. Although she acquiesced, by her resolute expression, it was apparent that Georgia was not planning to let this go easily.

"Fine," she said, as she pivoted on one foot, and indignantly withdrew herself from Simon's office. He did not watch her go, nor did he see her stick out her tongue at him as she disappeared around the corner.

He felt dreadful about lying and sneaking about, but Simon entered the lobby of the Benson that evening with a visible spring in his step. Luckily, he was able to slip away from school unobserved. According to Cordelia, the elderly part-time lady who came in thrice weekly to type up Simon's correspondence on the office Royal No. 10 cast-iron typewriter, apparently Georgia had been quite incensed after their happenstance that afternoon and had left school immediately after classes let out.

And Simon was uneasy about calling on a woman staying alone in the hotel. How would it look? It surely would not appear aboveboard for a school principal to rendezvous with a strange woman in her hotel room. Even though the town had a measurable population, gossip still had a way of spreading quickly.

Fortunately, when he arrived, the lobby was bustling with activity. Simon assumed there must be a party going on, or some sort of event happening in the hotel ballroom because kitchen staff and other hotel employees were busily traversing to and fro through the lobby carrying assorted linens and chairs and candles and other commodities. This was ideal. With so many people rushing about and the desk clerks clearly distracted, it should be relatively easy for Simon to slip by virtually unnoticed. Gliding past the large gilded mirror he stealthily made his way up the spiral staircase to the second floor.

Although it had been more than a year since he'd been here, it seemed like only yesterday that he had accompanied Imogen down this same hallway to her room after she'd injured her ankle. He had been delighted to find her again after so many years apart, and there was no discounting the obvious attraction that had existed between them, then and now.

He remembered how disheartened he'd been when he had returned the next day only to discover that she had gone and the strange circumstances of her disappearance. He had hoped to find her only to come to the crushing realization that he never would. And yet, here she was, back in his life once more, but at the very worst possible time.

Glancing about, he saw no one on this floor; a good sign. Making his way down the protracted, carpeted hallway past the potted ferns, he arrived at her door, room 213. All at once, he felt like a nervous schoolboy; jittery and unsure of himself. It was silly. He began to sweat beneath his shirt collar. Simon reached into his vest pocket and pulled out a handkerchief to mop his neck and brow. Taking a deep breath, he rapped lightly on the wood door.

Before he could react, the door flew open and Imogen grabbed the lapels of each side of his jacket, pulling him inside and closing the door behind him with her foot. Once inside, she greeted him with a playful, but lingering kiss on the lips. This woman, Simon mused, she is so always full of surprises!

For Imogen, the day had been unbelievably long. At noon, she had gone to the hotel's café and eaten lunch, alone, which apparently was frowned upon for women in 1913—every time she looked up from her delightful Macedoine salad and Fricandeau of veal sandwich, somebody was giving her a disgusted look. There were so many rules, it seemed; so many ways to commit some social sin, especially if you were a woman. There were guidelines for the way you lifted your skirt when you crossed the street so that your ankle didn't show, unless it was muddy; for laughing too loudly, or at the wrong time; for the proper way to move and speak and dress. It was hard to keep up. Nonetheless, Imogen wasn't going to let a few dirty looks spoil her day or from getting out and enjoying the pleasant fall afternoon.

After lunch, she left the hotel and went for a leisurely walk. It was late October, the sun was shining, and the leaves were in full, splendid decay. Burnt oranges and bright yellows and bold reds aglow in a symphony of color, a light breeze occasionally separating a few from their branches and sending them gently cascading down, making the otherwise everyday world seem like a magical place.

Autumn was Imogen's most favorite season. She remembered a few good ones from her childhood, the ones spent with her dad raking up big crunchy maple leaves in the front yard and pushing them into lovely piles that she would then send her small kid body careening into, scattering them everywhere all across the yard again. With dad's corroboration, it took hours to finish the raking-the-leaves chore, but neither of them seemed too concerned. As she walked along, Imogen wondered if her dad, wherever . . . or *whenever* he was, thought about her when it was fall. She hoped he did.

When Imogen pulled her lips away from Simon's, the look on his face was priceless—full of shock, surprise, amusement—a kaleidoscope of reactions that made her laugh. Most likely, pouncing on Simon the minute he arrived, wasn't proper etiquette, any more than dining in a restaurant alone, refraining from raising her voice or using crude language, or gasp, not kissing prudently was!

"I'm sorry," Imogen apologized, lowering her eyes. "I don't know what came over me." Simon had been surprised by the kiss, sure, and her laughter at his reaction had been rather perplexing, but he wasn't angry with her, not at all. Cupping her chin in his hand, he guided her gaze back to him.

"I am not angry Imogen," he said. "In fact, I am delighted that you kissed me first."

"You are?" Imogen said coquettishly. Never in her life had she felt the least bit timid, but her knees felt stunningly weak now.

"I'll admit it," he said. "On the way here, my thoughts were fraught with fear about whether or not I would kiss you." He was being the timid one now. It was sweet.

"Please, sit down Simon," she said, gesturing toward the settee. Simon was puzzled. A gentleman always waited for the lady to be seated first.

"After you," he said politely.

Imogen sat down and Simon followed suit. And they sat. And they sat some more. Without speaking. Awkward didn't begin to describe the bubble of silence that floated between them until they both started speaking at once.

"I'm so glad . . ." Imogen began.

"How was your . . . ?" Simon started. It was a clash of back and forth you go, no you gos until Simon broke through.

"How was your day Imogen? What did you do?"

Although he seemed impressed by her uncommon mannerisms, it occurred to her that maybe she shouldn't appear too "modern." Thinking it might be wise to tamp down her enthusiasm a bit, speak more softly and subdued, like a lady, she answered softly, "It was divine." She couldn't recall ever using the word "divine," before in conversation, but it sounded right.

"I then dined at the hotel café," she continued in a mellifluous tone, "followed by a lovely stroll about town." She knew her measured response sounded affected, but she didn't want to make a mistake that would give Simon a reason to doubt she was from this century, at least not now; not yet.

Simon sensed how uncomfortable she seemed. He had no clue where Imogen was from, but it was clear she was not well versed in the particulars of social etiquette—rules Simon himself found to be rather trifling anyway. But that's what he liked about her. There seemed to be no pretense with Imogen. She was her authentic self. She didn't try to pretend or suppress her zeal.

"That sounds nice," he said nodding at her, a small smile beginning to form at the corners of each side of his mouth. "Now please bring Imogen back and let her tell me again how her day was."

"Thank you," she said, expending a robust sigh of relief. "I recognize that you don't know me that well and . . . " She was faltering and losing her words again, ". . .well I'm just . . . I'm . . . I guess, not as fancy as the people that you know."

Simon tossed his hair back the way he did and laughed out loud. "Fancy? Oh my," he replied. "I'm not at all fancy," he said. "In fact, my upbringing was nothing short of unfancy!"

Imogen was genuinely surprised. He seemed so sure of himself. She couldn't imagine that he didn't come from some upscale family of good breeding—all that stuff that people in this time seemed to put so much stock into.

"Really?" she asked. "You seem so . . . so all together."

Simon laughed again. "It is true, as the principal of the school, I do have a certain decorum that I must follow."

Imogen smiled but the lull in the conversation created another long, uncomfortable silence. Sensing her discomfort, Simon stood up then and walked over to where Imogen was seated. Kneeling down in front of her on one knee he took her hands in his.

"I have never met anyone like you, Imogen," he said earnestly. "I cannot explain it. When I am in your presence I am like putty. When I am away from you, I cannot keep thoughts of you from seizing my mind."

If his mind was being seized, Imogen's was reeling. She couldn't believe this was happening to her. This was so much better than any of the rom-coms she'd ever watched. Never a big fan of the romance genre, she had endured and indulged her friend Rachel's obsession when she had dragged her off to the movies to see films like *Bridget Jones' Diary*, *Love Actually*, and *When Harry Met Sally*. If she had to watch them, she preferred dramas like *Titanic*, which at least had an historical backdrop.

Yet, as much as she loved hearing these words from Simon, inside she was panicking. She wasn't at all sure that she should even be here, in this time, feeling this way. It was happening so fast. These new emotions she was experiencing were both exhilarating and terrifying at the same time.

Simon, this place, had awakened something in her. She felt alive. Yes, that was it. For the first time in so many years she felt like being alive mattered; recognizing that it wasn't enough to simply exist. Of course, she had good times with Fletcher, but from the beginning, something had always been missing. Now she knew what that missing thing was—passion. Not in a purely sexual sense, but passion for everything, for learning, for adventure, for life. She had no idea what the plan was and she couldn't think beyond now and maybe a day or two in the future. In Imogen's mind, it was a clear case of Nodus Tollens: The realization that the plot of her old life made no sense to her anymore.

As these thoughts raced light speed through her mind, Imogen sensed Simon drawing close to her. Live in the here and now, Imogen, don't overthink this, she reminded herself as his lips lightly made contact with hers. She closed her eyes and let herself go with it. This kiss was different than the first one was; slower, sensual, lingering, a rising symphony of longing; a kiss for the ages. She wasn't sure, but despite not believing in angels, she may have heard them singing! And those butterflies, the ones that had been flitting around in her belly for the past few weeks, they were back.

Now Simon was apologetic as they drew apart. "Forgive me Imogen," he said. "When I am with you I cannot control myself. It's as though you have cast a spell upon me." He gave her a sly smile. "Are you a witch?"

For some reason, being asked if she was a witch was like the most hilarious and cheesiest question ever. It reminded her of the line in *The Wizard of Oz* when Glenda, the good witch, asked Dorothy, "Are you a good witch or a bad witch?" and Imogen lost it in a fit of giggles. Simon caught the contagious giggle bug and commenced laughing along with her.

Finally, when their laughter had subsided, Simon asked, "Why are we laughing?"

Imogen had to think about the timeframe of the *Wizard of Oz* for a moment before speaking. If memory served, the movie didn't come out until 1939, but L. Frank Baum published the first of the Oz books around 1900. Okay good, check.

"I was just thinking of *The Wizard of Oz*." Simon scratched his head in confusion. "The books?" Imogen prompted.

"Oh, yes, yes, of course," he said. "We have copies in our library at school, for the children, but I have not read any of them."

Imogen explained the good witch/bad witch reference and Simon laughed at that. What she really wished she could tell him though was how at night before she went to bed her dad had read a chapter of every single Oz book in the series to her, but in 1913 Baum had not yet completed all the books in the series.

"You enjoy reading then?" Simon inquired.

"Oh yes," Imogen responded quickly. "I spent a good deal of my childhood lost inside books."

That seemed to please Simon because he reached into his coat pocket and withdrew a hardbound book and handed it to her.   "I was not certain, but I think you might enjoy these."

The book was titled *Love Poems and Others* by D.H. Lawrence.

"He is a modern poet," Simon said. He reached out to take the book back from her, "May I?" Imogen nodded.

He opened it and in a clear and modulated voice, began to read one of the poems, "Kisses in the Train":

> *I saw the midlands*
> *revolve through her hair;*
> *the fields of autumn*
> *stretching bare,*
> *and sheep on the pasture*
> *tossed back in a scare.*
> *And still as ever*
> *the world went round,*

my mouth on her pulsing
throat was found,
and my breast to her beating
breast was bound.
But my heart at the centre
of all, in a swound
was still as a pivot,
as all the ground
on its prowling orbit
shifted round.
And still in my nostrils
the scent of her flesh;
and still my blind face
sought her afresh;
and still one pulse
through the world did thresh.
And the world all whirling
round in joy
like the dance of a dervish
did destroy
my sense - and reason
spun like a toy.
But firm at the centre
my heart was found;
my own to her perfect
heartbeat bound,
like a magnet's keeper
closing the round.

If at this moment Imogen had any doubts about her feelings for Simon, they all but dissipated after he read the final word in the poem and closed the book. In fact, it seemed like a good time to melt into his arms and jump immediately into bed with him.

However, if she wanted to keep her secrets she would need to rein in her fervor, for now. Finding within herself a jot of restraint, Imogen stood up and calmly thanked Simon for the book.

"That was wonderful Simon," she said, "thank you, I will treasure it."

Simon handed the book back to her and also stood up. "I am delighted that you liked my gift." He took her hand and bent down to kiss it affectionately. Taking a cue from Imogen's demeanor, Simon gave her a half smile as he plucked his derby from the chair, spinning it a half turn before slapping it on his head, and made his way toward the door.

"May I call on you tomorrow Miss Imogen?" he asked in a return to their previously reserved dialogue.

"Of course," Imogen answered as she followed him across the room. He opened the door and stepped out, but leaned back in and asked her, "Where are you from Imogen Oliver?

Imogen grinned as she pushed him gently out the door. "I told you," she said. "I'm from Oz."

Eyeing the claw-foot tub in the corner, Imogen sighed, fanning her brow. Perhaps a cold bath was in order.

31

Imogen awoke the next morning feeling remarkably refreshed. Last night's leisurely soak in the tub had been heavenly. Quiet reflection was definitely underrated. Without the routine distractions of music, the television, her phone relentlessly vibrating with notifications, she was able to truly relax for a change. Although she had wanted more than anything for Simon to stay last night, it seemed like things were moving pretty fast—too fast even for relationships in her own contemporary time. Although hooking up wasn't out of the ordinary; falling in love at first sight certainly was, wasn't it?

She dressed in a simple day frock. Although the days had seemed warmer than usual for October, there was a chill in the air. She was glad she had the jacket to slip on over it. In her preparations, Imogen had brought money along—a modern dollar became a period-correct dollar, which of course, went much further here, but if she chose to stay longer she would need to purchase additional clothing. And she would also have to make some decisions about where she would live. She couldn't stay in the hotel indefinitely. Was she actually making plans to stay? It sure seemed that way.

After she was finished dressing and pinning up her hair, Imogen took the stairs down to the lobby, which was abuzz with patrons checking in and checking out on this busy Saturday morning. Imogen walked over to the hotel clerk's desk. The clerk behind the counter was Marvin, the same one that had checked her out so thoroughly when she had first arrived.

"Hello Marvin," she said breezily. "Do I have any messages?"

As expected, Marvin raised a mistrustful eyebrow, but he dutifully checked the box for her room and indeed there was a note for her. As he pressed it into her hand, his fingers lingered on her palm a little too long.

Quickly pulling her hand away, Imogen leaned in close to the smirking clerk and said in a low, calm tone, "If you ever touch me like that again, I will kill you." She'd heard that line in a Bruce Willis movie once. She leaned away. Marvin's stupid grin had evaporated, but Imogen's hadn't.

"Have a nice day," she said pleasantly, as she turned and sauntered away from the desk.

Imogen sat down on a bench outside the hotel and unfolded the note. Of course, it was from Simon. Brunch? 11:00 a.m.? S. L. Elliot.

Across town, Simon faced the small, cracked mirror above the basin, adjusting his collar and straightening his tie. He knew that instead of preparing to visit Imogen again today, he should be marching directly over to Georgia's house and breaking off his engagement with her. It was the right thing to do, yet every part of him resisted. He hated to think that his relationship with Georgia was merely a plan B in the uncertain event Imogen disappeared again, but sadly, it was true.

Imogen was an enigma, a delicious mystery to be solved, but he couldn't trust that she wouldn't vanish again. He needed more time with her, to get to know her. He had questions, lots of them.

He hoped that some of those questions might be answered today as they spent the day together. It had been correct for her to insist that he leave last night. Their escalating passion for one another was threatening their better judgment. He didn't want to regret anything with Imogen.

Simon pulled his watch from his vest pocket. 10:30—that should give him plenty of time to walk the seven blocks from his small studio apartment to the Benson hotel. He had his motorcar parked at the garage, which he used for driving to work, but for short trips around town, he preferred to walk. The Broadway Street building wasn't a terrible living space for a single fellow. He did have to share the bathroom with several other tenants on the third floor, but the bed wasn't intolerably lumpy and the rent was comparatively cheap.

Ever since becoming betrothed to Georgia he'd been scrimping and saving wherever he could on his paltry principal's salary to purchase a home. That seemed to be Georgia's primary focus, that and making wedding plans, a constant barrage of endless details that was making Simon's head spin.

"Simon, do you prefer the white petunias or the purple dahlias? The Kennebec salmon or chicken croquette? A honeymoon in the country or the city? Tapered candles on every table, or no? Simon, are you listening? Simon!"

He could almost hear her grating voice reverberating inside his head. Not unlike the sound of fabric ripping, it made him cringe. His mother had been a seamstress, and to Simon's ears, the noise the tearing of fabric made was akin to nails on a chalkboard, but not nearly as wrenching as the tangible and most unpleasant physical feeling it aroused. It was obvious to him now more than ever that Georgia had been merely a rebound response to Imogen's disappearance; a distraction to keep him from ruminating on his shattered heart. Yet, her cringe-worthy voice withstanding, he couldn't help feeling like the deceitful cheat that he was for sneaking around behind her back.

But as he approached the final block and in the distance, saw Imogen seated on a bench outside the hotel, all prior feelings of guilt melted away. She didn't see him yet. She was gazing straight ahead, looking away, out into the street. An unanticipated rush of elation surged through Simon. She was a vision, but what Imogen possessed transcended her physical appearance. It wasn't that she was wearing the right clothes or the proper hat. Rather, it was because when her hair was carelessly coming unpinned and falling across her brow she didn't seem to care. She wasn't sitting up prim and straight. Her knees weren't completely locked in place as though they were being held together with steel bolts. There was a gayness about her; she was an enchanted soul with a strong and curious mind.

She possessed a comfortable acceptance of herself that was different from other women he had known, with the exception of his mother. In fact, Imogen reminded him a bit of her—a charming, but stubborn free spirit who kept everyone, including her son, in a perpetual state of bewilderment. Imogen had stirred up something within him that he hadn't known was missing. As he drew closer, she slowly turned to look in his direction, a broad smile forming on her lovely face.

Damn, does he ever look grand, Imogen thought as she watched Simon approach. She had known some extraordinarily handsome men in her time, but in that vest and suit, no one did dapper like Simon. Freed of his usual, tidy pulled-back ponytail, his hair hung loose about his shoulders. The taller than usual silk top hat paired with a pair of round, blue-tinted wire sunglass/spectacles reminded Imogen of the 21st century steampunk hipsters of her time, except the appeal was authentic; it wasn't pretend. Simon was the real deal.

She remembered the first day she'd lain eyes on him surrounded by his tittering entourage of girls. He oozed charisma that day too, but although he looked nearly the same today as he did then, she sensed there was something else hidden beneath that stalwart persona; a sensitive soul perhaps; someone who, like herself, tucked their pain away in a private, secret compartment. Imogen stood up as Simon approached. He dipped down low, tipping his hat chivalrously and she remembered to do the customary little curtsy thing back. He extended his arm. She effortlessly took it and they began to stroll along down the sidewalk together.

"What would you like to do today Miss Imogen?" Simon asked in his most elegant and gentlemanly voice.

"Well," she answered teasingly, "I think I'd like to peruse a bookstore or two, look at the geese on the pond, maybe ride in a motor car, and oh, eat ice cream!"

Simon smiled in amused delight. "I think we can do all of that."

They did do all that and then some, interspersed with lively conversation about a range of topics from poetry and literature to modern machinery—Simon was fascinated with the accelerated growth of contemporary technology. In the last five to 10 years, he explained to Imogen in great detail, they had seen the invention of passenger airplanes and seaplanes that could land on water, the electrical ignition system for automobiles, movie cameras, zippers, the toaster, motion pictures, the gramophone, and wireless telegraphy. Not to mention the vacuum cleaner, tea bags, and the electric washing machine. "Had she tried that new drink called Pepsi?"

At times, Simon became so enthusiastic about topics he waved his arms wildly in the air. It delighted Imogen to see him so fascinated by all the new modern gadgets and innovations, things that she took for granted. But a bit of a nerd girl herself when it came to techy gadgets, she understood his excitement.

Wandering into a bookstore, Imogen made a beeline to the book displays and was immediately impressed with the exquisite quality and the tactile feel of the leather-bound books. Simon passed her an odd, embarrassed look when he caught sight of her smelling the ink on the inside pages of Jack London's *The Call of the Wild.*

"Whatever are you doing, Imogen?" he asked, clearly flummoxed by her strange behavior.

"I love that new book smell," Imogen answered. "Really?" Simon said.

Imogen cocked her head to one side and gave him an incredulous look. "Have you really never smelled a book before?"

Imogen handed it to him. "Go ahead," she urged as Simon brought the book up to his nose and sniffed. His eyes grew wide and he sniffed again, breathing in deeper this time. "Oh my," he said, "you are right, that is delightful."

"See," Imogen said, pleased that she could introduce him to a new sensation. He picked up another book and sniffed it too. Imogen had to smile when she caught sight of what it was—H.G. Wells' novella *The Time Machine*—one of many she had read while researching time travel.

"This is one of my favorites," he said, closing it after taking a deep whiff of the inside and placing it back on the display. "Have you read it?" he asked.

"Uh-huh," Imogen answered.

"A fantastic tale," he murmured. "It certainly sparked my interest in fourth dimension travel. Do you think that time travel could actually be possible?" he asked.

Quickly changing the subject, Imogen picked up a copy of *The Jungle*, by Upton Sinclair. This is a great book," she said to Simon without thinking. "I read it a couple of years ago."

Simon shot her a confused look. "How could you have read it a few years ago Imogen? It just came out."

Imogen backtracked, "Oh, no . . . what I meant was . . ." She had to think fast. ". . . was that I . . . read a review of it in the paper the other morning and it was quite favorable."

Simon seemed to accept her explanation and they moved on and began to discuss other new releases such as Edgar Rice Burroughs' thriller *Tarzan of the Apes* and Margaret Sanger's *Family Limitation*, a highly controversial book about reproductive health. In the future, Imogen needed to be more careful.

After departing from the bookstore, the couple decided to stop in for lunch at a small sidewalk café. It was late in the year for comfortable dining outdoors, so the two went inside and chose a table by the window, each ordering a hot buttered rum while they waited for their orders.

"I am curious, Simon," Imogen asked, "how did you come by your middle name, Le Bon?" It was a mystery Imogen had wondered about since they'd first met.

Surprised, but delighted that she'd remembered that morsel of information about him, Simon had to admit that he hadn't a clue. It was the name his mother had chosen. He had not asked her about it and she had never explained to him where it came from.

Simon picked up the newspaper that was lying on the table. "Imogen," he said. "Have you seen the new puzzle in the paper? It's called a crossword."

All through lunch Simon continued to share his marvel of not only literature, but science. According to Simon, it was a very exciting time to be a teacher. He spoke of a German physicist by the name of Albert Einstein—had Imogen heard of him? Imogen let him go on, pretending she had not. In addition to his theory of relativity Simon described how Einstein had also published work on Brownian motion, observing that a tiny crumb floating in a hot liquid like tea is jiggled around chaotically.

"The crumb is being pushed by energetic and invisible particles, thereby establishing evidence for the existence of atoms!" he said.

Over dessert—hot fudge sundaes again—their conversation shifted to Darwin's *On the Origin of Species*, an interest in evolution, which they both shared, and how a year ago, they came to be at Doran's lecture.

"I was interested in the theory of evolution," Simon said. "It seemed to be a solid scientific concept, one that I might consider adding to our curriculum, but to be honest, I went to Doran's lecture for a rather different reason."

"And what was that?" asked Imogen, curious. As much as she loved hearing about Simon's interest in inventions and science and crossword puzzles, she longed to learn more about what made him tick.

Simon leaned back in his chair and began, "You may recall that I had mentioned before he was lecturing on evolution, Doran was a preacher," he said.

"Is that so?" Imogen asked. She knew this already, of course, but played along.

"Yes, he was very much the showy type of preacher; completely intimidating. But people seemed quite taken with him. They lined up outside the church doors waiting to get in on Sunday mornings," he said. "My mother took me to hear him speak when I was a little boy and he was both terrifying and mesmerizing. I was scared to death but I couldn't take my eyes off of him," Simon said with a snicker, clearly amused by the memory. But then his face darkened. "They became friends, my mother and Doran," Simon clarified before stopping midstream in his story to gaze out the window.

"What's wrong Simon?" Imogen asked.

"This is a story better left for another day," he said. He smiled halfheartedly and reached across the table to grasp Imogen's hand. "I have wearied you long enough with my stories," he said. "I want to know more about you Imogen. Tell me about your parents."

Knowing full well that Simon would not be getting the full rendering of her childhood and her parents, she was happy still to talk about them, especially her father. "They were photographers," Imogen began.

"What? Were?" Simon interrupted.

"Yes, they died."

Simon's smile faded. "I am so sorry Imogen."

Imogen appreciated his sympathy. "I was young and my grandmother Iris raised me."

Simon seemed to perk up. "Iris? The same as our mutual friend!" Imogen realized she'd slipped up at once. He had known Iris, her grandmother, when she was a young woman, when Imogen had unwittingly stepped into Grammy's photo when she was in college and Andre and Simon were there.

"What was your grandmother's last name?" Simon asked.

"Fisher," Imogen lied, "my maternal grandmother."

"Ah," he said nodding. Simon seemed to accept that explanation, but then inquired, "Was Iris Graham a friend of yours then?" Holy shit, this was getting risky, Imogen thought. She forced herself to return to that day in 1901.

"Actually," she began, "I didn't know Iris that well. We were acquaintances and I happened to be in the park that day that we met."

"Iris was such a lovely woman," Simon gushed. "Andre was devastated when she disappeared."

Imogen nodded and quickly steered the conversation in a different direction, away from her grandmother.

Later that afternoon Simon escorted Imogen back to the Benson. "Meet me for dinner tonight?" he asked before leaving.

"I thought you might be tired of me after spending the entire day together," Imogen said.

"Never," Simon said, kissing her hand.

32

As evening descended upon the Crystal Dining Room at the Benson Hotel, it was transformed into a veritable wonderland. With the lights dimmed, the twinkling flickers of a hundred candles strategically placed around the room cast leaping, spinning, pirouetting shadows on the walls and floors and ceiling, creating an enchanted otherworldly ambiance. Tables set with fine linen and crystal rimmed the edge of the polished wood dance floor where a full orchestra—groups of woodwinds, brass, percussion, and strings—performed on the elevated proscenium.

Seated across the table from Simon, Imogen felt like Cinderella at the ball. Her evening gown, a sumptuous silk organza, was a pale mauve with a full skirt and an open back. Dainty pearl earrings and a fancy, jewel encrusted hair comb picked up the reflective light dancing from the candles. Completing her ensemble, opera-length, white gloves that went way up above her elbows like she was dressed for the prom, a pair of dainty satin slippers, and a beaded purse. If there was one thing about this era that Imogen liked best it was that people really knew how to dress up. And despite the tight corset, which she loathed, she felt like a princess in a fairy tale.

Having skipped out on prom both her junior and senior years

during her dark, I-hate-everything-and-everyone phase, she missed out on that whole shopping for a dress, getting your hair and nails done, corsage wearing, riding in a limo experience. People still dressed up in her time, but it was in more of a flashy, trendy, be-seen sort of way. The only time she saw real ball gowns anymore was once a year watching the celebrities pose on the red carpet at the Oscars.

Looking as debonair as ever in his black tuxedo coat, trousers trimmed with satin ribbon, silk cummerbund, and swanky bow tie, Simon seemed to take pride in his appearance, unlike a lot of the guys she knew back home, who wouldn't know the difference between a sports coat and a suit jacket; who existed year-round pretty much in khaki shorts, a T-shirt or sweatshirt, depending on the weather, and flip-flops, always.

The ballroom, the lights, the fashion, a man she was falling hard for—the night felt, dare she say it, magical? Sensing his gaze, Imogen tilted her head sideways catching Simon staring at her intensely, his face filled with emotion.

"You are stunningly beautiful, Imogen," he said.

Embarrassed, Imogen was compelled to laugh it off. No one had ever called her beautiful, let alone "stunningly" anything before. She saw herself as more the cute type. But the combination of the elegant duds, the candle's soft glow, and the wistful way Simon was eyeing her, she had to admit that at this moment, she felt different and special and perhaps even a little beautiful.

"Oh, I have something for you," he said, breaking the spell and drawing something up from the chair beside him. He placed a box wrapped in a velvet ribbon on the table between them.

"What's this?" Imogen uncharacteristically squealed. She wasn't used to surprises.

"Open it," Simon said.

Imogen eagerly untied the bow and slid the cardboard box from its cloth wrapping. On the front of it a comical little cartoonish guy held an Eastman Kodak Co's No. 2 Brownie camera. Imogen lifted the lid and took the camera out. The Model D was covered in supple brown leatherette cardboard. It also came with an instruction booklet and one roll of 120-exposure film.

In her own time, she had seen Brownie cameras only in the display cases of antique shops and thrift stores. She had not used a real camera in years, partly because after her parents died, she had lost interest, but with everything digital now, most of the time she used the camera built into her smartphone to take pictures. She'd always thought it might be fun to try one of these old film cameras though. Her parents shot exclusively in film and she had learned darkroom techniques from helping her dad. Plus, the studio darkroom was still accessible—finding film might be the difficult part.

Imogen thanked Simon. "This is incredibly thoughtful," she gushed. Earlier today, they had wandered into a camera shop and Imogen had mentioned that she would like to try out a Brownie camera. She didn't expect Simon to go back to the establishment later and buy it for her. Ever the gadget aficionada, Imogen had to chuckle as Simon couldn't wait to explain to her how the camera worked.

"You hold it here and wind this key, see, and this is where the film goes," he said excitedly, opening the wooden film compartment inside to show her. With his vast knowledge garnered working as a photographer's assistant he prattled on. Little did he know that her parents carted around a profusion of sophisticated professional photographic gear—lenses, tripods, lights—meaning she knew far more about the inner workings of a camera and its accessories than she let on to him.

They chatted about the camera until dinner arrived, a cornucopia of goodness, from veal chops, chicken croquettes, asparagus tips and minced lamb to watercress salad and a vanilla custard tartlet for dessert. After dessert was finished, the orchestra started playing again and couples took to the dance floor, immediately transforming the room into a canvas of color as the skirts of the elegant ladies swirled in an eddy of motion.

Simon stood up, pushed his chair aside, and extended his hand to Imogen. "Shall we?" he asked. Imogen took his hand and he pulled her onto the dance floor. This would be another test for Imogen. She had never actually waltzed before. It was something that was on her list to do, but had never gotten around to. As it turned out, it wasn't a problem because Simon was a skilled dancer. All she needed to do was follow his lead. In his arms, they glided effortlessly across the floor.

"What is this song?" Imogen asked.

"Meet Me Tonight in Dreamland," Simon whispered softly into her ear.

"It's wonderful," Imogen sighed. She felt as though she was dancing on a cloud, in a perfectly enchanted dream that she hoped she would never awaken from. As cliché as that sounded, she was beginning to understand why romance novels were so popular. Life wasn't always wonderful. It was messy sometimes, and awkward, but at times like this, when it was very good, it was something we all desired; something we all wanted to happen to us at least once in our lifetime.

The song ended, but Simon did not loosen his grip from around her waist. He gazed into her face before saying the words, "I love you, Imogen."

A tiny gasp escaped Imogen's lips. Her eyes darted up and away. Love. Was that what this was? She liked the sound of it, but at the same time, it was terrifying. "I . . . I'm not sure what to say Simon."

"Take a deep breath and say that you love me, too darling," he said without hesitation.

"Simon says, say I love you?" Imogen teased back, a small smile forming at each corner of her mouth.

Simon returned the smile. "Yes, Simon says," Simon said. Just then the orchestra struck up again, launching into the "Blue Danube Waltz." Imogen knew this song. Grandma Iris used to play it all the time on the piano.

"Well?" Simon asked.

Although the music drowned out the sound of her voice, caught up in the music and the movement and the moment, Imogen mouthed the words Simon was waiting to hear, "I love you!" And with that, he lifted her up into the air and twirled her around across the floor.

Unbeknownst to the blissful couple who had eyes only for each other, lurking behind the curtain stage right, someone watched them as they danced and laughed, oblivious to everything and everyone around them. After the song ended, Simon took Imogen's gloved hand and led her back to their table where after-dessert drinks awaited. He pulled the chair out for her and she slid into it, her dress making a satisfying rustling sound.

"That was wonderful," Imogen said breathlessly.

Sharing in her delighted giddiness, Simon sat down and boldly leaned in for a kiss.

Suddenly, a voice above their heads boomed, "Who are you?"

Startled, Imogen and Simon recoiled when they looked up and saw who was speaking. Towering over them with her hands locked on her hips was a furious Georgia Bitgood. Like a malevolent sorceress swooping in to spoil the party, the tall—she was at least half a foot taller than Imogen—menacing woman seemed entirely out of place in her drab, everyday schoolmarm clothes and long, black braid cascading down her back. Simon abruptly stood up, knocking his chair over, which made a sharp bang as it hit the hard wood floor.

"Georgia!" he said, stunned.

"Who is she?" Georgia demanded, pointing an accusatory finger at Imogen.

"Uh . . . she's a friend," Simon managed to utter.

"Oh, a friend, huh?" Georgia said incredulously, her tone clearly demonstrating she was having none of it. "I have never witnessed 'friends' dance like that before!" she said, her voice growing increasingly louder amd shriller. The orchestra stopped playing mid-note and the room went eerily silent, all eyes focused on the drama unfolding at the couple's table.

In an effort to diffuse the situation, Simon tried to usher Georgia out, "Come Georgia, let us take this outside . . . " But she brushed him away angrily.

"No! I'm not going anywhere Simon until I know what is going on. Who is this woman?" she demanded again defiantly.

Imogen wasn't sure what to do. She was feeling as perplexed as Georgia. As far as she knew Simon had broken off their engagement. He hadn't actually said, but she had assumed he had.

Imogen looked up at Simon, searching his expression for reassurance. "What's going on Simon?" she asked.

Trapped between the penetrating stares of both women, Simon stood frozen in place. He was torn. Should he nudge Georgia out the door and risk losing Imogen or tell Georgia to go to appease Imogen. What to do? A pickle he was in.

Like a Mexican standoff, the three of them stood a few feet

apart regarding one another for an awkward few seconds, until finally, Imogen broke the impasse. Standing up, she grabbed her purse
and wrap from the chair and stated, "I will leave you two to figure
this out."

As she started to leave the table, she glanced over at Georgia.
And rather than anger in her face, Imogen saw something else. The
woman nodded at Imogen, lobbing her a look of solidarity that
seemed to say, "I know that this is all Simon's fault, not yours."

Imogen left them and Georgia turned her attention to Simon.
Removing the engagement ring from her finger, she tossed it onto
his dessert plate where it made a pinging sound and rolled around a
couple of times before settling in the center of his praline sorbet. In
a sudden change of heart, she reached over and plucked it from the
ice cream before tucking it into a pocket of her skirt.

"Goodbye Simon," she spat, turning and stomping away, her
boots making a heavy clomping sound against the backdrop of the
hushed room. Simon turned away, stunned that two women had just
walked out on him. And then, thwack! something hard struck him in
the back of the head. He twirled around to see Georgia rushing out
of the ballroom door, and her black, lace-up boot was lying on the
floor at his feet.

"Ouch!" he cried, rubbing the back of his head where the boot
had made impact. Simon expended a restrained sigh. Well, even
though she'd kept the ring, it seemed clear that his engagement to
Georgia was officially called off. And for the first time since this
drama began to unfold, he looked up and noticed that every person
in the room was looking at him.

"Uh . . . sorry for the scene folks," he mumbled, hastily grabbing
up his coat and derby and making a mad dash for the exit.

33

Another long night of watching, waiting, wondering. Another night parked down the street from Imogen's house. Teddy had been by three times already this week and had not spied her once. With the exception of the front porch light, the house was dark; no flickering TV, no movement. He'd checked her mailbox for mail—there was none, and newspapers hadn't begun piling up on the porch, so where was she? From his own experience, he knew that recovery following a trip could take several days and conceivably, she could be staying at her boyfriend's house, or perhaps she even had a separate place elsewhere that she used for departure and return.

When he had sneaked inside her home and office last time he hadn't noticed any anchor photographs lying around anywhere. Of course, he couldn't be sure, but Teddy had a nagging suspicion that Imogen hadn't gone to any place in this time. Anxious and antsy, he fretted whether he should consider a second trip to 1913 to maybe just poke around a bit. Maybe she was planning to stay there for good, he thought. That could be a good thing, but on the other hand, it could also be a very, very bad thing, because what if she was hooking up with Simon? Teddy speculated. It would only be a matter of time before they tracked down Doran and together they figured the whole thing out. Then she'd come back for sure, and everything would unravel.

❧

After Tiffany Rose "disappeared," missing person fliers with her senior portrait on it were plastered all over town. On a tip from some kids who said they thought they saw someone that looked like her at the park, the police showed up one day at the photography studio asking a lot of questions, but with no body and no evidence, there was no proof that Teddy had anything to do with it. Still, Niles, who had witnessed the argument between Teddy and Tiffany the day before she went missing, was suspicious. After the police left, Teddy went back to sweeping up as usual until Niles pulled him aside.

"Teddy," he said, "let's go into my office for a chat." Teddy followed him into his office and Niles shut the door.

"Sit down," Niles instructed. Teddy sat down and waited. His boss seemed distressed, which made Teddy feel uneasy. He could feel sweat beading at his temples. Niles hesitated, took a deep breath, and then dropped the photograph face up on the table.

"I know I asked before, but now I'm asking one more time before I go to the police," he said. "Do you know anything about this?"

Teddy leaned forward in his chair to view the photo. It looked like the same photo Niles had shown him before when he'd first figured out how to travel; the one with the girl in the old-fashioned clothes.

"The girl in the photo looks an awful lot like Tiffany Rose, Teddy," Niles said sternly, "the one you brought here and argued with, the one who's missing." Niles voice got louder, "What did you do, Teddy?"

Before Teddy could answer, Imogen unexpectedly appeared at the office window. She was jumping up and down and gesturing to her dad.

"Stay right there, Teddy," Niles instructed, "I'll be right back." He dashed around the desk and left the office to go deal with his daughter.

Teddy fidgeted in the chair waiting for Niles to return. He tried to stay calm. Niles was just outside the window talking to Imogen. He could see him turning back periodically to glance in, probably making sure that Teddy didn't bolt. Teddy wanted to bolt. This was not good. Not good at all. He looked at the photo again. It was her, Tiffany Rose. But how? What had she done? She must have gotten hold of a camera somehow and left the photo in the exact same location as the studio thinking that it might be discovered later. But how the heck would she have even known where the studio would be? As far as Teddy could tell, he'd left her in an empty field.

Teddy considered all this as he waited and tried to come up with a feasible explanation. After a few minutes, Niles returned. Imogen and Jade were still peeking through the glass, but Niles waved them away and the two scampered off.

"Okay Teddy, I'm going to ask you again, what do you know about this photo?" Niles said.

Teddy shook his head. "I … I don't know anything," he muttered.

"What do you mean you don't know?" Niles asked. "Is this her or is it not?"

"It looks like her, but it can't be her Mr. Oliver," he said as earnestly as he could muster. He explained that they had broken up and gone their separate ways. That was it. He was sticking to his story, no matter what, that whatever happened to her was as much of a mystery to him as everyone else.

Niles, who had picked the photograph up now and was tapping it repetitively against his palm, looked back at Teddy with a stern expression for a moment before saying, "Alright Teddy, I guess I'll have to take your word for it." He shoved the picture into his coat pocket and stood up. "You can go, for now."

Teddy stood up and opened the office door and met Mr. Oliver's wife Francis, who was on her way in.

"Hello Teddy," she said in that smooth way of hers.

Teddy tried to avoid making eye contact with her, but couldn't help himself. "Hi, Miz Oliver," he murmured under his breath as he thrust his head down and hurried away.

Back in the storeroom, Teddy set his broom aside and wedged himself into his hiding place. Pulling out the doobie hidden in the hole in the wall, he lit it up and took a couple of long drags to calm himself down, but he knew, it was only a matter of time before his employers would figure out the truth and go to the police, or worse, tell his mother. Teddy knew what he had to do.

It was a snap to jimmy the lock and slip inside the office unnoticed, as he knew it would be. The studio was dark, but Teddy had brought along a flashlight; he didn't want to turn on a light and arouse suspicion. And there, just as he also knew they would be, in their office on the desk in plain sight were two photographs—one a beach landscape; the other a school photograph of Imogen's stupid little friend Jade, who had recently moved away unexpectedly.

Teddy looked around double checking that no one else was in the studio. It was empty and silent, the only sound coming from the hum of the refrigerator they kept out here for snacks and lunches.

Confident that he was alone, but knowing that he had to move quickly in case they reappeared, he grabbed up a small trashcan and placed it on the table. Pulling out the cheap disposable cigarette lighter from his pocket, Teddy flicked it, holding the plastic button down and watching the flame for a second before setting it to both of the pictures he held in his hand. He felt some remorse for trapping Mrs. Oliver. There had always been this incongruous little spark between them. Had things gone differently, Teddy might have liked to pursue that flicker of possibility. As the sides of the photos began to curl, the flame getting perilously close to his fingers, he dropped them both into the can and watched them burn until there was nothing left but a pile of ashes. He smiled in spite of himself. Nice try Tiffany Rose, he thought. If I can help it, nobody will ever find out about you.

Teddy expected there would be questions, but was amazed to learn that the grandmother had made up an elaborate lie about what happened. A small news story in the paper had said that the couple, Niles and Francis Oliver had died in a car accident while traveling out of town. When the studio was padlocked Teddy breathed a little easier. Eventually, he moved out of his mother's house to the neighboring town of Stambourg, where he opened up his pawnshop. Time travel, as it turned out, was a great way to make money, boatloads of it, if you were careful and smart enough, like Teddy, to fly under the radar.

Teddy flipped through the stack of pictures he held in his hands—each one a photographic rendering of the same hotel, but shot at different times and different angles. Pinpointing precisely when to go back was a crapshoot. It had been easy to follow her last time because he knew specifically when, where, and why Imogen was going because it hinged on her attending Doran's lecture, which had a specific date. Now, her inducement would likely be to find Simon and presumably recommence their relationship, which had blossomed during that first trip. His best bet of locating her, he figured, was within that year following the first trip. He'd choose a random date from the first six months and if she wasn't there then, he'd try the latter part of that year.

It wasn't an exact science, of course, but it would narrow it down some. He didn't like going that far back. To be honest, he didn't really enjoy time travel at all—because, the headaches. And the thought of having to potentially return multiple times was unappealing, not to mention the whole getting involved thing. After the Sutro debacle, he had sworn off getting tangled up in messy affairs of the past—the fire, death on the beach. It was too much. Now days he never changed a thing; get in, get out. Yet, here he was, doing it again, getting involved.

Teddy put the car in gear and headed back to Stambourg for the night. He should get some rest. Tomorrow was a travel day.

34

Once outside the dining room, Simon wasn't quite sure which way to go, although Georgia throwing her shoe at him had solidified his decision about which girl to follow. Assuming Imogen had retreated to her room, Simon raced around the corner, and taking two steps at a time, bounded up the stairs to the second floor. That this felt like déjà vu was not lost on him. A year or so ago, he had followed this same trajectory, to devastating results, as he was loathe to recall. He could only hope that Imogen would stick around long enough this time for him to explain about Georgia. By the time he reached room 213, he was in deep panic mode, but he paused, reminding himself to remain calm.

Taking a deep breath, he knocked on her door and waited. No answer. He knocked again, slightly louder this time. Still no answer. He was beginning to fear the worst, but decided that rather than jumping immediately to conclusions, perhaps it would be prudent to first go downstairs and take a look around. The desk clerk may have observed her in transit.

When Simon got down to the lobby he immediately recognized the desk clerk Marvin. Did he live at that desk? Simon couldn't help wondering. It seemed like he was always there.

Glibly, the bored Marvin inquired, "May I help you, sir?"

Simon leaned against the big oak desk. "Yes, have you seen a woman who is staying here at the hotel—a Miss Imogen Oliver?"

Although he curtly answered "No," it was obvious that Marvin was trying hard not to react. Curling up his nose ever so slightly made Simon suspect he might know more than he was letting on.

"Nuts! Are you sure?" Simon asked, giving Marvin a second chance to come clean.

"Well . . . I might have seen her pass by earlier," he admitted.

"Which way was she going?" Simon asked, excited at the possibility that Imogen may not have left anywhere for good this time.

Marvin shrugged. "She got into the lift," he said as though he had no real interest whatsoever in the comings and goings of the hotel guests, though Simon suspected Marvin knew about everything that went on in the hotel.

"Are you certain you saw her go upstairs?" Simon asked. "I've been up to her room and she did not answer when I knocked.

"I'm certain," he said, turning his back on Simon and pretending to check the room key slots.

It could be that she was angry and choosing not to come to the door. Or, it could be like before. She had cleared out. Marvin had said he didn't see her leave, but no one had seen her leave last time either.

He turned around to head back up to the second floor when he noticed the back of a woman that looked like Imogen rounding the corner. Simon sprinted after her.

"Imogen," he called out, but she didn't turn around. He caught up to her and touched her shoulder. The woman that turned around was not Imogen, although she was wearing a gown similar in style and color, it definitely was not her. The woman gave Simon a sharp look of disdain.

"Oh, terribly sorry," he said, quickly snatching his hat from his head and tipping it slightly in her direction. "I've mistaken you for someone else."

"Indeed!" exclaimed the woman, who appeared to be about three decades older than Imogen.

Simon backed away uncomfortably. Rather than waiting outside her room, he decided to return to the lobby in case she may have exited the hotel. He sat down on an overstuffed chair and pretended to be engrossed in a copy of *Vogue*, a woman's magazine he snatched up from the table. Feeling increasingly anxious, Simon fidgeted, periodically pulling the watch from his pocket and checking the time. After about a half hour he went back upstairs to Imogen's room and knocked on the door again. Still, there was no answer. He placed his ear up close against the door's thick, hard wood to see if he could detect any sound of movement inside. Nothing. After about 10 minutes, he went back downstairs again to wait around in the lobby. He didn't have long to wait this time.

He was absent-mindedly thumbing through the magazine when he glanced up and saw Imogen strolling in through the hotel's revolving doors. Oh thank heaven, he thought, relieved that she hadn't vanished a second time.

However, she was not alone. She held the arm of a stocky man. Simon remembered him. It was the odd little man with the misshapen mustache and the poorly tailored suit who had been at Doran's lecture, and then later, in Imogen's room when Simon had discovered she was gone last time. Imogen did not notice Simon at first. The two were engaged in an animated conversation. She didn't appear enamored by him, but merely chitchatting in a friendly, new acquaintance sort of way. He must have said something droll because Imogen threw back her head and laughed. She stopped mid-laugh when she saw Simon, who was walking over to greet them.

"Simon," she said, self-consciously untangling her arm from the man's sleeve. The relaxed demeanor of her cheerful escort seemed to deflate as soon as he encountered Simon. He stepped back and away from Imogen as though he had been caught in an act of doing something wrong.

Simon took a step forward. "Imogen," he said, "I've been waiting here for you." The look of concern and relief on Simon's face was heartfelt. Teddy thought it might be a good time to take his leave. As he turned away and started to go, Imogen caught his jacket sleeve and pulled him back.

"Where are you going, Mr. Jenkins?" she asked.

Teddy wasn't sure what to say. "Why I . . . I was just going up to my room, Miss Oliver."

Imogen smiled sweetly at Simon and then introduced them.

"This is Leeroy Jenkins," she said. "We ran into each other outside and decided to take an evening stroll together."

Simon coolly extended his hand and Teddy shook it. "I believe we have met, once before," Simon said. "About a year ago, Mr. Jenkins? After the Doran lecture?"

"Oh yes, of course," Teddy muttered. He knew what was going on between Imogen and Simon, but the knowledge didn't make the situation any less uncomfortable.

"Very nice to see you again," he said, nodding at Simon. He removed his hat, tipping it in Imogen's direction as he slowly backed away. "Goodnight, Miss Oliver," he said as he turned and ambled away from the scene.

Teddy could barely contain himself after leaving the couple in the lobby. Honestly, his timing couldn't have been any better if he'd planned it. After his misfire during the first part of the year when he'd come back and found no sign of either of them, Teddy had been hesitant to make the planned return trip in the latter part of the year. He hated traveling this far back anyway and had decided if it didn't pan out this time, that was it, end of story, he'd let the chips fall where they may. But as luck would have it, the random date he'd chosen to return had not only been right on the money, but his good fortune didn't stop there—he arrived out front of the Benson shortly before Georgia Bitgood exited the hotel in a huff, wearing only one shoe. He'd barely had time to get his bearings when she nearly knocked him over.

"Excuse me," Teddy said approaching her cautiously, hat in hand, "I think we've met. Are you Miss Bitgood."

"Who are you?" Georgia snapped, clearly seeing red about something.

"Leeroy Jenkins, at your service," he said, passing his hat in front of him like a shrewd carnival barker displaying his wares.

"Do I know you?" Georgia asked, a confused look on her face.

"I believe you are a friend of Mister Simon Le Bon Elliot, are you not?" Teddy inquired.

Hearing Simon's name made Georgia's jaw clench in suppressed rage. "Ooooh, that scoundrel!" she cried. "I never wish to lay eyes on him again, ever!" She began to hobble away in her one shoe when Teddy leaped in front of her, blocking her way. Suspecting that this might be a serendipitous meeting, Teddy turned up the charm.

"How would you like to get back at the scoundrel and that woman he's been seeing?" he asked, knowing precisely the right words to say to raise the hackles of a woman scorned.

"How do you know about that?" Georgia shot back suspiciously.

"Why, don't you remember her?" Teddy said, his voice as smooth as butter. "She was the one I helped you corral in the alley-way, about a year ago, or so?"

"Oh yes," Georgia said, "I do remember you now."

Teddy put on his most sincere face—a well-rehearsed combination of pity and understanding—and said, "You want to break them up, don't you?"

Georgia, hung her head, and in a barely audible voice, mumbled, "Yes, I suppose so."

Teddy seized the moment. "I can help you then," he said barely able to contain his glee.

"Why do you wish to help me?" Georgia asked distrustfully.

"I have my reasons," Teddy said. "Let's go have a chat, shall we?" He took hold of Georgia's arm and led her away to strategize.

As Teddy and Georgia conspired, Imogen, who after exiting the ballroom, had retreated to her room upstairs, tried to distract herself with one of the magazines she'd pilfered from the lobby, but it was no use. She was a restless bundle of nerves. She didn't know what was happening, whether Simon had decided to follow after Georgia or her, although it didn't matter. She wasn't planning to vanish like she did the last time, but even so she didn't want to make it too easy on Simon. Clearly, he had not told Georgia about their relationship.

Imogen felt sorry for Georgia. Beneath the anger, Imogen could tell that Georgia was really hurting. Simon was wrong to not tell her, but she guessed that might be partially her fault. They had been spending nearly every waking hour with one another since she'd arrived. What she needed was some fresh air to clear her head. Pulling on her belted jacket, Imogen left her room and made her way down the hall to the lift. The doors closed and unbeknownst to either party, as Imogen was riding down to the first floor in the lift, Simon was ascending the stairs to the second floor. In the lobby, she sensed eyes upon her. She turned around and that nasty desk clerk was glaring in her direction. Imogen raised her hand, smiled and gave him a slow-motion parade queen wave, which felt incredibly right in the long white gloves. He waved back halfheartedly.

Outside, Imogen took a deep gulp of the evening's cool fall breeze. She caught a hint of smoke in the air from a distant chimney. Her plan was to go for a short cab ride, and then return to the hotel. If Simon did not show up tonight, well, she would take a nice bath and see what transpired tomorrow. But as she was about to step off of the curb and hail an approaching hansom she felt a hand clutch her arm, pulling her back. Thinking it might be Simon, she spun around crying out, "Simon!"

But the person tugging at her was not Simon. It was that man— the one from Doran's lecture who had given her the silver coin. He looked unchanged—same ill-fitting pinstriped suit and derby, although his mustache looked real this time, not hastily pasted on as she had remembered it being before. Something else seemed recognizable about him, but she couldn't quite put her finger on it.

"I'm sorry Miss . . . ?"

"Oliver," she finished for him.

"Miss Oliver," Teddy said, removing his hat. "I did not mean to startle you. I believe we met, about a year ago if memory serves, at the Doran lecture downtown."

"Yes, I believe we did," Imogen said.

"My name is Leeroy Jenkins," he said, extending his hand.

Imogen shook his hand, remembering to use the proper turn of the century protocol, which was allowing the man to gently grasp the woman's hand, sort of like shaking hands "lite" between the sexes.

"Leeroy Jenkins?" Imogen said. "I've heard that name somewhere."

Teddy began to wordlessly panic. Uh-oh, he thought to himself. He hadn't considered that Imogen might recognize the Warcraft reference.

"Oh," Teddy interposed innocently. "It was my grandfather's name," he lied.

"I see," Imogen said. "Well, what can I do for you Mr. Jenkins?"

Teddy couldn't believe his dumb, good luck. Not more than 10 minutes ago, he'd hatched a plan with Georgia and now, out of the hotel doors walks Imogen herself. And she looked stunning, by the way. In comparison to the dour, shoeless Georgia, Imogen was a vision in her plum-colored ball gown. He couldn't help envisaging that it was he that she looked at adoringly, rather than Simon . . .

"If you don't mind, I was just out for an evening stroll when I saw you," Teddy said. "Would you care to join me?"

Gazing down the street and then back toward the hotel, Imogen pondered his proposition. What if Simon showed up? What if he did? Maybe she'd give him a bit of time to worry. Smiling, she linked her gloved arm in his. "Don't mind if I do."

35

Imogen started to comment about this Leeroy Jenkins fellow, but before she could open her mouth to speak, Simon reached out and took her hand in his.

"It's not what you think Imogen. Please don't leave again," he pleaded. "It's over between Georgia and me."

Imogen's expressionless face made it difficult for Simon to read what she was thinking, but when she finally smiled, he knew everything was going to be alright between them.

His earnest pleas convincing, Imogen reached out and gently stroked his whiskered chin. "Simon," she said sighing, "I won't leave again."

Simon was overcome with unexpected emotion, something that was quite foreign to him. Never, had he felt such affection for any one person. He wanted her in every way possible, but mostly right now, in the physical sense. That was wrong, he knew, but the yearning welling within him said otherwise; he sensed she felt the same.

"Come on, let's go up to my room," she suggested.

"Are you certain?" he asked.

"I am," she answered. Under the ever-watchful eye of Marvin, the couple boarded the lift together and headed upstairs to room

213.

Attempting to unlock the door to her room was testing Imogen's patience as she fumbled with the cumbersome key, jiggling it back and forth in the lock with little success. Simon wasn't helping. She was distracted by his warm breath as he planted a series of soft, slow kisses in a line along the nape of her neck, not to mention the close proximity of his body against her backside, which was threatening to set Imogen's lady parts atwitter.

Seeing her frustration, Simon stopped nibbling on her neck to say, "It's those silly gloves you're wearing, pet. Let me try." He took the key from her hands while still holding on to her from behind, jimmied it once, and like that, voilá, it opened.

"My hero!" Imogen said playfully. Once inside, Simon quickly drew Imogen to him. This time it was he that kicked the door shut with his foot.

He caressed her neck with his lips again, this time all along the sides and up around her ear lobe, to which he offered a wee lick and a nibble. Imogen pulled her shoulders up and squealed, "That tickles Simon!" which made Simon want to do it even more as he lobbed an array of kisses and various smooches her way, leaving her gasping in a fit of uncontrollable giggles. They were both laughing now.

"Simon, I'm serious, stop," she said as she tried to wriggle away from his grasp. Not intending to let her get away, Simon stopped tickling and teasing and he gently kissed her on the lips. Soft and sensuous quickly turned into hot and impassioned and the next thing they knew they were both crazy, madly, frantically turned on. Consumed by passion, he grasped the back of her head causing her hairpin to slip out; her hair cascading to her shoulders, which stirred Simon even further.

"Oh my god, Imogen," he said breathlessly into her ear. With that, he picked her up in his arms and transported her over to the bed, placing her down on it gently where he joined her, lying down next to her. They canoodled like that for a while. Imogen could feel Simon's rising erection against her thigh and instinctively she reached down and stroked him through his trousers. Simon's body stiffened, and he abruptly stopped kissing her neck.

"What is it? What's wrong?" Imogen asked as Simon sat up and stared straight ahead.

"Imogen," he said.

"Yes?" Imogen said, wondering what had suddenly come over him.

He turned and looked her straight in the eye and asked, "Are you a virgin?"

Imogen's mouth dropped open. "Well, no, Simon, I am not," she answered honestly.

Simon seemed shocked. Having never been in a situation such as this before he wasn't sure how to react. Outrage was his go-to. Leaping from the bed he stood peering down at her. "Who have you been intimate with?" he demanded to know.

Oh, he was really pissing her off now. "Are you serious?! That is none of your business!" Imogen responded angrily, jumping up from the bed now too and facing him on the opposite side of the bed.

"Then I cannot be with you," Simon stated emphatically, folding his arms across his chest and turning away from her in a stubborn stance.

"Why not?" Imogen inquired.

"Because you are not a virgin," Simon repeated without looking at her.

Judiciously, she understood that Simon's abysmally archaic behavior was a condition of his upbringing and the times that he lived in, and she could go along with most of it—the clothes, the absurd rules and dumb etiquette, but this was pure nonsense. They were both adults. She had hoped that their feelings for one another could transcend this century's silly societal norms.

Imogen placed one hand defiantly on her hip and inquired, "Alright then, are *you* a virgin?"

Spinning around to face her, Simon snorted, annoyed that she had thrown his question back at him.

"Well no, I'm a man," he said, indignant.

"Are you religious?" Imogen asked.

"No, but . . ."

"Then I don't see the problem?" she said in a calm, rational manner. "If there isn't some deity up in the clouds judging whether or not I 'save' myself for marriage, then what difference does it make to either of us?"

"It's not proper," Simon lamented, visibly deflated and sounding more like a whiny child than an adult man.

Imogen felt bad for him, but continued, "As far as I can tell, whatever happens between us is a private matter, correct?"

She had a point, although it bothered him that he had been forced to yield to a woman's logic. It was usually the other way around. But he sensed that there was something different about Imogen from the moment he met her—from the first time in the park, and then a year ago in the square when, immune to his charms, she had brazenly stood her ground following his dismal attempt at wooing her. Her intelligence, her fierceness, her independent streak, the dichotomy of sweet girl and wild woman—each of these attributes had been what had drawn him to her in the first place. She was right. It was silly to let other people's rules dictate their bond.

Simon rushed around the bed, scooping her in his arms and holding her tight to him. "Accept my apology, Imogen," he whispered. When he drew her close and kissed her tenderly, Simon felt a sudden rush, like he had been liberated, as if Imogen had given him permission to be human, to toss aside the archaic constraints. He was excited by the notion of throwing caution to the wind, of exploring with Imogen something feral and untapped that percolated beneath the surface, just waiting to be unleashed.

"Take off those silly gloves," Simon ordered. Ooh, Imogen was liking how demanding he was being.

"These gloves?" she asked, lifting her arms coquettishly and pointing at them. Simon smiled slyly and nodded, "Yes, those gloves."

Imogen cheerfully obeyed. Taking her time, she leisurely peeled them down her arm, from her elbow to her wrist, then pulled each finger off one by one before dropping them onto the floor in an improvised strip tease she'd seen performed once in an old black-and-white movie on TV.

Simon was a captivated audience. He had seen a hootchie-kootchie act like this once too. When he and his buddy Frank were 12 they had sneaked under the tent at a traveling circus to watch the racy adults' only show featuring an exotic dancer billed as Chartreuse De Monde. When their adolescent snickering drew the attention of the barker, he immediately dispatched Olaf, the circus'

7-foot strong man, to roust them both from the tent. But the five or
so minutes of what they'd witnessed had made quite an impression!
And now, here was Imogen, doing a much spicier, more rousing
rendition than Miss De Monde ever could.

Pushing Simon down into an empty chair she began to slowly
undress, slipping each sleeve from her arm in a seductive and prolonged tease. The satin gown slipped effortlessly to the floor. She
kicked off her slippers, and lifting each leg onto the bed she leisurely
unclasped her silk stockings from the garters, tossing each one at
Simon to gleefully catch. Simon observed with spellbound fascina-
tion as she began unlacing her undergarments, one by one, untying
each silk ribbon, starting at her thigh and working her way up to the
last one beneath her bodice. Taking her sweet time, she coordinated
her efforts to match Simon's reaction, enjoying the fact that his eyes
were glued on her only, made more thrilling by the fact that what she
was doing, in this century, was considered quite risqué.

Simon had never felt such excitement and anticipation. This was
something new and electrifying, yet part of his antediluvian upbringing tugged annoyingly at his collar, reminding him that this wasn't
normal behavior, and troubling thoughts that made him question
Imogen invaded his thoughts. How did she know how to do this?
Why was she not a virgin? Still, he could not take his eyes off her.
Maybe all of that would make sense later, but for now he dismissed
it, focusing all his attention on the ravishing woman who stood
bathed in a pool of moon rays that shone a spotlight through the
window, casting spells and weaving lunar magic into the otherwise
ordinary hotel room.

The last of Imogen's garments tumbled dramatically to the floor
and she stood before him like a goddess, unsheathed and beautiful.
Simon had to remind himself to breathe. He rose from his chair;
silk stockings falling from his lap, and cupped one exquisite breast,
carressing the other with his hand.

"You are the most dazzling creature I have ever seen," he said.
Encircling her waist with his arms he walked her backwards and
deposited her gently onto the bed. She watched him disrobe in silence until he was standing bare before her, clearly aroused. Imogen
was equally stirred. She reached behind Simon's head and untied the
leather band that held his ponytail, releasing his shoulder-length hair.

Raised on her parent's rock music, Imogen couldn't deny that what
she loved best was the band members' long locks. Tonight, Simon
Le Bon was her own personal rock star, and he was sexy as hell.

Sensing her shared enthusiasm, Simon began to kiss her neck,
her earlobes, moving downward, running his tongue along her belly.
Imogen was surprised by Simon's thoughtful tenderness. She had
imagined men of his time being misogynistic and woefully clueless
about pleasuring a woman. Not so with Simon. She recalled one of
the first things she'd noticed about him physically was the shape and
appearance of his hands, hands she had fantasized about touching
her the way he was now.

As he inched down further and further, her entire body began
to shutter with anticipation. Never had she ever felt such yearning
and she wasn't sure she could be as patient as Simon. More than
anything she wanted him right now. As though sensing her need, the
slow train left the station and Simon could no longer restrain himself either. He swiftly entered her and together they rocked room
213. Climaxing in a synchronized crescendo of wild whimpers and
raucous groans, Simon collapsed, sweat raining from his forehead
before rolling over spent on his back beside her.

"Oh Imogen," was all he could say in between breathless gasps
of air. Imogen was having difficulty catching her breath as well.

"That . . . was . . . intense," she managed to say.

"Quite," Simon agreed.

They smiled at one another and Imogen whispered, "Want to do
it again?"

36

Beneath the down-filled quilt Imogen contentedly nuzzled against Simon's chest as he dozed. Warm and cozy, so relaxed she could easily fall back asleep, it was another lazy, rainy Sunday afternoon in a string of them. From the bed, Imogen could see droplets of rain pinging against the windowpane. In the time since she'd returned to 1913, they had already fallen into a happy comfortable routine, as couples do. Closing themselves off, away from the world and people who might judge their love.

Over the last month, Simon had made peace, more or less, with Georgia. At least she seemed to be accepting their breakup. Simon tried to avoid her as much as possible, and she seemed equally inclined to give him a wide berth. Imogen had begun working at the store where Simon had purchased her camera. She didn't need to work. Honestly, she had plenty of money. The money she had brought with her could sustain her for a long while, especially considering she could buy a handbag for as little as $1.39, underwear and hosiery that cost anywhere from 35 cents to $2, a coat for $6.

But she was becoming increasingly bored with hanging around the hotel reading. She had to admit she was really beginning to miss those little modern distractions, like her cell phone, the ability to binge-watch a series on Netflix, or shopping online. Even going out and exploring the city was starting to lose its charm, mainly because the weather was turning colder. It was November now and Imogen was seeing frost in the mornings.

One day when she had gone back to the store to drop off her roll of film for developing she had struck up a conversation with the proprietor, Tomás Donovan.

"Are you enjoying your Brownie?" he had inquired.

"I love it!" Imogen gushed. She truly did. She never realized how much fun it could be to have to actually pause before taking a photo, to stand completely motionless and Zen-like and focused to set up each shot. It wasn't like digital where you could take an un-limited amount of shots, upload only those you wanted to keep, and delete the rest. With only 12 or 13 exposures, one had to be selective about what or whom they photographed.

During their conversation, Mr. Donovan had seemed surprised that Imogen was so knowledgeable about cameras and the develop-ing process, that she knew about exposure times and light sensitivity, and the types of chemicals that went into the various processing baths. She was about to be on her way, when he stopped her.

"Would you like to come to work for me?" he had asked, "as my assistant."

It was part-time, only two or three days a week, but Imogen was thrilled at the prospect of working, of filling up her days with some-thing more than hot clam nectar and the newspaper in the morning, followed by afternoon tea and a stroll; and especially, doing some-thing for which she actually had an interest.

She helped with orders, assisted in the darkroom when needed, and filled in at the counter when Mr. Donovan needed a break. She was pleasantly surprised too, how much she enjoyed interacting with the customers. Normally, being around people made her anxious. Perhaps it was because it was a different era and the environment fresh and new to her, but she enjoyed watching people, observing the men's and women's fashions, the outfits on the little children. She liked seeing the excitement in their eyes when they marveled at the cameras; she liked answering their questions and showing them how the cameras worked. It also helped keep her mind off other things that had been troubling her lately.

The newspaper was filled with the news from Europe, which had been embroiled in war now for two years. The United States had been supplying Great Brittan and the other Allied powers while remaining neutral, but talk of entering the war was brewing in the states. As a history major, Imogen knew what was coming. The US would enter WWI next year, in August 1914. More than four million military personnel would be mobilized. There would be more than 110,000 deaths; including 43,000 who would succumb to an influenza pandemic. She knew also that the Selective Service Act would pass next year and likely Simon would be drafted. All males aged 18 to 45 were required to register for military service.

Simon rolled over on his side to face Imogen and wrapped his arms around her. "Good morning, darling," he whispered sleepily into her ear.

With his touch, Imogen's worries dissolved like morning mist. She craved nothing more than waking up in his arms, and Sundays never came soon enough. Because she was still staying at the hotel, to get around being harassed by the nosy desk clerk Marvin they had befriended Otis the hotel elevator operator, who let Simon use a hidden back stairway that was for hotel staff use only. She knew she needed to find another place to live soon, but a part of her resisted. Although this new life felt permanent, mostly during the times she was with Simon, at other times it felt temporary.

She snuggled against him, and with her index finger traced a path through his forest of chest hair. It was soft, not at all coarse, and curly, and there wasn't too much of it or too little. A small thatch also ringed his belly button, which Imogen liked to fiddle around with as well. At this early stage, it was about learning all about each other—likes, dislikes, opinions, values, those diminutive nuances that can only be observed close up—all that, including, of course, each other's bodies. Imogen, however, was reticent about showing off all of hers. First of all, despite her initial striptease act, she had been making an effort to tone it down a bit so that Simon wouldn't suspect she was from the future. Second, she was trying to conceal the small tattoo etched on her hip. Neither of these modern constructs had crossed her mind when she'd first traveled back.

Simon drew his arms up, clasping his fingers together behind his head against the pillow. "Are you enjoying your employ at the camera store?" he asked her.

Imogen turned to her side and cradled her head in her hand. "I like it," she said, genuinely enthusiastic. "I grew up around cameras, but I never thought I'd actually be interested in photography the way my folks were. I was an only child and so I was the primary focus of their photographs. I remember as a little girl getting so tired of their constant picture taking and saying, 'enough, that's enough.'"

That made Simon laugh. "I can picture you saying that."

Noticing how very natural it felt telling Simon about her childhood, Imogen continued. "I had a friend named Jade," she said.

Simon cocked his head sideways and raised his eyebrows. "That's a rather unusual name," he commented.

"She was black," Imogen said.

"A negro?" Simon inquired, without a hint of bigotry.

That word, so alien to her and spoken out loud caught her off guard, but she understood that Simon meant no malice.

"We were inseparable for a summer," Imogen went on. "We did lots of things; building tents made of blankets in the living room, running from dawn until dusk; dancing, being silly, watching TV, just kid stuff," she said.

Simon was confused. "What is TV?" he asked.

It had tumbled out of her mouth so quickly in conversation Imogen had momentarily forgotten where and when she was. Fortunately, she was quick with an explanation, "Oh, well TV," she threw off dismissively, "that stands for The View. So when we were going out to play we would say we were going out to watch TV."

"Ah, I see," Simon said, nodding his head, unconvinced. He was becoming accustomed to Imogen's strange outbursts and references to things that didn't quite add up or make sense. He attributed his acceptance of it to being raised by a mother who often made similar random odd observations about things, too, as though she knew about something far off for which he couldn't know.

"I would like to learn everything about you Imogen, and certainly, more about your family," he said, prompting her to continue her stories.

Imogen was more than pleased to talk about her dad. He was fun rolled up in a sunny day, always up for adventure and shenanigans of any stripe. She told him about their numerous excursions, of hiking up and down mountains, leaping over streams; of examining bugs and looking for fossils and animal tracks. She told Simon the story about holding their breath through the tunnel to avoid the trolls, conveniently omitting the part about it being in a car. Imogen's happy childhood tales amused Simon, although they were in stark contrast to his own wretched upbringing. It made him glad to know that some children grew up in normal environments.

"What about your mother, Imogen?" Simon asked. "What was she like?"

The cheerful, lively features of her face noticeably dissipated with Simon's inquiry and he felt bad.

"Forgive me for prying, Imogen," he said. "Was your mother unkind?"

Imogen shook her head. "No, it wasn't like she was mean to me or anything." Imogen sighed. She'd never really examined their relationship too much growing up. Probably because she relied on her dad to serve as a buffer between herself and her mom.

"My mother was . . . I guess you might say, detached," she said. Imogen took whatever crumbs Francis dropped, and they were few and far between. "She pushed me away," Imogen said sadly. "I guess I needed more from her than she could give."

Simon sat up and pulled Imogen in close to him where she rested against his shoulder. He stroked her hair tenderly with his fingers for a moment before saying, "My mother was that way, too."

Imogen was curious. The only time he had ever mentioned her was when he had taken her up to her room that first time, after she'd injured her ankle at the lecture.

"Don't get me wrong, she rarely let me out of her sight," he began. "In fact, she smothered me. It was as if on the one hand she was afraid of losing me, yet on the other, she secretly wished I wasn't there. I often sensed that she both loved and hated me. She loved me because I was her child, but hated me because I was a burden, and perhaps I reminded her of someone that she did not wish to be reminded of."

Imogen frowned. "Your father?" Imogen asked. "Where was your father, Simon?"

"That," he said, "is a question for the ages." Simon looked away, straightening the quilt with his fingers, clearly uncomfortable with the direction their conversation was taking.

Recognizing this was a touchy subject, Imogen backed off. "You don't have to tell me about it if you don't want to, Simon."

But he was determined to tell her. They needed to understand one another, and learning about their respective families was an important part of that process.

"I don't know who he is," Simon began. "She wouldn't tell me. I remember asking her, begging her to tell me so that the other children would stop calling me a bastard."

Imogen couldn't hold back a gasp. "That's horrible," she exclaimed. No one called fatherless children bastards anymore, or at least not in her time. It brought back the memory of that lady with the ginormous hat she had encountered on one of her early time-traveling excursions. Hadn't she called that young woman's child a bastard? It seemed so cruel and archaic, and it broke Imogen's heart thinking about what Simon had endured.

But then Simon smiled as if a happier memory had unexpectedly floated past. "My mother, she was peculiar and angry most of the time," he said, "but she could also be sweet and loving, too. She indulged me with treats when she could afford it, perhaps to make up for her dour demeanor. In some ways, you remind me of her."

Imogen smiled. "Really, how so?" she asked.

"She was strong-willed, quite intelligent, and independent. And like you, she was a bit of a maverick too." He winked at Imogen.

"Now that is interesting," Imogen said with a chuckle. "Was it because she wouldn't follow all the silly rules, too?"

Simon nodded, but he was serious again. "You at least follow some of them, but she refused to follow any rules at all," he said unsmiling, "and that was to her detriment."

Simon described how like Imogen's parents, his mother also did photography but that rather than enjoying it, she seemed obsessed by it, but not just any photography, photos of herself and Simon only. He explained how she worked as a seamstress in a factory and saved every penny to pay for a studio sitting. If she had any money left over after that, she spent it on Simon.

When the first hand-held cameras came out, she saved up to buy one. "She asked strangers on the street to take photos of us," he said. The first selfies, Imogen thought.

"Do you have a picture of her?" Imogen asked.

"No, it was strange," Simon said. "We had all those photographs taken, but I never saw any of them. I don't know what became of them."

"What happened to her, your mother?" Imogen asked.

Simon seemed drained from talking about it, but he continued. "She was institutionalized," he said. "One day, a tall man in a dark suit came and took her away."

"How old were you Simon?" Imogen asked quietly.

"Seven," Simon answered.

"Oh my god, Simon. That's awful. What happened? Where did you go?"

Simon looked down at his hands. "I was sent to an orphanage," he said.

"And your mother?"

"I did not see her ever again," he said. He tried to hold back the tears as long as he could, but the more he tried, the more they seeped from his eyes, spilling down his cheeks.

"I'm so sorry Imogen. Forgive me," he sobbed into his hands as Imogen held him tight and stroked his neck.

"It's all right, Simon," she said as she comforted him. His shoulders heaved and after a moment, he wiped the tears away and took a moment to compose himself before looking into Imogen's eyes and admitting, "I have never told anyone that story."

Imogen squeezed his shoulders. "Thank you for trusting me," she said softly.

Simon sighed deeply and kissed her hand. "That's why I went to the lecture that night," he revealed.

"Doran's lecture?" Imogen asked. "Why?"

"I think he was the man in the suit that took her away."

"Wow," was all Imogen could say in response.

"You seem surprised? Do you know Doran?" Simon asked.

Imogen fumbled for words. No, she didn't really know him.

She'd only come back to do business with him; to get the stereo-scopic plates, but she couldn't tell Simon about that.

"I was interested in his lecture, that's all," Imogen said.

Simon paused before adding, "I was distracted that night, but I have not forgotten about him."

37

Teddy tossed back black coffee laced with Scotch from a stained teacup as he watched people and cars wayfaring up and down the busy street from the window of his cheap second-story flat. Another day in borings-ville, he thought. The St. Mark boarding house was a dump, but despite having plenty of money, it would do him no good to rent a fancy penthouse and draw unwanted attention to himself. The result was renting a room, complete with a shared bathroom, a Murphy bed, and a hotplate, fairly common accommodations for many urban dwellers. He missed his apartment above his pawn shop; he categorically missed his big-screen TV as well as myriad other modern conveniences like his electric shaver and his cell phone and his computer for surfing porn sites online.

The worst part of this era was that so much of it involved one-on-one engagement, something which Teddy was never really up for. He had discovered a couple of entertainment venues that didn't require interaction: the Nickelodeon or the movie theater downtown. The films there were tedious and silent; the production values wont. How did people exist back here? he pondered often, although he had to admit he did enjoy the films that starred the sexy femme fatale Theda Bara. Even by 21st century standards, that Theda was a mega-hotty for sure.

For the past month, he'd been shadowing Imogen to see whether or not she planned to stick around in 1913, and so far, it looked like she was. Although she was still living at the hotel, she'd gone out and gotten herself a part-time job. He knew she was seeing Simon, although they had gotten fairly sneaky about their weekend trysts. He'd observed that they were in cahoots now with Otis, the hotel's elevator operator, who let Simon take the staff's back stairs up to Imogen's floor.

It was time to bring Georgia into his plan. He had spoken to her several times already and she was anxious to know when the time would be right to execute it.

Upon their first meeting, Teddy had instructed Georgia to stay away from Simon as much as possible to let things cool down a bit until he could formulate a suitable plan. And as much as Georgia had stepped away from Simon, he knew inside she was a seething ball of rage and he was prepared to coax every bit of that pent-up anger out of her. He was meeting her today and he hoped that soon both he and Imogen would be saying goodbye to 1913 for good, that is, if everything went as planned.

Teddy took out his pocket watch. Time to go. He poured the remaining coffee down the sink and left the cup on the small foldup table. Grabbing his overcoat and derby, he headed down the creaky wood stairs to the street to join the wave of humanity already on the move. From there, he briskly walked the four blocks toward the train tracks. To avoid any hint of impropriety, they had agreed to meet in the most public place they could think of, the train station. As Teddy neared the terminal, he saw Georgia standing on the platform waiting for him. She waved him over to a nearby bench.

"Hello Mr. Jenkins," she said flatly. Honestly, what Simon had even seen in her was beyond him, Teddy thought.

"Miss Bitgood," he said removing his derby and fluttering it in front of him in an adapted bow. He gestured for her to sit down, and then followed suit, taking a spot on the bench a good several feet away from her, so as not to look like they were together.

Without turning her head to look at him, Georgia asked, "What is your plan, Mr. Jenkins?"

Teddy avoided eye contact with her as well. "The young girl students are quite taken with Mr. Elliot, is that correct?" he asked.

Georgia tilted her head sideways and answered, "Yes, why?"

"Can you arrange for an outing where they, you, and Mr. Elliot can be at a certain spot and time?"

"Do you mean a field trip?" Georgia asked, shifting her eyes sideways to look at Teddy without turning her head.

"Yes, that's it exactly," he said. "I know Miss Oliver's schedule. I would like for her to pass by and see him interacting with you and the girls. Can you arrange an encounter?"

Georgia continued facing straight ahead without looking at Teddy. "Yes, I think I can," she said, "but it will take a bit of time."

"Excellent," Teddy said. "Every Tuesday and Thursday afternoon at 3 o'clock, she passes through the city square on her way back to the Benson Hotel."

Without looking at Teddy, Georgia stood up and casually walked away in one direction. After she departed, Teddy stood and went the other way.

38

Mid-November fall foliage was in full glorious swing; a dazzling mix of red, yellow, orange that littered the sidewalks with a patchwork of multicolored leaves. A constant gentle, but chilly burst of wind blew up, sending more leaves whirling down from the trees and making it look like the world was raining confetti.

Last week, Imogen had purchased a snug gray cloak and leather kid gloves to fend off the cold bite that infused the air most mornings now when she headed out to work. She could take a car, but Imogen preferred to walk. She liked the exercise, but also taking in the city sights, a bustling carousel overflowing with humanity and cars and trolleys and horses. She loved how alive the city felt; the cacophony of sounds, the aroma of smoke that permeated the city from multiple fireplaces reminding her of drinking hot cocoa with marshmallows bundled up and snuggled close to her dad by the campfire. She loved hearing the rustling sound of her petticoat brushing against her long skirt as she walked, and the clickity-clacking of the heels of her boots on the paved sidewalk.

She had become acquainted with the merchandisers—the sweet elderly lady in the millenary shop arranging the latest hats in the window display, the cobbler sweeping outside his shop, the florist inside arranging the fresh-picked flowers. She always carried her Brownie with her and had asked each of these people to pose for her at least a few times, along with any children that she could cajole into holding still for a few moments.

Life was going along pretty well. She liked her job; she and Simon were carving out a relationship, although as much as she hated to admit it, a few issues and differences had cropped up between them already. She feared that if she did not speak up soon, not even love and passion would be able to fix things. They seemed like small things, but they were beginning to pile up. For instance, he had become irritated with her for saying "good gracious," which evidently was considered profanity; she'd run across the street in front of a carriage, which was considered risky and uncouth; and on several occasions she had accidently lifted her skirt marginally higher than necessary while climbing the stairs and—gasp—exposed her ankles.

Adding to that, he was, at times, interminably arrogant, an insufferable know-it-all, correcting her often; telling her how ladies were supposed to behave, reminding her that she should forever acquiesce. She wondered why now, when the rules of etiquette were seemingly becoming more relaxed, he held on to such antiquated standards of protocol, but she suspected that it might have something to do with his mother, who according to Simon, tossed the rules out the window every chance she got.

Likewise, a relationship with her was probably no picnic either. Imogen was messy. He had commented on that. Often. She had tried to do better, to tidy things up before he visited. What she felt was stimulating conversation he seemed to misconstrue as arguing. She was smart and stubborn, all of the things he claimed to love about her, yet also seemed to be the most annoyed by. These things chipped away at her judiciously concealed veneer of confidence and she wasn't sure how long she could take it before she exploded.

If that wasn't enough, Imogen had other nagging doubts about whether she could even thrive for very long in this world of the past. At first, she had only missed small distractions like her cell phone and TV, but as time passed, she was starting to realize ever more things from her old life that she was giving up. Simple pleasures like getting up early and going for a run or hiking the butte, yoga pants and comfortable shoes, wearing shorts and sandals in the summer, going out for a beer unescorted; small simple things really, but things, nonetheless, that she was realizing she'd never be able to do again here.

Granted, women in her time hadn't quite broken through the glass ceiling, and misogyny and rape culture and sexual harassment and assault were prevalent still, yet she missed having the freedom to come and go whenever and wherever she pleased without the limitations of having to dress a certain way or being forced to follow a rigid set of rules of behavior that dictated every waking moment of a woman's life.

Perhaps what she missed most of all, however, was Luxe. Sure, he was just a cat, but she missed him terribly. She missed how he would curl up in her lap or on her chest at night and touch her face with his little paw to remind her to continue petting him. She hoped that Fletcher was taking good care of him, feeding him the fancy food, giving him the treats he loved, brushing the tangles from his fluffy, white coat.

All the way to work, in her head, Imogen ruminated on each and every doubt as she walked along, probably "riskily" because she wasn't paying attention; wondering if she had made the right decision coming here or how much of herself she was willing to surrender before she lost her identity entirely. Simon did not know the extent of what she was giving up to stay here with him, one of which was giving up searching for her parents. Because you couldn't hop from a photo you were already in to another, she would have to go back to her own time first. Telling him the truth could fix that, she supposed, but if she ever did, how would he take it? Would he think her a lunatic and have her committed to Crestview like his mother had been?

When she arrived at the store Mr. Donovan greeted her with a hearty "Dia dhuit ar maidin (good morning) lassie" in his thick Irish accent. Working here took her mind off Simon and her other worries for a while. Mr. Donovan treated her like the daughter he'd lost and Imogen was beginning to acknowledge that the kind old man was becoming a stand-in for her own long-lost father.

At a quarter of three, Imogen closed out the cash register—a hulking precursor to an IBM clothed in a fancy polished brass case that she loved to operate, pushing the buttons, hearing the ding-ding of the bell when the drawers opened to make change. The bell reminded her of a scene in Frank Capra's mawkish film *It's a Wonderful Life* when Nick the bartender made the cash register's bell ring over and over, mocking the film's sappy tagline "Every time a bell rings, an angel gets its wings."

She removed her work apron, grabbed her cloak and satchel and called out a leave-taking farewell to Mr. Donovan who was working in the back room. "Slán abhaile Imogen," (safe home), he called out as she was leaving.

"So long, Mr. Donovan," she replied, closing the door behind her. The temperature had risen, warming it up enough that Imogen didn't have to wear her cloak. The sun was soothing against her back, and despite the doubts and worries of this morning, she couldn't help feeling lighthearted as she began her afternoon walk. It was too nice of a day to go back to the hotel right away, she thought. Perhaps she would do some window-shopping and then sit on a bench and feed the birds in the town square by the fountain and people-watch—she had her camera with her, so maybe she could convince a few people to pose for her.

As she rounded the block, the square came into view, and it appeared to be abuzz with activity as other people enjoyed the unseasonably warm autumn day. As she drew closer, she spotted someone familiar. She'd recognize those round sunglasses and that dark ponytail anywhere. It was Simon. He was situated at the center of a group of girls—probably his students. They must be on an outing today from school. But he didn't seem to be paying much attention to them. It appeared he was engaged in deep conversation with one person in particular. Imogen couldn't believe it. It was Georgia Bitgood; she'd recognize that woman and her long, fat braid anywhere. And her arm was looped casually through his, like they were a couple.

She was aware of her lips moving as she silently cursed under her breath, goddamn it, what is going on? She wanted to stay calm, but when everyone you love has been ripped from your life, there is an almost instantaneous proclivity to overreact. What if Simon was getting back together with her? He had been so exasperated with her lately. Perhaps he wished to be with someone who fit in; someone who understood the social norms better than she could ever possibly hope to. Assumptions ran dangerously amok in Imogen's head.

As she drew within closer range of the circle Imogen could see that Simon hadn't noticed her arrival, but some of the female students had, and rather than disengage they clustered together in a tight circle as though protecting their principal and teacher from some threatening intruder. What was this nonsense? Why were they protecting them? She marched toward them and they drew tighter together, but Imogen was angry now and despite the girls efforts at thrusting her back she pushed through to the center of the group. When she broke through, Simon turned around to look.

"Imogen!" he said, clearly startled. "What are you doing here, darling?"

"I might ask you the same question . . . darling," Imogen said in a contemptuous tone.

Georgia hovered slightly behind him, her arm still linked in his, and glared at Imogen. The old Imogen, the one who had built an impenetrable wall around her heart as protection from ever getting hurt, would have probably turned and walked away, given up, but she had made a fairly substantial investment in this relationship. Hell, she'd traveled across time to be with him—not that he knew that—but he was the only fucking reason she was here.

Love was hard for Imogen. Jade, dad, mother, Grammy—everyone leaves. Everyone dies. She loved Simon; he was her kryptonite. But perhaps she'd made a mistake. Maybe it wasn't meant to be after all.

Momentarily forgetting where she was and any prissy proper decorum that was expected of her, Imogen blurted, "What the hell's going on Simon?"

Simon's face changed from mildly surprised to stunned disbelief. The students and Georgia stood by, mouths agape, silently watching the drama between the two of them play out. Imogen was pleased to see that he'd pushed Georgia away dismissively, but something wasn't right because when he reached her, instead of gently speaking to her, he grabbed hold of her elbow and unceremoniously escorted her away from the circle. Although he wasn't clutching her so tightly that it hurt or anything, the forceful way he was towing her away, made her even more incensed. Managing to wriggle away from his grasp, she stormed ahead of him.

"I don't like your tone, Imogen," Simon said, his voice deepening in a mannish, authoritative manner that Imogen had not heard before.

Imogen stopped walking and faced him. "What do you mean, you don't like my tone?" she asked.

Taking her arm again and lowering his voice, he pulled her aside, "I mean, I don't like the way you speak to me around others."

"I'm certain I don't know what you're talking about," Imogen said with much irritation.

"I don't mean to be harsh," he said, "but there is no respect from you. Quite frankly, it's embarrassing."

"Oh, I know exactly what you mean," Imogen said, pulling her arm back in an effort to extricate it from his grip. Pent-up anger was burbling up to the surface and she was beyond caring now.

"Do you know what's embarrassing?" she asked. "It's that silly entourage of yours—the young girls, Georgia Bitgood. 'Oh Simon, yes Simon, whatever you want Simon,'" she said launching into her best mocking, trifling girl impression. "You think it's disrespectful because I don't fawn all over you like they do, right?"

Before he could answer, Imogen continued. "And the worst part is that the whole time they're throwing themselves at you they know full well that it's all a tease; they won't follow through."

"Because only whores do that . . .?" Simon said.

Like a runaway truck barreling out of control down a steep grade, the words tumbled from his lips before he could stop them. Everything at that point turned ultra-surreal. The words that Simon already regretted hung in the air between them as if suspended by invisible wires. Imogen's jaw tightened, her body became rigid with fury and resentment and she did something completely impromptu; she slapped him, hard. When she had seen that happen in the movies, it had always seemed hollow and staged, but she got it now; it was all raw and reflexive and it happened so fast that she withdrew her hand in dismay.

She was sorry, not sorry. And although she should have said something tamer, like, "How dare you?" what spilled from her mouth instead was, "Fuck you, Simon. Go to hell!"

With tears welling in her eyes, the only thing Imogen could think to do was run. She turned away from Simon now and sped off. She must have been a sight. It wasn't every day that people in 1913 saw a young woman racing full-bore down the street, holding up her skirt, which was hiked up around her knees in her fists, boots flying like the wind. But Imogen didn't care. Screw this and screw him. She'd had enough of this place and time.

The buckets of tears that spilled from her eyes caught in the wind before they could even hit her cheeks as she ran and ran and ran some more without stopping. She glanced back once in Simon's direction as she took the corner and saw that he was following after her, which spurred her to run even faster. At home she ran the trails, another thing she missed, and she'd run in a couple of half-marathons. No fucking way was Simon going to catch her. She glanced back to see him slamming head-on into a pedestrian on the sidewalk. She didn't hesitate to seize the opportunity to widen the distance between them.

Bursting unladylike through the doors and into the hotel lobby, her hair unpinned and hanging wildly in a tangled mass, parts clinging unattractively to the sweat on her body, Imogen gasped for air. She placed her hands on her knees and bent her head down to take a minute to catch her breath. Marvin, the desk clerk, started to open his mouth to say something, but after seeing the fuming, gnarled look Imogen shot in his direction, decided against it. She turned then and ran as fast as she could from the lobby, disappearing up the stairs.

Simon's mind raced. "Oh my lord, what have I done?" he thought before instinctively turning on his heels and giving chase. He had never seen a girl run so fast in his life, but Imogen, of course, was no ordinary girl and she was already a block ahead of him. From a distance, he could see her turning the corner as he sprinted after her, narrowing the gap between them slightly. She turned to look back in his direction once before turning left at the corner of Pearl and High streets. Simon wasn't accustomed to running. He could feel the sweat already beading up on his brow. He was panting and his legs felt heavy, like a couple of 50-pound bags of flour were strapped to them. Nobody ran, especially not women. They played croquet or golfed or did archery to stay fit. So how was Imogen so fast?

Preoccupied by these thoughts, he took the corner without stopping, barely slowing down and promptly plowed straight into the portly man, knocking him backward onto the hard sidewalk. Simon tripped too, tumbling over him, his boot grazing the man's head as they both went down. His derby and glasses flew off, bouncing and landing a few feet away.

Simon got up and apologized profusely to him, "I'm so very sorry" he said as he reached out and grasped the man's extended hand to help him up. He was about to apologize again and resume chasing after Imogen, when he noticed who the fellow was. "You," he said.

"Nuts!" Teddy said, brushing off his tweed jacket and touching his bruised forehead before placing his derby back on his head. "That was a floorer!"

"I'm quite apologetic Mister . . ." Simon said.

"Leeroy Jenkins, at your service," Teddy said with much flair and elan.

"Jenkins, right," Simon repeated. "As you can see, I'm in a bit of a hurry . . ."

"Indeed you are, indeed you are," Teddy said scratching the hair on his chin. "Why the rush, old man?" Teddy said, grasping Simon's shoulder with his pudgy fingers. "Buy me a drink? Make up for that nasty spill you caused?" Teddy said with a clever smile.

Perched on the barstool beside Leeroy Jenkins at O'Malley's bar, Simon fidgeted impatiently, tapping the thick wood bar, bouncing one knee up and down, and checking his pocket watch every five minutes or so. Jenkins had successfully made him feel guilty for knocking him down and tearing a hole in his jacket, insisting that Simon buy him a beer, "to compensate."

Granted, he had kicked the poor fellow in the head with his boot. Still, the clock was ticking. Any other time, Simon may have been inclined to sit a spell with this Leeroy Jenkins. He did, in fact, have many questions, like why was he lurking about all the time. He'd attended the Doran lecture and spoken to Imogen that first time he'd seen her, and then again the night of the ball when he escorted Imogen back to the hotel, but his mind was elsewhere and he just wanted to get this over with.

For the next 20 minutes Jenkins yammered incessantly about the weather, the stock market, the impending war—anything and everything. But when he slapped Simon's shoulder with his stocky hand, Simon's patience had worn thin and he abruptly slid off the barstool.

"Thank you kindly for allowing me to make amends, Mr. Jenkins, but I must be on my way now."

Teddy ceased talking mid-sentence, but before he could say another word, Simon was gone. Once outside, his feet barely hit the sidewalk before he broke into a brisk run in a frantic race to catch up with Imogen.

Simon swept into the lobby, breathing heavily, sweat trickling down his brow and neck and soaking the edges of his collar. He bent over, placing his hands on his knees to catch his breath. Anticipating what Simon was going to ask before he asked it, Marvin simply motioned in the direction of Imogen's room up the stairs. Simon waved a gesture of thanks, and sprinted out of the lobby, leaving Marvin shaking his head.

Still out of breath, but determined to find her, Simon raced up the stairs and down the hall to her room. Room 213. The feeling of deja vous in this situation was again, not lost on Simon, and the fear that it might be playing out in the same fashion as before terrified him. He hesitated before knocking. He needed to stay calm. He took a deep breath and then rapped softly on the door.

"Imogen?" he called out, his lips close to the gap between door and wall. "Are you there?" No answer. He knocked again, slightly louder. Nothing. He had raised his fist and was just beginning to start pounding on it when he spied Marvin exiting the lift. Following closely behind him was Leeroy Jenkins.

Marvin approached Simon. "How may I help you, Mr. Elliot?" he asked gently. They had been here before.

"It's Miss Oliver," he said.

"You've misplaced her again?" Marvin inquired, eyebrow raised.

His shoulders visibly sinking, Simon sighed deeply and answered, "Yes, I suppose I have."

He glanced over at Leeroy. "Why are you here, Jenkins," Simon asked.

Teddy knew he shouldn't have followed Simon, but he could not help himself. Of course, he needed to know if his plan had worked.

"Um," he stammered, "Well, I saw Miss Oliver fly by earlier

and well I . . . I felt compelled to come to the hotel to check on her, make sure she was all right."

Simon scowled at him, "Compelled, eh," he mumbled under his breath.

Marvin pressed past Simon and began to rap on the door. "Miss Oliver, are you in there?" he called through the door. He waited a few seconds before repeating. Still no response. Removing a skeleton key from his pocket, he placed it in the keyhole and turned it counterclockwise. He pushed the door open and Marvin, Simon, and Teddy guardedly entered the room, but there was no need to search, the evidence was clear. She was gone again. The only indication that Imogen Oliver had ever inhabited this room was sitting in the middle of the bed, the Brownie No. 2 camera and the room key she'd left behind.

Simon collapsed on the bed beside the abandoned camera and placed his head in his hands. "Why?" he moaned before suddenly leaping up and turning on Teddy.

"You!" he said, seizing Teddy roughly by the collar. "Who are you? You know more than you're letting on. Where is she? Where is Imogen? Tell me now!"

His eyes blazed with anger. Marvin jumped in, attempting to loosen Simon's grip on Teddy, but Teddy had managed to wriggle free on his own. Stepping away, he bellowed, "She's from the future, you dumbass!"

Simon was confused. "What? What are you saying?" he cried.

"She didn't tell you, did she?" Teddy asked casually.

Enraged, Simon reached out again to grab him again, but his hands met air. Like an evanescent bolt of lightning, Leeroy Jenkins had departed.

39

She was back, but she did not open her eyes. Not right away. She could still feel the blurry edges of time rolling up and fading around her. And when she finally tried, her eyelids were stuck together. When she brought her hand to her face, it felt wet and she realized why—tears wept 100 years ago and the sad realization that the past no longer held anything good or sweet or fine for her.

Imogen managed to collapse onto the futon as the pain roared back along with the tears. In her mind she saw his face, the devastated look of someone that did not understand, that he could never understand because she would never tell him the truth. Her migraine was severe—worse than she'd experienced ever before. Drawing the fuzzy blanket up over her head to keep out the light Imogen curled up on her side in a fetal position on the futon where she wept anew.

Several hours later, the pain had subsided enough that she could drive home, where she immediately crawled into her own bed and fell fast asleep. Hours later when she awoke, the room was completely dark. Night had fallen twice as she fitfully slept, and Imogen knew what she needed. A drink. Well she didn't really need a drink, but she . . . yes she did, she definitely needed a drink.

Hastily getting dressed, she scooped the car keys from the Anguiano clay pot by the hutch and headed to her car thinking she might just grab a six-pack at the neighborhood store around the corner, but as she neared the entrance, she changed her mind. She needed to be in a bar, around other people who were drinking too. She did not want to be alone tonight. As much as she loved her cat, his company would not suffice. She pulled into the parking lot of the first dive bar she could find. Lime green flashing neon illuminated the sign above the door—Froggies—perfect. She sent Fletcher a text to see if he'd join her and then went inside.

Walls of dark paneling greeted her as she entered the dimly lit, one-room tavern. It took a second for her eyes to adjust, but it was your standard dive bar—a vintage jukebox sitting big and useless and silent in one corner, two shabby pool tables beneath low-hanging faux tiffany glass lights suspended unsteadily by two slim chains from the ceiling, a well-worn dart board.

Imogen made her way to the rear where the bar was tucked into an even darker and bleaker corner. The only light, which originated from the backlit Coors sign, reflected off the stained mirror behind the bar, revealing a row of chrome barstools, the cracked and peeling green vinyl on the seats shored up multiple times with duct tape.

Besides the motley couple furiously pumping coins into two video poker machines and the bartender, only three other patrons inhabited Froggies on a Tuesday night. An older guy, ruddy skin, stringy gray hair, and a beard wearing camouflage overalls sat at the farthest end of the bar eating pretzels and nursing a scotch. To his left a glassy eyed younger man, probably mid-30s in a dirty tank top and baggy trousers sat silent and sullen, head down, staring intently into his glass of beer.

And finally, perched daintily on the edge of her barstool, a middle-aged woman in a faux leopard coat, her hair a muddle of teased confusion, scarlet lips, and eyes done up with the darkest most dreadful blue eye shadow, was leaning in close to chat up the heavily pierced/tattooed and much younger, bartender.

As Imogen drew near, in unison they turned their heads to check out the fresh and unfamiliar. Imogen knew she wasn't looking her best. She hadn't bothered to freshen up. In fact, her eyes were red and puffy from crying. She'd basically rolled out of bed, pulled on an old sweater and jeans and a pair of uggs. She had not even bothered to comb her hair, but from the looks of it, she should fit right in with this crowd.

Setting the cocktail with a lopsided umbrella injudiciously plopped into it down on the bar, the freakish clown doll patted the barstool next to her. "Come on over here and sit by me, little girl," she called out to Imogen.

Ponying up between her and gray beard, Imogen ordered her first shot of Patrón.

Two hours and many shots later, Imogen was drunk. Wait, no, sloppy drunk. And friends with everyone in the bar. And now she couldn't stop giggling at her cell phone, which she had set down on the bar. It just kept vibrating and pulsating and dancing, and at the moment it seemed like the most hilarious thing Imogen had ever witnessed in her life. A blurry face too kept popping up every time it buzzed, but Imogen couldn't make out who it was.

"I think it's for me," she said to Jonette, the beehive lady and Imogen's new best friend, who was equally inebriated herself and fully amenable to extending Imogen a special Froggies invitation into the inner circle of the bar's regulars.

Jonette snorted along with her. "It looks like a boy," slurred Jonette.

"I LIKE boys!" Imogen shouted, waving her shot glass above her head, and they both cackled wildly, that is until the merriment turned to tears.

All of a sudden, Imogen flashed on why she'd come here. Simon. It wasn't like she could dial him up on the cell phone. Cell phones weren't even invented where he was. Imogen put her face in her hands and bawled uncontrollably, "Simon, oh Simon."

"Who's Simon," somebody asked.

A few minutes later, Fletcher entered the tavern. When she didn't answer his calls or his text messages, he got worried and came to find her. Fletcher had driven by this dive nearly every day on his daily commute, but never ventured inside. From the looks of it, there was a reason why he'd never stopped in. Besides being a dive, it also had a sort of a depressing vibe about it. It reminded him of the bars in that movie *Barfly*. He and Imogen had watched it together during one of their date nights, staying in, eating pizza and popcorn, and drinking beer curled up together on the couch.

He was a little apprehensive to see her. He'd been thinking about their relationship, such as it was. He would always love Imogen. He knew that, but he was prepared to move on. And yet, seeing her now it was hard to resist rushing over and throwing his arms around her. She was seated at the bar with her back to him. From where he stood, he could see that her hair was a mess. In fact, it looked like a ferret had made it its home. And she was weaving precariously back and forth on the barstool waving around a shot of something in her fist, and loudly belting out *Girls Just Wanna Have Fun* with some crazy drunk lady in a leopard-skin coat.

Fletcher approached Imogen from behind and tapped lightly on her shoulder, startling her and causing her to spin around violently, upending her drink and nearly falling off the stool. Fletcher reached out in time to catch her fall.

"Who are you?" she asked, looking at Fletcher with a squinty eye. "Oh . . . I know you," she said, poking his chest with her finger. "You're Flesher," she said, slurring his name so that it came out sounding like Flesh instead of Fletch. Her speech was garbled and unclear, but Fletcher could make out some of what she was saying. "What are you doin' here, Flesher?"

"I'm here to pick you up Imogen," Fletcher answered, trying to sound reasonable and detached.

The crazy hairdo lady chimed in. "No, nooooo, you can't take my friend away," she moaned. "We're not done singin' yet," she said as she tried to pry Imogen away from Fletcher with one of her long, glittery fingernail-polished claws.

"Yeah!" Imogen nodded in agreement, her head bobbing, "thas right Flesher, me an' this lady here, we are not done singin' yet. And I spilt my drink . . . I need a drink!" Imogen yelled at the bartender.

"She needs a drink!" the woman parroted.

Fletcher managed to pry her fingers from his arm, push her away from Imogen, and interject, "No, she doesn't need another drink. Come on Imogen, let's get you home."

"But I don't wanna go home," Imogen wailed as Fletcher attempted to peel her body off the barstool.

"Yes you do," he told her impatiently. Imogen had managed to wrap her ankles around the post, and between tugging her and the loud shrieks of "let her go," coming from the woman and several of the other bar patrons who had joined in, Fletcher gave up.

"Fine!" he said, exasperated. "Stay here and drink, but don't call me again." He let go of Imogen's arms and she slid unceremoniously off the barstool landing in a lump on the floor. The other drunks cheered as he walked away, but as he was nearing the door, he heard a voice calling out to him.

"Flesher, Flesher, don't leave me here," Imogen whimpered from the floor where he'd left her. Fletcher sighed and walked back over. He lifted Imogen up and managed to get her legs moving.

A boozy chorus of, "Goodbye Imogen," trailed them as they left the bar.

Imogen began to sob. "I sorry Flesher," she said as he half walked, half dragged her out to his car.

"It's okay," Fletcher said, tucking her legs into the passenger side, stretching the seat belt across her chest, and buckling her in. Imogen's head lolled forward as Fletcher shut the door and came around to the driver's side.

"Where's Luxe? Where's my kittycat Flesher," Imogen fussed, her words overlapping.

"Luxe is fine," Fletcher assured her as he started up the car. "Lie back and be good now. I'll get you home."

Home, however, was the wrong word. Imogen immediately straightened up in her seat and bawled, "Home? I don't wanna go home. Take me to the Benson, that's where I wanna go. I wanna go to the Benson."

Fletcher looked over at her. "Why?" he asked, "Why do you want to go to the Benson? Let me take you home Imogen so you can sleep it off."

Imogen was having none of it. A few people had come out of the bar now and were watching them. Imogen's emotional state was quickly escalating and she was inconsolable.

"Take me!" Imogen screamed.

Two guys standing outside the bar who had been observing their exchange strolled over to Fletcher's side and rapped on the car window. Fletcher rolled it down a crack.

"Everything okay in here?" one of them asked suspiciously. "She okay?"

Fletcher nodded, "Yeah, everything is fine; no worries." He nodded at them and they backed away from the car slowly.

Completely frustrated, Fletcher gave in. "Okay, okay, I'll take you wherever you want," he said, impatiently starting up the car and backing out of the parking lot.

Imogen stumbled into the Benson's lobby and immediately shouted, "Room 213!" at the hotel clerk behind the desk. She slumped over the counter and gave him a pleading look.

"I'm sorry ma'am but room 213 is not available," the clerk informed her.

"213, 213, I want room 213," Imogen chanted. "Is that you Marvlin?"

Seeing how drunk the girl in front of him was, the clerk looked over at Fletcher and smirked. Fletcher raised up his hands and said, "Excuse us, just one minute."

Prying the disheveled Imogen away from the desk he led her over to one of the plush lobby chairs, plopping her down into the layer of soft cushions. "Stay," Fletcher commanded before walking back over to the desk.

"I'm sorry, sir, but that room hasn't been cleaned yet," the clerk said.

Fletcher scratched his chin and asked, "Can't you get somebody to clean it up real quick?

"Sorry," the clerk answered, "The maids aren't here yet. They don't come on until midnight."

Exasperated, Fletcher shot the clerk a pleading glance. "Look dude, can you help me out here?" I don't know why she wants that particular room, but clearly it's important to her," Fletcher explained.

"Here," Fletcher reached into his pocket and pulled out a crumpled wad of bills. "Here's an extra $75 bucks, it's all I have on me. You can put the rest on my credit card."

The clerk frowned. "Well, okay, I'll see if I can get someone up there, but it may not be as sanitary, and you'll have to wait for a bit."

Fletcher offered a relieved smile, "That's okay, no problem, we'll wait. Thanks man. I appreciate it."

The clerk nodded and picked up the phone at the desk to call housekeeping.

Fletcher approached Imogen who was still semi-propped up in

the chair. Her head was down, loose hair hanging forward across her face, legs akimbo. Fletcher lifted her chin and Imogen looked up at him through tears.

"Didyougetit?" she asked, her words coming out as one long sentence, "room 213?"

"Yes, I got it," Fletcher assured her. "Good, Imogen said, managing a half smile, her head lolling sideways as she slumped even further into the easy chair.

Ten minutes later, the clerk walked over to where Fletcher was seated. "Sir, room 213 is ready, you can go on up."

Fletcher thanked him and took the passkey. He pulled Imogen from the chair and together they stumbled over to the elevator.

"Where's the lift?" Imogen demanded loudly.

"The lift?" Fletcher looked at her confused. "What lift? What are you talking about now Imogen?"

"The lift, the lift, the gate to take us? It haz to open to go up, up, up!" Imogen's arms were flailing as she reached out.

The elevator doors opened. "I dunno Imogen, just get in," Fletcher said as he pressed her forward.

"The lift, the gate? Where is it?" Imogen's voice trailed off from the quiet lobby as the doors closed leaving the desk clerk shaking his head.

On the second floor, they walked the narrow hallway down to room 213 and Fletcher pushed the card into the slot and Imogen started wailing again, this time it was about the key. "Where's' the key with the little heart; that's not the right key, Flesher," she muttered.

"Just go in Imogen," Fletcher said exasperated, pushing her through the doorway. They entered the room and Imogen looked around. "It's not right," she said.

"What now Imogen? What's not right?" Fletcher asked, irritated.

"The room," she cried, "it's not right. Where is that funny couch and the roses and the face washy bowl thingy?" She pointed at the modern dresser that the TV sat upon. Fletcher, now losing all patience with the drunken Imogen, sat her down on the bed and began to pull her boots off one at a time.

"I don't have a clue what you're ranting about," Fletcher repeated.

"It's not right," Imogen whimpered. He pulled off her socks and her jeans and shirt, turned back the covers, and pushed her inside.

"There," he said, pulling the covers up to her chin and patting her hand like a doting father tucking his stubborn child into bed.

Imogen immediately tossed the covers back, sat up straight, and peered down at the plain white cotton bed cover. "Where did the lace go?" she said angrily.

Stifling an urge to laugh, Fletcher shushed her. "Just sleep it off Imogen," he told her.

Imogen flung her head back onto the pillow, a wisp of matted hair covering her face. But she closed her eyes and within a few minutes Fletcher could hear her softly snoring.

Sometime in the middle of the night or possibly in the wee hours of early morning—she wasn't sure—Imogen woke up confused in the dark, unsure of where or when she was. Instinctively, she reached for a familiar form lying beside her in the bed and burrowed herself against his backside. When he turned and wrapped his arms around her frame, holding her tight, and then kissing her, she kissed back. "Oh Simon," she mumbled.

Fletcher stopped mid-smooch and firmly pushed her away. "No," he said. "We can't do this." Imogen muttered something unintelligible, rolled over on her side, and promptly fell back to sleep. Fletcher got up, dressed in the dark, and crept out of room 213, leaving Imogen alone to sleep it off.

Wherever the heck she was, the room was super bright and even though Imogen refused to open her eyes to face morning, she couldn't ignore the incessant rata-tat tapping sound of someone knocking at the door that had awakened her from a deep, intoxication-induced slumber. She felt completely discombobulated. Last night was like a hazy dream. Where was she anyway? The inside of her mouth was dry as the Saharan desert. She needed water, stat.

Squinting, she could barely make out the time projected on the ceiling from the soft glow of the digital clock: 8:28 a.m.

Too early," she mumbled turning over on her side and pulling the pillow around her ears to drown out the knocking. Reaching out, she ran her hand along the sheets to feel if anyone else was in the bed with her. Nope. She was alone. Well, that was probably a good thing, she thought. She vaguely remembered being put to bed by someone. Who was it? Someone from the bar? Jesus, she could not remember. The last thing she recalled was drinking shots and singing songs with some lady with crazy hair and ruby red lips.

The tapping started up again. "Okay, okay," she said, annoyed. Throwing the covers back, she scooted off the bed and stood up. Instantaneously, the room became a funhouse, spinning round and around. "Oh shit," she said, collapsing back onto the bed. She brought her hands up to her face and rubbed her eyes and head. Clearly, getting up was going to suck, but whoever was banging on the door wasn't going away.

After sitting for a few seconds, she made a second, slower attempt at standing up. She eased herself up to a standing position, slowly this time, and holding on to the bed for support. She still felt a little lightheaded, but the room had stopped spinning around like a top. She made an unsteady path to the door where she stood on her tiptoes and peeked through the peephole. It was a hotel person, Imogen surmised, because he was wearing a clean, white shirt with a name badge.

"Just a minute," she called out in a raspy, drank-too-much-Whiskey-infused voice. Without time to locate her clothes, Imogen turned around and yanked the blanket from the bed, wrapping herself up tight in it like a burrito before unlatching the door. When she flung the door open, the hotel employee stepped back, startled by the disheveled hot mess standing before him wrapped up, probably naked underneath, in only a blanket.

"Um, um," the dude stammered uncomfortably. "I'm very sorry to bother you, miss."

Her head was beginning to ache, she could really use some water, and she had to pee. "Look . . ." Imogen narrowed her eyes and squinted at his badge, "Sean . . . can you make this quick?" she said dully.

"Uh, yeah sure, okay," Sean spluttered, "Are you Imogen Oliver," he asked. Impatient, Imogen bobbed her head up and down. "We've been waiting for you to show up," Sean said.

"Excuse me?" Imogen said, confused and a little annoyed. Why did that statement make her feel like she was receiving a welcome to hell notice from the Hotel California? "Waiting for me to show up? What the hell are you talking about?" Imogen asked.

With that, Sean produced a stack of weathered, yellowing envelopes bound with an old ribbon and extended them for her to take. Imogen unfolded her other arm from inside the blanket, tucking the end in on one side to keep it from falling down.

"What is this?" she asked as she took the letters from him.

"Take a look," said Sean.

The letters made a crunchy sound as Imogen gently rifled through them. Each letter, about eight in all, was written in old fashioned cursive with real ink, and all the envelopes were neatly addressed to her.

"Where did these come from?" Imogen asked.

Sean explained that they had been locked up in the hotel safe for years, along with a handwritten note instructing whomever was in charge at the time to hand-deliver them to Imogen Oliver, who, when she showed up, would be staying in room 213.

"Thank you," Imogen said, still gazing trance-like at the letters, forgetting all about the hotel employee.

"You're welcome," Sean called out as the door closed in his face. Quickly remembering her manners, she opened up the door again.

"Oh sorry," she said, "just a sec." Imogen ran about the room frantically trying to locate her purse, finally finding it shoved underneath the chair. Pulling out $2 she hurried back and tipped him.

She closed the door and backed up to the edge of the bed to sit down, holding the letters in her lap. Despite being well preserved in a safe for more than a century, the edges were turning yellow and cracking in spots. It seemed so bizarre to think that not so very long ago, she had been in the place where these came from, when the paper was crisp and fresh and new. Extracting one of the letters from the envelope, Imogen carefully opened it. Of course, it was from Simon: *My beloved Imogen*, it began in his familiar expressive manner. She could picture him saying the words out loud as she read them:

I fear I will never see you again. I beg your forgiveness for the unkind words I said. I never meant to harm you. Please give me a second chance to make amends. Come back to me. Forever yours, Simon.

He must have left them there for her at the front desk of the Benson, hoping that she would return. As she read the words, tears began to flow down her cheeks. She could go back, she supposed. But she'd given it a shot, and as much as she loved Simon, was it worth it to sacrifice herself? Give up who she was, relinquish her needs and disappear into his world? Grammy had come back because she said she wanted to give her parents grandchildren. Now that she knew her own parents were still out there somewhere, would she want to give them grandbabies someday as well?

With a million what-if's dancing around inside her head, she laid the letters aside and slumped backward atop the expansive king-size hotel bed. Glancing over at the clock she noticed a piece of paper on the nightstand. She reached across the bed and grabbed it. It was a note from Fletcher: *Imogen, Hope you feel better tomorrow. Dropping Luxe off at your house tonight.*

She dropped the note on her chest and lying there on her back, staring up at the uninteresting plastered ceiling, that in another time had been elaborately trussed with carved bosses, stenciled decorations, and mirrors, Imogen contemplated what to do next.

40

His mouth, formed in a perfect "O", Marvin shot a swift glance at Otis, whose eyes, like Marvin's mouth, were wide as the Grand Canyon. Otis turned to look at Simon, who could only shake his head in stunned disbelief. All three gaped at the empty spot where only moments before, Leeroy Jenkins had been standing in the flesh before completely vanishing into thin air!

"My lord," Otis gasped.

"Where did he go?" Marvin asked. Simon nervously twisted his ponytail into a tight knot with his finger.

"What do you suppose he meant, Mr. Elliot," Marvin said, "when he said she was from the future?"

Dropping back down on the edge of the bed, Simon stroked the small patch of hair on his chin with his thumb and index finger as he tried to make sense of what had just happened. But as he sat there pondering it, the creeping realization that Imogen was gone, perhaps for good, trumped Simon's need for immediate answers surrounding Jenkins' strange departure.

But Simon stood up and proffered an explanation. "Gentleman, I have no idea what happened here, but the only conclusion I can come to is that Mr. Jenkins ran from the room."

Marvin was incredulous. "Ran outta the room? How? He evaporated into thin air. We all saw it!"

Otis, nodding his head up and down in agreement with the wiry desk clerk said, "Yes, we all saw, Mr. Elliot."

Simon looked back and forth at both men before evenly stating, "What we thought we saw here . . . did not happen. Jenkins ran from the room. We simply didn't notice."

Marvin and Otis regarded each other for an instant before they both nodded, acknowledging what Simon was getting at. Who would believe their story? Nobody, that's who.

Before Marvin closed the door to room 213 and locked it, Simon scooped up the Brownie No. 2—Imogen's camera—from the bed and he left the Benson Hotel. For the next month, he went through the motions of eating, sleeping, going to and from his daily job as principal at the Normal school. He had spoken to Georgia Bitgood a few times in passing, but she had been as sullen and quiet as he had, much changed from the loud, aggressive woman of before, and neither spoke of Imogen. Each week, Simon sat down and composed a letter to his beloved, leaving it with Marvin at the front desk at the Benson in the hope that she might return.

And every week when he dropped it off he asked Marvin the same question, "Has she been here?" and each time Marvin sadly shook his head, no.

Four weeks later when Simon arrived at the hotel he was surprised to find it bedecked in Christmas finery. Above the revolving doors, a huge wreath of conifer branches adorned with holly, pinecones, and sprays of berries beckoned lodgers inside the warm and showy lobby where a towering fir tree festooned with shimmering ornaments of jingle bells and candles and cherubs was the centerpiece. A snow-filled diorama of a Christmas village, complete with buildings and a church and tiny people ice-skating on a frozen pond sat on the mantle of the stone fireplace, surrounded by a bevy of bright red poinsettias.

Consumed with despair, Simon had managed to completely forget all about Christmas. Rather than making him feel festive and enthusiastic about the new year, the swags of greenery with pine-cone and burlap bows and garlands woven through them that trailed down the banisters of the grand staircase, leading up to room 213 especially, had the opposite affect—he felt even more despondent. He had hoped he and Imogen would be spending the holidays together as a couple, two ardently in love individuals merrily window shopping, taking a ride in the horse-drawn sleigh through downtown, making snow angels, ice skating in the park, perhaps decorating their own small tree together. Without her, those dreams were dead and gone.

After dropping off another letter and getting the nod from Marvin that he'd come to expect, Simon stepped out onto the sidewalk in front of the hotel. In contrast to the cheery, joyful scene he'd left inside, outside it was cold and dreary, the sky a drab slate. When a light snow began to fall, Simon turned up the collar on his tweed jacket and began the long slog back to his flat.

Like every other day since Imogen had gone away, as he walked along, Simon replayed everything over and over in his mind. In particular, he couldn't seem to shake Jenkins' strange parting words, "Didn't she tell you? She's from the future." The future. How could that be? Simon wondered. Frankly, the idea that time travel might actually exist thrilled him, but how was it achieved? And where was the time machine? The improbability of it messed with his head when he thought about it too long.

All things considered though, it was beginning to make impossible sense—Imogen's abrupt comings and goings; her odd remarks on topics for which Simon had no natural knowledge; her quirky ideas about women's roles and how they ought to be treated; and, of course, Leeroy Jenkins's curious exodus. It was all quite mysterious and inexplicable, yet as he mulled things over, memories of his own mother's unusual mannerisms and snatches of conversations from long ago crept into his consciousness, and there was no denying the similarities she and Imogen shared. And although his mother had never said it outright, he sensed that her obsession with having their pictures taken, plus the fact that there were no photographs to show for that effort, might have something to do with all this, as crazy as it sounded, with traveling through time.

The wisps of petite snowflakes that had been wafting gently

down from the dark sky earlier when Simon emerged from the hotel had turned now into fat spiraling masses of wet, bent on assaulting his eyebrows and lashes and cheeks and nesting in his collar and hair. An arctic wind had blown up too and as he trudged along, still wholly absorbed in his own thoughts, Simon breezed right past the camera store, not realizing his blunder until he nearly smashed into a hard brass light post planted at the corner of 10th and Mill, a good several yards beyond the store. Backtracking, he returned and entered the establishment. A soothing blast of warm air pleasantly slapped Simon in the face when he opened the door and a bell attached to it alerted Mr. Donovan, who was busily sorting items for the display window.

"Simon!" he shouted gaily as he made a beeline toward him. For an elderly gentleman with chronic rheumatoid arthritis plaguing both knees, he shuffled over quickly, grasping Simon's hand with an unexpectedly robust grip.

"How are ye?" he asked.

"I am well," Simon answered, even though his declaration was mostly a lie.

"Have ye heard any news of young Imogen?" Donovan asked eagerly.

Simon's shoulders flagged and he shook his head. "No, I'm afraid not, Mr. Donovan."

When Imogen had disappeared, no one thought to notify her employer. When she didn't show up for work, Mr. Donovan became understandably worried. Finally, after several days, he went searching for her at the hotel and the hotel clerk directed him to contact Simon. Although he was relieved that nothing bad had befallen her, he was downhearted to learn that she had gone away. He had not only lost a suitable employee, but someone who had reminded him of his poor, unfortunate daughter, who back in Ireland, had succumbed to smallpox before her 16th birthday.

"Aye, she may not have been Gaelic like my Fianna Maire" he said, "but Imogen, she had the sparkle of an Irish lass in those blue eyes!"

Simon had not thought about Imogen in that way, but come to think of it, yes, she did have an exceptional spark. Arguably, before Imogen, life had been uninteresting and mostly predictable. Like an endless road to nowhere stretching out before him, Simon envisioned a life of marriage to Georgia Bitgood, a slew of children, and the drudgery of working as a school principal until he was old and gray and could work no more.

Simon was lost again in thought when he heard Mr. Donovan ask, "What can I do for ye today, Simon?"

"Oh, yes," he said, looking up. "Forgive me, I was thinking of something else." He dug a receipt from his coat pocket and laid it on the counter in front of Mr. Donovan. "I've come to pick up the photographs I dropped off a few weeks ago."

Mr. Donovan brought the note up closer to his eyes for a better look. "Yes, yes, they came back yesterday," he said, turning and scurrying to the back room to retrieve them. A few minutes later he returned with a small package with the name KODAK stamped in bold black letters on the front.

Several weeks earlier, on a whim Simon had decided it was high time to see what was on the Brownie No. 2 Imogen had left behind. Admittedly, he was also quite curious to see what she had been photographing; it seemed like she took the camera with her everywhere, which made it a mystery why she would leave it behind. Unless she couldn't take it with her? he speculated. Or was it because it was a gift from him and she perhaps wanted no reminders of their relationship? At any rate, convinced she probably wouldn't be returning for it anytime soon, he left the 120-film roll at the store for Mr. Donovan to send off to Kodak for processing.

Mr. Donovan slipped the package across the counter to Simon, but as though petrified to open it, Simon stood silently observing it for a moment until Donovan finally said, "That will be two dollars, Simon."

"Oh, of course," Simon replied, fishing out coins from his pocket and placing them in Mr. Donovan's outstretched palm.

"Thank you, sir," he said, quickly grabbing up the bundle and turning around to leave. He sensed that Donovan was also curious about what was in the photos, but Simon was reluctant to share. He wasn't sure how he would react to potentially seeing her face in one of the images, and the last thing he wanted was to give in to his emotions in front of Mr. Donovan.

Before opening the door to go, Simon turned back, and raised his hand in a gesture of so long. "Thank you again, Mr. Donovan."

Donovan returned a sympathetic smile at Simon and returned the wave.

Alone in his cramped kitchenette, Simon gazed at the package from Kodak that had been sitting there for two days. Yes, he had been avoiding it: he had to go to work, he had to go to bed, he had to eat, he had to pick up the post, no time now, got to go. But with a heavy sigh, he reached over, picked it up, and unwrapped the stack of about 15 or 16, two and a quarter, by three and a quarter-inch black-and-white pictures.

The first picture was of a young girl wearing a sailor suit of the type his female students wore. She was smiling, her head tilted slightly and resting against the railing of what looked like a bridge, a river flowing behind. He regarded the next few—busy street scenes of blurry moving cars and horses and people; children playing on the sidewalk; people throwing pennies into the fountain at the plaza; the cathedral ceiling at the Benson. They seemed ordinary in their simplicity, but Imogen clearly had an eye for composition, because the angles and the position of the subjects gave them a definite rule of thirds, artsy feel.

Even Simon, who was not exactly a patron of the arts, could tell that these should be enlarged and hanging in a gallery some-where. He flipped to the next picture. It was Imogen. Through the magic of photography, he could look upon her sweet face over and again—the spray of tiny freckles zigzagging across her nose, that tiny gap between her teeth that she'd shown him how she could spit water through once. What had she called it? Her mad skill? Looking at her now in a photo reminded him of how much he had lost.

Why did he say it? Why had he been such a horse's ass? If Jenkins was correct and she was from the future, how far into the future? Far enough that women might actually share equality with men? It was true, women were making progress in their fight for the right to vote. If she came from a time where even that was taken for granted, of course she would have had difficulty adjusting to this time.

With much melancholy and regret, Simon reluctantly set the photo of Imogen aside. The next two were candid shots of the two of them together. They were standing on the sidewalk outside the camera shop. He remembered that day well. She had asked Mr. Donovan if he would take a photograph of them together. In the first she had tried to stay still and serious, but at the last second, he had pinched her side making her giggle, which caused the photograph to come out blurry. But even with the blur, her vibrant disposition was on fearless display—a woman who was smart and funny and full of life, and always up for spontaneous adventure. A tear escaped Simon's eye and rolled down his cheek. Not since he was a child had he allowed himself to cry, but he broke down now and wept as he stared into the lovely face of his beloved Imogen, with whom he'd probably never see again. If what he suspected was true, he would be long dead before she was ever born.

Planning to skim through the rest of the photos later, Simon started to set them aside, but one other caught his eye and he brought it up close to take a better look. Even though it was grainy and shot from a distance, he could clearly make out who it was. Seated on a bench at the train station, there was no mistaking that it was Leeroy Jenkins and he was leaning in toward Georgia. He took a closer look at several others and in nearly every one, Jenkins could be seen lurking somewhere in the background. Curious. Who was this fellow? And why was he so interested in Imogen and Georgia?

The first time he'd run into him was at the lecture on evolution—the same time he met Imogen. It appeared that he always showed up when Imogen was present. And why were they both attending a lecture by Doran, a person with whom Simon was also curious about? What was the connection? Simon wondered how Doran fit into this. He had gone to the lecture himself to find answers, but abandoned those plans after meeting Imogen.

Perhaps H.L. Doran was the key. Simon snatched up the loose photos, tucking them together into a neat stack, and stowed them in his vest pocket. If Herbert Doran was still around, he would find him.

41

Exhausted, disheveled, and hungover after last night's embarrassing lapse in judgment—how many shots had she taken? She couldn't remember, Imogen thought as she pushed the door of the late model Honda Civic open and got out, thanking Stanley, the nice, but overly chatty retired Uber driver for the ride, and handing him a $10 tip. She'd made the mistake of telling him that she had overindulged last night. The result: Stanley regaling her with half a dozen or more tales of his own drunken, wayward youth. Fascinating as it was, it was difficult for Imogen to focus much when it felt like an atomic bomb was exploding between her temples. Now she remembered why she had finally taken her own "I'll never drink again" advice and now only partook of the occasional foo-foo, umbrella embellished mixed cocktail.

"Remember," Stanley called out to her as she turned to walk away, "lemon tea and dry toast." Imogen offered up a weak smile and nodded, not entirely convinced that Stanley's hangover home remedy would work, but willing to at least give it a try.

"It's the first thing I'll do," she said, giving him a small wave and heading in the direction of her car, the only vehicle left in the dirty, water filled pot-hole laden Froggies parking lot, the result of an overnight downpour that made everything in the world appear more gritty and dreary than usual, according to Imogen.

Opening the passenger side door, she carefully laid the fragile stack of papyrus on the seat. Glancing over at them every few minutes or so, Imogen put the car in gear and headed in the direction of aspirin, ice water, couch, blanket, and maybe lemon tea and dry toast if she had the energy, in that order.

After first carefully securing the letters in an acid-free box to protect them from decaying any further, Imogen popped a couple of aspirin and headed straight for the couch where she quickly dozed off. When she awoke later and checked the time on her phone, it was late afternoon.

"Oh shit," she groused rolling back on the couch. She'd slept the day away, but rest had helped a lot. Her head, reduced now to a mere annoying dull ache, was no longer pounding, but her stomach felt a little queasy.

Imogen got up and traipsed into the kitchen. Rummaging through her cupboard, in the back she found a box of lemon tea. Although she was more of a coffee person, she had kept some around for her friend Rachael, who was a big tea drinker. It also reminded her of Simon, who was a connoisseur of tea—Earl Grey to be exact. They had this ongoing tea vs. coffee debate that ran the gamut from age, origin myths, and controversies to varieties and popularity. Had he known she was a barista she might have told him that the future held more than just coffee: black; that there were hundreds of different varieties of exotic and designer beans and a multiplicity of coffee drinks—macchiatos, cortados, Frappuccinos, espressos, lattes and cappuccinos. It was an engaging topic of discussion that they purposely knew would never be resolved, yet they loved arguing endlessly over it. It made her feel sad thinking about it, yet she couldn't help smiling at the happy memory.

After filling up the teapot with tap water and putting it on the stove to boil, she popped a piece of bread into the toaster. Standing in the kitchen, she all at once remembered the note Fletcher had left about dropping Luxe off. Where was he? Normally, he would greet her at the door, wrapping his tail around her leg, and mewing for supper. Had he been here when she got home? She hadn't noticed.

"Luxe, Luuuuuxe," Imogen called out as she walked throughout the house checking the closets and under the bed, "here kitty, kitty. Where are you, Luxey?"

The high-pitched escalating whine and loud hissing of steam emanating from the kettle's spout summoned her quickly back into the kitchen to remove it from the burner. Where was that cat anyway? She wondered. She wasn't terribly worried . . . yet. He always showed up eventually when he got hungry enough. Luxe wasn't one of those pampered inside cats, content to sit in the window all day and watch the world outside go by. He was independent as hell and he liked to roam. Hmmm, that sounded familiar. Trying to make him do something he didn't want to do was like, well . . . herding cats. When he wanted out, he yowled, loudly. It was probably the most annoying sound Imogen had ever encountered. Even if she didn't want him to go out, she eventually gave in because he just would not stop the obnoxious mewing until she did. After pouring the boiling hot water into her mug and drowning the teabag in it, she grabbed the piece of toast, put it on a plate, and sat down at the kitchen table to eat.

Imogen took a sip of the warm tea, deeply breathing in the healing properties of the lemony aroma and then taking another bite of the plain toast. It was a dash bland, but Stanley had been right, it was fixing the queasiness in her stomach. Plus, she hadn't eaten anything since yesterday, so getting something down was probably a good idea anyway.

Now that she was feeling better, she wanted nothing more than to delve into the rest of the letters that Simon had sent. After hollering for Luxe out both front and back doors, she finally gave up and headed to the bedroom and the box that contained the eight letters. Before Grammy had died she'd been in the process of preserving Imogen's parent's photographs and memorabilia in acid-free paper and boxes. That way, the clerk at the craft store had explained in great detail, they wouldn't yellow and disintegrate.

Imogen folded her legs up lotus style on the bed and opened up the box, carefully lifting the bundle of letters out, pushing the box aside, and placing them in front of her. She opened a yellowing letter, which was dated eight weeks ago . . . well, eight weeks and give or take a hundred years, she noted.

In Simon's fine handwritten script, it read:

My Dearest Imogen, How might I begin to sincerely apologize for the dreadful words I spoke to you? I am ashamed that such crass terms escaped my lips. I understand that you must surely think that I was speaking what I believed to be true of you, but I hope, nay, implore you to please believe me when I tell you I do not think ill of you. You are the most delightful, beautiful, intelligent creature I have, or shall ever meet again. Wherever you have chosen to go, Imogen, if you can find it in your heart, please consider returning, if only to let me explain myself and to beg your forgiveness.

Yours Respectfully, Simon Le Bon Elliot

Imogen imagined Simon seated at his oak principal's desk, taking his fancy pen and dipping it into the black inkwell, his hand moving across the clean white paper with flourish, the way he did everything. As she read through the first few letters, it moved her that he was laying his heart bare—probably something that a gentleman of that time was quite unaccustomed to doing. After a few letters, Imogen could no longer stifle her tears. Every deeply expressed "I want you," every excruciating "I love you," every "I need you Imogen," felt like a thousand daggers stabbing straight through her heart. Flinging her body dramatically backward onto the bed, she pressed the letters against her chest, and sobbed; great big, wet, amplified, pitiful forlorn sobs; not-caring-if-the-neighbors-hear sobs; bawling like a motherless child.

"Goddamn it Simon," she heard herself howling into the empty corners of the room. "Why does everything have to be so hard?" she cried out, turning over on her stomach and burying her face in the pillow to cry some more. She felt silly and dramatic being this emotional, despite the fact that she was all alone. No one could hear her, and maybe that was the point. She rolled back over on her back and stared up at the ceiling to let that thought sink in.

Squinting, she trained her eyes on the area of the ceiling where the patterns of plaster formed what looked like a skull if you looked at it one way, or three skulls if you looked another, and at yet another angle it was a beastly kitty that sort of resembled the Cheshire cat in *Alice in Wonderland*, glowering down at her.

The phenomenon, commonly known as pareidolia, was the

reason why people claimed that Jesus magically appeared on their grilled cheese sandwich, or they saw unicorns or angels or whales within cloud formations, or a human face on Mars. Humans cognitively look for patterns in objects, whether real or imagined and Imogen had been doing it since she was a kid. To the skulls and the beastly cat, she repeated the word again out loud: "Alone; I'm all alone in the world, an orphan," she said sadly. Grammy was gone. Jade was gone. Parents, somewhere, but gone, nonetheless, and she had no clue where to even begin to look for them. They might as well be dead. She did have Fletcher and Rachael, but only sometimes.

In the middle of her anguish, Imogen felt a rough, sandpaper like thing touch her arm. "Meow." Imogen turned to look. "Luxe!" she squealed, sitting up and scooping him up in her arms. "You're back! Where have you been you bad, bad kitty," she scolded him half-heartedly through her tears as she burrowed her face in his fur.

"Meow," Luxe replied, nuzzling up close and letting her stroke his soft fur coat. Yep, she had missed this cat a lot. For the next hour, Luxe stuck to her like glue. Poor kitty, he had truly missed her, too. She could tell. He'd even brought her a gift, a small garter snake that he dropped proudly at her feet. Even if he was only a cat, it was almost as though he could sense that his mistress was sad and heartbroken.

After a while, Imogen felt better and was able to pull herself together and read through the rest of the letters. With each one she began to notice his pleading became less intense, as though he had gotten past the initial pain and was coming to accept that she would not be returning, but in the last letter, clearly something else had changed, like Simon had uncovered something.

It was brief and to the point:

Imogen, I have information of dire import to relay. Look nearby for photographs of a woman and a child and find out what you can about Crestview Sanitarium. If these letters are finding their way to you, please find a way to return!
Lovingly, Simon

Crestview Sanitarium. Where had she heard that name before?

Oh yes, of course, Doran had mentioned it. He had said that he had had something to do with sending a few people that he thought were in need of psychiatric care there, but had later regretted it. And Simon's mother had been sent there. She wasn't sure how Simon expected her to relay the information without taking it back to him in person, but she'd think about that later. Imogen loved a mystery and she loved research.

Luxe was not happy when Imogen pushed him off his cozy spot nestled on her chest, but even a roll onto the bed wasn't enough to disturb his nap. He spun around in a circle a couple of times before settling into the cushy blanket and turning himself into a furry ball, content knowing his owner was nearby.

She started with a search on turn of the century sanitariums. The search engine returned pages and pages of hits, and like any new topic that piqued her interest Imogen got easily sucked into reading about the history of mental illness. It turned out that calling a hospital a sanitarium was really just a nice word they used to gloss over its darker operation as a lunatic asylum. Calling it a sanitarium made it sound pleasant, like a nice place for rehabilitation and recovery, a day spa, if you will, when in reality it was a place for locking up anyone unfortunate enough to be regarded "mad," many of whom were women with no influence in the matter. Whatever male person was in "charge" of her, be it a husband, her father, a brother, he could legally have her committed for any old innocuous infraction like say, being disobedient or for infidelity. Using the lunacy laws on the books at the time, men had a perfectly acceptable and legal way of conveniently ridding themselves of their female partners!

Imogen was shocked to read about one lunatic asylum in West Virginia that listed examples of some of the symptoms of mental illness that could be used against patients: laziness, egotism, disappointed love, female disease, mental excitement, greediness, imaginary female trouble, quackery, jealousy, religion, masturbation, bad habits, to name a few. And they were subjected to all manner of "cures," from hydrotherapy—cold or hot baths—and douches to cure hysteria to applying leeches to the temples to treat what they called "cerebral congestion." Many were restrained by straitjackets and chains or sentenced to prolonged solitary confinement. Horrible things.

Starting around the mid-1930s patients were guinea pigs for electroshock therapy and lobotomies, a procedure that involved drilling two holes in the patient's skull and inserting a sharp tool into the brain, which was swept left to right to sever the connections between the frontal lobe. Imogen remembered reading about Rosemary Kennedy, sister of President John F. Kennedy who had undergone a prefrontal lobotomy when she was 23 because of mood swings and violent outbursts. The procedure failed and Rosemary's mental capacity was diminished to that of a two-year old, resulting in institutionalization for the rest of her life.

Before the introduction of asylums, mentally ill people were usually hidden away under the care of relatives. The first asylums were set up with humanitarian intentions as places that could care for the mentally ill and potentially cure them. However, good intentions were lost amidst the increasing asylum population, inadequate staff, and lack of understanding of mental health. The overcrowded public hospitals were often unsanitary and had bars on the windows. The staff was poorly paid and frequently treated patients harshly. Imogen remembered Grammy telling her about her sister Lillian's mental illness. They had not resorted to sending her away to one of these horrible places, but being hidden away without getting the proper care, she ended up killing herself anyway. It was fascinating reading and like most historical topics that interested her, Imogen spent a good amount of time immersed in it.

Finally, after she'd pretty much exhausted the subject, and remembering again why she had started researching asylums to begin with, Imogen typed Crestview Sanitarium and the name of the city into the search engine. She discovered, that the hospital had been shut down in the early 1960s and the building had been converted to what was now the town museum.

Simon had also said to look for photographs. Hmmm, I wonder, Imogen pondered as she got up and made her way down the hallway to the guest bedroom. Pulling the step stool over, she climbed up, reaching back into the far corner of the shelf in the closet and pulling out the shoebox where she'd placed the old tin box labeled "Studio photos." Imogen carried the box over to the bed and plopped down next to Luxe, who was too lazy to stir from his tight ball. When he heard Imogen lifting the lid of the box though, he lifted his head up and mewed. Getting into boxes and tote bags and open doors and drawers was Luxe's favorite pastime, but when he started to make a move to get in it, Imogen pushed him away. "No," she said sternly. Denied, he busied himself with a bath instead.

It had been several years since she'd looked at these, right after Grammy's funeral, as a matter of fact. After learning that her parents were still alive, she had gone out to the studio, which had been shuttered since they disappeared. Inside, she'd found this tin hidden inside the wall. At the time, she thought it was strange, but she had been so wracked with grief over Grammy's death and trying to keep up with college, she didn't have time or energy to think about what they might mean or who these people might be. She had put them up in the back part of the closet and forgotten about them, until now.

All of the photos appeared to be of the same curly-haired woman, but clearly taken at different times and locations. In one, she stood solemn and alone and extremely pregnant in front of what looked like a barn. In others, there was a child. In another, the child was an infant and in several later ones, perhaps the same child as a toddler, and then the boy about six or seven years old.

A couple were professional studio shots, expensive in those days, but most were taken inside in what appeared to be a living room where she was sometimes seated; in others standing. In one with the baby, she stood next to a large hearth. Several framed photographs of people graced the mantle. Others were taken outside. In one, she was standing next to a large tree; in another on a bridge overlooking a river, and the one at the barn. It seemed that most of the photos were nonspecific in nature; they could be anywhere, but one of the outside shots caught her eye. In this particular one, the woman and the boy, who was older in this shot, stood together on the steps of a building. Imogen brought the photo up closer to her eyes and squinted. Behind them was a plaque with some sort of writing on it.

Imogen leapt off the bed and ran out to the living room to look for a magnifying glass, sending an alarmed Luxe scampering. She found one in Grammy's organization caddy, filled with pens and pencils and other odd assortment of necessities like a sewing kit and paper clips and tweezers that she had always kept handy near the couch. She returned to the bedroom with the magnifying glass and held it over the photo. Although the boy was blocking part of it and it was a little blurry, Imogen could make out several words: "Crestview Sa . . ." Imogen gulped. With the magnifying glass still trained on the photo, she noticed something else. The boy looked a lot like Simon—the dark hair, the brooding, sad eyes—it was uncanny. The woman, presumably the boy's mother, had one hand on the boy's shoulder and the other was touching her hair, her index finger looped around a curly strand.

42

Simon stood at the top of the rickety second-story hallway and rapped on Herbert Doran's door. Finding Doran had been a much easier task than he thought it would be. A quick inquiry at the postal office was all it took. The postmaster directed him to this address, a rented a flat over the mercantile in town. Frankly, Simon was underwhelmed with his lodging. For an accomplished speaker such as Doran, Simon had expected him to reside in something a bit more stately. He raised his hand to knock again when the door opened and Doran peered out.

Simon quickly introduced himself. "Hello, Mr. Doran. My name is Simon Le Bon Elliot."

"What can I do for you Mr. Elliot?" Doran inquired without fully opening the door.

"I am here to find out about my mother," Simon said candidly. "Tiffany Rose Elliot was her name. I think you might have information about her."

Doran guardedly emerged from behind the door.

"Come in, Mr. Elliot," he said, a trace of melancholy seeping into his voice as he ushered Simon inside the apartment. "I've been expecting you."

The interior of the apartment was larger and more impressive than it appeared from the outside. Nothing fancy—a hook rug on the floor, a few chairs, a comfortable-looking davenport; but the most impressive component, the two full walls lined completely from floor to ceiling with shelves full of books.

"Please," Doran said gesturing for Simon to sit.

Simon sat down on a wingback chair, which was much more comfortable than it appeared.

"Can I get you anything?" Doran asked. "Tea? A Coca-Cola?"

"Tea would be lovely," Simon said, reminding him fondly of the endless debates with Imogen over the merits of tea over coffee.

"Tea it is," Doran said. As he turned and headed toward the kitchen, Simon noticed that he walked with a slowed pace and his shoulders seemed to concave. He had also observed that Doran's appearance was markedly changed. His hair was longer and a bit unkempt, and he now had a shaggy, untrimmed beard. He also appeared drawn and haggard, tired; so unlike the fiery, charismatic lecturer with the booming voice he remembered from a few years ago.

Simon heard the whistle from the kettle going off and a few minutes later, Doran emerged from the kitchen carrying two steaming mugs of hot tea, which he set down on the small wooden table located between Simon's chair and the one Doran had now occupied.

"Sugar?" Doran asked, offering it up from a dainty, rose-patterned canister that was already on the table.

"No thank you," Simon replied. He preferred honey in his tea, but was not inclined to ask Doran to get up and go get it even if he had it.

Even though it hadn't infused completely, Simon took a small sip of his tea and nodded. It wasn't Earl Grey, but it was good. Did he detect a hint of chestnut?

"How do you like it?" Doran asked. Despite his diminished stature, the man's voice still carried the deep timbre of his former self. Simon nodded.

"It is Gu Zhang Mao Jian," he said, "a green tea harvested on the banks of Qiushiu River in the Wuyi Mountains of China."

Wrapping his hands around the mug, Doran inhaled the aromatic steam, took a dainty sip of the hot brew, closed his eyes briefly indicating his approval of the blend, and then set the cup down gently on a saucer on the table. He glanced up at the ceiling for a minute before speaking, "Now that we have the pleasantries out of the way, Mr. Elliot allow me to tell you a story," he said, leaning back into his chair, folding his arms together, and crossing his legs. "A story about your mother, Tiffany Rose."

"I first laid eyes on Tiffany Rose in August, 1885," he began. "Ripe with child, she was seated third row center in the sweltering heat of the tent, sweating so profusely her skin glowed as she furiously fanned herself with the paper revival program. It wasn't only her lovely unkempt mane of natural curls or the fact that she was pregnant that caught my attention, it was that she was unaccompanied.

"In those days I was what they called a fire and brimstone preacher. My daddy, also a minister, encouraged it and I was fired up with the spirit of the lord and looking to save souls!" he said with a chuckle. "My sermons were filled with dire warnings of the consequences of sin, of judgment and eternal damnation, and the glory of repentance. We'd come to a town and set up the big tent and people from all over flocked to the meetings. At revival, the tent shook with praise music from a trio that played fiddles and tambourines. I'd whip the congregation into a collective frenzy of amens and hallelujahs, and when they were so overcome by the power of the Holy Spirit, almost all of them would rush forward to confess their sins and beg Jesus for salvation. It was a good show.

"Afterward, individuals would step forward to offer testimony about the ways that God had intervened in their lives. We'd wrap it up with a stirring closing hymn like *How Great Thou Art* or *The Old Rugged Cross*, and the crowd would shuffle home feeling uplifted and protected from Satan's temptation for another week, until next Sunday came round.

"On this occasion that I first saw Tiffany Rose, I was immediately struck by her quiet grace. Although she was noticeably large and uncomfortable with child and trying hard to manage the intense heat, she had a resolute appearance of strength and determination about her that I had never observed in any woman before. Throughout my lively sermon she sat stoically in her chair, slowly waving the fan back and forth, her face never changing expression, even when I hit the high points and the rest of the crowd around her had commenced leaping from their seats, arms lifted heavenward, whirling and gyrating in the aisles. I was captivated by her.

"After the music was over and everyone started filing out of the tent I noticed she was having difficulty getting up out of her chair. She had shifted her large belly sideways and was gripping the chair in front of her trying to ease herself up. I also observed that not one single soul lent a hand to help her. They walked past her as though she was invisible. I straightaway rushed to her side and assisted her in standing upright. She thanked me and turned away, but I had to know, why had she not reacted to my theatrics and compelling speech the way the rest of the crowd had? I lightly touched her arm and she quickly pulled it away as though my slight touch of her skin hurt her. I apologized profusely.

'I am quite sorry, ma'am,' I said, 'I did not intend to startle you.' Without smiling, she looked straight into my eyes and said, 'You are hiding something Preacher Doran.' Of course, I was taken aback. I did not know how to respond. 'Whatever do you mean,' I asked. She handed me a slip of paper with an address written on it. 'Come tomorrow and I'll explain,' she said. It was one of the few times I saw her smile. She turned then and left the tent."

Doran paused and Simon leaned forward in his chair and interjected, "Did you meet her the next day?" he asked, anxious for Doran to continue the story.

"I did," he said.

Doran seemed to enjoy keeping Simon in suspense. He had always loved watching the look of anticipation on the faces in the crowd as they hung on his every word, taking their cues from him. It felt like real power and had he been of the evil persuasion, it would have been easy to manipulate people into doing his bidding. Doran took another sip of his tea, swallowed, and set it back down on the saucer and continued.

"The address led me out to a falling down old farmhouse just on the outskirts of town. When I arrived I found no one home. The place was entirely deserted. Thinking perhaps she had been mistaken about the address, I started to take my leave, but then I heard a voice call out my name. It was her. She was standing inside the door of a barn that, compared to the house, was in good shape. I approached her and as I drew near I noticed that in her hands she was holding what looked to be a small wooden box with a handle and brass devices resembling a compass.

"I was perplexed, but before I could say anything she held it out to me and asked, 'Will you take my photograph please?' Of course, they are commonplace now, but in 1885 I had never seen a hand-held box camera before. 'Where did you get this,' I inquired. I turned the remarkably lightweight box camera around in my hand. It must have been quite costly and I was curious how a young woman, expecting and alone could have possibly come by such a thing. 'Never mind that,' she said irritated, 'please, just take the picture.' I was not sure how to operate it, but after she demonstrated how to hold it and to use the waist-level reflex viewfinder to take the photograph, she toddled over to the barn wall where she posed still and solemn."

Doran sighed deeply before adding, "It was the first of many photographs I would take over the years of your mother . . . and you." He glanced over at Simon to gauge his reaction.

Simon was still leaning forward in his chair, listening intently, elbows on his knees, staring at the floor as if searching his mind for a memory. When he finally looked up at Doran after a few moments, he said, "I remember you. You were Herbie, the candy man."

Herbie was a nickname Tiffany called Doran. Simon held a few nebulous memories of the tall man with the deep voice who sometimes came to their ramshackle house bearing sweets—lemon drops and jelly beans and salt water taffy—things that his mother could never afford.

"Yes," Doran said, nodding.

"But you stopped coming."

"I was married with small children at the time," Doran responded.

Simon nodded with understanding. "You were lovers then," he interrupted.

"No," Doran shot back, "we were not ever that."

Simon was baffled. "But you were married and seeing my mother? I don't comprehend."

Doran smiled. "She was my friend," he said. "My marriage was in trouble long before your mother ever came along." He hung his head and breathed deeply again as though the words he was about to say were made of lead.

"I prefer the company of men," he divulged. "I am a sodomite, a sinner. I should not have married, but I thought if I preached against it long enough and hard enough, it would go away; I'd be cleansed, but unfortunately, it never did."

He looked into Simon's stunned face and said, "Your mother, Simon, she knew without me telling her, but she did not judge me harshly like the others did."

Simon was well aware of the seriousness of sodomy. In some regions, a sodomite could be sent to prison, as was the case of the celebrated playwright and author Oscar Wilde, who in 1895, was convicted of gross indecency with men and imprisoned for two years to hard labor. In other locations, it could mean a death sentence. Despite his initial shock, Simon tried to fathom the backlash Doran must have faced as a minister accused of engaging in such activity.

Doran continued his story. "The truth about me didn't come out until years later when I was caught in a compromising position with a young deacon. I quietly left the ministry, but I lost everything—my wife, my family and friends. And I decided religion was no longer for me. That's when I began studying evolution and lecturing on it." Doran paused and then added, "but Tiffany knew all of my secrets, and she held them close to her, as I did hers."

"Hers?" Simon inquired.

"She told me a wild story Simon, about being pulled through a photograph . . . from another time, from the future. She said a bad man had brought her through and abandoned her here. I didn't believe her, of course, but I humored her because I cared deeply for her. It crossed my mind a time or two that because she was the only one who did not think ill of me, perhaps she truly was from a future where people like me were accepted for who we are, not for who we love. She had this notion that if she left photographs in the vicinity where she had been brought through, someone in the future might find them, come back and rescue her, and take her home."

Simon began to nod his head. It was beginning to make sense

now—the photographs, the odd word choices and obscure cultural references that sometimes slipped out of her mouth. Still, the future? That was a complete impossibility, wasn't it? Another question puzzled Simon. "How did she know that you were hiding something?" he asked.

"Did she know something from the future? I don't know," Doran answered. "Perhaps men like me are more easily identifiable in her time. She never said."

Doran continued. "I do regret that I humored her and encouraged her to leave the photographs, because as the years gathered I came to realize that it was not helping to indulge her. This was not merely some imaginative flight of fancy of hers. She truly believed that she came from the future. Around the same time, a gentleman who said he was a friend of your mother, and an agent of the Society for the Prevention of Abused Children approached me, suggesting that Tiffany was in dire need of mental help. Because I believed in carrying out social gospel, which mandated that as a Christian it was my duty to help people in need and to work to change society as a whole, I pursued his request, and I eventually convinced her that it would be in your best interest to get help. She trusted me."

Now Simon understood. "That was you who came for her, when I was seven, and that's why she didn't put up a fight."

"Yes," Doran said, "As her minister, I signed the papers to have her committed to Crestview Sanitarium. They assured me they'd do everything they could to help her."

"And I was sent away to the orphanage," Simon said sadly.

An awkward silence followed before Simon spoke again. "Is she still there? My mother, is she still at Crestview?"

"I do not know," Doran said. "I visited her on several occasions, but the last time I went to see her, they informed me that she no longer wanted visitors, not me, or anyone."

Tears began to form in the corners of Simon's eyes. Ever since he'd let himself come apart after Imogen left, it was as though the dam had broken, and now the tears came easily and all the time—when he looked at sunsets, heard a particular moving piece of music, petted a cute puppy. It was becoming downright embarrassing. "I must see her," he said, his voice cracking as he wiped his eyes with his sleeve. "How can I see her?"

Doran jumped up from his seat. "We'll go together!"

Simon hesitated. "Wait," he said, motioning for Doran to sit back down. "The agent, who was he?" Simon asked. "What was his name?"

Doran raked his fingers like a comb through his scruffy beard and gazed upward at the ceiling struggling to recall.

"It's been very long ago, but if memory serves, I believe it was something with a 'C'," he said, "Cramer or Crush? Crusher?" He snapped his fingers. "Gordy Crusher. That was it!"

Simon frowned, but withdrew the envelope containing Imogen's photos from his pocket and opened it anyway. "I have something to show you," he said, removing the photos and passing them over to him.

Doran reached out and took the envelope from Simon's hand while simultaneously pulling a pair of reading glasses from his pocket. Scanning several photos he looked back questioningly at Simon.

"Is this the man that came to you about institutionalizing my mother?" Simon asked.

Doran nodded. "Yes, yes that's him, but I don't understand . . . ?"

"What was his motivation for having my mother committed?" Simon asked. "He shows up in nearly every photo, always skulking in the background. I saw him at your lecture talking to Imogen. He was there when Imogen disappeared the first time. He was back when she returned, but he said his name was Leeroy Jenkins. What is his connection to my mother and Imogen?"

Doran leaned back in his chair and scratched his forehead before speaking. "When I met Imogen, she was using an alias, Daphne, I believe it was. She purchased my stereoscopic plates and I recall noticing many similarities between she and your mother," he said. "As farfetched as it sounds Simon, I believe your Imogen and Tiffany Rose may be time travelers from the same time period."

"And Leeroy Jenkins or Gordy Crusher?" Simon asked, "How does he fit into the picture?"

They looked at each other and Doran said, "Do you think he could be the same man that dragged your mother through the photograph?"

"I don't know," Simon said. "but we have to warn Imogen. I don't know why he's following her, but if he was able to track her down here, he may be following her now, wherever . . . or whenever she is now!"

Simon told Doran that he had been leaving letters at the hotel for Imogen for the past few weeks, thinking that she might return, but now the realization that the letters may have to travel across more than a century gave him new understanding about why she had not responded. Doran suggested that if she had returned to her own time, she would likely be at her home and thus unaware that there were letters addressed to her and waiting at the hotel.

"I have an idea," Doran said, "let's go for a drive."

"Where are we?" Simon asked after pulling to the side of the road and cutting the engine on the motorcar.

"This is the place where Tiffany Rose and I left the photographs," Doran said.

Simon glanced around the site at the remnants of an old farmhouse that had fallen in upon itself and a barn that was still intact. It did seem familiar to Simon. He had only been a child, but he had an imprecise memory of this place, of his mother carefully placing photographs around the inside of the barn—some of them up high in the rafters where she climbed up in her long skirt—others near the floor or tucked into a board. Each time they had returned, the photographs from the last time they came were still there where she had left them. When he had asked her why they did this, she had given only a one-word reply: help.

Doran and Simon got out of the motorcar and made their way carefully across the muddy field. It was winter still and cold. The snow had melted, but neither was dressed properly for traipsing through wet and mushy, overgrown fields. When they reached the barn, Simon pulled the heavy door open and peered inside. Silvery cobwebs filled up most of the room, but fortunately the gaps in the weathered barn provided enough shafts of light to illuminate the interior. Simon climbed up in the loft and searched every corner while Doran swept the corners on the ground floor, and as expected they each returned with a handful of photos, although some were in better shape than others.

"Some of these look as though they've been nibbled on by vermin," Simon said to Doran pointing out the gnawed edges.

"The ones I found aren't in terribly bad shape," Doran said as they compared their respective lots. "But if they've deteriorated this much in this fairly short amount of time, it's likely they will not survive the next 100 years."

"Right,' Simon said. "What should we do?"

"I have an idea," Doran said. "Remember, we passed a store on the way out here? We could put them inside empty tins. That way, they will at least be protected from the elements rather than left lying around loose."

Simon liked the idea. They drove the mile or so back to the store and purchased three tins. When they arrived back at the farm, they dumped the tins contents: coffee, baking powder, and tobacco, and placed half of the photos in one, and half in another. The third would be for the latest photos taken by Imogen with the Brownie. Simon pulled the envelope from his vest pocket and was readying to add them to the tin, when he had an idea.

"Perhaps we should leave a message for Imogen in with these?"

"Brilliant, Simon!" Doran said.

Fortuitously, Doran had with him his lever-filler safety pen and ink dropper. Not knowing who the future recipient might be, but hoping that it would work and it was Imogen who found them, Simon's penned messages on the back of several photos read simply:

Who is this man?

43

Although Imogen couldn't be completely certain that the people in the photographs were Simon and his mother, while she still had the magnifying glass out, she decided that it might be prudent to take a closer look at some of the other photos as well to see if she was missing anything. She examined each one carefully with the magnifier, searching for any anomalies. They appeared to all be much the same, that is, except for one. In this particular shot, the woman and the boy were standing by a bridge, the embankment in the background. Along the banks stood several trees, but as she moved the glass in tighter, the details of another person began to emerge. Although his body was partially concealed behind one of the tree trunks, she could see the outline of a man wearing a hat. To her naked eye his face seemed marginally blurry, but magnified, she could identify a few defining features: a rounded face, dark eyes, thin mustache slightly askew.

Imogen gasped. "Oh my god!" It couldn't be, but wow, it sure looked an awful lot like that Leeroy Jenkins character that she kept running into every time she had been back to Simon's time, and the incongruous part, if this was indeed him, was that he looked exactly the same in this older photo as he had a few weeks ago. What was he doing in a photo with this woman? Imogen bit her lip and pondered if what she suspected might be true. This was clearly no ordinary person. It had to be another time traveler. But who was he?

Imogen had an idea. Reaching for her laptop she typed "Leeroy Jenkins" into the search engine. A slew of hits popped up. Of course, she thought, that's why the name sounded so familiar. Leeroy Jenkins was the character name of a player in the video game *World of Warcraft*, who notoriously screwed up a detailed battle strategy with a group of other players. The name could be a coincidence, she thought. When she had asked him about it, she recalled him saying something about being named after his grandfather. On the other hand, only someone from this time, and most likely a computer gamer, would choose that name as an alias, much the way Imogen grabbed names to use from current literature and popular culture.

That time she had taken a stroll with him he had been nothing but charming, although admittedly he made her feel sort of uncomfortable and she wasn't quite sure why, maybe the way it seemed like he was trying way too hard to be familiar with her. It was strange. He didn't seem so much interested in her as a potential date, as much as wanting something from her.

Something strange was going on here. What was the connection between Leeroy Jenkins, Herbert Doran, and this woman, potentially Simon's mother? Imogen had been debating about whether or not to return to 1913. Certainly, Simon would want to have these photos of his mother. Imogen owed him that much, but discovering Leeroy Jenkins in the photos changed everything. She hadn't deluded herself into thinking she was the only one who could time travel. Her grandma and parents had been able to, so surely there must be others. She'd just never encountered anyone else. It was settled then, she'd take the photos back, although she realized she wouldn't be able to take the originals back because they already existed at that time. She'd need to make copies.

Although she felt better having made a decision, there was another impetus for wanting to go back. As much as she tried to dismiss it, she had to concede that since she'd returned her heart had felt as heavy as a ship's anchor. What was it about Simon anyway? She had always thought of herself as a strong, independent, progressive woman, not some foolish female who fell into the romance trap so easily.

She didn't need anyone. She could take care of herself, and up until meeting Simon she'd done a pretty excellent job of keeping people at bay, not allowing anyone to penetrate the roadblocks she'd fastidiously installed, but he crushed it. Maybe that silly saying was true, the heart wants what it wants. But why did the heart want someone who was so impossibly far away and out of reach? She had tried making a go of it in his time. And certainly, she had known going in it would be different. She hadn't anticipated that it would be so complicated.

And if she returned he would want her to stay, of course, but that would mean giving up the search for her parents, not to mention her business, her lifestyle . . . unless? Unless she told him. And would it be so terrible if she did? Couldn't she come back from time to time? And maybe he already suspected as much. He had said in the letters that he had information. Besides, she reasoned, once he saw that she had possession of the photos his mother had left, it would be a dead giveaway; he would know that she was from the future.

Her grandmother's heartwrenching story haunted her. Grammy had once said that you can become so enamored with a time and place that you may want to return to it again and again, but the first rule of time travel is, don't get involved with the people. Imogen understood that now. Like Grammy, the idea of one day having children had crossed her mind and it would be much easier to leave Simon now when their relationship was new rather than later, as grandma had done. Imogen knew now that leaving Andre had shattered Grammy's heart. Was she destined to do the same?

Despite her eccentric proclivities, Mimi Pinky had been mostly reliable about tending to Luxe while Imogen was away, and because she was a fellow cat person, she always made sure to spend a few extra minutes petting him and giving him some extra attention so that he wouldn't feel lonely. Normally, she would call her up ahead of time, but today Imogen was in a hurry.

Imogen hoped Mimi wouldn't be in one of her nosy, chatty

moods and she could drop off the house key and be on her way. Parked in the driveway was a black sedan, one she hadn't seen before. Good, Imogen thought, if she had company, it could be a relatively short visit this time. Mimi Pinky answered the door wearing one of her signature furry leopard bathrobes accentuated by a lovely pair of bunny slippers.

"Come in," she said, opening the screen door wide and pulling Imogen into her dingy, always cluttered living room. It took a minute for Imogen's eyes to adjust to the dimness. Mimi's curtains were the blackout variety, designed to keep all light out. The only light came from the television, which churned out nonstop reality/game/talk shows all day and night long. Mimi pushed a stack of magazines that were on the couch aside and patted the seat, gesturing for Imogen to sit down. Mimi might be somewhere on the hoarder spectrum, but it wasn't as bad as it could be. While there were mini-stacks of things in every corner, at least there was still a visibly clear path for walking throughout the tiny house.

Imogen sat down and said, "I was just wondering if you might look after Luxe for me."

"Of course, dear," Mimi Pinky answered. "You know how much I love that old guy of yours. I could just hug him all day long," she said wrapping her arms around herself to demonstrate how huggy she could be. Imogen wondered if Luxe put up with her hugs, because as much as he liked cuddling sometimes, hugs weren't really his thing. While they were sitting there, Imogen heard the sound of a lawn mower engine roaring in Mimi's back yard.

"Oh, you have company," she said. "I'm sorry to bother you, Mimi, but I have a lot to do today and thought I could drop off the house key on my way out."

"Oh, it's not really visitors," Mimi said, rolling her eyes and leaning in close like she had a big secret, and touching Imogen's arm, "it's just my no-good son Teddy. Imogen had not seen Teddy since she was a child and he was a pimply teenager.

"Oh, how is Teddy?" Imogen inquired in a conditioned gesture of civility. She had never liked Teddy much. He was a bully as she recalled, and yes, she could acknowledge that people can change, but still, she had never been even mildly interested in what became of him. It was a loaded question. Mimi launched into a five-minute invective about her son. Teddy lived a quiet life over in Stambourg, the next town over, had never married, so zero grandchildren, which was a pity because Mimi Pinky would be an excellent nana. But, despite him being a bachelor with no strings attached, she still didn't see him as often as a mother would like to see her son. She was getting on in age and she sure could use his assistance more often.

About half way through her tirade, the back door swung open and in walked, presumably, Teddy, hot and sweaty from mowing. Wearing a tattered blue handkerchief around his head and a pair of dark sunglasses, Teddy was quite a sight in his striped shorts, tennis shoes, crew socks, and a dirty T-shirt with sweat rings that snaked around his collar, chest, and armpits. He looked like he hadn't shaved in a while and his face was covered with shiny droplets of perspiration. Stopping short when he saw Imogen sitting on the couch, without speaking or removing his sunglasses, he ducked quickly into the kitchen.

Clearly appalled at her son's rude behavior, Mimi called out to him. "Teddy! Don't you see that we have a guest? Don't be rude. Where are your manners?"

"Just a minute, ma," Teddy called out from the other room. Imogen could hear the opening and closing of the freezer, then running water, and the clink-clink of ice cubes tumbling into a glass. A few moments later, he emerged from the kitchen carrying a tall glass tumbler of ice water.

Mimi happily began to chatter incessantly. "You remember Imogen Oliver don't you, Teddy?" she said, "she lives down the street. I feed her cat Luxe, such a sweet kitty he is. Of course you remember her. Didn't you work for her parents one summer when you were a teenager? Teddy? Do you remember the Oliver's, Teddy?"

"Hello Teddy, how are you?" Imogen asked politely.

In between gulping large swigs of water from the glass, Teddy managed to bark out a gruff "hello."

Mimi prattled on. "Imogen brought the key over. I'm taking care of Luxe again," she babbled. "She's going on another business trip."

Imogen managed a feeble smile, hoping to find an excuse to escape Mimi's oppressive home soon.

"A business trip, huh?" Teddy said. "Where you going?"

To Imogen's ears, the tone of his question came across more

like an interrogation than a friendly inquiry. And it made her feel uneasy.

"Chicago," she said, offering up the standard story she had used on Fletcher all the time. Teddy nodded without saying any more. It seemed like a good time to make her exit.

Imogen stood up, a clear signal that she was leaving. "Well, here's the key," she said, handing it over to Mimi. "I'm leaving tomorrow, but I'll leave dry food out for Luxe for tomorrow night." She looked up and Teddy, who was still standing there presumably looking in her direction, although it was hard to tell where he was looking exactly because of the dark sunglasses. She smiled anyway, and started to turn toward the door when she heard him ask, "So, what are you doing in Chicago? What's your line of work?"

She had thought their conversation was over, but apparently not. He was asking a lot of questions, but she had a script of answers ready and waiting in her head.

"A cannabis conference," she replied without a hint of hesitation. "I own a weedery." With marijuana now legal in the state, it was completely legit, not to mention, a trending business.

Teddy nodded his head approvingly and said, "Cool, well have a good trip." With that, he turned and disappeared out through the back door again.

The next day, Imogen put out some dry food and water for Luxe, which he ignored, instead, forlornly looking up at her and mewing, almost as if he knew she was leaving again. He rubbed up against her leg, wrapping his tail around her calf. Imogen leaned down and gave him some pets.

"You be a good kitty for Mimi now, Luxe," she said. "I'll be back soon," she told him, but didn't know if that was true or not. It's a good thing cats didn't understand words because Luxe would have known for sure that she was lying. Suddenly overcome by emotion, Imogen scooped him up for a final hug, which he didn't love, but then giving him some always appreciated rubs and a good scratching behind his ears, chest, and under his chin.

She felt like crying and she wasn't sure why. Setting Luxe down, she turned and walked out the door, locking it behind her.

44

Teddy arrived early at his mother's house to find Mimi Pinky seated at the red Formica table doing the crossword puzzle. "I brought donuts!" he called out to her as he strolled in, plopping the pink box on the table.

She was surprised to see him. "My, aren't we chipper this morning!" Mimi said. Teddy rarely came over unexpectedly, let alone two days in a row, and he'd never brought donuts before. She was always happy to see him, of course, but a little suspicious too.

"Why are you here, Teddy?" she asked.

Hauling out the charming persona he'd cultivated during his treks back to the 20th century, Teddy smiled and touched his mother's shoulder, saying, "Can't a son visit his ma and bring her donuts?"

That seemed to appease Mimi. She patted his hand and eagerly flipped open the box to get to the yummy goodness inside.

"Oh, I shouldn't," she said as she poked the maple bar with her finger. "Well, alright, but I should go over and feed Luxe before I do," she said, starting to get up from her chair. Teddy stopped her.

"Oh no, you enjoy the donuts, ma, I'll go feed the cat for you," he said chirpily.

"Oh would you Teddy Bear? That would just be the sweetest thing."

"You betcha!" Teddy said, happily grabbing the key off the peg where she always hung it. "Enjoy the donuts!" he hollered back to her as he left the house.

He'd been watching her for weeks since she'd returned from 1913. He knew that she'd gone out and got roaring drunk at the bar when she first got back—he'd followed her there and observed her boyfriend folding her into his car. She hadn't done any traveling since, until now. For sure she wasn't off to a weed convention. As if. It was all he could do to hold back a snicker when she had told him that yesterday. For all he knew, Imogen could simply be working another case. It seemed like she'd gotten over Simon, moved on, yet he couldn't be sure. It wouldn't hurt to give the studio a quick check to make sure there wasn't anything else incriminating lying around in there.

Like any good neighbor would do, Teddy sauntered up to Imogen's porch presumably to check on her house, breezily picking up the newspaper and tucking it under his arm while he unlocked the door with the key. Since his last break-in when he didn't find any anchor photos lying around, he was fairly confident that Imogen departed and arrived elsewhere so likely wouldn't be home for a little while anyway.

When he opened the door, the cat jumped off the chair and scampered over to him mewing loudly for food. He didn't like cats and this one looked like he hadn't missed many meals.

"Not here to feed you," he snapped at Luxe, who padded after him as he made a cursory scan of the house. Nothing seemed out of place. He opened up a few closets and peered inside. He entered Imogen's room. It was a controlled mess. He walked over and opened up several of her dresser drawers, which contained the usual things—jeans, shirts, socks. Hoping he'd uncover a drawer full of sexy panties, Teddy was disappointed by Imogen's boring choice of plain cotton sports bras and undies.

Leaving her room, he scanned the area for the cat, but it wasn't around anywhere, probably found another room to lie its lazy cat ass down in, he thought as he locked and shut the door behind him.

He headed around back to the studio and was surprised to see that the blackberry vines had been cleared away. It had been tricky maneuvering to get inside last time. Teddy unlocked the padlock and went inside, leaving the door ajar to allow some natural light in. It was the same as the last time he'd been in it, full of cobwebs and dust. He was just beginning to nose around when he heard a noise behind him. He spun around in time to see a white puff scurrying across the room. The cat.

"Damn it," he said out loud as he turned and gave chase. Luxe was pudgy, but he was fast. At one point, Teddy had him cornered, but when he lunged for him, like all cats, Luxe instinctively zagged, galloping in the other direction into the back room to hide.

"I'll get you, you stupid cat, one way or the other," he shouted, as he fumbled along the wall for the light switch, found it, and with a flick, lit up the space. And then, he heard a loud metallic crash. He ran behind a divider expecting to see the cat, but instead discovered that a panel had been knocked off the wall and a tin box with its contents spilling out onto the hardwood floor.

"Oh god" Teddy said dismayed. More pictures. How could there be more pictures? he wondered as he walked across the room picking each one up.

"Holy shit," he said, "it's me." He was in all of them—sitting at the train station with Georgia Bitgood or skulking in the shadows behind someone. This was not good, not good at all. Imogen must have taken them with that stupid Brownie camera she carted around with her everywhere. But how did they wind up in the studio? Did she place them here before she left 1913 to retrieve them later? If so, why were they still here? Why hadn't she come out and gotten them? Unless she wasn't the one to leave them.

As he flipped through them, one dropped from his hand and onto floor, landing with the backside up. Teddy picked it up and read what was written on it: *Who is this man?*

There was no doubting it now. They knew something. Like hot magna, panic bubbled up to the surface in Teddy's chest and his mind began to reel, veering off in several directions at once. He began to pace to and fro, back and forth. Waiting for the shoe to drop was not an option.

No, they were probably figuring it all out right now, and then she'd come back and tell Mimi everything. The time for passive observance was over. If he followed her, maybe he could prevent her from getting back here to tell on him. But if he could take care of the situation back there, no one here would ever find out.

45

As she concentrated on the photograph in front of her, the office began to contract and the edges faded away. Surprisingly, Imogen was getting used to the physical discomforts—the prickly sensations and dark descent—that accompanied each time trip. And this time, she was confident she'd be arriving at the right time. A year can make a world of difference in people's lives, as she had discovered the last time when she made the erroneous assumption that she could pick right back up with Simon, only to find that in that short span of time he had gotten engaged to be married to Georgia Bitgood.

Welcomed by a frosty gust of winter wind that whipped willy-nilly around her ankles Imogen arrived on the sidewalk outside the entrance to the Benson. Just another face in the crowd, busy people bundled up from the cold in heavy coats and furs passed by her without taking notice. Evidently hem lengths in the latter part of 1913 had begun to slowly creep up because although her dress was still tailored and modestly longish, her ankles were now exposed to the elements. She reached up and felt the fur hat on top of her head. Hats were still in, and today she was glad for the warm belt-hugging coat. But as she quickly realized, even being outside for a few minutes was enough to send her scurrying toward the warmth of the hotels' lobby.

After warming her hands for a minute in front of the massive fireplace, Imogen headed over the desk to check in. A familiar gruff face looked up and met her gaze. It was Marvin, the terminally dour desk clerk, but this time, when he saw her, his eyes grew wide in astonishment. Dropping the key he was holding in his hand, Marvin rushed from around the open side of the desk, leaving the astonished guest he had been helping to gape at him with curious surprise.

When he reached her, he threw all hotel protocol to the wind, flinging his arms around her, nearly knocking her hat off, and crying, "Miss Oliver, it's you!" That she was confused by this odd and unexpected encounter was an understatement. Why was Marvin being so nice? she wondered. Marvin didn't even like her. What had happened after she left to illicit this sudden change in him?

But before she could respond, Marvin had taken hold of her elbow and was ushering her like a VIP over to a nearby chair.

"Sit down right here Miss Oliver and I will ring up Mr. Elliot straightaway," he said grinning broadly. "He will be most delighted to see you," he said gleefully, clearly tickled. "Oh, he most certainly will!"

Not sure what to make of Marvin's attitude adjustment, Imogen shrugged and made herself comfortable in the cozy chair by the toasty fireplace while Marvin made the call.

Across town, Teddy landed outside of his rented flat. "Christ, it's cold," he sputtered when he felt that initial blast of cold slam into his face. Quickly entering the building to get out of the cold, he trudged up the stairs to his old room, all but forgetting that he no longer lived there, and thinking he might have to rent it all over again. "Damn," he said to no one as he headed back out into the cold. The biting wind froze his nose and ears as he trudged along, and when he saw a window display, Teddy ducked into a dry goods department store.

Six stories high with an impressive white brick exterior, the

McMartin-Daniels store was a modern marvel. Much cleaner and nicer than the sprawling big box department stores of his day, these luxurious multilevel buildings carried everything from clothes and household items to hardware and farm machinery. Teddy had to admit that he had become enamored with the fashion stylings of this era. Sure, T-shirts, cargo shorts, tennis shoes, and a hoodie were comfortable, but he rather enjoyed dressing up. It made him feel elegant and manly and moreover, respected. And today especially, he could use a good hat to keep his ears and slightly balding head warm.

A lavish floor comprised the store's gentlemen's department, which was filled with everything from fine silk suits and hats to accessories encompassing belts, ties, shoes, vest pocket fobs, and cufflinks—anything a man might need. At the center of the vast room, Teddy spotted a large display with rows of hats in a variety of styles and colors. He wandered over and selected a gray derby, picking it up and running his chubby fingers along the brim.

"How much?" he asked the sales clerk who had been inconspicuously trailing him since he came in.

"Oh yes, sir, an excellent choice!" the clerk crooned. "That particular derby is in our Manchester line and is priced at a very affordable $4."

Teddy loved the soft feel of the fabric on the hat. In fact, he adored this hat, but it was woefully impractical. Save for looking dandy and maybe keeping the top of his head a little bit warm, it wouldn't do in this weather. Reluctantly setting the derby aside, he moved on, perusing the rest of the selection of hats on the display table. Finally, he tried on an ugly hat with fox fur earflaps. It wasn't exactly classy, but Teddy had to admit, it was much more suited for the elements, not to mention, would provide a far better means of disguise.

"I'll take this one," he barked at the clerk. "And these glasses too," he said, impulsively snatching a pair of rounded spectacles from a display next to the sales counter. Unruffled by Teddy's snippiness, the patient clerk took Teddy's money and watched as he quickly departed to another area of the store.

Taking the moving stairs, Teddy ascended to another massive floor devoted exclusively to everything hardware. Like a Sears on steroids, Teddy could almost feel the testosterone building up inside him. Over here bicycles and buggies, over there, tools and firearms. It went on and on and Teddy was convinced that if he only had more time he could conceivably spend an entire week exploring this one floor alone. Unfortunately, he was on a mission and the luxury of time, ironically for a time traveler, was not something he had right now, not with Imogen and her cohorts almost certainly plotting against him at this very moment.

Following the labeled signs, Teddy made his way to the guns and ammo section. He marveled at the array of weaponries, single- and double-barrel shotguns, a Winchester Model rifle, pistols from Browning and Mauser and Colt's 45 caliber automatic pistol, and even a small Remington Derringer that would fit quite nicely in his vest pocket. With World War I waiting just around the corner, the interest in weapons and military equipment had skyrocketed as Teddy noticed the abundance of survival type gear. A gun would be good, but what he really wanted was a knife, a sharp one. As a kid, it had thrilled him considerably to find bugs and snails and frogs and other small animals to stab repeatedly with his trusty Buck knife. Making his way over to the knife section, he selected a pearl handle hunter's knife for 70 cents.

Once outside, Teddy donned his furry hat and shades, concealed the knife in his coat pocket, and began to make his way in the direction of the Benson Hotel. No need to find the landlord, he surmised. This time, he wouldn't be staying long.

Imogen was flipping dispassionately through the pages of the latest women's magazine, admiring the new fashions for 1914 when she felt a familiar hand upon her shoulder, a touch so au fait it sent copious shivers all the way down her backside. Turning around, she looked into Simon's sexy, lovely, wonderful face, and nearly lost it when she saw real tears in his eyes. He had missed her! And she had missed him. It had been only weeks since she'd seen him, but it didn't matter. Driven solely by impulse and emotion, Imogen flew from her chair, nearly toppling it, reaching out for him, wrapping her arms around his collar, and clinging to him like he was the last life jacket on a sinking boat. She knew she was making a spectacle, but didn't care.

"Oh my god Simon, I love you, I love you," she cried, burrowing her face into his collar and breathing in the conversant scent of all things him. Simon lifted her face, holding her chin with both hands.

"Imogen, my darling. Don't ever leave me again," he said before launching into a series of kisses, on her eyelids, her cheeks, her earlobes, before navigating back to her awaiting lips.

So lost in the moment and each other, neither one noticed the gathering crowd until they heard the faint sound of applause. Untangling from each other they glanced around the room at the group of happy, smiling, clapping people, Otis the elevator man and Marvin the desk clerk among them. It was embarrassing, but at the same time, moving. People loved love and being in love, and watching other people in love. And Simon and Imogen—in love.

Marvin cheerfully handed Imogen the key to room 213. "Here you go Miss Oliver," he said.

Imogen smiled. "Why don't you call me Imogen," she said. "We're friends now, right?" Marvin nodded.

"Okay then," she said, giving him a genuine smile before taking Simon's arm and heading toward the stairs.

Shortly after Simon and Imogen had disappeared upstairs, Teddy entered the hotel lobby wearing a heavy coat, glasses, and a large Ushanka, the Russian hat with fox fur earflaps that he'd purchased on his way over to keep his ears warm. As he was writing his name down, he couldn't be sure, maybe he was just being paranoid, but it sure felt like the desk clerk's eyes were boring into his head. Teddy had chosen a different alias this time. Leeroy Jenkins had been retired. Today he was Emmett Brown, the doctor from *Back to the Future*. It sounded just old-timey and common enough not to stand out as a recognizable name should Imogen, for some reason, check the register. It was risky business staying at the hotel, he knew, but he had to be able to keep tabs on her and wait for the right time to get her alone.

When he had finished signing the book and glanced up, the desk clerk had already turned around and was grabbing a room key from the slot.

"Room 302," he said, placing it on the desk in front of Teddy. Teddy reached for the key, and was about to turn away, when Marvin asked "Have you stayed here before, sir?"

Teddy felt a wave of paranoia rush over him again. Perhaps he recognized him. After all, not so long ago, as Leeroy Jenkins, he had vanished right before his eyes.

"Um, no," Teddy said in a deep, but uneasy voice.

"Very good, Mr. Brown," Marvin said brightly, "you'll want to take your first right, and the lift will take you up to the third floor. Or if you prefer, the stairs are adjacent."

Teddy relaxed. Whew, he was only offering directions. Teddy palmed the key from the counter, gave Marvin a friendly salute, turned, and headed for the stairway.

Like two excited schoolmates heading out to recess, Simon and Imogen took each other's hand and flew up the stairs. When they reached room 213, the two of them, smiling slyly at each other like a pair of Cheshire cats, could barely contain their excitement. Simon fumbled with the clunky heart-shaped skeleton key trying to open the lock and when the door finally opened, they burst into the room, immediately jumping on the bed and rolling in each other's arms, giggling uncontrollably.

Simon rolled over atop of Imogen and looked into her eyes. "I can't believe you're here!" he said, his voice ecstatic.

"I can't believe I'm here either," Imogen answered softly. He bent down and fervently kissed her lips.

Their lovemaking was electrifying, tapping into a bottomless well of yearning that only time spent apart from one another can produce. First emotionally charged, tugging frantically at buttons and ties, unloosening corsets and collars and casting off old inhibitions, clinging to the other as if this was their last day on earth; next wild and reckless and intense, a release of pent-up desire, and then slowing down to easy and deliberate as Imogen picked up where

Simon left off and they fell easily into the familiar rhythms of the other's body, as if to say, "Oh yes. I remember you now."

Afterward, after taking a few minutes to catch her breath, Imogen relaxed peacefully against Simon's shoulder, abundantly content to stay here, well, for infinity! If they had the necessary life-sustaining provisions, it wasn't a terrible idea, she supposed. Thus far in her life, Imogen decided, this was the best place to be. She looked over at Simon. His eyes were closed, but he wasn't asleep. She could tell, because he was smiling.

"What are you doing?" he asked.

"Watching you," Imogen purred. Simon turned on his side, pulling her in close, and wrapping his arms tight around her.

"I could stay here with you like this forever," Simon said.

"You are a mind reader. I was thinking that same thing," Imogen said, "but we should probably talk about what's been going on since I left."

"Oh must we?" Simon moaned, closing his eyes again and hugging her tighter.

Imogen smiled and wiggled away from his clutches. "Yes," Imogen said, "we must." She sat up and began to get dressed.

Out of the blue, Simon blurted, "You have a tattoo!" he said leaning over and touching it with his finger, "right there." She'd forgotten about the small stylized heart tattoo on her right hip.

"Yes," she answered honestly. They were way past pretending that she was from around here. Still, Simon seemed dumbfounded. Circus sideshow performers or sailors and soldiers were the only ones that got tattoos, and usually crude renderings of anchors or hearts accompanied by their paramours' names, patriotic symbols, mermaids, or exotic ladies.

"It is exquisite Imogen," he said. "The color and the artwork are extraordinary."

Most of the time, Imogen forgot that it was even there. She'd gotten it on a whim when she was 16. After a night of partying, she and two of her friends had decided it would be a great idea to get tattoos. Her counterparts had gone all out and gotten full-on tramp-stamps across their lower backs, a popular trend among young girls at the time. Imogen, however, who wasn't quite as freewheeling as her crazy, drunk friends, decided on a smaller, less trendy ink. She was happy with hers, whereas after a few years, her friends, who had long since outgrown low-rise jeans and crop tops, had come to despise the adolescent rendering as well as the derogatory connotation of the name, and planned to have them laser removed.

Imogen finished dressing and leaned against the edge of the bed. "I don't know how much you know, if anything, but I have to tell you something that I know will sound completely crazy."

But before she could begin, Simon interjected, "You're from the future, correct?"

Boom. There it was. The future. Out in the open. It wasn't as bad as she thought it would be, especially considering now that besides their rather unconventional relationship, there was something else going on here. Imogen nodded, wondering how much he already knew. "Yes," she answered frankly. Imogen stood and walked over to her coat, which was draped across the settee. From a pocket she pulled the envelope of photographs and handed them over to Simon, expecting that it might be difficult for him to view the images of his mother. She remembered he'd mentioned that he'd never gotten to see any of the shots she'd taken over the years.

After thumbing through them, however, he looked over at Imogen and smiled broadly. "I can't believe they survived!"

That wasn't the response she was expecting. "You've seen these before?" she asked, "but I thought . . ."

Simon gently interrupted her. "Tell me your story first, Imogen, and then I will explain.

"Okay, well I found the tin box with the photos inside a wall at my parent's photography studio when I went in there after my grandmother died," she said. "I thought it was strange, but I didn't know who the people were. They didn't mean anything to me at the time that I found them, so I put them up in the back of my closet and forgot about them," she said, "until I got your letters at the hotel, that's when I decided to pull them out and take a closer look. I realized it was you and your mother."

Simon looked down at the array of photos spread out on the bed and sighed. Even though he'd seen these before, viewing them again still dredged up painful memories of being endlessly caught up as a child in his mother's obsession.

"Sit down Imogen," Simon said gesturing and patting the bed.

"I have a bit of a story too." Imogen sat down. "My mother and Doran were friends," Simon told her. Over the years, she took more photographs of us and she left them in a barn. Although I had been with her a few times when she left the photographs, I was too young to remember where the place was, but a few weeks ago, Doran took me there and we found them. They were scattered around in random places and some of the earlier ones were starting to fade and degrade from the elements. We thought it might be prudent to put them in tins to protect them, so they would be intact if and when someone in the future found them." Simon looked over at Imogen to assess her reaction.

She stood up and began to mull this new information over and over out loud. "So, this barn where you went, it must have been there before my dad's studio was built, but how could the tins get into the walls unless the studio was built around or an extension of the original barn? Or, had someone else found them and hidden them?" Imogen sighed deeply. This was even more complicated than she could fathom and she was the time traveler.

Simon shook his head. He had no answers either. Neither of them could know what happened in the intervening years between when he was there and when Imogen found them. But even more curious, Imogen wondered, what was the connection between herself and Simon's mother? Flipping through the photos, she singled out one in particular and handed it to Simon.

"Look carefully at this one," she said, nervously biting her lip. "What do you see?" Simon recognized it as being one of the loose pictures he and Doran had gathered up and placed in tins.

"Simon! Look at the tree in the background," Imogen said excitedly.

Simon squinted as he held the photo up closer to his eyes.

"Do you see him?" Imogen asked.

She watched his eyes growing wide as he focused in on the half-hidden silhouette behind the tree. Tapping the photo with his finger in a gesture indicative of comprehension, Simon said, "So if you found these, then you must have found the other ones Doran and I left there, in the very same location?"

"No, I have not been out to the studio since," Imogen said nodding her head. "What photos are you talking about?"

"I'll show you," Simon said, bounding out of bed excitedly and forgetting he was still naked. Quickly pulling his britches on and fastening them, he rushed over to the same chair and from his vest pocket, produced a single photograph, the one he had held back from Imogen's camera. It was Imogen's turn to be stunned.

"Holy shit, it's him!" Imogen cried out. Simon cringed, giving her a startled, irresolute look as if to say he would never become accustomed to a woman swearing, but at this point, Imogen didn't care. The pretense of feigning that she was a refined lady was over. Aligning the two photos side by side on the bed, there was no doubting that in both images, it was clearly the same person.

One floor above the room where the freshly reunited lovers were becoming reacquainted, a mix of rage and excitement was building as he lie on his bed masturbating to the imagined moans and groans of the couple below. Though he could not actually hear them, he knew what they were doing with each other. Initially, his fists had balled up so tightly he had dug his fingernails deep into his sweaty palms, drawing blood, but rather than doing something potentially stupid and costly like punching a cavernous hole in the hotel room wall to ease his rising resentment, he redirected his anger. Unbuttoning his trousers, Teddy begun to fantasize that Imogen was doing to him what she was probably doing to Simon right this very moment.

He could picture her deliciously curved body; between her silky legs, a beautiful flower welcoming the busy bee, but his depraved fantasies, like always, took a darker turn. IT was no longer a flower, but in its place, a shark with a bloody, gaping mouth and the face of his mother. Oh why did she always have to show up and ruin everything? Watching his erection dissipate, a disheartened Teddy buttoned up his trousers and pressed his back hard against the pillows on the bed.

Simon didn't deserve someone like her, he thought, although he was a handsome one, all right. And Teddy took some pleasure in knowing that somehow a couple of underwhelming individuals, clearly lacking in the looks department, could produce such a striking specimen.

Though he had no clear connection to Simon, despite the biological one, it excited him again to think that in a way, even as his son was fucking Imogen, he was fucking her, too. Not only that, but it thrilled him to think that very soon, she would cease to exist.

46

As much as both would have preferred to stay between the warm covers divinely entrenched in each other's arms for the rest of the afternoon, Imogen and Simon managed to eventually get up and reluctantly prepare to set out in the cold to their destination—Doran's apartment. While they had been upstairs in their room spooning, a light, but wet snow had begun to fall, accumulating on the sidewalk making it slippery and a challenge to maneuver. Imogen had forgotten in her time away how precarious it was to simply walk around in high-top boots. And although she had mastered them fairly well, when the sidewalk was slick, it could be perilous. She smiled when Simon entwined his arm with hers and gently guided her.

On the way over, Simon filled her in a bit on Doran and his mother's history, as well as the disturbing revelation that Doran had a proclivity for his own sex, which made Imogen chuckle.

"Is that funny?" Simon had asked confounded by her blasé reaction.

"Or is that something that is common in the future? Do men . . . openly . . . do that?" he asked completely serious.

"Oh Simon," Imogen had said, punching his arm playfully and

brushing it aside for now. Fortunately, it wasn't a long walk and they arrived at Doran's apartment posthaste.

"Imogen Oliver, I presume," Doran said, extending his hand to greet her.

Imogen smiled, a bit embarrassed, "Yes, Mr. Doran," she said as though they were starting over and just now meeting for the first time. The last time they met, she had been using her Daphne Blake alias. He had taken her out to the lovely English garden, and during their discussion of evolution, had disclosed that his family and congregation had abandoned him over his views, which at the time Imogen had thought seemed pretty harsh and probably not the whole story. After Simon spilled the beans on the way over that Doran was gay, his story finally made sense. Doran shook Simon's hand, welcoming them both before leading them into the small living room.

"Please," he said, gesturing for them to sit down on the small divan. "Can I get you something warm to drink? Tea? Coffee?" he asked them. But before either could reply they heard a slight tapping sound at the door.

Doran flashed his guests a perplexed look. "Who could that be?" he said as he approached the door and opened it. Simon and Imogen heard a woman's voice before Doran ushered none other than Georgia Bitgood into the room.

Simon immediately jumped up from his seat. "Georgia! What are you doing here?" he demanded to know. Imogen certainly wasn't expecting this either. Did Georgia and Doran know each other? she wondered. Why was she here?

Georgia glanced at Simon and nodded a greeting at Imogen. "I am very sorry for interrupting," she said. "I saw the two of you walking and I followed you here."

"Why?" Simon asked, perplexed.

Georgia stumbled over her words. "I . . . I wanted to speak to you, to apologize, to you especially Miss Oliver."

Imogen arose from the divan. "To me? Why?"

"May we speak to one another . . . alone?" she asked Imogen, her eyes round and pleading.

"Would you excuse us for a moment?" she asked Doran.

"Of course," Doran said.

Reaching out and placing her hand in hers, Imogen gently

guided Georgia toward the privacy of the kitchen. Once they were out of earshot of the men, Imogen tried to let go of her hand, but Georgia resisted, holding on tighter.

With a shy, but genuinely earnest smile, Georgia said, "I wanted you to know that I don't feel bad about not marrying Simon, although I am marginally distressed that I will have to spend my life alone."

"Alone? But why?" Imogen asked, clearly confused by this bit of news.

Georgia explained that her father, a preacher, had insisted that his only daughter marry and produce for him grandchildren. She had behaved so badly out of fear of her father's retribution and the stigma of spinsterhood that would surely burden her for the rest of her life. Yet, on the other hand, marrying would likely end her vocation as a teacher.

"I love teaching," she said, "but I have no desire to marry or have children of my own."

"I don't understand," Imogen said. "They won't let you teach if you marry?"

"That's right," Georgia said, "and there is something else." She squeezed Imogen's hand, and leaning in close, whispered, "My love would only be true if it might be reciprocated by someone such as you."

Imogen's eyes grew wide with dawning realization. "You mean you're gay?" she asked.

Georgia frowned. "No," she said, shaking her head and loosening her grip on Imogen's hand. "I am sad."

Imogen immediately recognized her gaff. Of course, the word "gay" meant something entirely different than it did a hundred years from now. She gave Georgia a warm hug, and Georgia hugged back.

"I understand what you're saying; I really do," Imogen said, "but don't worry, there are other people out there like you."

From the blank stare on Georgia's face, it was apparent that Imogen's words weren't registering, but that was okay; it was a way too complicated topic to address right now anyway.

"Come on," she said, looping her arm in Georgia's and pulling her along with her back into the seating area where Doran and Simon were awaiting their return. Both men stood when the women reentered the room.

"Georgia will be joining us," Imogen announced. Simon gave her a bewildered "look" like "What? Why?" but Imogen smiled, ignoring him and escorting Georgia to a nearby chair.

"Well then," Doran inquired again, "tea, coffee, Coca Cola anyone?"

After everyone had their beverage and had settled in comfortably, Doran first turned and addressed Imogen.

"For Miss Bitgood's and my benefit, before we begin, I wonder if you might please explain how you happened to come to us Imogen."

Okay, this was it, Imogen thought, time to come clean, all secrets revealed, and honestly, she was looking forward to it. It would be a relief to be unburdened, and she couldn't think of a better group of people to share it with.

Imogen set her coffee cup on the side table and cleared her throat. "I was four the first time I stepped through a photograph in my grandmother's photo album," she began.

For the next hour or so she explained to her rapt audience how she had accidently wandered into a photo, three times: first as a child, once during high school, and then again in college when she had first met Simon. She did her best to fill them in on what she knew about the way time travel worked. She told them about being nine years old and coming home from school and informed that her parents had died in a car accident, but finding out later that it was all just one big lie, because her grandmother had confessed before her death that not only were her parents still alive, but lost somewhere in another time. And someone had deliberately trapped them there.

She explained that she had initially started up her business, Dead Relatives, Inc. in the hope of finding her parents, but that the satisfaction of helping people had gradually become an equal motivator.

". . . I came back to attend Herbert's lecture because his great nephew, a client of mine, hired me to find out what had happened to his uncle's stereopticon equipment. And you know the rest," she finished, picking up her coffee cup and taking a sip of the now cold brew.

The room was quiet as Simon, Doran, and Georgia tried to process Imogen's fantastical story. Simon finally broke the silence.

"How fast can cars in the future go!"

"Yes, and what is the future like? What year are you from? Are women equal? Can they vote?" Georgia added excitedly.

"What happens physically when you enter the photograph, Imogen? Do you have to prepare? Are you wearing clothes from the future when you arrive?" Doran inquired.

Not anticipating that kind of reaction to her story and frustrated with being bombarded with questions from all sides, Imogen tossed her hands in the air in exasperation, stood up, and marched off into the kitchen. Georgia shrugged and looked over at Doran and Simon, who were doing the same, until Simon realized their error and bounded from his chair.

"Imogen," he called on his way to her. "We're sorry Imogen, please come back."

He found her standing at the sink basin staring blankly out the window, tears rolling down her cheeks.

"Imogen," Simon said, gently touching her shoulder and turning her around to face him. He lifted her chin and said, "I am truly sorry, my dear. All of us . . . we got so caught up in your story . . . we didn't mean to distress you." Imogen looked up at Simon and leaned her head against his chest.

"I guess I didn't expect that talking about my parents and everything would be so tough," she sobbed. "In my whole life I only told one other person that story."

Simon held her tightly. "While you were reliving the pain of losing your parents, all we could think about was what the future is like," he said, "It was thoughtless of us." Doran and Georgia, who had been hovering in the doorway listening immediately rushed over to console her, too.

"I'm sorry also, Imogen," Georgia said, taking Imogen's hand in hers.

"I likewise am deeply apologetic," said Doran, reaching out awkwardly to squeeze her shoulder.

Imogen wiped her cheeks with her hand and smiled, "It's okay you guys." She was feeling embarrassed now. "I just haven't told many people and I guess I didn't expect I'd get this emotional."

They all nodded and told her it was all right to be emotive and besides, she was among friends. They returned to the living room and chatted about mundane things until Imogen was ready to resume.

"So after my parent's disappeared, Grammy locked the photography studio up. But after she died when I was sorting through her things I found the key and decided to go out there," she explained. "That's when I found the tin of old photos hidden inside the wall. Mice had gnawed on it or something, but a part of the wall had fallen away, exposing it. I didn't recognize the people in the pictures, so I stored them up in my closet where they sat for a few years. I had forgotten all about them until I received Simon's letters," she explained.

"He said I should look for photos of a woman and child and for information on Crestview Sanitarium. I remembered seeing a sign and some words in one of the photos from the tin. After digging them out and looking at them closely I recognized that the people were Simon and his mother. These were the photographs he had spoken about, the ones she had hidden and that he had never seen. I knew I had to bring them to him."

From her pocket, Imogen produced the first of two photos and handed it to Doran. Simon and Tiffany were standing in front of the Crestview sign. Doran nodded sadly and said, "I remember. This was the last photograph of them. She asked me to take it to the barn one last time."

Imogen could sense that Herbert was in a lot of pain, but she wasn't quite finished yet. "There was another one in particular that stood apart from the others," she said as she handed the one of the two of them posing on the bridge from her pocket and handed it over to Doran. Georgia leaned in closer to look. "I also found something curious," she said. "Do you see someone else in the image?"

"Leeroy Jenkins!" Georgia gasped. "He was the one who encouraged me to threaten you," Georgia said, her voice becoming distraught, her brows knitting up with anxiety. "I am so sorry for stomping on your toes Imogen. Please forgive me. It was quite-wrong-headed of me."

"It's all good, Georgia," Imogen said, smiling at her new friend. "It's water under the bridge as far as I'm concerned."

"I thought it was strange when he showed up again two years

later, around the time you returned, Imogen," Georgia said, "and he offered to help me break you and Simon up."

With the flood gates opened everyone in the room had a story to share of an encounter they'd had with Leeroy Jenkins.

"The first time I saw him was when he showed up at your lecture, Herbert," Simon said, "and he was there again later at the hotel when Imogen first disappeared . . . er, went home, I guess?" He looked over at Imogen and she nodded. Simon then produced the photographs that he and Doran had discovered among the developed photos from Imogen's camera.

"Look," he said as he passed them around, "here he is sitting on a bench at the train station with Georgia."

"Oh my," Georgia gulped, astounded that these photos existed. "He met me there to tell me what Imogen's daily routine was, so I could arrange to make it look like Simon was still seeing me and cause you to fight, and maybe make you go away for good." She glanced over at Imogen and Simon before hanging her head in shame. Imogen reached over and gave her arm a reassuring pat.

"And he was there again after our fight, Imogen," Simon said. "In fact, I bowled him over when I was chasing after you. I felt terrible and so agreed to buy him a drink to recompense. He was a complete boor. I couldn't wait to get away from his company. Evidently, he followed me back to the hotel because he showed up at your room after I found your camera on the bed," Simon added, his voice rising with excitement at retrieving a memory he'd let slip by.

"He said something curious that I didn't understand at the time. Right before he vanished into thin air, he said that you," he pointed at Imogen, "were from the future!"

Imogen placed her hands on her hips. "Okay, so who is this guy?" Imogen asked. "It's a safe bet he's a time traveler and it seems he knows that I am too."

"The question is," Simon added, "what does he want and why is he trying so hard to keep us apart?"

So far, Doran had kept silent during the conversation, preferring instead to sit back and quietly listen to each person carefully, as if gathering up all the information before choosing to weigh in.

Imogen turned to him and asked, "What do you think, Herbert?

You knew Simon's mother. Did she give you any clues?"

As if preparing for a sermon, Herbert Doran took a deep breath, cleared his throat, and in his deep, reverberating preacher voice began, "I first laid eyes on Tiffany Rose in August, 1885. Ripe with child, she was seated third row center in the sweltering heat of the tent, sweating so profusely her skin glowed as she furiously fanned herself with the tent revival program. It wasn't only her lovely unkempt mane of natural curls or the fact that she was pregnant that caught my attention, it was that she was all alone . . ."

Although Simon had heard the story already, for the next half hour or so, the group listened, enthralled by Doran's story about how Tiffany had appropriated him to the edge of town to take her photograph, a place she would return to again and again over the years to deposit the pictures inside the barn. He told them how they became friends over shared secrets—his, a desire to be accepted for who he was and who he chose to love; and hers, a wild story about being violently pulled against her will through a photograph from the future and then left alone and abandoned in the past.

"She believed that if she left photographs in the area where she came through, someone in the future might find them and come back and rescue her," Doran explained. "I didn't believe her at the time, of course, but I humored her, and I got to know this young fellow," he said, smiling and gesturing in Simon's direction.

"It wasn't until I saw his picture on his lecture flier that I recognized him, the man my mother called Herbie," Simon said. A look of embarrassment crossed Doran's face, but he grinned when Simon added, "He brought me treats and candy. I thought he was the candy man."

Imogen glanced over at Simon and smiled too, glad to hear that his childhood held at least a few good memories. Turning back to Doran, she asked, "So what happened to Tiffany?"

Doran sighed. This part of the story was difficult to tell. "A man approached me and suggested that she might require mental help."

"Let me guess, Leeroy Jenkins, right?" Imogen said sardonically.

Doran nodded. "Yes, I believe now that it was indeed him, but he went by a different name then—Gordy Crusher. He said he was from the Society for the Prevention of Cruelty to Children and that they had received reports that his mother was suffering from melancholia, mental excitement, and strong opinion."

Imogen couldn't help rolling her eyes at that. Those were just a few of the ridiculous claims she'd read about that men at that time could cite for having a woman committed to an asylum.

Doran continued. "He said that her employers and fellow employees at the shirt factory where she worked as a seamstress had become concerned for her and the wellbeing of her child after she had made claims of being from the future. The society felt that she may be doing irreparable damage to her young son and that she should be institutionalized and the child removed to a children's institution."

Doran paused, his face crestfallen, but he continued. "As a Christian cleric, I was duty-bound to sign the papers to have her committed to Crestview Sanitarium. They assured me they'd do everything they could to help her. At the time, I believed it would only be temporary, that they would evaluate her and she would likely be released." The group sat silently, each attempting to digest Doran's story.

Doran concluded, "After Simon came to me a few weeks ago, we went out to Crestview together. Regrettably, they informed us that Tiffany Rose had left the sanitarium years ago, had probably been transferred out and they had no records."

Imogen informed the group that according to her research the old Crestview hospital had been shuttered in the early '60s and the building was later repurposed. It now housed the town's museum. "I was going to Google more about it, but I got all distracted by the photographs of Simon and his mother," she said. When no one responded, she looked around and noticed they were all staring at her.

"What?" she asked, mystified.

"The 1960s?" Simon asked.

"What's a Google?" Georgia questioned.

She kept forgetting that their frame of reference was completely at odds. "I'm sorry Simon, yes, the 1960s, and Google, well . . . It's a thing," she said. Hoping to avoid having to go into a lengthy explanation of modern technology, she quickly changed the subject.

"Okay, so this guy, this Leeroy Jenkins who we've established that we've all had encounters with, is clearly a time traveler," she said, "and in my experience, travelers use aliases. You recall Daphne Blake when we first met, don't you?" she said gesturing to Doran, who nodded.

"When I first met him, I thought his name sounded familiar, but I couldn't place it," she said. I remember asking him about it and he said something about being named after his grandfather, which made sense. It sounded like an old-timey name . . . no offense to old-timey names," she quipped, flashing a grin at her audience.

"Anyway, it wasn't until later that it dawned on me: Leeroy Jenkins is the character name of a player in the video game *World of Warcraft*, who notoriously screwed up a detailed battle strategy with a group of other players. Only someone from my time, and most likely a computer gamer, would choose that name as an alias."

"Video game?" All three repeated, looking at her in confusion again.

After Imogen gave them a brief explanation of what a video game was, Simon asked, "So Jenkins isn't his real name?"

"Probably not," Imogen acknowledged, "and neither was the name he used before that when he was posing as an agent." She explained how she often borrowed names from current literature and popular culture when traveling. "Gordy Crusher sounds like a pop culture name salad that he tossed together."

"Well, whatever his name may be," Doran said, "Simon and I believe this Jenkins fellow is dangerous and he may even be the same person that brought Tiffany Rose here and left her, and perhaps is returning again and again because he feels compelled to cover up his unforgiveable deed."

It hadn't occurred to Imogen until right now that perhaps that was why this guy kept showing up wherever she was. But who could it be? Other than her parents and grandma, she knew of no others with the gift.

"Herbert," Imogen said, "did Tiffany Rose ever mention who brought her here?"

All eyes were glued on Doran. Leaning forward in his chair and placing his hands against his head, he closed his eyes and stared down between his legs at the floor as if engrossed in some distant thought, searching back through the recesses of memory for a snippet of conversation, a recollection, a name. He stayed like that for a few moments before finally jerking his head up and shouting out, "Teddy!"

47

"Who is Teddy?" Simon and Georgia asked in unison.

"The man who brought her through the photograph, she said his name was Teddy," Doran repeated. "I remember now, but it took me a while to recall because she told me his name only a single time."

He continued, "It was when we first met, when were out at the barn site and she told me her crazy story about how she got here. As I mentioned previously, I was skeptical, but also intrigued about how she came up with such an imaginative tale. I asked her why someone would want to do such a thing to her and she said, 'Teddy didn't want the baby and he was afraid I would tell his mother.'"

Though the name Teddy meant virtually nothing to Simon, Doran, and Georgia, Imogen gulped, her jaw dropping as the disturbing truth about what Doran was saying began to gradually sink in. Teddy! Of course, Leeroy Jenkins is Teddy. Teddy Bear. Teddy Diamond. Mimi Pinky's Teddy.

Had she not run into him at his mother's house just the other day after years of not seeing him, it might not have been so marked—all the questions he'd asked her about her line of work and where she was traveling to and why, the reason he never removed his hat and sunglasses the entire time they were chatting. It was obvious now he didn't want her to recognize him.

And because his mother looked after Imogen's cat, he always knew when she was traveling. Fletcher had said there was someone watching the house and she had brushed it off as wild speculation, but now, in retrospect, it made complete sense. He had worked for her parents that summer that they disappeared. Tiffany Rose was probably one of the high school girls that had come in to sit for her senior portrait. Oh my god . . . And the worst part, it meant that Teddy . . . Teddy likely was Simon's biological father!

Noting the dramatic shift in her demeanor, Simon asked, "Does that name mean something to you, Imogen?" he asked, concerned.

Imogen stood up, but she was dizzy and she felt sick to her stomach. She clutched her abdomen and sat back down. Her mind darted back to that summer and the disgusting behavior she and Jade had witnessed in the studio. She remembered now why she had felt glad when Teddy Diamond had left the neighborhood for good.

Simon stood up and took her arm, helping her back into the chair. "What is it, Imogen? Are you alright?" Georgia had arisen from her seat as well and rushed to her side. "Are you sick?" she asked.

She answered both of their questions. "Yes, I'm sick," she said, "and no, I'm not all right."

Herbert got up from his chair, too but headed to the kitchen instead, returning quickly with a tall glass of cold water that he handed to Imogen.

"You know this Teddy fellow, don't you?" he said.

"Yes, I think I do," Imogen answered after taking a sip of the water.

"What can you tell us about him?" Doran asked.

Imogen exhaled long and deep. Her stomach had stopped doing little flip-flops for now, but she still felt strange. She hadn't thought about him in years, but the memories came flooding back.

"Theodore Diamond, or Teddy," Imogen began, "was our neighbor. She told them about his bullying, his looney mom, his cruelty to animals, and about the time he'd nearly set her on fire with a lit firecracker.

"One summer, my parents, who were photographers, hired him to work in their studio," she explained. "My friend Jade and I used to spy on him." she smiled at the memory of Jade. She told them about the high school girls who came in to pose for their senior portraits and how Teddy would take the rejected prints home with him.

"We were just being naughty kids, you know, trying to annoy him, but after a while . . . he started doing things."

"What sort of things?" Simon asked.

Imogen hesitated before continuing. "Things that a teenage boy shouldn't be doing in front of children," she said, her voice trailing away . . . "exposing himself to us."

She could tell by the stricken looks on her listener's faces that this went way beyond the realm of taboo behavior.

"Did you tell your folks?" Georgia asked.

"No," she answered, "before I could, my friend and her family moved away unexpectedly, without telling anyone. I was quite devastated. And well, I was nine."

Herbert rose from his chair and began to pace. "He sounds like a horrible person, but what makes you think this Teddy is the same one who kidnapped Tiffany?"

"I also ran into him the other day at his mother's house. Mimi Pinky takes care of my cat."

Simon, Georgia, and Doran looked at each other. "Mimi Pinky? Is that a real name?" Simon asked.

"Unfortunately, it is," Imogen said, smiling weakly. "So anyway, I was dropping my house key off to her when her son Teddy came in from mowing the lawn outside. I had not seen him since he was a teenager. He was wearing a handkerchief thing on his head and dark sunglasses that he never took off, but it was so unusual, he started asking me a lot of probing questions about what I did for a living and where I traveled to on business. I thought it was an odd encounter at the time, but now, in light of everything we've discussed, it seems to carry more weight."

She turned to face Herbert, asking him, "When Tiffany told you her story, did she say what year in the future she was from?"

Doran stopped pacing and began tapping his fingers against his temple. He stood like that for a while before saying, "Now that you mention it, I do remember her telling me a year once. It was later on, when she was being committed to Crestview and at that point, she had dropped all pretense and was openly stating that she was from the future. I want to say, 1997 perhaps?"

Imogen leapt up from her chair. "Oh my, 1997, you say?"

"Yes, I think that's what she said, why?"

Imogen took a deep breath before speaking. "That was the same year my parents disappeared, and even though everything was a blur for me afterward, I think Teddy left home shortly thereafter."

"Do you think he might have been responsible for all of their disappearances?" Doran asked, "not just Tiffany Rose?"

Imogen shook her head, "I don't know. I was a kid, but I do remember seeing him in the studio talking with a girl that looked a lot like Tiffany. I also saw him arguing with my father."

The pieces were starting to fit. "If he did this to Tiffany because she had threatened to tell his mother, perhaps my parents suspected him as well. And to ensure that they wouldn't find out, he may have destroyed their anchor photographs to trap them wherever they were."

Simon, who had been quietly listening throughout the entire discussion, abruptly stood up, and without a word strode away into the kitchen. Alarmed, Imogen immediately got up and followed him. He was the one standing by the sink now, hands in his pockets, staring out of the window.

"What is it, Simon?" she asked, gently placing her hand on his arm.

Simon turned to look at her, his face as sullen and disconsolate as she'd ever seen it. "If what you say is true," he said, "this man . . . this monster who betrayed my mother, and perhaps your parents, too . . . this Teddy, he is my father, right?"

During the excitement of the discovery phase, Imogen had completely forgotten about Simon and that unpleasant aspect of their revelation.

"I'm sorry, Simon," she said. Simon turned around and faced her, wrapping his arms around her waist and pulling her in tight next to him. She laid her head against his chest and they stood like that, holding on securely to each other for a moment or two without speaking.

Finally, Simon pulled away from her. "You are going to leave, aren't you?" he said, his face fraught with the look of someone in pain.

Imogen looked down at the floor. "Yes," she replied, "I have to."

"Will I ever see you again?" he asked.

"I don't know," Imogen said. "I can come back, but I'm not sure yet if I want to stay. It's complicated Simon, but I swear, I will track him down and make him pay for what he did to your mother!"

She hated having to be so goddamn brutally honest, but she was done lying and concealing information from him. It had to be all out there.

"Take me with you," he blurted.

"What?" Imogen said, taken aback by his direct pronouncement.

"Take me with you," Simon repeated, pulling her in close to him again.

Imogen pushed away from him. "I can't," she said, shaking her head.

"Why not?" he demanded, his voice raising an octave higher.

"Because I . . . well . . . because I don't know what might happen," she confessed.

The intensity of his gaze, his piercing eyes, made her want to do everything and anything he asked, if only she could.

"If my mother was pregnant with me when this Teddy fellow brought her through the photograph, then that would mean that I was conceived in the future, correct?"

Imogen nodded in agreement.

"That being the case," he continued, "theoretically, I should be able to return to the time that I was conceived in."

Imogen could not argue with his logic; it made perfect sense, but how could they know for sure if it had never been tested?

She looked into his distraught, pleading eyes. "Simon," she said, "it sounds possible, it does, but how do we know it will work that way for sure? It's super risky. How do we know that you won't revert back to an infant, or worse, die? I couldn't live with myself if something happened to you."

Simon's shoulders slumped and he looked down at the floor, defeated. When he lifted his head to look up again, he spied Doran, with Georgia stationed behind him, standing in the doorway.

Back in the living room, Imogen expressed aloud, "Why would Teddy go to all this trouble? Who would I tell about time travel? I don't have anybody to tell. As far as I know now, he's the only other person like me."

"Plainly his mother," Doran ventured, "and that may be the worst thing that could ever happen to him."

"Mimi Pinky? He was never very nice to her, as I recall. They weren't close," Imogen said.

"Perhaps they were closer than you think," Doran said.

48

As the afternoon began to fade into early evening, the room grew steadily darker and the assemblage hungrier. Deciding to head out together for dinner at the hotel, the group bundled up in their coats and gloves, fur hats and mittens and scarves and made their way single file down the rickety stairs to the mercantile on the ground floor and out onto the wintery street.

In the hours they had been cozily ensconced in the warmth of Herbert's apartment, a freezing rain had replaced the falling snow, enough time to encase the brittle tree limbs and coat the streets and sidewalks with a thin layer of ice, and creating a hazardous condition for anyone on foot.

"Perhaps we should hail a cab?" Simon suggested, although as they glanced around, it appeared they were the only individuals out on the street braving the elements this night.

"We can walk," Imogen said, taking Simon's hand in hers as they ventured judiciously together out onto the slick sidewalk, "everyone just be careful, okay."

The near empty streets were eerily quiet, the only sound coming from the occasional tree branch cracking from the weight of the ice it bore, and the crunchety crunch crunch of their boots in the snow as they cautiously navigated the sidewalk in silence, each ostensibly lost in their own thoughts, trying to make sense of the day's long list of stunning disclosures.

Two blocks out, the electric street lamps came on, illuminating the opaque sidewalk, although even with the light it was still difficult to see the hidden patches of black ice, and as daylight slipped away, the temperature had already dipped down several degrees.

Taking the lead, Simon had moved ahead of the party to blaze a trail for them to follow on the snowy sidewalk. Doran followed behind him, with Georgia and Imogen bringing up the rear. Despite her coat and gloves, Imogen was cold and shivering and miserable. And after observing Georgia, who was wearing heeled boots, struggle to keep her footing, several times having to grab hold of Herbert's arm for support, Imogen stopped walking.

"Maybe we should see if we could catch a ride!" she called ahead as little puffs of cold breath ringed her face.

Georgia called back to Imogen. "It is fine, Imogen," she assured her, "It's not far now. I can make it." The others continued on without stopping or turning around.

"Well, okay," Imogen said. Her words had barely caught up to them when from behind a gloved hand clamped over her mouth and an arm encircled her neck. She felt a frigid piece of steel pressing up hard against her throat as someone dragged her from the sidewalk and down a darkened alleyway. She struggled to get away, but the grip tightened.

"Don't fight me," a muted and menacing voice snarled in her ear. The hand moved away from her mouth and she wanted to scream, but the tip of the sharp knife piercing her skin, prevented her from vocalizing. Her mind raced. Why wasn't anyone coming to help her? Did they not notice that she was missing all of a sudden?

Her assailant dragged her deeper down the darkened alley, farther away from her friends and the lighted street. This is it, Imogen envisaged. I'm gonna die back here in the past and no one will ever know. She knew she should have prepared herself for the possibility, but it was one of those fleeting things that tend to be easily dismissed by life's many distractions. Almost lulled by the inevitability of her imminent death, he stopped dragging her and the sound of a man's familiar voice brought her back.

"I don't want to kill you, Imogen," he said, "but I have to, you know I have to." He pressed the sharp blade hard against her skin.

"Teddy?" she croaked.

"I'll do it," he panted breathlessly into her ear. "Don't try to stop me!" But the feeble, unconvincing tone of his voice sounded more like someone pleading to be talked out of it.

Terrified, but helpless to get away, the minutes felt like an eternity to Imogen, though every second she was still alive meant Teddy was hesitant to follow through and more time for Simon and Herbert and Georgia to realize she was missing.

"Teddy," she pleaded, "You don't want to do this." If she could distract him he might not overreact if her friend's showed up.

"Shut up!" Teddy snapped at her. Seconds later, Simon burst onto the scene of the unfolding drama, and instinctively rushed forward to help Imogen.

"Put it down!" Simon bellowed.

"No," Teddy shouted defiantly, pressing the knife snugger against Imogen's throat. "I have to do it." He took a step backward toward the wall.

Noticing the knife in Teddy's hand, Simon backed off, giving him extra room and hoping that he could talk him out of harming Imogen.

"No, you don't have to," Simon said calmly.

"Yes I do, Teddy barked back at him. "She'll tell."

"No she won't tell," Simon assured him, trying to keep his voice even and composed.

"Oh yeah, she'll tell Mimi. I know she will," Teddy said, his voice cracking and taking on the quality of a petulant child.

"Tell Mimi what? Who's Mimi, Mr. Jenkins?" Simon asked slow and soothing-like, hoping to defuse the situation. "Imogen doesn't know anything."

Teddy frowned. "But the pictures?" he asked, confused.

"What pictures," Simon asked, "there are no pictures."

Appearing confused by what Simon was saying, Teddy started to lower the knife. But wait, he knew there were pictures. He'd found them in the studio. Realizing that Simon was trying to trick him, he swiftly brought the knife back up to Imogen's throat, this time nicking her skin and drawing blood. Georgia let out a panicked gasp when she saw Imogen flinch.

Vacillating between anger and infantile behavior, Teddy squeezed out a tear and his hands started to shake. It appeared he was losing all control of his emotions.

"Yes, she does too know, and you know," he wailed. "All of you know what I did to Tiffany, and you know that you're my goddamn kid," he said, angrily pointing at Simon, "and she knows what I did to her parents, and so . . . and so, I have to kill her here, right now so she won't go back and tell." He was blubbering now.

Teddy's grip on her was becoming so constricted, Imogen thought she might burst, and when the blade started gashing deeper into her flesh, she let out a primal howl, "Nooooo."

Just then, a boot came hurling through the air, striking Teddy squarely in the forehead and knocking him backward. Slipping on the ice, he lost his balance. He tried to hold on to Imogen for support, but as he tumbled backward, the knife in his hand came down with him gouging into Imogen's neck.

Simon and Herbert both made a mad dive for Teddy, pushing him away from Imogen, and wrestling the knife away from him. Georgia rushed over to Imogen's side.

"Here," Georgia said," pulling a dainty white hand-embroidered handkerchief from her skirt pocket and pressing it against Imogen's skin to stop the bleeding.

"Oh no Georgia, it will ruin it," Imogen cried.

"Nonsense!" Georgia said as she applied pressure to the cut.

Turning away from Teddy, who was still lying in a prone position where he'd fallen on the cold, icy ground, Simon asked Imogen, "Are you alright?"

"Yes, I'm okay," Imogen said.

In the relatively short span of time it took for Simon to look away and back again, Teddy was gone.

"Where is he?" Simon shouted at the empty spot where Teddy had just been just seconds before.

"I don't know," Herbert said, shaking his head back and forth in confusion. "He was here and then, like that," he snapped his fingers, "he was gone!"

Georgia flung her hands up to her cheeks. "What the blazes?" she gasped. "He evaporated!" It was one thing to discuss time travel in the abstract, quite another to witness an individual dissolve into thin air right before your eyes.

It was Imogen's turn to provide comfort. "It's okay," she said, placing her arm gently around Georgia's waist, and also noticing that Georgia was wearing only one boot.

Imogen was the first to speak. "I have to go *now*. I have to follow him," she said.

Simon shook his head. "No, Imogen, not now, not yet. You're hurt."

"You heard him," she wailed. "He admitted that he trapped my parents! I have to find out what he knows."

Simon grabbed her hands and looked into her face, his eyes pleading. "But Imogen, can't you wait?" It pained her to look at him. He was so sad. She shook her head and looked away.

"He'll get away if I don't follow him now," she said.

"Let me go with you," Simon begged.

"Oh Simon," she said, hanging her head, "we talked about this already. I can't let you take that risk."

Goodbyes were never her strong suit. Imogen glanced around at this group of people she had grown to admire so much and said sadly, "Thank you for everything. Thank you for helping me." She gave Herbert a quick hug, saying, "Take care Herbert. I'll see what more I can find out about Tiffany and Crestview."

He nodded. "Thank you Imogen," he said.

She turned to Georgia. "Take care of yourself," she said, grasping her hand. Georgia flung her arms unabashedly around Imogen's waist, hugging her tightly.

"Oh, I wish you didn't have to go," she said, starting to cry. "I've never had a real friend before." Imogen felt the old pain of losing Jade bubble to the surface and it was all she could do to fight back tears.

"You're going to be just fine," Imogen reassured Georgia, giving her a small peck on the cheek. She started to turn away, but stopped. "How did you get your shoe off so quickly? she asked.

Georgia smiled. "I always keep the laces of one loose, just in case," she said. "A spinster can never be too careful."

"You have a great arm."

Georgia smiled. "After I attended a minor league game with my father I was hooked." she said. "Some of my girl students and I have a catch after classes."

"Keep at it and maybe one day you'll have a league of your own," Imogen tossed out, even though Georgia wouldn't get the movie reference.

She turned and Simon gathered her up in his arms and they clung to one another for what seemed like a long time, but in fact, was only a moment. Cradling her head in his hands, Simon softly kissed her lips, leaned in close, and whispered, "I love you Imogen. Please, please say you'll come back to me."

Trying to squelch a tsunami of tears, Imogen took a last look at everyone before squeezing her eyes shut. She had to go. She was ready. And as she concentrated on a single photograph sitting atop her desk 100 years from now, the familiar sensation of time and space separating and folding in, commenced and Imogen felt herself being drawn away.

In that final moment when her body was becoming translucent, Georgia and Herbert noticed Simon impulsively reach out and grasp ahold of Imogen's arm. Imogen's eye's fluttered open in disbelief before they both disappeared.

Frozen in place, an unspoken feeling of "wow, what just happened?" passed between Herbert and Georgia. Herbert walked over and picked up Georgia's boot, which was still lying near the spot previously occupied by Leroy Jenkins/Teddy.

"Nice landing," he said, handing the shoe to her.

"Thanks," Georgia said as she sat down on a crate to put it back on on bare foot. When she had finished lacing it up, Herbert extended his hand to her giving her a boost up.

She cocked her head to one side. "So you like men," Georgia said.

"I understand your preference is women," said Herbert, chuckling. "We should be friends."

Georgia smiled. "We should."

As they turned and headed back toward the street, Herbert asked, "Have you any interest in aviation?"

"Aviation," Georgia pondered. "Hmmm, perhaps. Why do you ask?"

"I've been thinking of learning to fly."

49

I mogen grabbed on to Simon and held on tight. As long as she could feel his touch, she knew he was still with her, although she couldn't shake the stomach-churning feeling that before this was over everything could go terribly wrong. Traveling through time was never a pleasant journey. She could only imagine what Simon was experiencing. But she kept her eyes closed and when the dark particles of time finally waned and she felt a solid surface beneath her feet, she slowly opened her eyes. Simon, though still holding on to her, collapsed into a pile on the floor at her feet, passed out and stark naked.

"Simon!" Imogen cried, getting down on her knees and shaking him. "Simon, wake up!" When she let go, he fell over, rolling over onto his side like a limp, wet noodle. "Oh my god, Simon," Imogen moaned. Not sure what to do to revive him, she slapped both of his cheeks, then leaned over and checked to see if he was breathing. He was, but just barely. That was a good sign. Still feeling wobbly and unsteady herself, she managed to get up. Grabbing a plastic cup from her desk, she sprinted into the bathroom to fill it up with cold water. She returned to his side and began splashing cold water onto his face. She patted his cheeks some more, but still there was no response.Imogen began to panic. What if he's dead? Oh shit, I killed him. This is why she didn't want to risk it.

"Wake up Simon, please," Imogen wailed as she began to rock back and forth uncontrollably. "I told you not to come," she sobbed. Resting her head on his chest, she wept. "Why didn't you listen, you big dumbass?" Her shoulders involuntarily moving up and down to match the rhythm of her sobs, she didn't feel it at first. But then, he moved and she felt the tips of his fingers touching her back and she shot upright.

"Simon!" His eyes were wide open now, but they appeared glazed over and unresponsive. He stared blankly past her, not blinking, as though looking through her. "Simon, can you hear me?" Imogen asked again, waving her hand back and forth in front of his face like a magic wand. At least he was alive, but what was this? Was he paralyzed? In a coma? What? And then, before she could react, Simon projectile vomited directly into Imogen's face. "Ahhrrrggg," Imogen wailed, instinctively bringing her hands up to wipe away the nasty bits of bile clinging to her face, as Simon rolled over, continuing to retch onto the powder blue office carpet.

"Are you okay?" Imogen asked, wrapping an arm around his shaking shoulder.

Simon limply nodded his head. "I'm alright," he said weakly.

He was in one piece. He was alive. He wasn't an infant. Imogen was glad for that, but relief swiftly turned to anger. "Goddamn it, Simon!" Imogen yelled, as she jumped up and briefly left the room to wash the vomit off her face in the bathroom basin. "What the hell were you thinking?" she scolded on her way back from the bathroom.

Simon sat still and doleful, head down, gazing at the floor. But as she looked at him there—nude, hair askew, she couldn't stay mad long. He'd been through a lot. She recalled the first few times she'd traveled. She hadn't thrown up, but she remembered that physically, it had not been a pleasant experience at all.

"I'm sorry," she told him, her voice softening as she bent down beside him taking his hand in hers. He looked up at her with sad, confused, puppy-dog-like eyes. She helped him get to his feet and he wobbled a bit as she guided him into the small bathroom. Wetting a hand towel, she cleaned up his face and dabbed up some of the vomit that had dribbled and splattered down his chest. She looked up when he started snickering. "What's so funny?" she asked him.

"I was just thinking how fortuitous it was that we never made it to dinner," he said. "The only thing I had in my gut to throw up were those stale cookies we had at Herbert's house! And by the way, where are my clothes?" he asked, looking down at himself.

Forgetting her anger, Imogen realized she was glad he'd taken the risk, and she wrapped her arms around him. "You are 'hee-larious' Simon Le Bon Eliott," she said laughing. "Come on," she said, guiding his still unsteady frame over to the futon. "Lie down here for a bit." She covered him up with the fuzzy blanket and then nestled down at the other end near his feet.

"Thank you for allowing me to accompany you," he said. Imogen pretend glared at him. "Allowed you? Are you kidding me?" She patted his ankle and closed her eyes.

50

Imogen's eyelids fluttered open. What time was it? She arched
forward and glanced around the darkened room, unsure where
she was. She didn't have to look up at the office clock to know that
it was far later than she wanted it to be. Leaping up from the futon
she toddled gingerly over to the vicinity of the light switch, feeling
blindly around the wall with her fingers until she felt it. She flipped
it on and the room became bathed in a sheet of blinding fluorescent
light. Simon opened his eyes, but quickly closed them again.

"From whence is that dreadful light emanating?" he sleepily garbled. She forgot that Simon probably wasn't accustomed to bright,
office light.

"It's fluorescent lighting," she explained, "and you're right, it is
quite dreadful, but we have to get going Simon," she urged. "We've
wasted too much time already. For all we know, Teddy may be long
gone by now."

Simon rubbed his eyes as he tried to acclimate to the harsh
light. But as he did, they grew ever wider as he looked around and
scrutinized the modern office furnishings. Everything from the
picture frames to the desk was made of metal. He got up from the
futon, still a little jaggy, but much better, and wandered over to take

a look out the small second-story window. He gazed below at what appeared to be a smooth, surfaced street where nothing but sleek motorcars in a variety of colors whisked back and forth, until a light that changed from green to yellow then red stopped them, prompting a deluge of more motorcars to cross their path in the opposing direction. Hypnotized by it, he couldn't pull himself away, until Imogen pressed up to him from behind.

"We have to go," she reminded him.

"Have you seen this?" he asked her, wide-eyed and childlike, "the cars and the lights going . . ."

"Yeah, yeah," Imogen said impatiently, handing him a pair of sweatpants and a sweatshirt that she kept in the closet for times like this when she had time-traveled in clothing from another time and ended up coming back naked. Simon inspected the clothing, running his hand over the fabric.

"What is this? It's so soft?" he asked.

"Uh, cotton? Sweat clothes fabric, I don't know, Simon, just put it on."

The pants fit okay because they were stretchy, but the legs were too short, and the too small sweatshirt's sleeves reached only as far as his forearms and it stretched taut against his chest. Simon tossed his arms out to the side in a pose and asked, "How do I look?"

"You look ridiculous," Imogen snorted, but it'll have to do for now. Come on," she said, steering him to the door and pushing him through it. After locking the office door she led him down the hallway to the elevators.

"What is this?" Simon said when the bell went "ding," and the doors smoothly rolled open.

"It's the elevator," Imogen answered without thinking. Simon peaked inside.

"Where is the lift operator?" Imogen rolled her eyes. She understood that everything here was new to Simon, but she didn't have time to explain every little thing to him. "Simon!" she said. "There will be time for marveling later, but we're in a hurry; now get in!" He cautiously stepped inside and watched as the doors closed shut. The ride down wasn't bad, very smooth, and he grinned happily as the doors appeared to magically open to allow their exit.

Simon followed Imogen across the parking lot to her Mazda.

She used her key fob to open the doors. She could tell by the look on his face that all of this was overwhelming for him, but they didn't have time. He got into the passenger side and immediately started to touch everything. He felt the fabric on the seats and ran his hand along the car's dash, admiring the workmanship.

"Here," Imogen said, "let me help you." She tugged the seat belt up and across his chest and buckled him in. He started to speak, but Imogen placed her fingers to his lips to stop him. "Don't say anything more," she warned. "Now listen to me Simon," she said sternly. "I understand that all this is a lot to digest, I really do, but somehow, some way, you have got to stay focused. I promise I'll explain everything to you later, but right now it's important for us to find Teddy, okay? Can you do that?"

Sulking, Simon nodded, but once Imogen started up the car and they were heading down the road, he couldn't stop himself from expelling little gasping noises every time he saw something new and surprising out of the car window.

Although they were still several blocks away from her street, Imogen could already see where the huge, angry black ball of billowing smoke was coming from. And as they turned the corner they were greeted by a tangled mess of fire trucks and police cars, lights flashing, a throng of onlookers standing on the curbs watching as the fire personnel sprayed water on flames shooting out from the vicinity of Imogen's house.

Quickly pulling over, she shot out of the car, running full speed down the street. "Wait!" Simon called out as he struggled with his seat belt. It took him several seconds to extricate himself from it, but when he was finally able to get it unfastened, he exited the car and raced after Imogen. As she neared the scene, it became clear that it was the studio that was on fire—the houses, so far, were safe. And if the houses were spared, that meant that Luxe was safe too. She could only hope.

Sprinting toward the barrier the first responders had set up she was immediately stopped in her tracks by a very large police officer.

"Sorry, you can't go past here, miss," he said, grasping her arm and yanking her back.

"That's my house!" Imogen shouted, her voice eclipsed by the sounds of the fire, the trucks, and the crackling police radio.

"It's not safe," he said, creating a wall between himself and her as she stood helplessly watching the studio burn, the flames licking at the roof and along the sides, a million memories of her father, helping him make beautiful photographs magically emerge from the bath in the darkroom.

Straining to see through the thick column of smoke, to her right she spotted her—Mimi Pinky, wearing her signature shabby pink housecoat and furry slippers, standing on the curb across the street alongside a few other neighbors. But when Imogen turned back to look at the blaze, she saw something that would forever be seared into her brain—a firefighter, coming toward her, and in that instant, everything around her seemed to slow way down. In his arms, he carried something—a furry and white and limp something; the pads of its four little pink paws singed. Imogen began to hyperventilate.

"Oh noooo," she shrieked, rushing forward and breaking through the police and fire barrier in an effort to reach Luxe. Seeing the anguish on her face, the firefighter carefully laid the cat down on the grass and began to administer CPR. Another rushed over with a small pet oxygen mask, which he placed over Luxe's nose and mouth. They diligently worked to revive him, but it was no use. He was gone. With tears in his eyes the firefighter looked into Imogen's stricken face.

"I am so sorry, ma'am. It was burning so hot, we couldn't get inside and when we finally did, we found him lying by the door. He'd been in there for quite a while before we got there."

Imogen thanked him, telling him it was okay, she appreciated that they'd done everything they possibly could. Lifting up Luxe's lifeless limp body she clutched him close to her, burying her face in his matted and badly burnt fur. "It's okay, kitty; it's okay Luxey," she said, gently rocking him back and forth in her arms. She stayed that way for a time before a woman police officer stepped forward.

"Why don't you let this lady here take him for you now," she said, touching Imogen lightly on the shoulder. "She's a veterinarian. She'll take good care of him." Imogen didn't want to ever let Luxe go.

"No," she cried, gripping the dead cat in her arms tightly. Simon intervened then, and leaning down next to her he placed his hand on top of hers.

"Imogen," he said quietly, "let this lady take him. She's promised that we can give him a proper burial."

Imogen regarded the vet's kindly face as she slowly and gently withdrew Luxe from Imogen's arms and carried him over to a waiting van. Imogen collapsed against Simon's chest and began to weep.

"Why?" she sobbed, "why was he in the studio?" And then she abruptly stopped crying. "Why *was* he in the studio?" she asked out loud. "He was supposed to be in the house. He could not have gotten into the studio, unless . . . unless someone let him in." Simon had no idea what she was talking about.

"Teddy!" she bawled. In an instant Imogen was as livid as Simon had ever seen her. Grabbing him by the hand, they flew across the street, heading in a straight trajectory for Mimi Pinky, who was still standing unaware on the curb making small talk with the neighbors.

"Where is he?" Imogen demanded of the startled Mimi.

"Who, where is who?" Mimi asked, startled.

"You know goddamn well who," Imogen screeched, her face red hot with anger. "Teddy!" she said, "Where's Teddy? Tell me now!"

Mimi started to back away from Imogen, "I . . . I don't know," she stammered. "I mean . . . he was just here . . ." She whirled around in a little circle, searching the vicinity. "He must have gone back to the house . . ."

Imogen didn't wait to hear more. She bolted toward Mimi Pinky's house with Simon following right behind her. They ran up to the porch and entered the house without knocking.

"Teddy!" Imogen cried as she searched through the living room and kitchen areas. "Where are you, you son of a bitch?" she screamed, wildly flinging open various doors to closets, a bathroom, Mimi's bedroom, searching every room for him. "Damn!" she said to Simon as she came out of the last room in the hallway, "maybe he isn't here after all."

Simon grabbed hold of her hand and squeezed it. "We'll find him," he assured her. As they turned and started heading for the living room Simon stopped in his tracks, causing Imogen to bump into his backside. "Did you hear that?" he whispered.

"What?" Imogen said turning to glance about the empty room. He took her hand and led her to the front door.

"Let's go," he said loudly, opening the front door and closing it again. "Shhh," he whispered, placing his index finger to his lips. Together, they softly tiptoed into the kitchen and waited there quietly, the only sound coming from the back and forth click-click, swish-swish of the eyes and tail on the Kit-Kat clock hanging on the wall above the refrigerator.

After a few minutes passed, they heard the creak of a door slowly opening, and then, Mimi Pinky burst in through the front door. Imogen and Simon quickly ducked behind the door, squeezing in next to the stove. In her high-pitched, sing-songy voice, Mimi chimed, "Teddy? Teddeeeeee? Where are you Teddy Bear?"

A small, cracked voice responded, "Ma?"

"Teddy, what are you doing in there?" Mimi Pinky asked, her voice trailing as she disappeared down a hallway.

"Migraine," they heard Teddy moan before Simon and Imogen bounded into the room to confront him. Startled, Teddy tried to make a break for the bedroom, but before he could slam the door shut, Simon pushed his arm and shoulder through, prying it open. He grabbed Teddy roughly by his T-shirt and spun him around. Losing his balance, Teddy stumbled and fell to the floor, landing with a thud next to the bed table. Clutching his temples, he stared down at the floor, and began to whimper and cry.

But Imogen had no sympathy for Teddy Diamond. "I hope you choke on your tears, you sick fuck," she screamed at him. "You murdered my cat!"

Teddy cringed, shrinking further into the space between the bed and the end table.

"I know what you did to Tiffany Rose," Imogen continued, "and I know you did the same thing to my parents!" Imogen shrieked.

With that, Teddy stopped whimpering. He glowered at Imogen and began to ball his hands into two tight fists. In an instant, Teddy's demeanor changed completely—from pathetic loser one minute to raging psychopath the next.

Using the wall to stand up, he screamed back at Imogen, "Your mother was a whore! That whole summer that she was sniffing around me like a cat in heat she was cheating on your dad in San Francisco," he hissed. "And you" he said, turning his attention to Simon, "spawn from hell—your mother was even worse than hers. The little bitch thought she could tell on me and get away with it, well I showed her, didn't I?"

Imogen was undeterred by his foul words. "You're a pathetic little man," she spat. "You don't deserve to have a son like Simon." Years of unexamined anger and hurt and frustration came rolling to the forefront and she exploded at Teddy. "It may be too late for Tiffany, but not for my parents," she screamed. "Where are they Teddy? Where did you trap them?"

Unexpectedly, Mimi Pinky who had been silent up until now was all present and standing like the Great Wall of China between Imogen and her child. "What is she saying Teddy?" Mimi demanded. Mimi's hands were shaking and her lip was quivering, but her eyes were like two giant saucers lobbing pestilential gas rays in Teddy's direction.

"Teddy Bear, is this true?" she challenged her son. Incredibly, Teddy recoiled from Mimi, his previous bluster all but melted away. As he cowered in the corner, Imogen and Simon watched him return to the sobbing, blubbering loser Teddy from just a few minutes ago.

"What did you do to that girl Teddy?" Mimi demanded to know. Teddy said nothing, but when she looked over at Imogen for answers Imogen was more than happy to spill the beans.

"He knows how to time travel," she blurted. "He got Tiffany pregnant and took her to the past and dumped her there."

All of a sudden, Mimi Pinky was no longer the loveable meddlesome, weirdo neighbor lady. She was pissed off.

"Don't listen to her, ma," Teddy wailed. "She's a girl and girls lie!"

Mimi was having none of it. "And what else did he do," she asked Imogen firmly.

"My parents were time travelers," Imogen continued, "and he trapped them, too."

"Is this true Teddy?" Mimi asked, bending her frame back around to address her son. Never mind what he'd done to Imogen and her parents, or Tiffany and Simon, apparently his concern centered solely on getting back into Mimi's good graces.

"Please don't be mad, mommy," Teddy pleaded as he sneakily reached into the drawer of the nightstand and pulled out a stack of photographs.

Imogen saw what he was doing. "Don't let him do that!" she cried as both she and Simon lunged toward Teddy. But Mimi was blocking their way.

"You have to tell me where they are!" Imogen screamed in a panic, knowing what Teddy was about to do.

Slowly lifting his hand, he gave Imogen a creepy little wave and then flashed a cruel smile in her direction before promptly vanishing into the random photograph he held in his pudgy hands.

The photo fluttered through the air in a downward spiral before landing face up on the shag-carpeted floor. Imogen struggled to get around Mimi.

"Move out of the way," she cried. "I have to follow him before he gets away!"

Simon didn't wait for Mimi to move, instead he leapt up onto the couch, bypassing her, blasting across the cushions to the floor where he reached down and snatched up the photo that Teddy had disappeared into. It looked like any ordinary tropical beach, but when Simon turned it over, in small faded letters, barely legible, it read:

Bikini Atoll, 1954

A layer of soft sand cushioned Teddy's landing as he tumbled onto a beach somewhere, sometime. Before opening his eyes, he let the soothing warmth of the sun roll over his cheeks; he breathed in the salty smell of the sea, and felt comforted by the fine grains of sand brushing against his arms. His headache was gone.

They could tear up the photo and trap him here forever for all he cared. What did he have to lose? The hell with them, he'd live out his days in paradise.

Teddy expended a deep, contented sigh, fully expecting to see ocean waves and swaying palm trees when he opened his eyes. Instead, a flashing red light slowly came into focus. It appeared to be a camera lens mounted to a concrete enclosure.

He heard a noise behind him, bleating? Shifting in the sand, he twisted around to see from where the sound was coming. "What the fuck?" Teddy said. A small white goat was tethered to a sign that read:

WARNING! Atomic Test Site

It was the last thing Teddy Diamond saw before the blinding flash of brilliant cosmic light exploded in the sky, sending a shockwave of radioactive heat, first luminous and incandescent and then opaque, across the island paradise.

EPILOGUE

66 That was really nice of the fire department to pay for the
plaque," Imogen said to Simon as they walked along the path
leading out of the pet cemetery.

Simon squeezed her shoulder. "You can visit him whenever you
like," he said.

Imogen shook her head and made a face. "Nah," she said. "Luxe
was a good cat . . . no . . . he was the BEST cat, but I'll get another
one someday," she said. "We have more important things to do right
now," she said. "Teddy said San Francisco. That's a start."

"We?" Simon asked, stopping and taking her hands in his.

"We, if you want it to be," Imogen answered.

Cocking his head to one side and twirling a strand of his ponytail, Simon teased, "Hmmm, will it be Elliot & Oliver or Oliver &
Elliot?"

"What do you think?" Imogen said, lightly punching his arm.

"I think if we're ever going to find them," Simon said. "I guess
We better get started!"

ACKNOWLEDGMENTS

To my husband and best friend Jeff Bolkan, who has inspired and helped me in too many ways to count. I could not have done it without you, honey.

Thank you to my grandma, Violet Thomas, my first teacher.

Huge thanks to Gail Curtis, who bookended this project—at the beginning when I was tossing around ideas at Movie Club (although we don't talk about Movie Club)—and in the final stages, giving me divine feedback during several very long phone conversations overflowing with lovely synergy.

Much gratitude to my family, Cory and Courtne Huffman, Kaylee Huffman and Steve Crum, and Daniel and Jenny Stoltey, for their love and support.

Many thanks to Lisa Brunswick for being my #1 reader and to Paul Wade for coming up with the name Dead Relatives, Inc. Thank you to Laura Brewster for her calm reinforcement; to Marlitt Dellabough, Laurie Notaro, and the Bolkan family as well as countless friends, family, professors, and coworkers who, over the years, have shaped, influenced, or contributed in big and small ways to my life experiences.

Finally, thanks to my childhood friends: Kevin Scarlata, who promised in high school that one day he'd make a movie out of my book; and Beth Kincaid Glaeser and Marianne Wright Dixon, who were always there when I needed them most.

Teaching in Alaska
What I Learned in the Bush
Julie Bolkan
Among the first outsiders to live and work with the Yup'ik in their small villages, this book tells Julie's story of how she survived the culture clashes, isolation, weather, and her struggles with honey buckets—a candid and often funny account of one *gussock* woman's 12 years in the Alaskan bush.

10 Takes: Pacific Northwest Writers
Perspectives on Writing
Jennifer Roland
From novelists to poets to playwrights, Jennifer Roland interviews a variety of authors who have one thing in common—they have all chosen to make the Pacific Northwest their home.

Washington's Festivals, Fairs & Celebrations
Janaya Watne
Northwest native and fierce outdoorswoman, Janaya Watne has written an information-packed exploration of Washington's vibrant festival calendar. Tourists as well as the well-established who are looking to find the perfect week, weekend, or one-day trip will enjoy this handy guide.

Oregon's Festivals, Faires & Celebrations
J.V. Bolkan & Sharleen Nelson
From truffles & brews to mosquito fests & digeridoo, in Oregon there's always something to do! This handy travel and event guide includes more than 90 listings—everything from craft brew & wine fests, food- and flower-based celebrations, and music/film festivals to family focused events.

COMING SPRING 2018
from GLADEYE PRESS FICTION

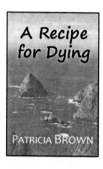

A Recipe for Dying
Patricia Brown
The sleepy seaside town of Sand Beach has a problem. Older folk are dying, seemingly peacefully, but is it really the work of a serial killer? Eleanor, a retired teacher, stumbles into the mystery. With the help of an eclectic cast of friends she sets out to discover who and what is ending so many lives.

- Visit www.gladeyepress.com for fantastic deals on these and other GladEye Press titles.
- Follow us on Facebook: https://www.facebook.com/GladEyePress/
- All GladEye titles can be ordered from your local book store and Amazon.com.

GladEye Press

CPSIA information can be obtained
at www.ICGtesting.com
Printed in the USA
FFOW01n1521210418
46297681-47799FF

9 780991 193165